S0-ABB-542

Freddy
A good friend
Cheers
Bill

When Olive Leaves Beckon

When Olive Leaves Beckon

William Boudreau

authorHOUSE®

AuthorHouse™
1663 Liberty Drive
Bloomington, IN 47403
www.authorhouse.com
Phone: 1-800-839-8640

© 2013 by William Boudreau. All rights reserved.

No part of this book may be reproduced, stored in a retrieval system, or transmitted by any means without the written permission of the author.

Published by AuthorHouse 03/27/2013

ISBN: 978-1-4817-3275-8 (sc)
ISBN: 978-1-4817-3274-1 (e)

Any people depicted in stock imagery provided by Thinkstock are models, and such images are being used for illustrative purposes only.
Certain stock imagery © Thinkstock.

This book is printed on acid-free paper.

Because of the dynamic nature of the Internet, any web addresses or links contained in this book may have changed since publication and may no longer be valid. The views expressed in this work are solely those of the author and do not necessarily reflect the views of the publisher, and the publisher hereby disclaims any responsibility for them.

“If a man does not keep pace with
his companions, perhaps it is because
he hears a different drummer.
Let him step to the music which he hears,
however measured or far away.”

Henry David Thoreau
American author

Dedicated

To the Memory of

Alfonso

Spaniard, ex-mercenary & gentleperson

Assassinated in Africa

In the throes of mass hysteria

INTRODUCTION

Throughout history, a special breed of warriors has played a role in determining the outcome of events. These men thrive on adventure and employ well-developed martial skills. A requisite for success includes fearlessness, self-assurance and an absence of qualms on killing. The motivating factor is the generous monetary compensation offered for their services.

In a social context, mercenaries blend in the fabric of everyday citizens. Upon completing a mission, they resume their normal lives until called for another mission. The lure to settle down is compelling for some, inviting these seasoned warriors to abandon their militaristic ways and accept a more pacific lifestyle. Some will heed the call, while others will persist in pursuing adventure and trust their luck will continue.

This is the tale of such individuals, as I knew them during my diplomatic career. All of the characters and the African venue, except the scenario in Chapter One (see Author's Note), are my creation based on my experiences and imagination. This tale occurs in central Africa, Belgium and southern Europe, while the timeframe is the late 1960's.

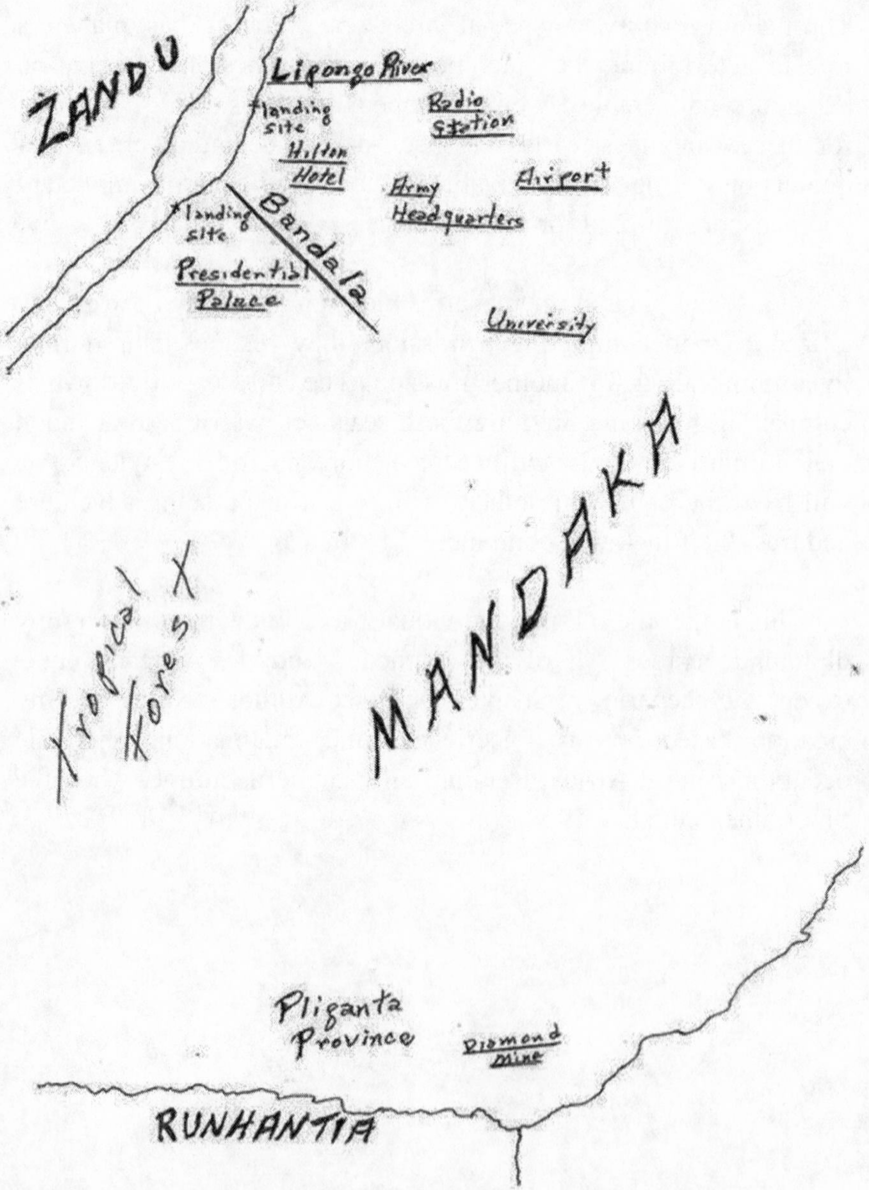
ZANDU
Lirongo River
landing site
Radio Station
Hilton Hotel
Airport
Army Headquarters
landing site
Bandala
Presidential Palace
University
MANDAKA
Tropical Forest
Pliganta Province
Diamond Mine
RUNHANTIA

PART I

AFRICAN ADVENTURE

"When You Play,
Play Hard;
When You Work,
Don't Play at All"

Theodore Roosevelt
American President

"However Brilliant an Action,
It Should Not
Be Esteemed Great
Unless the Result
Of a Great Motive"

François de la Rochefoucauld
French Author and Moralist

CHAPTER ONE

The American Consul was usually the first official to arrive at the American Embassy in Leopoldville, now Kinshasa, Democratic Republic of Congo. Despite a full day of celebrating July 4th, he was at the embassy by 7:30 am on July 5, 1967. The Marine Security Guard informed him the American Consul at the Consulate in Bukavu, in eastern Congo, wanted to speak with him on the two-way radio.

"Hey buddy, what's happenin'?"

"A day late, but we've had fireworks this morning. I awoke to the sound of distant gunfire," reported Phil Hunter, the Bukavu diplomat. "A short time ago, Katangese militia—Congolese *gendarmes* from Katanga province—and white mercenaries took control of Bukavu. There might be more to it."

"Are you guys OK, Phil? Have you been threatened?"

"We're fine. Let's see where this is going."

"We can get you out with our Air Attaché's plane."

"Not to worry. I'll let you know."

"This could be related to the recent capture of Moïse Tshombe by the Algerians. Mercenaries tend to remain true to the former Congolese leader after working for him."

"I don't think they would be foolish enough to threaten us."

"Phil, let's not have any derring-do. Get back to us with anything you pick up. I'll advise the ambassador and we'll get back to you. *Bonne chance, mon ami!*"

Living in exile in Spain, Tshombe was in flight on his private plane over the Balearic Islands when the aircraft was hijacked and taken to Algeria on June 30. He was a prisoner of the revolutionary government in Algeria under a death sentence imposed *in absentia* by a Congolese court. The affair became an international *cause célèbre*.

Major Johannes van der Veldt, the South African mercenary leader in Bukavu, dropped by the consulate. He looked the part of a warrior in his fatigues, clean-shaven face smeared with streaks of black grease over a ruddy complexion, blond hair, robust and full of fire. A movie-star-handsome Italian comrade named Captain Mario Rossetti accompanied him.

The major spoke in a calm but resolute voice. "Mr. Hunter, no harm will come to you, your fellow Americans and other Europeans. Our action is limited. My task is to occupy Bukavu. Captain Rossetti will serve as our liaison."

"You'll have no trouble from us. What do you expect to accomplish and whom do you represent."

"This is a political action. We have a grievance with the Congolese Central Government. A couple of years ago, President Mobutu hired over 1,000 of us to fight the *Simba* rebels—lawless and brutal Congolese operating in eastern Congo. We've been successful in this campaign. Under international pressure, Mobutu disbanded one of our units. Colonel Bob Denard's 6th Commando red berets is due to be dissolved as well.

"The *Simbas* are assisted by the communists and radical allies. They want to establish a government in Stanleyville, now Kisangani, as Patrice Lumumba tried to accomplish. We had to take action to prevent this. We demand the release of Moïse Tshombe. If he's not set free, we'll establish a separate country in eastern Congo and spring Tshombe to govern this new country."

Hunter responded. "Let me be clear on our position. The United States policy and goals are to work with our allies to assist the Congolese in unifying their country. We'll not lift a finger to aid and abet your insurrection."

"Believe me, Mr. Hunter, we don't expect any assistance from your country."

Captain Rossetti spoke up. "I'll do my best to keep you informed and to address your concerns."

Mario Rossetti was a native of Verona, Italy. As he approached 40 years of age, he began questioning his way of life. He figured he was living on borrowed time; there would have been long odds he would still be around given his profession. At first glance, Mario appeared like a beginner's crossword puzzle; uncomplicated, an easy read with all blank spaces readily filled. For casual acquaintances, Mario was a fun-seeking, life-loving Italian. Some of his closer friends were aware of his 'business trips', but few knew their actual nature. It didn't matter because he was good company. Scratching through the gregarious façade, one would find an enigmatic and contradictory individual. People knew him as a lover of the arts, attending opera performances at *La Scala* in Milan. His personal favorites were Puccini's *"Tosca"* and Pagliacci's *"Cavalleria Rusticana"*.

Mario had a decent singing voice, a baritone with good range he considered average. Weren't all Italians good singers after all? His voice was pleasant and abundant enough for a friend to hire him as a gondolier plying the Venetian canals when he was at home. He was a romantic and yet, he had no qualms about killing if it was part of a mission. He began envying the lovers he propelled along the waterways of the venerable city. As they embraced, he couldn't avoid ruminating on what was missing in his life.

Mario returned to visit Hunter that afternoon at his residence adjacent to the consulate. "Even though the United States is opposed to your activity, there's no reason why we can't be comfortable and chat over coffee."

"That's fine with me, Mr. Hunter."

Mario gave an account on the day's activities. "We came into Bukavu with six dozen men. We felt resistance would be limited. No one has been killed or wounded other than Congolese soldiers. We've taken no hostages. The army contingent proved true to its reputation. Three soldiers were killed and a few wounded. The remaining soldiers did as expected; they dashed away into Rwanda. They wanted no part of the conflict."

"What about Stanleyville, Captain Rossetti?"

"The situation in Stanleyville was more violent and involved taking Europeans as hostages. Major Jean Schramme, a Belgian owner of a large coffee plantation south of the city, led one segment of white mercenaries and a few hundred Katangese *gendarmes*, joining forces with Bob Denard's mercenaries. They entered the ANC—Congolese National Army—camps on the outskirts of the city as the soldiers slept. Some 100 soldiers were killed in the initial assault. It was a massacre, like shooting fish in a barrel. Denard considered this a strategic ploy to warn the Congolese the bad-ass guys were back in town."

"I heard Denard received a severe head wound today during the fighting. If this is true, it could affect morale."

Mario confirmed Denard's injury and continued with his accounting of events in Stanleyville. About 500 mercenaries and Katangese faced 2,000 Congolese soldiers split up into two encampments, one on each side of the city along the river. The mercenaries were experts in hand-to-hand combat. They took out inattentive sentinels, using garrotes and knives as they approached each guard from behind. There was hardly a sound other than the gurgling of soldiers as they were expiring with their last gasps, blood spewing from slit throats and abdominal thrusts.

Gunfire broke out when slain sentinels were noticed, one by a soldier returning from the latrine and by a cook setting out to prepare breakfast at the other encampment. The camps awakened with the shouting. The mercenaries opened up with a barrage. Soldiers emerged from their tents sleepy-eyed and dropped in their tracks as they attempted to get in shooting positions. The mercenaries had the advantage of darkness and surprise. They knew circumstances would change as the firmament began to lighten with the approaching sunrise.

They accomplished their first objective: to lay siege to the army encampments. Their next step was to return to the city, which they knew well, and fortify themselves against a possible counter-attack from the soldiers. Denard's plan was to keep his main force in the city and dispatch small sniper groups to engage in hit-and-run action on the encamped soldiers. He felt this would wear on the morale of the Congolese troops and frustrate the Mobutu Government. Denard wanted to avoid a prolonged gun battle that would favor the soldiers with their 4-to-1 advantage.

As they began their planned retreat, soldiers returned fire. The mercenaries realized it wasn't going to be as easy as expected. The soldiers stood fast. They would swarm all over them in full daylight. The mercenaries and Katangese sustained casualties, including the head injury to Denard. They had aroused a sleeping dog that snapped back.

The ANC showed more poise than earlier days. Confidence grew when they saw their bullets penetrate the European interlopers resulting in injuries and death. Unlike the ANC unit in Bukavu, the Congolese soldiers in Stanleyville regrouped and fought back. They suffered many casualties but didn't despair. The soldiers received a strong shot in the arm when they learned of the mercenary leader's injury.

Bob Denard was a spirited and respected leader of his men. Under Denard's leadership, no one questioned the success of the mission. His injury was debilitating; the bullet caused partial paralysis. A pall enveloped his followers.

Denard seized a plane and retreated to Rhodesia. The mercenaries endeavored to follow Denard's plan. Firing from dense brush, the snipers picked off a dozen or so soldiers. They hadn't counted on soldiers being deployed around the encampments' perimeters so quickly. The soldiers managed to locate two of the sniper groups and fatally shot three mercenaries. The remaining men reported to Schramme that sniper action wasn't going to work as intended.

The mercenaries were compelled to recognize the changing circumstances. The Congolese Army was more proficient and it had much greater numbers. There were indications of assistance forthcoming from other countries. Mercenaries were losing interest. They abandoned Stanleyville.

Mario Rossetti met with Phil Hunter daily. They became more comfortable with each other. "Mario, I sense your heart isn't in this. You've lost your ardor."

"Phil, you're observant. I have become distracted."

"Do you intend to continue? Your insurrection is condemned by the international community."

"I came here to join Bob Denard in his effort to gain Tshombe's release. We don't seek international approval."

"You must sense it's a lost cause, Mario. You don't have enough men."

"Actually, this is my farewell visit, Phil. I'm getting out. Other mercenaries have left. The mission has changed since Denard's exodus."

"You'll have company crossing the border. Europeans are taking flight from Bukavu as things get worse. I've been recalled to Leopoldville and told to close the consulate, so I'll be gone in a day or two."

"Well, then, Phil, let's wish each other Godspeed, and safe journeys wherever they make take us."

"I'll drink to that. *Ciao*, Mario."

As Mario returned to his quarters, his mind wandered. He thought of his olive grove in Tuscany. He was surprised to hear a dial tone when he lifted the phone receiver in his room. Taking a chance that it might work, he placed a call to Pietro, his partner. Another surprise. He was connected.

"Hello, Anna speaking."

"This is Mario. It's great hearing your voice. Is Pietro close by?"

"I'm delighted to know you're still alive. We worry. Hold on, here's Pietro."

"Hey, *amico*, how you doing? Where are you?"

Mario explained his state of affairs briefly, adding he needed to speak with a friend.

"I think I'm finally battle-weary. I've always insisted I do what I enjoy most and I've avoided examining my lifestyle."

"Mario, I've pestered you about facing reality. Although you relished the change-of-pace when you were a gondolier, you'll recall you grew uncomfortable with the intimacy you shared with your passengers. So then, you escaped to Monte Carlo, where you could hide from your emotions working with casino security."

"I can always rely on you, Pietro, to get me to look at things differently. Well, you've been partially successful. Change may be coming."

"I look forward to embracing you, my friend, when you return from your 'wars'."

"I need to get away for awhile and see how I feel after a break. It's getting to me. I'm seeing more savagery now than ever."

As he concluded his chat with Pietro, his thoughts drifted to Marianne, a friend he met a couple of years earlier when she was teaching in the Congo's Katanga Province. They maintained contact after she returned to her home in Liège, Belgium. He was anxious to see her again. He wondered if she thought of him.

CHAPTER TWO

Mario was mentally and physically exhausted. He needed a respite. Prior to his arrival in Bukavu, Congo, he spent several months in Angola, fighting alongside South Africans, Rhodesians and other European mercenaries. They were assisting one of the liberation movements competing for freedom from Portugal. When he walked away from the Tshombe affair and left the Congo, he returned to Monte Carlo to square himself with his boss at the casino. He had taken a mutually agreed leave of absence but he knew time was running out. For the remainder of the year and the first half of 1968, Mario spent most of his time working at the casino, with occasional trips to Lucca in Italy's Tuscany region to assist his olive business partner, Pietro. He kept in contact with Marianne, his friend in Liege, Belgium, visiting her from time to time on short visits.

When François Morency left his apartment in Auteuil in Paris' XVIth *arrondissement*, he was certain he would be asked once again to put his life on the line for somebody else's cause. The venue was different from other missions but the scenario was the same. It was always about power. Sometimes it was working for someone who had power and wanted to retain or expand it. Then there were instances, such as the present one, when someone out of power wanted assistance to attain it.

He was upbeat as he strolled in his cherished 'capital of the universe'. On this day, June 27, 1968, there was no place he'd rather be than in his hometown. He knew he'd need to change his mind set for the anticipated mission; destination Africa.

François took the line 10 *Métro* to *Odéon* station. Upon entering the *Méditerranée* at 2 *Place de l'Odéon*, the *maître d'* led him to a small salon. His host, Jean Paul Kibali, a former Cabinet Minister in the Republic of Mandaka, was sipping a cocktail.

"Colonel Morency, I'm delighted to meet you. You come highly recommended."

A slightly built, light-skinned, middle-aged African rose to greet François. His neatly trimmed hair and gray speckled moustache, along with his spectacles and a tailored three-piece suit, despite the summer heat, gave the appearance of a banker. He seemed rather diminutive as he stood by his guest who wore a military field jacket and khaki trousers.

The battle-hardened soldier of fortune looked the part. Although he just celebrated his 45th birthday and his rusty hair was intermingled with a few strands of gray, he was an imposing figure. He carried a robust 200 pounds on his V-shaped frame; a bit over six feet, with broad shoulders, trim waist, and firm jaw line. He had the right academic credentials to ease himself into a successful career in a field of his choosing. As a graduate of the prestigious

Ecole Normale Supérieure, he had access to the elite of France. Yet his yen for adventure led to the military. A bachelor, François was conditioned by military discipline, which caused some rigidity in his manner.

"*Mon plaisir*, *Monsieur* Kibali. My fellow Parisians seem to be treating you well."

"Yes, my life in exile has been pleasant but it's time to return to my country. Before we begin, may I offer you an *apéritif*? I'm having a *Dubonnet*."

"*Merci*. A *pastis* for me. *Garçon*, *un Ricard*."

"How was your trip from Provence, Colonel? I believe you mentioned coming to Paris by train."

"Yes, I came up yesterday on the express. The train is more agreeable than the alternatives."

"I agree, Colonel. Unfortunately, we don't have the luxury of choice in my homeland. *Voila*, *votre boisson*. *Santé*."

The two men sat back and nodded politely to each other as they sipped their drinks. *Le Méditerranée* was a convenient location for Kibali's occasional meetings; his XIVth *arrondissement* apartment in Montparnasse was within walking distance.

"Colonel, I assume you have a good idea why I invited you to meet with me."

"Yes, I do. I've been informed of your intentions by my sources."

François had invaluable contacts within the French government, military and business community. He was in demand for his keen analytical mind and extensive experience.

Kibali explained his situation. "Jacques Tombola assumed power through a popular uprising led by university students. Much of the population rallied behind him as he spoke of land reform and accountability. The romance endured as some initiatives were effected. Tombola's allies became more entrenched, abusing their authority and alienating the population. Corruption is undermining our economy. Anti-government agitation has been growing despite repression.

"I can't ignore the suffering any longer. I've been encouraged to return and establish a new government. Important elements within the country have assured me of their support. Mandaka's valuable mineral resources and rich agricultural land have attracted potential outside suitors."

"I know Mandaka is in dire straits, Mr. Kibali. The French Government has soured on Tombola's incompetence. It's still providing technical and economic assistance but has threatened to end this aid as it has with military assistance. So, what is it you'd like me to do?"

"Before I discuss this, I want you to meet a close friend and collaborator. He awaits us in the nearby *Jardin du Luxembourg*."

François and Kibali strolled from the restaurant, crossing the *rue de Vaugirard* and passing by the *Palais*. As they approached the *Fontaine de Médicis*, François spotted a barrel-chested African man in his mid-50s standing in the shade of the plane trees. He was focused on the carved figure of Polyphemus crushing Acis and Galatea. Kibali made the introductions as they settled on a vacant bench on the eastern terrace.

"General Gaston Pastambu is an old colleague, dating back to our years as students at *l'Ecole Spéciale Militaire de Saint-Cyr*. The French considered us such good candidates for assimilation as 'Frenchmen', they enrolled us in Napoleon's elite military institution."

"Enchanté, général," François greeted Pastambu. "Given what Mr. Kibali and you are planning, it appeared you were identifying with Polyphemus."

"You're astute, Colonel. I assure you I was merely admiring the art work."

"General, Mr. Kibali has explained his intentions. Have you considered the pitfalls?"

"Mr. Morency, there's always risk in combat, regardless of how thorough the plans. Mr. Kibali and I have sketched out a rough scheme for you to work with, that is, if you accept our offer."

"I understand the risks, General. They're inherent in my line of work. How do you evaluate the people's response?"

"Surely you know how changes in government usually occur in Africa. Many African countries have a tradition of authoritarian rule and it's taken as a way of life when one such leader removes another."

"You're expecting indifference with some relief and appreciation?"

"Mr. Morency, we expect guarded enthusiasm with minimal resistance. Of course, this will depend on the efficiency of the operation."

"Good point, 'the efficiency of the operation'." François needed assurances. "In addition to being a mercenary leader, I served in the French army as a paratrooper for 15 years, including the Foreign Legion. I've enjoyed many successes and I've been through adversities and survived. Before approaching me, you probably learned that I'll not accept a mission unless I'm in complete control of the military operation."

Kibali broke in. "We understand this, Colonel. You're a seasoned warrior with a get-it-done attitude. We're aware of your exploits and outstanding record of leadership. We also know of the *Croix de Guerre des Théâtres d'Opérations Extérieures* you received for service in Indochina and the *Croix de Valeurs Militaires* awarded you for service in Algeria. So Colonel, we're well informed and that's why we're meeting."

"Well then, *Messieurs*, here we are. I've great confidence in my abilities. I rarely apply value judgments. The essence is compensation and a realistic and attainable goal."

Kibali responded. "We appreciate your candor. I assure you that you'll be content with our offering. I'm confident the goal is both realistic and attainable. I'm committed to the welfare of my people. At present, Mandaka is another 'backwater region', as you Westerners call us, on our 'Dark Continent'. We have assets, including diamonds, uranium, cobalt, and platinum plus petroleum reserves in undetermined quantity. Our rich agricultural land is reverting to nature since many of the plantations were abandoned. I'm a bit of an idealist, but I know a trustworthy government will allure foreign investors."

"Mr. Kibali, what's your take on your country's borders?"

"There are no controls. Smugglers, poachers and other mysterious figures are engaged in cross-border transactions with impunity. As you know, Europeans established artificial boundaries throughout Africa in 1885. My tribe resides in three different countries. We're still one people but we owe allegiance to different countries. Splitting up tribes and lack of security at the borders allow unhindered passage."

"If we proceed, we'll want to use some of your tribal members."

General Pastambu cleared his throat, making a guttural sound amidst the melodious twittering of the birds overhead in the trees. "We have concerns about the machinations of the Soviet Union and its allies to gain footholds in various parts of Africa. So far, we know such activity in Mandaka is minimal."

"General, the Soviets strive to get their 'technicians' and those of their allies installed wherever they can. The East Germans are considering an initial offering of personnel to assist your military. Mandaka would seem to be a compliant host."

"As I said, this is a concern. Tombola and his sidekicks have taken trips to Moscow and an East German delegation has visited Mandaka. Cubans are active in the area but we know of no sightings within our borders. The only result to date is a ten-month old treaty of friendship and cooperation with North Korea."

"Thanks for the briefing. This might be an interesting engagement. Give me five days. You'll have my answer then. If I accept, I'll provide you with my plan."

Prior to heading to the *Gare de Lyon* for his return to his villa on the Rhone River in Arles, François called a friend and colleague. He met Mario Rossetti when they were on Moïse Tshombe's payroll in the Congo's Katanga Province several years earlier. They served on other escapades in Third World countries. They bantered briefly.

"I've been offered another mission in Africa. Can you free yourself if I accept? I want you as second in command."

"Always good to be with you, François. I am a bit restless. Time to take a break and engage in some adventure. Let me know when and where."

"I'm heading back to Provence and I'll call you from there. The offer's appealing but I need to do my homework and touch base with my suppliers in Marseille."

"François, one more thing. When you're putting the team together, be sure to include Julio Valesquez, Preston Langford and Gundhart von Stoessel."

"Will do, *mon ami*. Give my love to Marianne the next time you speak to her. *Ciao*."

CHAPTER THREE

As the train wended its way south through the belly of France, François worked on his plan for the mission in the comfort of his *Wagon-Lit* accommodation. He reviewed the maps of Mandaka, correlating the sketch given to him by Pastambu and focusing on the locations of targets. He confirmed they were attainable from the river.

François returned to Paris, as agreed, to voice his acceptance. He had taken care of business in Provence, with other arrangements to look after in Paris. Meeting with Kibali and Pastambu in the former's apartment, he explained his plan.

"I've selected the early morning following the national holiday. A few soldiers will be on guard while others sleep. Tombola has made an exceptional move to mollify the citizenry. A German *meister brauer* will assist the local brewer, Prima Africana, with quality and output improvements. Soldiers aren't timid about celebrating. They feel it's an entitlement. Many will be passed out."

Pastambu chimed in. “Tombola’s making an effort to impress. He’s intent on demonstrating the love citizens have for him. He’s buying the people off with beer and good-time festivals. It’ll be a jubilee.”

Kibali added, “There’s growing concern Tombola is selling off our assets to the communists. The North Korean Foreign Minister will be there as a sign of fellowship. We could be heading toward another form of colonialism.”

François resumed. “I’ve identified four sites. All are essential. I’ll lead eleven men in seizing the presidential palace. Tombola is my responsibility. The palace will be our command center. The other critical targets are the radio station, army headquarters and the airport. Preston Langford will take the radio station with four men. Army headquarters is the responsibility of Gundhart von Stoessel and eleven men. Both men are veteran soldiers with solid military training and considerable experience. Preston is a graduate of the Royal Military Academy Sandhurst. Gundhart is a product of German nobility with a military elitist upbringing. Both are proven leaders in battle.

“I’m not assigning any men to the fourth target. General Pastambu can secure the airport with loyal elements. Thus, the General will be on hand for your arrival.”

“I don’t agree, Colonel”, as Pastambu reacted. “Yes, the four targets are important and must be controlled. There are at least two other areas. The capital city needs to be safeguarded and the university must be neutralized.”

“General, that’s true but hear me out. A key element to my acceptance is the size of my crew. It must be small to succeed. You can gather loyal volunteers to assist you. I’ve examined the layouts. I’m certain we can seize control of our three targets quickly.”

Kibali interjected. “I know a handful of officers I can rely on.”

François agreed there was a role for his military friends to play. Experience dictated François to be wary. He knew what he and his men could do but he was chary about accepting assistance from parties unknown to him.

“Friendly military units will need to step in once we’ve attained our goals. It’s our job to rid Mandaka of its current leadership. We won’t suffer any interference. When this is accomplished, it’s up to you to have sufficient support to sustain your return. No troops should be activated until the right moment. If they’re dependable, they’ll be what you need to establish yourself.

“General Pastambu will require assistance. Identify officers who will be loyal. Trusting wrong individuals would be perilous.”

Kibali wasn’t fully convinced. “You operate differently from what we are accustomed. I won’t engage any colleagues until you’ve accomplished your tasks.”

“You mentioned one officer in particular who’s a close ally, a regimental commander as I recall.”

“I have complete faith in Colonel Kingambo. His unit is based on the outskirts of Bandala.”

“I suggest you contact Kingambo just prior to our attack and have him stand by, ready to activate his troops. At the proper moment, tell him to deploy his men to the city and the perimeter of the university. Timing is critical. The four targets must be secure before suspicion is aroused. It’s also important the *gendarmes* don’t react prematurely.”

“We can depend on them. The commander is a good friend and member of my tribe. I’ll contact him and Colonel Kingambo.

They'll be discrete. The commander will keep his *gendarmes* neutral. The *gendarmerie* is apolitical, focusing on its mandate of dealing with law and order issues."

François felt the need to caution his employer. "This must be a surgical operation and I'll not tolerate screw-ups. Your trust in individuals better be well founded and they need to stay out of our way. If this backfires, we'll abort the mission, leaving you to devise another scheme without us. We'll leave you hanging dry. Let us do our job, we'll get you back in Bandala. One thing you should know is we'll pull out of an untenable position. If such were to occur, there would be many more Mandakan casualties and you wouldn't be welcomed as a hero returning home."

Kibali responded to François' admonishment. "I understand your concerns. I'm confident with the trust I have in my friends. These men won't betray you or me."

"This takes care of our business for now. I've secured a team of 29 capable men, including myself. Supplies, armaments and transport arrangements are set. I'll await confirmation that the funds have been deposited in my Swiss account."

Through his suppliers in Marseille, François arranged for the same make, model and caliber weapons for each of his men. He insisted they enter Mandaka unarmed. The armaments to be provided were the Israeli Uzi 9 mm sub-machine gun and the French 9-mm semi-automatic pistol, MAC-50, which served as the standard French army issue.

He used his contacts at the *Quai d'Orsay* to facilitate the assistance of the French Embassy in the neighboring country of Zandu. This provided the 'quasi-blessing' of an element of the French Government, while the French retained the option of 'official deniability'.

"The funds will be transferred today. We'll talk again before you leave for Africa. I'll travel to Jo'burg where chances of being recognized are slim and head to Nairobi."

"I'm pleased to assist with your return. *A bientôt!"*

"A bientôt, colonel, et merci."

Prior to departure on the mission, François gathered the men at his villa in Provence to go over the plan. They rehearsed the scenario on the banks of the Rhone.

"OK, listen up, guys, this is important," as François called for attention. "Synchronization is the key to our success. The charge on all four targets must occur at the same time to prevent warnings being sent. There'll be no radio communication when the mission's underway. The clock starts ticking when I give the signal to the first group, led by Preston. Departures will be staggered. The critical time for action is forty minutes after Preston's group departure. The action period mustn't exceed one hour."

CHAPTER FOUR

The tranquility of the moment would soon be transposed into a surge of activity deep in the heart of Africa. A group of European men lay at the edge of the river, eager to get on with the mission. A golden globe hovered overhead, beaming effulgently upon the earth. It was 2:00 am on a Sunday, a time when god-fearing people would be fast asleep. A full moon seemed to influence abnormal behavior in some individuals.

Unconventional events occurred in Africa with some regularity regardless of the phase of the moon. These warriors needed no external stimuli to prod them into action. They were professionals, veterans of many such sorties, and they were on the verge of facilitating a change of government in an African country. Over the previous three days, 23 team members had infiltrated into Mandaka. They did reconnaissance on the four targets and the topography.

Mario Rossetti sat silently in the Zodiac rubber raft as he awaited the signal. Two Zodiacs, each with three men and armaments, had crossed the Lipongo River from neighboring

Zandu. Members of the riparian communities on both sides of the river traveled back and forth regularly, usually by *pirogue*, for commerce or family reunions. Although Zandu and Mandaka were not on the best of terms, François was discrete in his dealings and movements in Zandu. Tombola spies couldn't be discounted.

Mario was pleased to have Julio by his side. Julio Valesquez and he were close friends, a relationship that endured beyond their missions together. At 36, Julio was two years younger than Mario, and he too was questioning his way of life.

While they weren't spitting images of each other, they had an uncanny physical resemblance. Mario was slightly taller at 1.85 meters (six feet) and about three kilograms (6.5 pounds) heavier. They both had dark wavy hair, with Mario having more curl to his. Their torsos were trim and sinewy. That one could be mistaken for the other was enhanced by their tanned complexions, brown eyes and masculine good looks. The smile was the giveaway. Julio's was warm and friendly whereas Mario's lit up the room, his pearly whites exuding vitality. While he downplayed his allure to women, they found it difficult to ignore his sensual magnetism.

A native of Barcelona, Spain, Julio served in the paramilitary *Guardia Civil* for several years enforcing Francisco Franco's dictates. He became disillusioned by the repressions imposed on fellow citizens. He transferred to the Spanish Legion, a branch of the regular army, akin to the French Foreign Legion, and sent to Melilla. The city enclave is one of Spain's *plazas de soberania,* places of sovereignty, in North Africa, surrounded by Morocco and the Mediterranean, and close to the Algerian border.

When François visited Melilla from Algeria to see a friend, Julio was invited to join them in a *taberna* for a *platica,* discussion, on mercenaries. Julio agreed to join François' newly formed group upon listening to François' overture.

A light breeze wafted across the river's edge with an acrid scent from fecundity and organic decomposition. Ripples on the river surface lapped on the sides of the Zodiac causing it to bob gently. Slight white caps were phosphorescent in the middle of the river by the light of the moon.

The presidential palace was visible from the riverbank. It sat astride a rise in the elevated terrain, which swooped down to the river's edge. The castle arose majestically above the level landscape, out of perspective with its surroundings.

As he gazed at the palace, Mario observed, "This is awesome. It exudes a sense of power and authority."

Julio saw it differently. "No way Mandakans have any respect for such opulence."

"Of course people resent it. You know something, Julio. It's a bit weird being here under a full moon. It was always a time for acting up and pulling some pranks."

"You said it. I would classify this action we're on as a bit more than a prank."

From a thrill-seeking youth, Mario entered into worldly and exacting manhood. His zest for life remained but he could ill-afford frivolity when on a mission. Minute details were critical to survival. He scanned the terrain by the light of the moon.

Julio called out to his two comrades, pointing at something on the river. An island was closing in on their raft. A bouquet of greenery with attractive lavender flowers was being presented as a token for a successful mission.

Mario was quick to react. "It looks nice, but we can't accept it. This is the inglorious water hyacinth and we mustn't let it entangle us with its spongy bulbous stalks. Keep it away from the raft. I'll stay on this side. Push it away with your paddles."

The floating island seemed intent on enveloping the vessel. The underwater mass reached out to establish itself under the raft. These islands were pleasant to look at, but this one was behaving like a sea monster. The two men poked and thrusted, nearly falling overboard. It became a physical battle, with both men fully engaged. They succeeded in dislodging the invasive flora. The river's current took over.

Mario applauded his mates. "Well done. Hoorah for us! We won our first battle . . . Let's review our next steps. When we get the signal, we'll jump out and haul the Zodiac through the bulrush to join our mates."

Julio noted that the lunar brilliance was diminishing. The expected cloud cover was moving in. "Mario, François was right about the clouds. We better get set to go."

Mario replied. "The palace is more intimidating in the dim lighting. Take note of the waterberry (syzygium) trees and their drooping branches. We need to get by those trees."

Visibility fell to a dozen yards. Mario received the go-ahead signal over his two-way radio, as did Preston in the other raft. Mario urged his two companions to move quickly and quietly.

"Let's get going. Hand out the weapons and stand ready to move on the palace."

As Mario and his two men joined François' group, Preston and his two men united with Gundhart and the 14 others a half mile upriver. Except for slight rustling through the brush by the men as they prepared for action, the nocturnal sounds of nature were all that was heard.

CHAPTER FIVE

The objective of the first group to depart was to secure the radio station, the furthest from the staging areas. The station normally shut down its limited broadcasts in the early evening, but it remained on the air through the night following a day of festivities. François respected Preston Langford's maturity and sound judgment.

Preston could be mistaken for a college professor. He was slightly older and taller, at just under two meters, than François. While not quite an antithesis, his physique was different from François', more of a Clark Kent to the latter's Superman. His svelte body was trim but wiry, topped with sandy, well-groomed hair and a buff/grayish facial complexion. An easy-going countenance contributed to erroneous conclusions. He was a mixer in society, something he did with no effort.

When setting up the mission, François explained that he had a specific task for Preston to handle.

"I need you on a mission, Preston. Are you available?"

"*Mais certainement, mon cher colonel.*

"You'll lead one of the groups and take control of the radio station."

"I see where this is going, François. I'll be reading a radio message to reassure the citizens and providing music to entertain them. Been there, done that."

"You've got it, Preston."

Preston Langford had the most formal military training within the group, with the possible exception of Gundhart. Preston served with distinction with the British forces. He was with the Fusiliers in southern Asia and the Legion of Frontiersmen in Africa as they battled the Mau Mau in Kenya in the early 1950's. He became disillusioned while defending the British Empire and turned away from a promising military career.

Preston had a flat in London but spent most of his time at his villa in Malaga, Spain, on the *Costa del Sol*. He was at his villa when he encountered François, who was vacationing in nearby San Pedro de Alcántara. The two met by chance at a *corrida de toros* in Ronda during the annual festivities of the *Feria Goyesca*. Preston was in a discussion with four men on the morality of bullfighting. François happened by and was beckoned by one of the men.

"François", said the man, "come join us. As you know, I detest the primitive barbarity of this spectacle. We're supposed to be civilized but this is a throwback to hedonistic times. Despite the brutality, the pageantry keeps drawing me here."

"Well, of course it's brutal but bullfighting is nothing more and nothing less than a sport. You'll agree there's violence in other sports. The question of morality applies only to the conduct of the *matador*."

As they chatted, François sensed he might have another recruit. He explained his mercenary operation. "Preston, I think you would fit in. When we're on missions, we leave morality concerns at home. Are you interested in joining us?"

He replied without hesitation. "Nothing to hold me back and I still have a sense of adventure in my blood. I've tried the easy life and I find myself yearning for more challenges."

It was 2:35 am when Preston Langford left the riverbed with his four men. He led them around the waterberry trees and through bamboo and elephant grass. He cautioned his men to stick close together and remain on the path trodden by villagers. To do otherwise risked entanglement in the impenetrable elephant grass and lacerations from its razor-sharp edges. Once clear of the riverine vegetation, a stretch of savanna lay ahead. Preston whispered to remind his men stealth was key.

"This should be the easiest target. We can't be complacent. The radio station will be lightly guarded but proceed with caution."

One of the men responded. "We've been around. This isn't our first operation."

"The mission's success depends on us. Can't give the radio operators a chance to give us away. Keeping one guard might be handy to gain access into the building."

Beyond the grassy field, small trees and shrubs girdled the station building. The hibiscus with its red blossoms and the pink-flowered oleander provided cover. A quick survey reflected no particular concern. Barely distinguishable in the cloud-filtered moonlight, four relaxed soldiers sat on the ground. The sound of a generator intruded on the rustic ambience. A modicum of illumination onto the darken exterior came through two lower windows.

Preston checked his watch; it read 3:13 am. He flashed two fingers followed by thumbs up to his four colleagues. Action would begin at all four sites at 3:15 am.

Time to strike. All five men moved simultaneously, covering ground so quickly, three of the guards didn't have a chance. Preston and his men knew to use their knives whenever possible, avoiding firing their weapons. Throat slitting was an acquired specialty and these men were proficient. It minimized resistance and enabled stealth.

Two of the guards went down immediately, gasping a final breath of air as their inert bodies collapsed to the ground. Blood oozed from the slashes, forming small puddles, which were absorbed by the dry earth. One of the guards managed to catch sight of his attacker an instant before being struck. With a quick reaction, he attempted to stand as he raised his weapon to fend off the attack, but his adversary was quicker. Adroitly avoiding the rifle thrust, the mercenary inserted his blade forcefully in the guard's upper left abdomen, driving it upward as he struck. The guard struggled to remove the knife but his life expired when the mercenary scampered around and broke his neck. The victim gesticulated with his hands as he bit the dust, his abdominal gash contributing more blood to the desiccated soil.

Preston continued toward the stairs. The youngest looking guard was wrestled to the ground face down, his arms pinned behind his back. A second mercenary assisted after disposing of his target with a neat slit across his neck and through his trachea. He held the point of his knife, still dripping blood from the kill, on the youth's neck, telling him to remain quiet and to stop squirming if he wanted to stay alive.

The four men and their captive joined Preston at the building entrance, pausing to read the pulse of the interior. Sensing no stirrings, they bolted up the stairs only to find the door locked. They had the captured soldier to serve as their passkey. Preston advised him to do exactly as instructed. With Preston and his men out of sight, the soldier rapped on the door but got no response. He banged on the door again, but harder. Apparently annoyed at being disturbed from his slumber, a gruff voice resonated through the door.

"Who is it and what do you want?"

The young soldier replied somewhat hesitantly. "I need to use the toilet, let me in."

The other snapped back. "Take a piss out there, the plants need watering."

Feeling more tension and refusing to be denied at risk of his life, the prisoner insisted. "It's not that, I have to take a crap so open the door for me, please."

A mumbled response followed. "*Merde*! For all I care, you can shit in your pants. But, I'll let you in, since we're in a holiday mood."

As the door swung open, one of the mercenaries grabbed the soldier by his shirt and yanked him out over the threshold. A second mercenary slipped behind the guard and dismissed him with a piano wire garrote around the neck.

Preston and two men rushed past the others into the building, firing bursts from their Uzis. A second soldier emerged, reeling out of a bedroom, unsteady from sudden awakening and a hangover. He waved a pistol and managed three wild shots as he went down under the spray of gunfire.

Gaining access to the broadcast booth became more urgent with the gunfire. Preston was hoping soundproofing would shut out the sounds. He assumed the booth was on the second floor when he noticed the absence of windows earlier. He lunged forward and dashed up the stairs brandishing his MAC-50 pistol. Three men were in the room. They were in civilian attire and seemed unarmed. The trio responded to the intrusion with looks of surprise and fear. It was obvious they heard nothing of the commotion. Preston saw no purpose in killing them as long as they remained docile.

On the lower level, the four mercenaries dispersed to check each room.

"Hey lads, look here", cried out one of the men. "We've got a couple of Sleeping Beauties. They're totally wasted."

They found two other soldiers, who had not stirred from their sleep. "They're comatose," chimed another. "Dead to the world."

"They can be thankful. Their stupor kept them from getting killed."

The fourth mercenary came in from another room. “Are you sure these guys are still breathing? It stinks like hell in here.” A rancid odor permeated the air. Several bottles with spilled beer and leftover food were strewn across the room. One of the soldiers was partially covered in vomit.

“Let’s get these guys tied up.”

With all soldiers either eliminated or incapacitated, one of the mercenaries broke out a deck of cards.

“Might as well play a few games of poker to pass the time.”

Meanwhile, Preston was securing the broadcast booth and ensuring no warning was sent over the airwaves. In a firm voice, he issued a command to freeze the men in place.

“Stay as you are and don’t move. Do exactly as I say and you won’t be killed.”

The men sat like stone figures afraid a nervous twitch might betray them and cause them their lives. Two of the men were sitting off to one side, and one of them displayed telltale signs of having soiled himself. Preston cautioned the man at the console not to place himself in jeopardy.

“Place your hands behind your head and hold them there. Push your chair backward slowly with your feet. That’s good. You can put your arms down. Pick up your chair, carefully now, and place it next to your two comrades. Sit down.”

Preston opened the door and called two of his men. He kept his pistol trained on the operators though he felt they posed no danger. He asked for a status report. “Are we secure?”

"Two terminated and two others unconscious and bound, along with our young guard. We're good, area swept and several weapons collected."

"Take these guys below and shake them down. Tie them and keep them away from the soldiers. Stay vigilant. I'll call if I need an operator to assist me."

He gave further advice to the operators. "Don't try anything foolish. You're getting a new president. We have no cause to harm you. *Vous comprenez*?"

All three remained rigid in their seats, nodding their heads and muttering their affirmation.

As the two men left the room with the three prisoners, they could hear Preston mumbling to himself. "Let's see what we have here. Time for music to soothe our listeners."

As the men settled back, one of them demanded, "We don't trust you guys. Let's have a new deal. Shuffle the cards."

They were checking their cards for openers when the mercenary facing the rear entrance saw slight movement of the door. He was reaching for his Uzi when a soldier appeared, firing his Kalashnikov AK-47.

He cried out, "Enemy! Hit the deck!"

The four men grabbed their weapons and dove for cover.

"Hans, behind you."

A second soldier entered through the front door and began firing. The two soldiers remained by the doorways scattering shots willy-nilly. Although relaxing, the mercenaries were ready with their weapons close at hand. They returned fire as they leaped behind the table and chairs. Thankfully, the aggressors were not very proficient with their AK-47s, as they had trouble holding their weapons as they sprayed shots all over the room. The mercenaries were more deliberate and quickly put the two soldiers down. The mercenaries didn't come away unscathed. Hans, the man with his back to the front door, took two bullets, one in his left shoulder and another near his right hip. When he went down, he dropped his cards on the table—a pair of aces and a pair of eights—Wild Bill Hickok's 'Dead Man's Hand'. Would he meet the same fate? A second mercenary was struck in his right arm.

One of the two uninjured mercenaries jumped up, shouting, "Quick, get the doors."

Another responded, "Where in hell did they come from? How the fuck did they get in?"

Someone else replied, "Had to have keys. We locked the doors. We'll still get chewed out."

"Yeah, Preston and François will have our asses. Let's get the bleeding under control."

Preston pushed two buttons on the console to stop the tape that was running, located the 'on live' switch and read his prepared remarks into the microphone.

«Je vous adresse au nom d'un des plus cher amis de Mandaka. Mon nom n'est pas important. Nous avons prie les actions nécessaire pour mettre en place un gouvernement représentant

les intérêts du peuple de Mandaka. Nous sommes ici pour assister le retour d'un champion pour votre cause. Il vous adressera prochainement pour expliquer la raison pour son retour et ses idées pour la future de votre pays. Jacques Tombola n'est plus le président de Mandaka. Nous implorons la coopération du militaire et la gendarmerie. Il ne faut pas résister car c'est un fait accompli. Le citoyen Jean Paul Kibali va diriger le gouvernement pendant cette période de transition. Soyez patient. Dans très peu de temps, M. Kibali vous parlera directement. Merci pour votre attention et votre coopération.»

Preston's French was polished, and he spoke deliberately, partly to heighten the moment but also for clarity of the message. The text was a collaborative effort between Kibali and François, giving assurances to the people of the country while urging non-interference in the period of transition. The message spoke of Tombola's overthrow and the return of a patriot, Kibali, who would speak to the nation in a short while.

Radio was the most urgent mass media element. Television didn't exist. Kibali loyalists were engaged to oversee the printing of articles in the newspapers, extolling Kibali's courageous return. Special editions would hit the streets at dawn. As in many countries of the world, Sunday was usually a quiet day with family and perhaps a church service. Church leaders would be alerted upon the successful completion of the coup d'état, with a request to give Kibali some leeway and time to explain his position.

Rather than playing martial music as usual in similar circumstances, Preston carried tapes of lighter symphonic music. He interspersed the music with the prepared statement.

Listeners tuning in would be serenaded with 'music to relax by' as he'd described it to François. His selections included works by his favorite English composer, William Boyce ("Concerto Grosso"), Tchaikovsky ("Swan Lake", "Sleeping Beauty",

"*Pathétique*"), Vivaldi ("Flute Concerto"), Brahms ("Violin Concerto"), Richard Strauss ("*Bourgeois Gentilhomme* and the Diner"), Debussy ("*La Mer*", "*l'Apres-Midi d'un Faune*"), Chopin ("*Polonaises*"), Beethoven ("Piano Sonatas"), Grieg, ("Wedding Day at *Troldhauger*"), Mozart ("Piano Concerto No. 21 and No. 23"), plus others of like nature.

The selections were intended to help create an atmosphere of national reflection. This was in contrast to news of violence, always exaggerated in such circumstances, as it made its way through the rumor mills.

The mercenary with the arm wound took charge of the situation. He directed his two able colleagues. "Help me with a tourniquet. I'm OK for now. Let's take care of Hans. The Peugeot parked on the side of the building must belong to one of the broadcasters. Get the keys. I'll inform Preston on our misfortune."

Preston was bowled over. "Goddamnit! It went so smoothly."

He accepted the explanation without further comment and checked the tape to be sure it had sufficient running time. "Let's go downstairs and look after Hans."

Preston inspected Hans' wounds and expelled a sigh of relief that the loss of blood was minimal. "We need to get him to a hospital. Do we have keys for the Peugeot?"

"Yes, I took them from the dead operator. A stray bullet got him in the chest."

Preston kept his cool. "You two get the car and bring it up front. Stay on your toes. There may be others lurking."

Preston untied one of the operators and told him he would serve as guide to the hospital previously identified in case of need. "I'm taking my comrade to the *Maison du Bon Berger*. I've located it on the map, but you'll help us get there."

Speaking to the two mercenaries as they reentered the building, "take hold of Hans and carry him to the car. Be careful handling him. I'll take our two mates to the hospital and return. The two of you stay here and make sure we suffer no more setbacks. Also, check the tape after awhile. It should be good for an hour or so. Other tapes are ready to be inserted. I'll alert François to our situation."

CHAPTER SIX

While Preston's group was making its way to the radio station, François and his team ascended the hill directly from the river. This route provided them with a steeper but shorter climb than other approaches. The men made their way through a variety of trees, acacia, bushwillow, ficus and mongongo that populated the lower half of the hillside. The upper portion was shorn of trees, presumably to afford a clearing adjacent to the palace. The regal manor loomed above as they scaled toward the soon-to-be former president.

Four men gathered at each of three locations along the periphery fence, creating entry points with wire cutters. No guards were walking perimeter duty but six soldiers were chatting, their weapons either slung on their backs or loosely held in their grip.

The soldiers were clustered around a finely designed water fountain of imported Italian marble. Its elegance was a remarkable sight, particularly in the heart of Africa. A statue of Neptune was at the center surrounded by a collection of nymphs. A basin circumscribing the statues was waterless, a condition due to lack of technical help and spare parts. Although its sense of grandeur was diminished, it stood as a symbol of comfort that was at odds with the scene about to be played out.

Mario thought whoever conceived the idea of the Roman god of the sea had to be wistful of faraway places. There was nothing maritime about this land-locked country.

As he surveyed the grounds, François spotted two other soldiers with different uniforms and of different ethnicity. He heard them faintly as they chatted, but was unable to identify the language. Fortunately, his aide-de-camp was a linguist. François motioned for him to come closer.

The French army had placed Michel Langlois in an intensive language-training program in Korean because of his aptitude for languages. He was sent to a small French army detachment in Pusan in the early 1950's and performed liaison duties for the United Nations-led forces.

"Michel, can you make out the language those two men are speaking?"

"Yes, I might if I get closer."

Michel crawled several yards along the fence, cocking his ear. The stillness of the night was in his favor.

"방법 당신이 저 여아와 어제 밖으로 만든 □? 그녀는 우선 저항했다, 그러나 샴페인의 병은 생각을 바꾸는 것을 도왔다□."

The aide returned to François and translated.

"How did you make out with that girl yesterday?"

"It was easy once I opened a bottle of champagne."

François' voice betrayed his anxiety and irritation. "*Allez-y, dites-moi!* I don't care about their sexual adventures. What's the fucking language?"

"OK, *pure et simple,* it's Korean, and they're not Africans."

Astonished by this, François nearly screamed out. "*Merde!!!* They must be North Koreans. With all of our preparations, there was no hint of a military presence."

François paused to reflect, realizing he had only minutes to figure out how to deal with this new twist. Killing them was out of the question; it had the makings of a major international incident. François had to neutralize them but he couldn't lose any time. He motioned to Mario. When he arrived, François explained the new development. From his vantage point, Mario hadn't seen the North Koreans.

"Change in game plan. Julio and you will take out the Koreans. I'll take two men with me to the presidential suite. The remaining seven men will handle the soldiers at the fountain and clear the area. The North Koreans must not be killed. Incapacitate them before they can react."

"No sweat, we'll take care of it."

"No time to lose. Get back and be prepared to move."

François gave the preliminary signal and saw the thumbs up from his men. They were on schedule but he was concerned other North Koreans might be present at the palace or at army headquarters.

All twelve men were poised to charge through the fence openings. Rather than stealth, the men were relying on suddenness and surprise.

The two North Koreans seemed aloof by choice, positioned a distance from the group of guards and closer to the perimeter fence. They weren't keen on being in Mandaka, anxious to conclude their brief visit to the god-forsaken country and return to the comfort of their homeland.

Mario cautioned his sidekick. "We need to make this work. No second chances."

"I got it. I'm not keen on testing their martial arts skills."

"Julio, our timing must be precise. I'll count down so we attack together. Get set. Our comrades are primed to attack."

Mario and Julio skulked toward their targets and leapt the few remaining yards as though propelled from a catapult. Just as they were launching, their comrades began shooting the guards, distracting the North Koreans. In effect, the Asians were blind-sided, a nasty move in American football but very much in play in combat. The impact of the flying tackles stunned the Koreans, who were confused by the commotion at the fountain. They were shackled before they were aware of what happened. Not being familiar with the language, Mario and Julio surmised they were not receiving accolades for their work.

Mario did his best to explain in French and English that the Koreans were not being held as prisoners, but were in protective custody for their own safety. The response came in the form of shrugged shoulders, quizzical looks and more shouting. He settled on a tried-and-true communication method, sign language. He motioned for them to move to the alee side of a parked truck, where he had them sit until they located a haven.

Seven men came out firing at the guards assembled by the fountain. The six guards never had a chance; they were mowed down before they could fire a shot. The mercenaries were proficient in hitting their targets. However, they knew the sudden intrusion in the nocturnal stillness would evoke a counteraction from unseen others on the premises. François anticipated another dozen or more guards in the compound. Three of the mercenaries succeeded in reaching the front side of the palace while the four others positioned themselves behind the fountain.

Other guards emerged from the ground level of the palace. The guard quarters were on the left side of the building and within view from the fountain. The guards neglected to extinguish the interior lighting and were sitting ducks in its glow. Two guards were shot as they came out. The light was turned off as a swarm of guards buzzed out of their hive, bent on overwhelming the opponent with sheer numbers. Several of the guards managed to gain cover behind some crates that were off to the side. Four other guards hustled to the back of the building and worked their way to the other side.

A battle ensued with the rat-tat-tat of automatic weapons. It was clear one side had the advantage over the other. It wasn't merely an issue of weaponry, although this was a factor. The Kalashnikov provided the firepower for the Mandakans. The AK-47 was developing a reputation in Third World countries as a replicable weapon, relatively easy to construct. There was a negative associated with the weapon; it had a tendency to jam at inopportune times. The Uzi, used by the mercenaries, was more dependable all around. However, the most important contrasts were in training and commitment. This was an African version of 'The Gang That Couldn't Shoot Straight'.

The Europeans were outnumbered better than two-to-one, not unusual for them. Both sides were shooting with no clear view of their targets. The lunar lighting had dimmed, making silhouettes difficult to detect. The Europeans gained the upper hand with their maneuvering. Those behind the fountain focused their firing on the doorway to the guard quarters to restrict egress. Crossfire by the three mercenaries at the edge of the palace kept the soldiers who had emerged at bay.

The dynamics of the battle changed when the four guards, who had scampered around the back of the building, began firing from the right side. The mercenaries became the target of crossfire. This drew the attention of three mercenaries: one behind the fountain, another near the front stairway of the palace and the third standing out on a balcony. The latter had entered the palace but François no longer needed him.

The four mercenaries at the fountain discussed their situation. One voiced his concern.

"We can't get in a piss-fight. Need to end this quickly."

The others shared their thoughts. "Darkness is our ally. Let's use it to our advantage."

"We're eight. Three are focused on the new position on the right. Two others at the front of the palace are keeping the left side covered. Three of us are here at the fountain."

"As you said, let's use the darkness and sneak up on their positions by the guard house."

"That sounds good. I'll stay here and keep firing, giving cover while you two crawl forward to get closer. Hug the ground and keep your arses down if you don't want an extra asshole."

Undetected by the mercenaries in the darkness, two guards had the same idea. They advanced toward the fountain, crouched off to either side to stay out of the line of fire. They kept their eyes on the fountain as they anticipated catching the mercenaries by surprise.

Unfortunately, these soldiers paid no attention to the ground beneath their feet. They stumbled on the two mercenaries who were crawling toward them. The mercenaries grabbed the soldiers by the lower legs as they attempted to pass. The soldiers hit the ground with a thud and were dazed by the fall. The mercenaries were quickly on their prey, slashing them with their knives.

The diversion on the right side of the palace continued with exchange of fire. The guards spread out and lay prone on the ground, using logs as shields. While they had protection, so did the mercenaries. This skirmish ended when a mercenary appeared behind the guards. The mercenary, who had been on the balcony, found a side exit from the palace. He advanced on the guards undetected. With his Uzi within ten feet of their backs, the decision was a no-brainer; the guards conceded.

Wiping bravado aside, the remaining soldiers became mindful of their situation; their numbers were diminishing and they were pinned down. Several guards had elected to sit it out in the guard quarters. The soldiers had no idea how many mercenaries there were. It was evident to them capitulation was the only option, other than annihilation.

«Nous nous rendons!»

They repeated their surrender. They saw five of their brothers fall in addition to six by the fountain, and three others suffered severe wounds.

One of the mercenaries called out, “Drop your weapons and come forward to the fountain. Those of you in the building come out now if you don’t want to be killed.”

A guard replied, “Don’t shoot. We’re coming out.”

«Ne faites pas de bêtises!», a mercenary forewarned the soldiers not to do anything stupid. "We have you covered. Be sure you're unarmed."

Julio came over to assist, leaving Mario with the Koreans. "I've got them covered. Get them manacled." Speaking to the soldiers, "Give us no trouble. Put your hands behind your backs and you'll be spared."

Mario told Julio to be sure the guardhouse was secure for confinement. Julio took two mercenaries with him to conduct the inspection. When they were fired upon from inside, they quickly backed away. One of the mercenaries pointed to himself, indicating he would leap back through the doorway while firing his Uzi and dive onto the floor.

Julio whispered in his comrade's ear. "There's more than one shooter and they're behind chairs to the left. Direct your fire there. We'll follow in, spraying the room."

The mercenary did as he said and drew return fire, but his lunge was good enough to land behind a divan. While the soldiers were firing at the intruder, the other two mercenaries poked their weapons across the threshold and let loose. The hail of bullets brought quiet to the room. Julio moved toward their targets; their guns were silent.

"We've got two more dead soldiers. A pity they didn't trust us."

"Yeah, too bad for them," one of the others responded. "They probably thought we're butchers, gunning down anyone we can."

The third mercenary commented, "We're so misunderstood!"

Julio reminded the two men of the inspection. "Be thorough. Check it out and let's be sure all weapons are removed."

"Where will we assemble them?"

"Let's pile 'em outside, away from the door."

With the guards in bondage and incarcerated, Julio returned to Mario and escorted the Koreans to another room in the guardhouse, keeping them separate from the Mandakans. The quarters were a suite of rooms lavishly appointed to curry favor with this 'elite' force. The premise being loyalty could be bought through special treatment and privileges.

Mario gathered Julio and the eight other mercenaries. "Some of you were struck in the fusillade. I see flesh wounds but nothing major. Look after each other to cover your wounds for now. Be careful, there could be other surprises. You two stay here and watch the prisoners. Don't allow contact between the Koreans and the guards. The rest of you scour and clear the grounds. Julio, come with me."

The two buddies vaulted up the stairs to join François. As they approached the presidential suite, the only sounds came from below as the Mandakan guards argued among themselves. There was total silence within. Mario and Julio prepared for the worse. They entered the building with weapons at the ready. Creeping through a hallway, they reached the main room. Nodding to each other, they stormed across the threshold, set to engage any resistance. They halted their charge in astonishment.

Mario's immediate thought was a tableau of a silent prayer meeting.

"Check this out" he intoned to Julio. "It's like the wake I attended last month for my uncle Antonio."

Julio agreed. "It's eerie. No action here. Sit back and contemplate."

François and Michel sat on the plush furniture in a salon. At the center of this congregation was the main prize, Jacques Tombola, in all his majesty. His throne-like chair was intended to give a sense of power. The figure itself wasn't one conjured when imagining an authoritarian ruler. There was no air of regality, given his dumpy and height-deprived body. Indeed, he was a caricature. Tombola seemed resigned to his fate, realizing it was in the hands of others, namely Kibali. François and Mario knew despots such as Tombola lived every day expecting challenges to their position and life. Perhaps this was a factor that led autocrats to paranoia and tyrannical behavior.

Mario couldn't get himself to feel sorry for Tombola, but he was impressed with his state of repose. As it was with certain figures in other walks of life, Tombola was defrocked for violating accepted standards of behavior.

Mario scanned across the suite. It was evident Tombola and his predecessors took good care of themselves. The draperies, furniture, carpeting, and tiling, were lavish and regal. With an eye for the arts, Mario thought the furnishings were mismatched. The light blue upholstered furniture with yellow bird-like designs was at odds with the rich burgundy drapery. As he approached François, Michel relinquished his seat so Mario could settle at François' side. Mario nodded his head and gave thumbs up.

Mario, with a good ear for music, recognized Antonio Vivaldi's "The Four Seasons, Concerto No.2 (Summer)" playing softly on the radio.

"Relaxing music. The battle goes on, but this is a nice change. Décor is luxurious but unsettling. I come up with garish. The interior decorator should be accountable for crimes against the senses. It's ostentatious, grounds for a popular uprising."

"My, my, Mario. Don't we have impeccable taste? If I can get your attention, Preston just called. Hans was wounded and taken to the Catholic hospital for surgery. The radio station is under control after a setback. How was it with you? What about the Koreans? Work out OK with the guards?"

"We're in good shape but met with a bit of resistance. Ended up with eleven guards down and a few others wounded. About a dozen or so conceded and are locked up. We sustained a few minor flesh wounds.

"Julio and I took care of the Koreans without a hitch. They don't seem to appreciate what we're doing for them, keeping them segregated. They look down their noses at the Mandakans. You know, race superiority and all that stuff. Now, tell me about your operation."

"Not much to tell. This is it. We walked through the entryway and this salon with nobody in sight. Three personal attendants were cowered in a corner of another room. As expected, our trophy was in the master bedroom, supine in his gross nakedness, oblivious to what was occurring. Given his reaction upon our entry and material on display, he was on drugs and alcohol. Lying on either side of him were these two young concubines, likely Asian imports. We convinced Tombola he should cover his eyesore of a body and we gathered in this room as we await a report from Gundhart."

Mario surveyed the scene and fixed his eyes on a pudgy, rather small African male, presumably in his 40's, and clothed in a scarlet velvet robe with gold trimming. From what Mario could see, there appeared to be no clothing underneath. Part of the fallen leader's genitals peeked out from their imperial covering, presenting a disgusting sight below a rotund belly.

"Tell me, François, doesn't Tombola remind you of something?"

"I don't know, Mario, maybe a troll or one of Snow White's dwarfs."

"What I'm thinking has to do with a television commercial. It was an American flour company, what was it, oh yes, Pillsbury. That's it, a pumpernickel 'Pillsbury Doughboy'."

Mario turned his attention next to the concubines. "These girls can't be more than early teenagers. Must be *cadeaux* from North Korea."

François observed, "Anything goes in the spirit of camaraderie. They're probably bargaining chips that helped clinch a deal. You know how that works. Sweeten the pie."

"Let's be honest, François. Can you imagine this guy doing the deed? Maybe he gets sexual satisfaction in some other way, but he can't be using his puny instrument for fucking. He's not only height deprived but his genitals seem to have left him a bit short. His rotund belly wouldn't allow the clearance he needs to get at the target."

"Mario, you're a hot shit! You just let it hang out."

"Tell me, François, what do you think? A partner would need tweezers to get to it."

"I haven't analyzed this in depth. You have more experience in such matters. It's hard to see how he could manage enough of an erection given what he has to work with."

The girls had to be frightened, but they sat placid, showing no concern. The three attendants, two female and one male, presumably Mandakan, sat on a divan in sharp contrast to the two girls and the dethroned 'eminence'. They were huddled together as if welded, their faces helping to distinguish one body from another.

The frozen expressions of foreboding reflected their perilous situation. None of these individuals posed a threat. All six sat in a semi-circle while François, Michel, Julio and Mario sat opposite them.

One of the men from below entered the suite. “We’ve swept the area and captured everyone on the compound. Five workers were hiding, but offered no resistance.”

“Two down, two to go. Still to hear from Gundhart and Pastambu. We should be pleased with how things are going. We hoped to avoid injuries to our men, but it’s something peculiar to our jobs. Stay here with me to guard these people.

“Michel, try your Korean on our prisoners. See what you can learn about their visit. Remind the men to remain vigilant. No telling what might pop up. The radio broadcast could get some *conards,* assholes, or *les curieux,* curious onlookers, to come out now their leader’s been toppled.”

Mario glanced at his watch. Only 24 minutes had elapsed. The assaults on the four-targets were launched at 3:15 am; it was 3:39 am in the continuing darkness of night.

CHAPTER SEVEN

Mario and Julio walked away from the group, selecting two chairs where they could chat. The salon's space afforded the two friends a measure of privacy. They last saw each other six weeks earlier in Monte Carlo. They never ran short of conversation material. The topic of *futbol* always found a place on their unscripted agenda. Among other topics were gastronomy, preferred travel destinations, other sports engagements and vintage wines. They also talked about other aspects of their lives, including how their life styles could be modified through some adjustments. Such thoughts eventually led to Marianne. As the two buddies chatted, it was easy for them to talk about things unrelated to their current engagement.

"Mario, I've been looking at different places to visit. You've been to several places in the United States and I've only been to Florida to visit my relatives. I just read about a couple of places that sound terrific. Have you heard of Marblehead, Massachusetts, and Charleston, South Carolina? I'm intrigued by the great write-ups on both places."

"I've been to Charleston and all I can say is it seems the locals want to keep their treasure a secret so they won't be invaded by northerners. It's a must place to visit with old plantations and historic mansions. More than that, there's a distinctive atmosphere, call it southern hospitality, that makes you feel welcome. I visited Marblehead when I went to Boston with my boss at the casino. It's a quaint, historic, seaside town that exudes both charm and old Yankee attitudes—this in contrast to southern hospitality. Both are worth the visit."

The two friends moved on to other topics, ending up on Marianne. Julio liked her and questioned Mario. He thought Mario was a fool for not settling down with her and raising a family. Mario developed a special relationship with Marianne Duhammel while serving in the Congo. At the time, she was a member of a Belgian contingent of schoolteachers sent to reinforce a nascent system of public education. She was back teaching in her hometown of Liège, where Mario visited her from time to time.

"So tell me, Mario, what's the deal with Marianne? She's a great *muchacha.* You can't expect her to wait forever. When's the last time you spoke to her? Maybe she has a lover. Would you know?"

"Easy now, Julio, don't get carried away. We keep in touch."

"The thing is, you don't have a clue if she's expecting anything more from you. Maybe all she wants is a handholding friendship. Could be she wouldn't marry you even if you pleaded with her. Has marriage been discussed?"

"Let's see if I can explain. There are things Marianne doesn't care about me and things I don't care about her. Despite this, we enjoy each other's company. We genuinely like each other and we engage in give-and-take on a host of issues. We're good friends and Marianne is dear to me. The answer to your question, Julio, is no.

Marriage is a topic we've managed to dodge. I haven't considered marriage because I feel my lifestyle precludes it. I can't speak for Marianne. I know she's been offered candidates, but she's dismissed them all. They probably don't measure up to her image of 'Mr. Right'."

"You're scared to admit how you feel. That's why you speak of doubts. You need to face it, pal, you're in love with *la Belge*."

"Lay off. I'm trying to sort things out. It's complicated. I know I need to make changes. I'll get together with Marianne in Liège when we finish here. We'll see where that takes us. My friend Pietro also needles me. He thinks Marianne is perfect for me, someone who would tame me. He has an ulterior motive. He goads me to settle down in Tuscany and work the olive grove with him."

Mario liked the sound of being an agriculturist and entrepreneur as he reflected on the thought of working hand-in-hand with his partner on their business investment. Mario and his childhood friend, Pietro DiSanto, from Verona, bought some acreage of olive trees a few years earlier. The business was solid and producing acceptable revenue. Mario was intent on getting Julio to invest in olives in Spain.

"Catalonia is a choice location for olive production. For example, the *Arbequina* grows well close to your home. If you're interested, we could form a partnership."

Julio responded, resolved to be non-committal. "I'll give it some thought".

Here they were, far removed from Tuscany and Catalonia, sitting in the presidential palace in Bandala, Mandaka, in the heart of Africa. Mario wouldn't let Julio off the hook until Julio relented.

"Good, then it's a deal, Julio. We'll go to Tuscany so you can see our operation and then on to Catalonia to check out the olives."

Julio admonished his friend. "No you don't. You're going to Liège. You can't avoid it. I'll go back to Barcelona and check things out. I'll join you in Tuscany after you've met with Marianne."

"You see, I do get excited over olives", as Mario reassured Julio. "Liège slipped my mind, but of course I'll go, *amigo*. I'll alert Pietro to your visit. We can discuss Catalan prospects when we get together. Another thing, Julio, there's something I nearly forgot with all this excitement. We can't afford to neglect things that are important in life."

"I have no idea what you're talking about, Mario."

"Of course you do. Just think about it a minute. It'll come to you. It concerns a subject very dear to us."

"Well, let me reflect. A subject very dear to us? We've covered just about everything. You're committed to see Marianne. What else could there be? Oh, I've got it. It has to do with *fútbol*. I remember now. It's the big match between Madrid and Milan."

"Exactamente, mi amigo! You and I will be sitting in *Stadio Giuseppe Meazza* in a few weeks. Your *compadre* Miguel and Real Madrid Club de Futbol will fall flat on their faces. *Associazione Calcio* Milan will run circles around your guys. Your *Los Blancos* will be humbled by my *Rossoneri*. I need you by my side to see your disappointment."

"Mario, no way I'd miss this. I'll cancel any plans I have. I'm anxious to see you pissed off with your *paesanos*. It'll be a moment to rejoice. *Buen valor, mí querido amigo.* Miguel is unstoppable. I'll take your bet if you feel so cocky."

"OK, Julio, you have a deal. Even money, US $1,000 to the winner."

"Agreed, Mario, and please no tears when you part with your money."

CHAPTER EIGHT

In his final conversation with Kibali before departing on the mission, François told him what he considered the real test of success. "Army headquarters is key. Things could get out of hand if we became involved in a protracted battle. Assuming all other elements of the mission go well, as I expect they will, victory will depend on Gundhart's operation."

The leader of the unit attacking the third target was reticent to divulge his background, but managed to impress François as the best military strategist of his associates. It was on record that Gundhart von Stoessel's father was a general officer in Adolph Hitler's army and received the *Ritterkreuz das Eisernen Kreuzes mit Eichenlaub.* The Knight's Cross-of-the-Iron-Cross with Oak Leaves was a high honor in recognition of valor and accomplishments on the battlefield.

Gundhart also served with the *Wehrmacht*. In a conversation with François on Algeria, Gundhart let it slip that he was involved with the *Afrika Korps*. No further information on either father or son had come forward other than that Gundhart's father died in battle during World War II. Gundhart was self-assured, highly disciplined and efficient. His manner was brusque but he was true to whatever cause he embarked on. While men respected his bearing and his deeds, some gave him a wide berth to avoid clashing with him. People were intimidated by his physical appearance. He came in the extra-large package size, weighing in at a rock-solid 104 kilos on a 1.97-meter frame. His shaved head, deep blue eyes, burnt orange-brown handlebar moustache and a weight lifter's physique were sufficient for any sane person to get out of his way. He wasn't the endearing sort but his deportment engendered trust; François had complete faith in him. The two men met on missions when both were operating out of white-ruled South Africa.

Gundhart knew that his group had the brunt of the work. The number of soldiers present at army headquarters at any given time was unknown. Intelligence indicated the number was changeable day-to-day, at least 50 or so and running in excess of 100. The site also served as a rest area for soldiers taking a break from posts in outlying regions. The headquarters complex wasn't fenced and consisted of several buildings, some used for lodging and others for offices, recreation or storage.

Gundhart and his eleven teammates knew the layout of the compound. The top priorities were command control and the commander's residence. The army leader was likely deep in slumber in his quarters. Gundhart undertook the task of capturing him.

As most African countries, Mandaka was a multi-ethnic nation with dozens of tribes and languages. There was no sense of national identity or national pride among the population. Kibali and

Pastambu belonged to the third largest tribe, favored by the French in colonial days. Tombola belonged to a minority tribe, considered an attribute by his student supporters. The Army Chief of Staff, General Etienne Luc Saferdatu was a member of the largest tribe. He was a sergeant in the colonial army, becoming an officer after independence. He rose in the ranks through a loose alliance with whoever was in power. He was careful to avoid being tainted by any untoward political acts. He ingratiated himself with Tombola by alerting him to an alleged plot.

As they departed the assembly area, Gundhart led his group through a stand of bamboo, thickets and shrubbery. The assortment of vegetation provided cover for the men as they proceeded from the river. Their advance became more deliberate when they entered an open field of grassland adjacent to army headquarters. The 100-meter savanna was interspersed with large 'upside-down trees', baobabs, and green monkey orange trees. The assault team moved on the target using the large tree trunks for concealment. The cloud-covered moon emitted a weak filtered light, affording limited visibility. Gundhart couldn't distinguish details of the military compound until he was nearly upon it. Loyalty was a fluid commodity. He was skeptical of anyone who alleged allegiance to Kibali. He knew his unit was the most vulnerable to betrayal by Kibali's perceived allies.

Gundhart motioned to his men to join him by an acacia tree. "Our teammates are about to go into action. We must take care of our end. The entire encampment appears to be in the arms of Morpheus, but don't be deluded; we'll be engaged in battle before we vanquish. Remember we're not here to overcome our opponents with force. Our goal is to get the military to capitulate quickly. When the troops awaken, we need to keep them at bay to work out a deal. Take action to defend yourselves, but keep in mind we're greatly outnumbered and we're not trying to decimate them."

One of the men spoke to confirm their orders. “It’s kinda weird, we’re on the offensive as we attack and then it becomes a defensive operation. Don’t shoot, but we’re allowed to take out as many of them as we can if we’re assaulted. Is that right?”

Gundhart nodded his affirmation. “You’re partially correct. Circumstances will determine our actions. We can’t afford to wage a sustained battle. Our number and the time element preclude this. Also, we’re not at war with these soldiers. We’ll inflict casualties only to the limit necessary to achieve our objective. There’ll be no wholesale killing. Shoot to kill only if your life or your comrade’s is directly threatened. We want these soldiers under our control. One final point. This is important. I want to see each of you walking out of here when we’re finished. Are we clear on this?”

Each man nodded his assent.

Gundhart continued, “I see four men standing by command control. Does anyone see any others? We need to identify anyone in the open before we proceed.”

“They seem to be the only ones.”

“Okay, here’s what we do. Eight of us will go as planned. Frantz, take three men and move out along the perimeter. Get as close as you can to the four men. Attack when you’re set. We’ll follow your lead. Join me after you’ve taken care of your man.”

Frantz was an Austrian who got along better than most with Gundhart.

“The rest of you spread out and find cover, behind a vehicle, a tree, anything. You must be ready to respond to any hostile action.”

A moment later, Gundhart gave the order to the seven remaining men. “There goes Frantz. Get in position.”

Frantz and his men dashed to the side of the building and were upon the four soldiers in a flash. The mercenaries showed their prowess once again, using their knives to slay the soldiers without a sound. Mercenaries were usually successful in man-to-man combat. Their vulnerability was in long sieges against a larger enemy.

The four men dragged their victims out of sight behind the building. One of the men joined the other seven and Frantz scurried over to Gundhart. Two men entered command control. Three soldiers were in the building with their weapons on the desk. They were relaxed, not expecting visitors. One soldier lunged at the interlopers. He struck a mercenary on his left side, knocking him to the floor and sending his Uzi flying across the room. The second mercenary whacked the soldier on the side of the head with his Uzi. The two other soldiers pounced on the mercenaries, resulting in a wrestling match. They tussled and jabbed each other as they rolled on the floor. One of the soldiers got hold of an adversary's MAC-50 sidearm and was grasping for the grip to fire. The other mercenary butted his head against his opponent's skull, stunning the latter. Turning around with his hand on his knife, he stabbed the second soldier in the back as the soldier fired. The shot missed his antagonist but struck the dazed soldier. The two mercenaries regained their footing and bound the three soldiers where they lay on the floor, unconcerned about their health conditions. Whether the soldiers lived or died was not their affair.

Eight mercenaries dispersed around the compound, taking positions opposite the barracks, behind three parked trucks. However, as two of the men were getting into position, they noticed a picnic area set back between two buildings. Unfortunately, some soldiers were still celebrating the holiday under a pergola. Both groups spotted each other. Despite limited range of vision, indistinct silhouettes could be detected. The Europeans hastened for cover before the soldiers were able to react.

The Mandakans had no idea who was out there, whether friend or foe. They were indulging in a generous supply of beer. In slurred speech, one soldier babbled, "Let's get 'em. Must be up to no good."

Another uttered, "Hand me my gun, I'll take care of them."

A more sensible voice said, "You can't just shoot without knowing what you're shooting at."

The second soldier retorted, "What difference does it make. That's what we do all the time."

He fired his weapon, bullets going in all directions. It was a case of 'shoot first and ask questions later', except this soldier had no idea what he was doing.

The shooting awoke some soldiers in the barracks, who came out partly clad with weapons in hand. The mercenaries kept their positions and held fire. The soldiers saw nothing and headed back to bed when the soldiers from the picnic area staggered toward them.

"We have intruders in the camp. We saw them."

"What did you see?"

"We saw men passing by."

"Where are they?'

"How the fuck do I know?"

One of the men from the barracks asserted, “You idiots are drunk. Who knows what else you’re seeing? Maybe dancing pigs?”

Another interjected, “I suppose it’d be prudent to look around to be sure.”

Several soldiers muttered, “I’m going back to bed.”

A soldier asserted, “I think I heard a gunshot a bit earlier, coming from that area”, as he pointed to the command control.

The nine remaining soldiers scanned the area and inched their way around the compound, checking buildings. They stumbled across the four dead soldiers. The stillness of the night was disrupted when they opened the door to the building. The two mercenaries sat facing the door with Uzis in their laps. The soldiers had their weapons ready but the Uzis beat the Kalashnikovs to the draw. Three soldiers fell. The six other soldiers rushed back to the barracks. One of the mercenaries gave chase, killing two more soldiers. He joined his mates behind the trucks. They remained concealed and held their fire.

The soldiers were now aware of a foreign presence. The mercenaries knew they would be engaged. They split up before the soldiers reacted. The rear entrances to the barracks needed to be covered. Five men stayed facing the front of the buildings and four men went to the rear. This put them in a good position to handle the soldiers if they attempted to come out.

As Gundhart reached the residence, he heard the initial burst of gunshots. This caused him to pause; his task had become more critical. Frantz joined him as Gundhart thrust his foot against the door, which shattered upon impact.

"Don't shoot him, I need him alive", Gundhart cautioned his colleague. "He's probably anticipating us after the gunfire."

They made their way through the living area and toward the bedroom. The door to the room was ajar and they could see the bed; it was empty. Where was the General? Gundhart burst into the room and, as he crossed the threshold, he was hit in the left thigh. Frantz pushed Gundhart aside and leapt into the room, firing his weapon. He hit the General's upper right arm, stunning and immobilizing him. Gundhart hobbled over to the General and disarmed him.

"Frantz, tie him up. We need to move fast. The shooting came sooner than I expected."

«Salauds!, you bastards! *Qui est-vous*?» the General barked out.

«Nous somme des amis de monsieur Kibali» Gundhart responded. "We're friends of your new leader. We don't want to fight you and your soldiers. Order your men to lay down their weapons."

«Va te faire foutre»

The General was visibly upset, lambasting the intruders for invading his home and telling them to go screw themselves. His anger overcame any pain he felt from his wound. He looked up and down at the two men, sizing them as more gunshots were heard.

Admonishing his captors, the General told them, "You're pitiful. You've no chance. I don't know who you are and what you expect, but you won't succeed."

There were three buildings in use as billets. The mercenaries trained their Uzis on the front and rear doors. They heard yelling from inside the buildings. Officers and sergeants were barking out orders and soldiers were bitching. No one came out.

One of the mercenaries whispered, “We have the advantage so far. They don’t know how many we are and they’re frightened.”

Another responded, “That’s usually something we can count on. Our opponents lack courage, training and discipline. It makes our job easier.”

“Don’t get carried away, my friend. They still have weapons that shoot live bullets. Even an inept coward can kill with a lucky shot.”

“Let’s hope Gundhart can get the General to concede before the troops realize that we’re only a handful.”

“Heads Up! The door on the right is opening. I’ll fire a burst and let them think about it some more.”

The mercenaries kept their eyes peeled on the six doors of the buildings. The doors remained closed. The sounds of the sylvan environment returned, bringing both comfort and apprehension.

Suddenly, the sounds of broken glass filled the air followed by a salvo of bullets whizzing hither and yon. The mercenaries fired at the windows from their hideaways. Whoever was in charge of the soldiers was trying to get a better grip on what they were facing. Soldiers were sacrificed as several were struck by mercenary fire strafing across each window. The doors in the rear of the buildings opened as soldiers attempted to gain egress. The mercenaries were ready for them. They pelted the buildings, front and back, causing the return fire to abate. Soon there was no more incoming.

The mercenaries felt they'd struck a punishing blow to the soldiers for initiating the action. They held their fire after a few minutes to reassess the situation. The shooting from the barracks stopped. It was a shoot-em-up that would stand up to any in old Western movie frontier towns. The exchange of volleys gave the soldiers a better idea on the location of the intruders. However, they faced the problem of getting out of the buildings to attack the enemy.

Gundhart explained Tombola's downfall to Saferdatu, who remained skeptical. "Where is your radio? A broadcast should help you understand what's happening."

Gundhart assumed Preston had accomplished his task. African music filled the room for an instant and then silence. Gundhart felt relief when he heard his colleague's voice reciting the announcement. The General was attentive but seemed confused.

Gundhart chimed in. "General, you still have doubts. We want to spare lives. You must order your soldiers to lay down their weapons. I assure you my men won't fire on them."

"I still think this is a ploy."

"All right, General, let's do this. I'll call my colleague at the palace and ask him to turn the phone over to Tombola. You'll learn from him what you're up against. You need to act if you want to avoid sacrificing more of your men."

"Make the call."

Gundhart called François and explained the impasse.

"The army commander is our prisoner. We're exchanging fire with his men. The General needs convincing. He's refused to order his men to lay down their arms. It might help him see the futility of resistance if he spoke to Tombola."

"OK, let's give a try."

François spoke to Tombola while holding the phone. "Your army commander is our prisoner and needs your guidance. Tell him both of you will be killed unless the army lays down its weapons. Do you understand?"

Tombola acknowledged, "Yes I understand. I realize resistance is useless."

As Tombola reached for the phone, he heard, «*monsieur le président, c'est Général Saferdatu*».

"What's the deal? What do you want me to do."

Tombola wished he could say otherwise, hoping he could get Saferdatu to turn the nightmare around. He heard gunfire over the phone, but no telling how the battle was going. He knew his personal situation was desperate. He was certain he would die if Saferdatu didn't capitulate. At one time, Tombola cared a great deal about his country and he knew deep in his heart he was the right man to lead it as it evolved. Intoxication of power intervened and the deeds performed to retain it accumulated. He now realized he'd become despotic. It was no longer the good of the country; it was only the benefits he could reap.

Tombola told Saferdatu, «*c'est foutu*!, we're screwed!, *c'est fini!*».

"They have the upper hand. We have a chance to come out of this alive if we surrender. Order your men to lay down their arms.

Jean Paul Kibali is the person behind this. He has supporters and financial backers. Nothing we can do now. Give it up."

Gundhart took back the phone, telling François, "I'll let you know the outcome. The Mandakan military needs to decide where we go from here."

François closed out the conversation, *«bonne chance, mon ami»*.

"Your fate is in your hands, General. Do we save lives or will there be more bloodshed? Tombola's government is finished. You will die if you fail to order a cease-fire. The ball is in your court."

"I need to get to the equipment in the next room."

"My comrade will assist you."

At that moment, nearby explosions interrupted them.

The soldiers returned to the windows in the barracks and lobbed hand grenades toward the trucks. One was a dud, failing to detonate after hitting the side of a truck. Another landed part way, creating a crater in the ground. The third grenade rolled under the front of one of trucks before exploding. It took out the truck's engine, causing it to ignite. The fire spread, engulfing the vehicle in flames. The luck of the mercenaries was still intact; the country's dire economic condition contributed to scarcity of commodities, one of which being petrol. The explosion was considerably less than it could have been thanks to the truck's nearly empty gasoline tank. Had it been otherwise, it would have been quite a bomb, blasting mercenaries and soldiers sky high.

The mercenaries scrambled from behind the burning truck and joined the others by the two remaining trucks, which were a safe distance. They resumed firing across the windows. They couldn't allow the soldiers access to the windows to wage a grenade bombardment. They also knew they would run out of ammo if they continued their enfilade, leaving them fully exposed.

Gundhart barked at Saferdatu, "No more delays. It doesn't sound good for your men."

"I'll do as you say."

Saferdatu grumbled as blood oozed through the coarse bandage wrapped around his wound. He addressed his troops over the loud speaker.

"Your attention. Listen carefully. This is your commanding officer, General Saferdatu. Stop your firing immediately. The foreigners have assured me they'll cease fire as soon as you stop. You are valiant patriots, and I'm proud of you. We're in a situation where it's best to stand down. I've just spoken to our president, his Excellency Jacques Tombola. He's a prisoner of these foreigners who represent other Mandakan leaders. He and I are well. We must capitulate. I'll not tolerate disobedience. I order all of you to lay down your weapons immediately. All shooting will cease."

The sound of Saferdatu's voice resonated across the compound. Another announcement succeeded in bringing a complete halt to the gunfire. He called on his officers to execute whoever didn't comply. No one moved, both sides held their positions. The soldiers awaited further orders from the general. The mercenaries looked for Gundhart to appear. Moments later, he and Frantz emerged from the building with Saferdatu between them. Gundhart was using a makeshift cane for support. Saferdatu was untied for appearance sake. Frantz stayed a step back with his weapon at the ready. The three men walked toward the barracks. Saferdatu ordered his men to leave their weapons behind and assemble in front of the buildings. He instructed the officer to reassemble the men in an open area that he indicated and have them sit on the ground.

When the soldiers were settled, Gundhart gathered his men by his side.

"Is everyone safe and accounted for?"

"Yes, it seems so", responded one of the men. "There are the eight of us, plus Frantz and you and the two in command control."

"That's not so. I was in the command control, but I left. Someone's missing."

Gundhart was able to take his weight off his injured leg as he sat in a chair taken from the barracks. He sent one of his men to command control to turn on the floodlights to expose the grounds.

"Frantz and you two stay with me. The rest of you search for our missing colleague."

The men rejoined Gundhart several minutes later, carrying a body. The Belgian was the oldest of the 29-man group but had shown that he was still able, though his reflexes had slowed.

"It's Roger Janssen. He probably died instantly from wounds to his forehead and abdomen. We faced some wild shooting and someone got lucky."

Gundhart was saddened by the loss. Though the men knew they weren't invincible, getting killed took away any illusions.

"Let's get Roger out of the heat and humidity. Carry him to the general's quarters and place him on the bed with the air conditioning. François will know what Roger indicated as his disposition. It's always tough to lose a colleague. In Roger's case, there's no wife or children. He was committed to this line of work until it caught up with him.

"Gather the abandoned weapons and pile them away from the buildings. Check all buildings for any other soldiers."

He assigned one of his men to stand guard over the weapons while six inspected the buildings. One man held the fort in the command control building.

Gundhart told Saferdatu to sit on the chair brought out for him. Gundhart had to make do until reinforcements arrived. Frantz and a comrade remained standing with their Uzis directed at the seated soldiers.

Standing by Gundhart, a comrade shared information he picked up when he was in command control.

"I checked the sign-in logs while I was there. The list came to 113. Frantz and I each count about 130-135. It seems loosely run."

"Some probably belong elsewhere and it was convenient for them to crash here after celebrating the holiday. Frantz and you need to keep a sharp eye until the others return from their inspections. Here comes another colleague. Shoot if any of them move. I'm going to touch base with François."

Gundhart was back on the phone with François, giving the greatly anticipated signal—army headquarters was ready for friendly troops.

François was still preoccupied with the North Koreans. “Gundhart, are all of the soldiers Mandakans or at least Africans? We have two North Koreans at the palace and there may be others in the country. Did you capture any non-Africans?”

“No Koreans, no Asians. They’re all African and likely all Mandakan.”

“That’s a relief. Tell me what happened since we last spoke.”

Gundhart briefed François on the situation, the firefight and grenades, Saferdatu being compliant, better than 100 soldiers sitting on the ground, the on-going inspection of the buildings, Roger’s death and ultimately, his own wound.

“Roger was a good man. It’s most unfortunate. We’ll honor him and accede to his wishes. Now then, what’s this about you? Why didn’t you mention your wound when we spoke earlier?”

“It wasn’t germane. We needed to take care of the matter at hand.”

“This puts a different spin on things, *mein freund*. I’m looking to get a military unit to relieve you. Hang tough for a while longer. We should be closing the book on this operation very soon. I’m taking a ride to check out the area and I’ll look in on you. Are you OK for now?”

“Yes, François, I’ll manage. Nothing I can’t handle. My head is clear and my trigger finger still works. I’ll lie down when my men finish their inspections.”

“I know you’re as tough as they come, Gundhart. Make sure that Saferdatu doesn’t sense any impairment in you. He seems the type who could quickly turn. A wrong word from him could rally his troops to rise against you.”

"I hear you, François. Frantz has his weapon trained on the General. Rest assured, my men and I can handle this."

"Auf vie de Shein"

"Gott mit uns"—God is with us.

CHAPTER NINE

Bandala International Airport was expanded with World Bank loans, anticipating a need for larger commercial aircraft. The International Monetary Fund provided funds in support of the Mandakan franc at the behest of France and other western countries. The intent was to bolster the economy through increased exports. This was a work in progress. The economy was stagnant with little activity at the airport. Mandaka was not high on anybody's list for tourism. Commerce was key but there wasn't much happening, at least officially. Thus, the airport's capacity was greatly underutilized and interest payments had to be made on outstanding loans.

The airport was the fourth scheduled target of the mission. François' men weren't involved in this operation, leaving General Pastambu to muster a unit. Although he wasn't pleased to be subordinate to François, he knew it was best for his friend Kibali. It'd be worth it if François pulled it off. He admired the boldness and bravery displayed by François and his men, but he was uneasy with the situation. After all, this was his country and these Europeans were foreigners.

When he was Army Chief of Staff, Pastambu stayed in Mandaka for a period after Kibali's departure into exile. The charges were fuzzy on details, but several army officers were accused of plotting to overthrow Tombola. The lead person's name in *le complot* never emerged. Speculation pointed to the upper echelons of the military. Pastambu became convinced someone was after his hide. Disguised as a pregnant woman, he fled across the river to Zandu by *pirogue* in broad daylight.

Pastambu returned to Mandaka from the opposite end of the country, crossing the southwestern border in a Land Rover. The three men accompanying him were also implicated in the alleged *coup d'état* nearly two years earlier and left the country. They made their way north over an unpaved single lane rutted road, taking three days to reach Bandala. They chose this route because of its rudimentary condition. The French carved out the road as a passageway through the jungle/forest covering much of the terrain. Pastambu was wary of discovery and felt he'd encounter fewer people along the way.

Numerous sections of the road were impassable for most vehicles. Abandoned lorries caused blockages as their axles were covered with the gelatinous muck produced by the rains on the roadway. The distance was just under 900 kilometers but numerous mud holes brought the vehicle to a standstill, requiring the three associates to push and rock it to freedom. On two occasions, the front winch, with chain wrapped around a tree, was needed to pull the vehicle out of deep ruts. At other times, they had to deviate from the road and serpentine around trees to gain passage. Road conditions imposed speed restrictions; the Land Rover rarely exceeded 30-40 kph.

The four-man group arrived in Bandala on the eve of the national holiday. Fearful of being recognized, Pastambu dispatched his three associates to contact known individuals for the airport operation. They recruited a dozen reliable men that evening, adding another ten the next day as they mingled easily with the crowds. Pastambu observed the happenings from a distance. He felt the 25 men he had were sufficient to handle whatever awaited them at the airport.

Pastambu arrived at the airport early Sunday morning to assess the situation. He was cautious as he crept toward the terminal. A few soldiers were standing outside, smoking cigarettes and chatting. He skirted around them and approached the building. A few more soldiers were sitting inside, swilling the copious local brew.

He retreated 100 meters down the road to welcome his men. His group had swollen to 47 men. Some recruits got others to join, all of whom swore loyalty to Kibali. Pastambu was overwhelmed; the number had nearly doubled. He didn't dare turn any away in fear their rejection might work against him and sabotage the mission.

"Thanks for coming. I notice each of you managed to get a weapon. Do you know why we're doing this? Does anyone have a problem with Kibali's return as our president?"

There were murmurs of approval. "We understand. It's been explained."

Pastambu continued, "I have more men than I need, but I can use all of you. There are soldiers stationed outside and inside the terminal building. When I checked, there were five outside. We need to disperse. Two of you will stagger, acting drunk, and approach the outside guards. This will distract them. They won't be alert because they've been drinking. Twenty of you will slip around, out of sight of the soldiers, ten to each side. Five of each group will move in on the distracted soldiers, while the remaining ten enter the building and apprehend the soldiers inside. That leaves 24 of you to move around the building to secure the airfield.

I'm placing my former aide, Claude Pelletier, in charge of this last group. I'll accompany the twenty man group."

Claude asked his boss for further clarification. "General, I gather we're to take the soldiers alive if we can."

"A good point, Claude, and it's important. You're correct. I want to avoid bloodshed on both sides. We should be able to do this without firing a shot. Be ready with your weapons and use them as a last resort. These soldiers are our brothers."

Pastambu's plan worked. Giggling and singing, the two men, dressed in dashikis, stumbled and swayed toward the terminal. The soldiers spotted the twosome as they came up the road.

« Regardez, nous avons deux ivrognes. Ils n'ont pas de soins dans le monde.»

Another soldier acknowledged, "You're right, these are happy drunks without a care in the world. Wish we could be like them."

Yet another soldier suggested, "Nothing to keep us here—no air traffic for several hours. Let's raid that beer supply inside. Who's to know?"

The two men were within a few feet of the soldiers. One of the men inquired, "Got a couple of cigarettes? We're fresh out."

At that moment, Pastambu and ten men surrounded the soldiers.

Pastambu told the soldiers, "We'll take your weapons. We won't hurt you. I heard you want to go inside the building and that's what we'll do. *N'essayez pas de bêtises*—Don't try anything foolish."

The ten other men moved inside the terminal with weapons drawn. Five soldiers were sitting; two of them fast asleep, the others chatting. Pastambu's men were upon them before they realized they had company. They surrendered their weapons and were joined by the five soldiers from outside.

Pastambu sent a few men to round up anyone in the terminal. He identified himself and explained Kibali's return. He invited the soldiers to join their cause. There was no hesitation; they climbed on board. Loyalty can be such an adaptable commodity.

Claude reported on the external situation. "Not a single soul out there. We didn't check the tower; someone should be there."

"*Merci*, Claude. Stand by. I've another task for you."

"I'll be here when you need me, *mon général*."

General Gaston Pastambu was pleased with the ease he and his men took control of the airport. There was no shooting, no killing, no wounded. As an officer in the Mandakan army, he valued the lives of the military.

Another one of his men reported on the search within the building. "We found six civilians. We're holding them in the passenger waiting area. All six, a snack bar attendant, two airline ticket clerks and three baggage handlers, were spread out on chairs sleeping."

Pastambu scratched his head, inquiring, "Why are they here? Nothing going on."

"They say they're better off here than at home, escaping the tropical heat and mosquitoes."

"Were any armed?"

"No, General. They're all clean."

"Are you certain there's no one else?"

"Yes, we searched everywhere."

"I'll talk to them later. Keep your eye on them and tell them they're in no danger."

Pastambu pondered his situation. He was considering the airport's location and the number of men he should retain. The new and larger airport was laid out some 32 kilometers from the center of Bandala. The only ground access to the airport was a 6.5 kilometer long, two-lane road cut through a woodland of trees and thicket. The area was lightly populated with a few small villages scattered within the copse.

"Claude, come here. Take some of the men in town as deterrents. Kibali alerted the *gendarmerie.* Tell them you're in Bandala to assist them. Set your men in pairs at strategic places, including the *banque centrale* and the *poste*. This'll give us a presence and should help keep things quiet. Keep a man with you and move about to check on the others."

Ever dutiful, Claude responded, *«Oui, mon général. Je suis toujours prêt pour assister.»*

"Very well, I appreciate your eagerness. Explain the task to your men. Stress that it's peaceful unless they're provoked and assaulted."

"There are vehicles by the tarmac. I'll take a mini-bus and a truck. There's another truck for your use."

"That's fine, Claude. Get on with it and move out," Pastambu ordered.

Pastambu assigned fifteen men to stand guard around the building's perimeter.

"Keep your eyes peeled. Let me know if you spot anything. Nothing can interfere with Kibali's arrival."

He assigned six other men to stay in the building and keep an eye on the workers. He held on to one of the men. Pastambu spoke to his young warrior, as a father would while entrusting his son with the keys to the family car.

"You have an important job to do. I want you in the control tower. The only scheduled flights this morning are two arrivals and one departure. The flight from Nairobi with Kibali aboard will be first, due in at 10:04 am. The other is an internal flight from the eastern region due at 10:57 am. No other planes are allowed to land. Pay close attention to the operator."

As they began to climb the exterior stairs to the control tower, Pastambu was still giving instructions to his underling. The stairs were unlit. The two men didn't notice someone standing on the upper landing. This other person was in military uniform. As he descended, he was unaware who was ascending until he was nearly on top of them. When he realized the men were interlopers, he hoisted his rifle and attempted to knock both men down the stairs. The soldier hit Pastambu with a glancing blow on his left shoulder, sending Pastambu stumbling down two steps. The younger man was less fortunate. The soldier struck a solid clout on the left side of his neck with the rifle butt. Pastambu steadied himself by grabbing the hand railing and lunged upon the soldier, whose thrust had caused him to fall on his victim. Pastambu hooked his powerful right arm around the assaulter's neck from the back. The stillness of the night was breached by the scuffle. A distinctive crack was heard as the soldier's neck snapped; his body went limp and lifeless.

Two of Pastambu's men on exterior duty heard the commotion and ran to the tower. They had their weapons ready to fire.

"Hold your fire. This is Pastambu. Lend a hand. I have a man wounded."

As they approached, Pastambu was laying his young associate on the ground.

"What happened?" asked one of the men.

"We were assaulted by a soldier, whose dead body lies over there. Our comrade is unconscious from a blow to his neck. Could have a spinal injury so take care. We need to brace his neck."

He looked closely at the two men, recognizing one as a former sergeant who had served under him. He asked him to stay while sending the other man to the terminal.

"Get whatever you can to immobilize his neck. Bring three men with you.

"As for you, I remember I tried to promote you to officer level. As I recall, I offered the rank of captain to entice you but you were steadfast in your refusal."

"That's true, General. I decided I didn't want a military career."

"Remind me of your name. It escapes me."

"It's Pascal Lefèvre. I retained my father's surname, which I find helpful in my business."

Pascal was the son of a French merchant and a Mandakan mother.

"I'm curious to learn what caused you to abandon a secure military career."

"With guidance from some of my late father's former associates, I established an import-export business 2½ years ago."

Pastambu responded, "Well, Pascal, here you are again on a military mission. Mind you, my offer still stands."

"Thanks, General, but no thanks. My business should improve with our country's new leader."

"It'll take a while to turn the economy around, Pascal. Entrepreneurs like you can help it along."

The other man returned with a blanket, a length of rope and three men.

"This will work. Tear off a strip from the blanket to bind his neck. We'll use the rest of the blanket to carry and wrap around him."

Satisfied with the improvised neck brace, Pastambu instructed the men. "Carry him into the building and take care setting him down. Get the truck on the tarmac and drive it out front. I'll join you shortly. Pascal, you stay here."

"What do you want me to do?"

"Stay with the traffic controller to be sure he behaves."

Pastambu briefed Pascal as he had the young colleague.

"We must be careful. The scuffle on the stairs probably gave us away."

Pastambu turned the doorknob and shoved the door wide open. He swept into the room, followed by Pascal, weapons pointed at two seated men looking back at them.

“Don’t move! Why are there two of you?”

The man sitting at the control panels spoke up. “This is my replacement. He had trouble sleeping at home in the heat so he came early.”

“Your shift just ended. Turn over the controls to your replacement.”

“Who do you think you are?” interjected the second controller. “You have no right to be here and we don’t take orders from you.”

Pastambu, somewhat irritated, riposted. “Yes I do and yes you will. I won’t take any crap from either of you. I’m General Pastambu. You’ll do as I say and you won’t question it. Do we understand each other?”

Both men responded in unison, “*oui, mon général”*.

“That’s much better. What’s the air traffic situation?”

The controllers confirmed the two morning flights and listed others arriving in the afternoon and evening. All were regularly scheduled flights and most were domestic. Except for the internal flights, few passengers embarked or disembarked in Bandala.

“This is what we’re going to do. My man will remain here with you—indicating the replacement. As for you, you’re no longer needed so you’ll go to the terminal building.”

The man completing his shift objected. "I need to go home to rest. I return to work this evening. In our job, we must be alert."

"You can rest in the terminal building. That's the best I can do."

Speaking again to the replacement controller, Pastambu gave him a stern warning.

"My man is instructed to shoot if you attempt to betray us. Just stick to your job."

"I don't want trouble. My wife and five children depend on me. I'll do my job and nothing else."

Pastambu patted the controller's shoulder. "That's good. I'm glad you understand. I can see you don't want your widowed wife to try to cope with fatherless children."

When Pastambu returned to the terminal building, he told the traffic controller to join the other six in the passenger waiting area. He checked on the injured man, who remained unconscious. The four men were by his side.

"How's our young warrior doing?"

"He's breathing easier and steadier. We've seen some movement of his feet."

"That's encouraging. Who's driving the truck?"

"I am, General", replied one of the men.

"This is what I want you to do. Take this piece of paper. I had a competent physician when I was here. His name and address are on the paper. I've written him a note. Let's get our patient on the floor in the rear of the truck. Carry him as you did earlier. Two of you stay with him and the other join the driver in the cab. Once the patient is in the hands of the doctor, two of you remain there while the other two return here with the truck. Any questions?"

"What if we get stopped along the way?"

"The streets should be empty at this hour. The *gendarmes* may be on patrol. If they stop you, show them the note. Are you all set? *Allez*, get a move on and remember you have a comrade on board with an injury that could be paralyzing or life-threatening."

The airport was secure. Pastambu was satisfied with the set-up. He settled on a chair to rest, away from the others. He phoned François, telling him the airport was under his control. He also told him about the mishap at the control tower.

Pastambu inquired on the rest of the mission. "Are all our targets secure?"

"Yes General, all four are under control. Kibali will be pleased. He's expecting you to contact some allies to step in at this stage."

"Thanks for the reminder. The mind is a little hazy from fatigue. I'll take care of the calls. Colonel Kingambo is eager to assist with his troops."

"I'm calling Kibali shortly. I expect he'll contact you after my chat with him."

Pastambu made phone calls to the four officers on his list. It took some time to reach two of them due to the early hour. His principal contact, Colonel Kingambo responded immediately.

In a flash, he nodded off in his chair. The arduous cross-country trek took its toll; he had lost some of his vitality. He needed to remain alert but his body craved repose. Sleeping on the job was a gross military violation, but he had no control over his fatigue.

CHAPTER TEN

Following his conversation with Pastambu, François took stock of the situation. He needed to assure himself no detail was overlooked. The *gendarmerie* remained an unknown. Time to get Kibali's friends involved—deploy troops to Bandala.

François recognized circumstances placed him as the person in charge of the country of Mandaka, at least for a few hours. He had no delusions on the temporal nature of his status. He was anxious to relinquish his command. As he listened to Preston's soothing symphonic music, relaxed and in a mellow mood, he glanced at his watch. He thought to himself—real good, under an hour. The time was 4:08 am; 53 minutes had elapsed since the kick-off time of 3:15.

There were other matters to take care of, notably touching base with Preston and Gundhart. François phoned Preston, who was leaving the hospital.

"How are our wounded comrades?"

"Not as bad as it seemed, François. They'll be OK but Hans might be here for a couple of days. I'm heading back to the station and leaving the two at the clinic. We can decide later what's to be done. How do we stand with our mission?"

"Preston, we did it. Mission accomplished. We've done our job. Army elements should relieve us soon. By the way, great music. I' m relaxed, if you can believe it."

Recalling their time spent together in Spain, Preston cajoled his friend. "You relaxed—no way. Not getting into macho bullfight music we both love—too stimulating for the occasion. Need to assuage and reassure Mandakans with 'mood music'."

François then contacted Gundhart. "Remind Saferdatu the soldiers are his responsibility and he's to see they cause no problems. Have him assemble the officers and top NCOs. He must convince them anyone posing a threat will be executed."

"Delighted to do so. Saferdatu will cringe as I give my brusque Teutonic rendition."

Seeking reassurance from Gundhart, François probed him further. "You sound fine, but can you handle yourself well enough?"

"No problem. I'm OK. Frantz is with me and we're licking our wounds while keeping the soldiers under control. We have an eye on a few potential troublemakers. Most of them are not hard-core military types."

"How's Saferdatu behaving? He's key to controlling the soldiers."

"He roared like a lion but he's become a gentle lamb. He has no delusions on life and death. He may be reconciled to becoming a Kibali ally."

"Be attentive. It may be a subterfuge. I'm heading your way shortly."

"I'll see you then. Be careful as you venture out."

"I'm working on getting medical assistance for you and our other wounded men."

"Dankerschon"

François knew his men always needed some type of medical care when on a mission. It could result from the women they interacted with, or from serpents and insects, or food and drinks, or gunshots and shrapnel. Medical care was an essential detail arranged in advance. French government officials identified capable physicians and medical facilities in Mandaka and in Zandu. These were mostly missionaries and NGO officials—non-governmental organizations, including French, Belgian, American and others from Scandinavian countries. He told them the new President expected them to take care of the wounded.

As he concluded the calls, his aide came to report on his chat with the Koreans. "They didn't want to speak with me at first, so I just sat by their side and carried on a monologue," Michel explained. "Gradually, they interjected comments on some things I said. Eventually, this is what I learned.

"They are part of the Foreign Minister's entourage and were sent to check on the guards they trained. They're not impressed with what they've seen. The Foreign Minister declined Tombola's invitation to stay at the presidential guest quarters, preferring the newly opened Hilton Hotel. He's quartered in the penthouse suite on the top floor. The guards said they are the only ones who were sent out. They're anxious to return to Pyongyang, where life is a lot less complicated."

François thanked Michel, taking notice of a change in lighting outside the window. A hint of daylight began to penetrate the darkened firmament, bringing with it a changing perspective on the situation, along with a new set of problems. There would be full daylight within the hour. He needed to finish his affairs before taking a ride.

François' next task was to tell Kibali to proceed as planned. Kibali left Paris a few days earlier for Johannesburg, and ultimately, Nairobi. He thought his chances of being recognized were less likely in Jo-burg, waiting there until Saturday to proceed. There were direct flights between Nairobi and Bandala, and Kibali would catch the 8:32 am flight. Even though it was early, François knew Kibali expected his call.

«Monsieur le Président, on vous attend ici à Bandala. Nous avons vaincu.»

François gave Kibali a briefing on the situation, telling him the mission was a success and the country awaited his arrival.

"I'll fill you in on the details when you arrive at the palace. Your friend, General Pastambu, did a fine job with his men at the airport. He'll greet you and escort you to the palace. We got Saferdatu to capitulate and order his men to lay down their arms. Jacques Tombola is here with me."

Kibali was elated with the news. Thanking François, he declared, *«Vous est très formidable. Vous avez ma pleine confiance ainsi que ma gratitude.»*

"Your Excellency, I appreciate your confidence in me and your gratitude. Tell me about the *gendarmerie*. Are we OK with them?"

"Oh, yes. As I told you earlier, François, it wasn't an issue that concerned me. The commander appreciated my call and expressed his thanks that I'm returning. He dispatched a dozen trusted men in vehicles to patrol the streets of Bandala. So, I believe we're fine in this regard."

Kibali told François that he would make a few calls as they had discussed. "I need to confirm important segments of the army will support me. You may think me peculiar, but I need reassurance I'm not touching off a civil war. I'll make calls to General Pastambu and a few other key officers. As I told you, one of these is a regimental commander at a base about ten miles from Bandala. Pastambu will have spoken to the colonel this morning."

François repeated a point he made during the planning phase. "If Pastambu and you trust this colonel to be fully supportive, and his regiment can be relied on, we can use his men staged at key points around the city."

"Yes, François, Pastambu and I agree. I'll ask him to have the colonel move his men to Bandala and the surrounding area. I'm being prudent with the military. I don't want to cause undue fear among the people."

François imparted wisdom he learned through his many years of experience. "Keep in mind loyalty is a fluid commodity. One's enemy yesterday can become one's ally tomorrow, and vice versa. Mandakan soldiers will blow with the wind. Strength in leadership is the most important factor."

"Be assured, my friend, I'm aware of this. The upper echelon of the military must be completely trustworthy. Pastambu and I have identified a few officers who are likely to betray us and must not be privy to our activities. I know at least a handful of officers who are solidly in my camp. Pastambu and I will meet with them as we begin to consolidate the military leadership, which is our top priority. Another issue is what to do with Tombola and Saferdatu. But that must await my meeting with them."

"Mister President, before you hang up, there's something else. The North Korean Foreign Minister is here with some of his people. They're staying at the Hilton except for two military guards whom we captured at the palace. They haven't been injured and we're holding them until your arrival. You may wish to contact the Foreign Minister to give him your assurances. See you in a few hours."

As François was putting down the phone, he heard *«A bientôt, mon comarade».*

It was Sunday morning, as Mandakans awoke to a new day. All three locations held by the mercenaries were away from population centers, so they were unable to observe the people's reaction to the overnight events.

Mario and Julio came by to check in. François shared his thoughts on the reception Mandakans might accord them. It would not be entirely submissive.

"Agitators will be stirring up crowds declaring, 'it's a foreign invasion'. *«Les étrangers européen»* will rally some people in appealing to their xenophobic fears. Nothing works better in coalescing a population than playing the 'foreigner card'. We're counting on the radio message and the morning newspapers to appease most of the population initially."

Mario added, "Hopefully, people will be happy to see the end of the Tombola regime and welcome Kibali with his 'Mr. Clean' reputation."

François responded, "Kibali is remembered favorably by many but his name was muddied by Tombola's people. Kibali's public advocacy of good government and transparency forced him into exile when elements in the government attempted to silence him permanently. His name couldn't be mentioned in the censored media."

"Here's to Mandakans identifying Kibali with the coup d'état, and not *les envahisseurs blancs,* the white invaders."

Julio chimed in, "I'll second that!"

It was time to head into town before crowds developed. François took Mario with him, leaving Julio in control. He spoke to his men on the lower level of the palace.

"I'm heading out to check conditions around town. I'll take a guard as my driver. Which one seems more amenable to help us?"

"This one is your best bet. No guarantees, but he might do."

"Very well, I'll go with him. Take him to an empty room where we can chat."

François and Mario sat down in the living room of the guard station. François spoke calmly to allay any fears the prisoner had.

«Quel est ton nom, mon jeune gens?»

«C'est Kwambe, mon général»

François corrected him saying, "Kwambe, I'm not a general, but I carry the title of colonel. You realize Jacques Tombola is no longer president and General Saferdatu is no longer commanding officer. Both are our prisoners. How do you feel about that?"

Kwambe replied, “I don’t care who’s in charge as long my people and my country benefit.”

“I’m going to trust you to do the right thing for your people and country. I want your help. Are you ready to work for me, Kwambe?”

“Yes, as long as you don’t kill any more of us”, Kwambe asserted as he began to feel a little more settled.

François instructed Kwambe further as he introduced Mario.

“You will call my assistant captain. I’m going to visit other locations around the city. Do you know how to drive?”

“Yes, I do, and I’ll be pleased to take you to town.”

«Très bien, obtiens la voiture et nous allons y aller». Kwambe saluted and left to fetch a vehicle.

CHAPTER ELEVEN

Kwambe Musambu was a member of a minor tribe. His village was in the most southern province of the country, 47 kilometers from the juncture of Mandaka's boundary with two neighboring countries. It was remote from Bandala in many ways, in addition to a distance of 945 kilometers. His immediate world was the village of 14 mud huts with thatched roofs and a few nearby villages carved out of the tropical rainforest.

Kwambe's formal education was more than most Mandakans, with eight years of missionary schools. American Protestant missionaries were in this sector of the country for a few generations and well received and respected. While their principal task was to proselytize, they provided the only access to education and medical care for the villagers; the closest location of government facilities was 78 kilometers.

Kwambe might have turned out the way of most Mandakans, with a feeling of inadequacy and a lack of opportunity. Diamonds altered his life. Discovered near Kwambe's village, the French barely scratched the surface with independence looming and the area's isolation. The Mandakan Government paid little attention to this potential treasure trove until a couple of years earlier. Anxious to reach out to elements of the local population, the central government recruited a few citizens in a special military training program. Almost overnight, Kwambe went from his tribal village life to a dogmatic training regime in North Korea. He was compelled to change his easy-going ways to conform to rigid military discipline. His main problem was the endless propaganda he endured as part of the training.

Before leaving the palace grounds, François and Mario chatted with Kwambe to know him better.

François asked him, "Based on what you're telling us, I'm having a hard time imagining how you handled North Korean indoctrination."

"I found inconsistencies and dogmatism unacceptable. What I was told conflicted with what I saw in contacts with the North Koreans. The communist teachings were at odds with the moral standards ingrained in me through my years at the missionary school and assisting at the missionary hospital."

Mario followed up. "How did you avoid being brainwashed?"

"Captain, it was difficult at first. I wanted to complete the military training but I sensed the indoctrination would turn me into a different person. I applied myself in the training programs and achieved high marks. I became more purposeful to repress the propaganda leveled at me. I spent a few moments each evening reviewing what I learned that day. In essence, I regurgitated, dismissing what I found objectionable. By doing this, I felt I could remain true to myself and the values of my family and tribe."

Even though he was only 21 years old, he was astute and steadfast enough to stick to his beliefs. Returning to Mandaka, he became a guard at the presidential palace. Now in his eighth month, he wondered whether this was another life-changing situation. He was pleased for this new opportunity. He considered Tombola pompous and brutal.

The road down from the presidential hilltop was well paved and tree-lined. The purple blossoms of the jacaranda trees rendered a majestic touch. Bougainvillea, hibiscus, agapanthus and bottlebrush trees formed a corridor for the entranceway. The colorful display paid tribute to the arrogance of power, since all else within view spoke of poverty in a blanket of drabness. The palatial workforce lived in a few dozen sun-baked mud shacks covered with dried palm fronds about 200 meters from the base of the hill. A stand of yellow-flowering mimosa trees served as a buffer between the palatial grounds and the shacks. As they approached the city, François and Mario observed a sharp difference in the landscape. It was awash with shacks nearly set one on top of another.

Mario remarked as he observed the vista. "You know me, François, I'm not an apologist for Africans, but their apathy and disaffection are understandable when your eyes are filled with such a scene."

"Life shits, Mario. Too many people, not enough resources and services."

"This is what Frantz Fanon was addressing in his writings."

"*C'est insupportable*! '*Les Damnés de la Terre*' (Wretched of the Earth) is regarded as a bible with its discourse on the dehumanization of colonialism. Fanon's contention is the downtrodden people would inevitably erupt in violence to affect changes. Mandaka is just about at that point, which should help Kibali in gaining acceptance."

"The communes are a collar that serves as a noose around the city, contributing to their own strangulation."

Mulling this over, François responded. "That's the problem. In a way, it is a noose, suffocating the economic life of the country. It boils down to heightened expectations."

Mario continued as he expressed his discomfort. "There's danger here with a void in leadership. Let's hope they won't realize this until after Kibali's arrival, when our task becomes a *fait accompli*."

"Troops will be taking over for us shortly, Mario. This will de-emphasize our presence. Kwambe, take us to army headquarters. Use the back roads; I want to avoid the center of town. We're good for now with few people on the streets."

A symbol of earlier Mandakan struggles lay ahead, *"L'Arc des Martyrs"*. This was the gateway to the city and one of the few reminders of the past. Dreams, promises, aspirations and good intentions all dissipated as quickly as a deodorant used to cover up malodorous rankness.

Kwambe took a right before the arch, leaving the fairly well maintained main road, and drove over a street with telltale signs of having been paved. Potholes retained water from a heavy rainfall two days earlier. As the vehicle passed over these depressions, clouds of insects arose, raising the specter of disease in the minds of the two passengers.

"These *banlieues* provide a glimpse of the country's economy", Mario remarked. "If Mandakans yearn for better living conditions, they should embrace Kibali's return with open arms."

As they proceeded in circumventing the center of the city, Mario continued with his observations. "It's 6:20 am, when people usually emerge to do their chores. This being Sunday morning following the celebration, we might get another 2-3 hours before they realize the country's leadership has changed. What they have now is the white man's word, which hasn't always been benevolent."

François asserted. "Kibali couldn't come any sooner. Not to worry, it'll work out."

Upon entering the compound, Kwambe drove up to command control. There was another vehicle with cross markings on its doors parked in front of the building.

"Looks like medical help is here", chirped Mario, pleased that Gundhart was being looked after so quickly.

François paused as he alit from the vehicle, gazing across the compound. He gave thumbs up to Frantz and the other men who kept watch on the seated detainees. He motioned to the closest man to come forward.

"Our driver's name is Kwambe. Until a few moments ago, he was an elite guard at the palace. I think I can trust him, but keep an eye on him while I check on Gundhart. Don't let him out of your sight; he could still turn on us."

As he climbed the stairs, he spoke to Mario. "This is encouraging."

Mario reminded François caution was the watchword. "Even if Saferdatu agrees to support Kibali, we don't know the man."

"No question. He's a bastard, in league with Tombola."

Gundhart lay on a couch attached to an IV with clear liquid dripping through the tube. He seemed at ease, probably the result of a mild sedative. A white woman, likely a missionary nurse, tended to the wound in his left thigh. François scanned the room and greeted Gundhart.

"Looks like you're in good hands, but don't get too comfortable because there's still work to be done."

„Solch sympathie, mien befehishaber," as Gundhart reproached his commander for his lack of sympathy.

The attending nurse felt tension and was about to admonish François for his insensitivity, when both men burst out in laughter. Gundhart lavished praise on his men.

"The doctor wants me at his hospital, the Catholic '*Maison du Bon Berger' (*House of Good Shepherd). He says there's a risk of complication if he treated me here. The bullet might have damaged the femur. I'm sure I'll be fine but it looks like you'll have to do without me for a while."

"You'll go to any length to get some time off."

"Watch yourself, François, don't be glib. You're fortunate. I would have shot another man for suggesting I'm a shirker, even in jest."

"*Jetzt ist meine feinen deutschen Freund, nicht bekommen, selbst aufgearbeitet.* Keep your cool my friend and don't get yourself worked up. All kidding aside, take care and follow the doctor's orders."

The French doctor came over to speak to François after administering to Saferdatu.

"Your friend needs a surgical procedure I prefer not to attempt here. His condition is stable but the injury is no trifling matter. The General is in better condition and I'll get back to him in a moment to close his wound. The bullet went through his bicep and exited, so in his case, it's patch up work."

François inquired further on Saferdatu. "How soon will you have the General's arm taken care of? I need him available to me after you're finished."

"All patients with gunshot wounds need a period of rest to recuperate. I've already begun treating the wound and I should be finished in another 20 minutes."

"These aren't normal times, doctor. I must have him when you're done. I appreciate your helping us."

"I have business to discuss with your patient before he goes to the hospital. Gundhart, tell me about Saferdatu. You've chatted with him. Give me a sense of the guy."

"I wouldn't bet my modest fortune on the man, but I'd make a side wager he could be relied on in the short term. He's an opportunist, adaptable to changed circumstances; he's not a zealot. He was Tombola's man because Tombola was in power. He seems to have accepted the situation as it is. He'll need to be stroked to win him over. He doesn't strike me as a person who would be involved in a counter-coup."

"Thanks Gundhart, I'll keep your comments in mind. Now, rest up and we'll get you to the hospital shortly. Sorry I upset you with my attempt at humor. You're the direct opposite of a shirker."

François joined Mario who was talking to Saferdatu. As Gundhart explained, Saferdatu seemed to have mellowed. François decided to test him. "General, you know the fight is over; there's a new regime. Jean Paul Kibali is appealing to the people to work with him toward a better Mandaka. We're here only to assist Kibali in his return. My men leave Mandaka in a few hours. I want you to speak to your soldiers."

"I've already spoken to them. You can see for yourself they're peaceful."

"I appreciate what you've done. It's important to keep them as they are. Tell them to give Kibali time to prove himself. They'll be released soon if they cause no problems."

"If you're inviting me to join Kibali's team, I need to know where I stand."

"It's not for me to speculate what Kibali will do in your case. Kibali and his team will decide the path Mandaka will follow, not us. As you know, General Gaston Pastambu is a close, personal friend of Kibali. He was involved with Kibali in organizing this mission. Significant support has gathered for Kibali in the military. This is as much as I know, General. Now, tell me what you think of these new circumstances."

"I accept what you say. I'll trust Kibali to honor my patriotism, my rank and accomplishments. I know Gaston Pastambu well and I trust he'll understand I was only doing my job when I took action against the coup plotters. If there's to be a new Mandaka, there must be forgiveness so we can move on. To answer your query, yes, I'll accompany you and speak to the men."

CHAPTER TWELVE

François was concerned with another venue. The presence of the North Korean Foreign Minister at Mandaka's showcase hotel elevated the Bandala Hilton to a place of importance.

"Mario, I can spare you while I accompany Saferdatu to meet with the soldiers."

"What's up?"

"The Hilton Hotel. It's 10-12 minutes from here. We want to avoid any problems with visitors. Talk to the manager and see what the deal is."

"Will do. Kwambe can drive me over the back roads. Who should I take?"

"Stéphane Chappuis is already with Kwambe. Take him. This might test Kwambe's loyalties. You know what to do if he attempts to betray us."

Still uncertain of local reactions, François added. "If you're threatened or see any sign of trouble, turn back. I don't want to lose you."

"There you go again, getting all sentimental. It's nice to know you care, *mon ami*. I think I'm in good hands with Kwambe."

As they drove out of the compound, a few more people were moving about listlessly. They continued through a more densely populated area, avoiding the center of the city. Mario noticed increased activity, but he considered none of it alarming. The smell of smoldering charred wood was in the air as smoke wafted lazily in the stillness. Fires were lit for the morning meal and to heat water for washing. Two goatherds were leading their flocks in search of a patch of grass. Several women were by the edge of a nearby stream, attempting to cleanse their clothing in the turbid water. Small groups of men, seemingly oblivious to anything around them, sat in tiny dirt yards, engaged in conversation and drinking heavily sweetened coffee.

"Stéphane, anything out there?"

"It's cool; nothing I can see."

"Hope this isn't the calm before the storm."

"Kwambe, stop at the kiosque. Get me a copy of the newspaper."

The headlines in the "*Bandala Presse*" read, "**KIBALI EST DE RETOUR!!!"** It was an article paying tribute to Kibali's unwavering moral character and his dedication to improve the lives of Mandakans. The article concluded, "Be patient and give Kibali your support. With your help, he will make Mandaka a better place to live." Mario was pleased that the article made it appear Kibali was already in the country. Another article recapped the road to independence, continuing with a vision of improvements Mandakans can expect.

Mario liked what he read. "People will see this is as Kibali's doing. If they think we're seizing power for our own sake, we wouldn't have a prayer of getting out of here alive."

When the Hilton came into view, the disparity of rich and poor, extravagance and survival was evident. While it lacked the grandeur of the palace, it was impressive nonetheless, with its manicured, lush lawns and bountiful array of flowers. As they came up the drive, their eyes gravitated to a fracas in front of the hotel. Three men, seemingly Arab, were preying on two 'European' men. Regardless of nationality, whites were lumped together as Europeans. Mario could see all five men were agitated, as they pushed and shoved each other. One of the triad unsheathed a knife and waved it at the Europeans, who seemed ready to attack their adversaries.

Mario told Stéphane, "Stay in the vehicle with Kwambe. I'll check this out."

As Mario walked toward the quintet with his weapon at the ready, the assaulters fled. He approached the two remaining men with caution.

"Who are you", asked Mario, "and what's this about?"

"I'm an American businessman. My name is Jack Thompson," replied the white man in his mid-40s with a bit of a paunch hanging over his belt. Mario thought he might have been an athlete in his day from his overall appearance but it had been some time since he had engaged in physical activity.

"And you?" Mario pointed to the second man with a slightly darker complexion.

"I am Anastas Violetes, a Greek businessman." Mario reflected that this one could likely handle himself in a confrontation.

"Why are you here?"

Displaying a degree of nervousness, Thompson responded. "We're both in import-export. We're here on business and only met yesterday during the celebrations."

"Why are you in the country at this time?"

Showing more composure than his colleague, and not wanting to irritate a man holding a gun, Violetes was quick to answer. "We're looking to develop business contacts. As it turns out, Mr. Thompson and I were given the names of the same people to look up through our sources."

"The three men who you were fighting, are they part of your contacts?"

"On the contrary", Thompson clarified, "it seems they're part of the competition. They were explaining that they didn't welcome our visit."

Mario instructed them to go back in the hotel. "You'll be safer there. Trouble could develop. There's been a change in government. I advise you to stay out of the way."

Violetes sought additional information. "I have commitments elsewhere so my time is limited. You seem involved with the regime change. What's going on?"

Mario gave them a brief run-down on the situation, insisting again that they remain in the hotel. As they parted, Thompson gave Mario his business card.

"I'm here a few more days. Let me know when it's safe to continue with my appointments."

Mario scanned the lobby and strolled over to the reception desk. A few people sat at a café on one side of the lobby. A service table had coffee, croissants and a stack of the "*Presse*" for the patrons. Three bellhops sat by the elevators, chatting among themselves. It was a relaxed setting. The manager was summoned.

«Bon jour. Je suis Philippe Ziegler, le gérant de l'hôtel.» Ziegler was a Franco-German Swiss and a Hilton Corporation management employee. "How can I help you, *monsieur?*"

Mario introduced himself and told Ziegler what was happening.

"Yes, I know. I heard the announcement on the radio and read the newspaper."

"Tell me, Mr. Ziegler, has there been anything suspicious? It seems very quiet."

"This is the way it's been. But wait a minute; there was a long distance phone call from Nairobi a little over an hour ago for the North Korean Foreign Minister who's staying with us."

"Do you know whether the Foreign Minister actually received the phone call?"

"My operator told me about it and assured me the call was transferred and received by someone in the Foreign Minister's suite. That's all I can tell you."

"Were there any other calls or any visitors that came to the hotel this morning?"

"No, Mr. Rossetti, it's been quiet with most of the guests still in their rooms."

"Have any Koreans been down to the lobby this morning?"

"We haven't seen any this morning. They may need to sleep in after whooping it up into the early hours. They kept our bellhops hopping with frequent calls for room service."

"Thanks. Call me at the palace if any problems develop. *Au revoir.*"

Stéphane and Kwambe were chatting when Mario returned to the vehicle. Their relaxed postures belied the fact Kwambe was the enemy a short time ago, shooting to kill Stéphane's comrades at the palace.

"What are you two scheming? You seem to be buddy-buddy."

"Mario, Kwambe was telling me about his life in the village."

Mario asked Kwambe, "Will your people feel the same as you about the change?"

"*Mon capitaine*, we're not a unified people, but a collection of tribes. The government in Bandala has little meaning for most of us. We relate to our tribal leaders and our villages. We know we are part of a nation, but it's a vague concept."

On the return drive to army headquarters, Mario noticed people gathering under a large tamarind tree on a lot in one of the communes. A man beckoned the people to congregate near him. As the vehicle drew closer, the crowd was larger than at first sighting. Several dozen vocal and animated men and women were assembled. The more the speaker waved his arms, the greater the crowd reaction.

Mario sensed trouble. "Those are angry looking people. What do you make of it, Kwambe?"

"A member of Tombola's tribe is stirring up the crowd. He's rallying the group to act against the foreigners before it's too late."

The vehicle accelerated suddenly as they spoke. Mario looked out the rear window and saw the crowd running after them, throwing stones and shouting.

"Kwambe, good going, getting us out of there."

"As we approached, I saw the group forming. It looked like a normal gathering. People in the neighborhoods share their thoughts and vent their frustrations. The mood changed when they saw us and listened to the speaker. Someone shouted, 'there they are, the foreign invaders. Let's get them before they get us'. Then I heard, 'let's get our weapons and chase them down'."

Mario was gaining greater appreciation for his driver. "You had the chance to act differently. Had they caught up with us, we would have defended ourselves. Many more of your people would've been killed."

"Like I said, I don't want my people killed."

They continued without further incident. The people they saw showed no interest as the vehicle passed. Danger loomed on the horizon. Mario was concerned.

"A crowd is easily manipulated into a mob. Agitators aren't shy about spreading rumors to fuel fear and chaos. We might be getting a battle we don't want."

CHAPTER THIRTEEN

Pastambu awoke startled and confused. Mind over matter hadn't worked. He was determined not to concede defeat, but his bodily needs overwhelmed his attempts to remain alert. He thought he had dozed only a few minutes, but recalled it was dark when he sat down to rest. Time passed and the sun had risen. Something awakened him. His phone was ringing and he managed to regain his wits to answer. It was François.

"Where have you been? I tried calling but I got no answer. I thought you might have run into a problem. What's going on?"

"François, not to worry. No problem here. I've been out checking on my men."

"I'm pleased to hear this, General. Kibali wants to speak with you before he leaves Nairobi. You should be available where you can receive his call."

"*Pas de problème*. Of course, I'll stand by for Kibali's call."

Actually, the purpose of François' call was to apprise Pastambu of the situation he was facing. "There's a developing problem at army headquarters that could spill into town, the airport and the palace. Some of my men were attacked when they were returning from the Hilton. An angry crowd attending a rally in a commune pelted their vehicle with rocks and threatened action. We believe the group is strengthening and gathering weapons as it heads our way. I have enough men and firepower to fight them off initially if they do come."

"If that's the case, François, what is it that you want from me?"

François hesitated a moment to reflect and decided to lay it out straight. "General, this is just a thought. What's your take on using one of Saferdatu's officers and some soldiers as a preventive force. I know it could be dicey, but there must be someone trustworthy here."

Pastambu wasn't sure if he was fully awake after listening to François. Did he hear correctly? Pastambu thought François was playing with fire with his suggestion.

"*Sacré bleu!* Do you realize what you're asking? *C'est idiot!* You don't know any of those soldiers, so how do you determine trustworthiness? Saferdatu is beholden to Tombola for his position. If you let him loose with armed men, or any of the captive officers, Saferdatu will be free to overwhelm you and storm the palace to free Tombola. I wouldn't put it past him to seek power if he had the chance. He knows where he stands with Tombola but his future is uncertain at best with Kibali. He has a streak of ruthlessness in him and is short on principles."

"Don't hold back on me, General. Tell me how you really feel."

"What more do you want from me, François?"

"Never mind. That was my attempt at levity. Anyway, when I was chatting with him, he agreed to allow Kibali a trial period to see what he can do. I persuaded Saferdatu to speak to the soldiers urging restraint and to give Kibali a chance."

"What does he expect from us?"

"General, the only concern he expressed was where he might fit in under Kibali. I told him it was up to Kibali and you to determine his position."

"Kibali and I agreed to leave any role I might play open. I have options to explore but I might stay on to help with the transition. It's not for me to speak on what's to be done with Saferdatu."

"If a mob confronts us, we'll be sandwiched between the rabble and the soldiers."

"Kingambo is deploying his men to Bandala. A few other unit commanders stand ready to proceed as needed."

"How soon can you get a detachment to assist us? His regiment has 1,500 to 1,800 men. He should be able to send a trusted subordinate with a unit to assist us."

"François, I'm looking out for you. I ordered Kingambo to do precisely what you ask. Your relief is on route and should be arriving shortly."

"We'll be happy to welcome the troops. We can make do until they arrive. When we're relieved, I'll return to the palace with my men, passing through the center of town."

"Colonel Kingambo should be there, probably installing himself in city hall. Tell him not to get too comfortable. He's due at the airport to greet Kigali."

"I'll do that. I'll see you at the palace."

"OK. I await Kibali's call and will bring him up to date."

Pastambu reflected on his situation. There was a blank period as he slept. He summoned one of his men from the passenger waiting area.

"It seems peaceful. Have there been any problems?"

"Nothing we couldn't handle, General. The off-duty traffic controller tried to bolt. He said he needed to get home to his family. One of our colleagues collared him as he sprang through the doorway. We tied him up to keep him from trying to get away again. Other than that, people have been sleeping and making escorted trips to the lavatories."

"What about the men outside?"

"No problem there either. I came over to report but found you sleeping. So, I took it upon myself to check on our men."

Reacting in annoyance and embarrassment, Pastambu changed his tone.

"What's your name and who put you in charge?"

"I took it upon myself to do what was right, General. I'm Guillaume Wabitale. I served in our army for four years and I'm now a school teacher."

"Very well, Guillaume, you should have awakened me but obviously I needed the rest. Thanks for looking after things for me."

"I told no one. There's something else. On my walk through the area, I discovered a vehicle that might be useful. There's a Citroën DS parked in one of the hangars and it seems operable. You might recall Charles de Gaulle rode in such a '*Déesse*' when the attempted assassination was eluded."

"Yes, I know the car and you're right, it's considered a prestigious vehicle. Do you know who owns this one?"

"It's registered to a French diamond merchant who probably left for Paris."

"Well done, Guillaume, go fetch it. We'll check it out to be sure it's safe. The '*Déesse*' will be appropriate to get our new leader to the palace."

Shortly after completing his phone conversation with Pastambu, François heard the ruckus in the distance. The mob wasn't in sight but its progress could be determined by the dust raised from the parched dirt road. As the frenzied stampede of people advanced, Mario recalled the *encierro,* enclosed street, at the *Fiesta de San Fermin* in Spain. Years earlier, he had managed to stay ahead of the raging bulls and reach the *Plaza de Toros,* exhausted but unscathed.

"François, this might be weird but I just had this thought. It's an analogy: the movement of the mob and the running of the bulls in Pamplona. This mob has been unleashed the same as bulls charging through the streets of Spain, with no rational thought of what lies ahead. They're both stampedes, leaderless and unruly. Mobs can be more brutal than animals."

"Well now, Mario, aren't you the philosophical one? This could be a sign of broader resistance or merely an aberration. Relief is on the way. We'll take care of the mob until the troops arrive. There are eleven of us to do what needs to be done."

"We need to keep the soldiers from charging us as we repel the crowd."

"Mario, the soldiers seem to have bought Saferdatu's message. There could be troublemakers. I'll take five men and you take the other four to keep the soldiers submissive."

"Our captives have seen their comrades fall, which should dampen their enthusiasm."

"Sounds good. We'll fire a few rounds as the mob approaches. This should give them pause to dissuade them from advancing. We'll use heavier weapons we appropriated from the armory if needed."

François called out, "here they come. Let's give 'em a scare."

The number was impossible to pinpoint but François figured it was around 200, mostly men and some women. They carried an assortment of weapons, the ubiquitous AK-47, rifles, pistols, but mostly machetes, spears and garden tools. François was intent on minimizing bloodshed.

"Avoid causing casualties if possible. These people are agitated. They're likely good citizens who tend to their own affairs, but are caught in the moment. They intend to do us harm and there must be no illusion about this. We need to show them this isn't a game and could get them killed. If they persist, target the agitators first."

Some elements in the crowd started shooting wildly, well out of range of the compound. François gave the order to fire warning shots. When the shooting began, seven captured soldiers took advantage of the distraction. They arose quickly and dashed toward the mercenary guards. The exchange of fire with the mob caused a reflexive glance by Mario and his men. Mario dismissed his inattention when he detected the motion among the soldiers peripherally. With his Uzi cradled in his left arm, Mario drew his MAC-50 with his right and fired one round at the lead man. The shot got the soldier between the eyebrows, just above the nose. The dead man's companions scrambled back to the pack, realizing they had no chance to overtake their guards.

Mario looked at Saferdatu. The General showed no emotion and did nothing to stop the soldiers.

"What are you going to do with these men for disobeying your orders?"

"It seems to me you've taken care of it."

Mario motioned to an army officer who was sitting with the group. "Come here, Commandant. I've noticed your demeanor. You seem to be sensible, realizing that this is a new ballgame. You saw what happened. Your general feels these soldiers can ignore his orders and get away with it. What do you think?"

«Ne vous inquiétez pas, Capitaine»

Telling Mario not to worry, the major walked over to each of the six men, who were trying to become invisible. He wrote down their names and gave each a harsh slap across the face. He called each a '*maudit cochon!*', stupid pig. He glared at Saferdatu as he reported to Mario. It was apparent the major didn't hold the general in high esteem.

"They've been humiliated in front of their comrades. This puts an end to their military service."

"Thank you, Commandant. Tell me your name."

"I am Commandant Florien Tanandu".

"Stay here by my side. Keep an eye on your fellow soldiers. I can't give you a weapon but you can still help keeping this situation tranquil. President Kibali will be pleased to learn of your assistance."

The crowd was undeterred by the warning shots, which landed short as intended. Shouting, laughing and jeering, the group seemed emboldened as it kept advancing. François spotted several men as the principal agitators. They were screaming above the din to charge the foreign enemy. Three of these were in front of the group, leading the assault. François knew he couldn't stave off a charging mob on one side and a potential swarm of soldiers on the other side with his small band of warriors. He was concerned about the repercussions of mowing down the mob. His experience told him that doing so would bring greater resistance within the population. It would reflect on past colonial atrocities. He had to take action and raised his Uzi. He shot two of the leaders through the chest, hoping to spare the rest of the mob. Most of the people in the crowd halted where they stood.

While individuals in the group began considering their vincibility, others resumed the charge on the compound. François was about to order his men to shoot at those advancing when he heard a rumble coming from the opposite direction.

"Hold your fire men; here comes the cavalry. The odds have changed and the crowd doesn't like them."

A convoy of armored personnel carriers and trucks approached the compound. The lead vehicle opened fire, strafing the ground just ahead of the mob. Some people stood fast, raising their arms and shouting back at both the foreign intruders and the military. This was short lived as the convoy drove past the group and entered the compound. Soon, only a few curious on-lookers remained. The rabble-rousers fled.

The commander in charge of the *compagnie* descended from the second vehicle. He saluted François with a polished gesture.

"I assume you're François Morency. Colonel Kingambo sends his compliments. He's impressed with what you've accomplished."

"*Capitaine*, your arrival is timely. My compliments to you and your good colonel. Yes, I'm François Morency. We were heading for a bloodbath. You saved many lives."

"I'm *Captaine* Edouard Bolotatu. My mission is to relieve you and take control of army headquarters. Under instructions from General Pastambu, Colonel Kingambo has ordered me to take General Saferdatu into custody. Where will I find him?"

"I'll fetch him. Mario, bring Saferdatu here."

François spoke to Saferdatu. "General, Captain Bolotatu and his detachment are now in charge. He has orders to take you into custody until your situation is resolved. He's assured me of your safety."

CHAPTER FOURTEEN

Captain Edouard Bolotatu and two of his men escorted Saferdatu into command control. They placed the former army leader in a side room. François accompanied the group and awaited the captain's return in the main room.

The general was upset with being held captive. "I don't understand why you're treating me this way. I professed my loyalty to Kibali and swear I'll be true to him."

"General, you know how this works. It shouldn't surprise you. You were Tombola's top military commander. Your fate isn't in my hands. I'll respect your rank while you're in my custody; beyond that, it's up to the new president, Jean Paul Kibali."

Saferdatu retorted in a rebuke to this inferior officer.

«Tu n'es qu'un gosse. Je veux parler à un officier supérieur.»

"General, you are my prisoner for the time being. Despite how youthful I may seem to you, I'm a seasoned and disciplined officer in the Mandakan army."

"Let me speak to Kibali to straighten this out. I believe it's my right to be heard and to meet directly with him."

"All in good time. You'll have the opportunity to do exactly as you request."

Awaiting Bolotatu to join him to go over details, François walked over to an urn on a side shelf and checked its contents. He was delighted to see warm coffee. He poured a cup and drank it as he preferred, strong and black. One sip told him it was one of his favorites, a Kenyan Arabica with its distinctive fruity acidic taste. He settled in a chair and lit a *Gauloise* cigarette from a pack he carried in his blouse pocket. François was an infrequent smoker but there were times when he found it pleasurable. This was one such occasion. Bolotatu joined François, poured himself a cup and sat across a table from François. He accepted the offer of a smoke.

"Captain, you're a lifesaver, more than you imagine. Your arrival spared many lives. It's always satisfying to conclude a mission on a high note."

"You were efficient, Colonel. I'd appreciate your insights on Kibali. You must know him fairly well to put your life on the line for him. I was a lieutenant when Pastambu left, but I don't know his connection to Kibali."

"I can't fill in all the details but I'll share what I know."

François briefed Bolotatu as the two relaxed, growing more comfortable with each other. He singled out Commandant Florien Tanandu as a good guy who provided assistance. He concluded by inquiring on the situation elsewhere.

"Captain, you know anything about the *gendarmerie* and at the university?"

"The *gendarmerie* is running motorized patrols in Bandala and other towns. We have our men in town and positioned on the outskirts of the university campus."

"Well then, Captain, my business is done. Must move on to prepare for your new president's arrival. You're now in charge."

"I salute you, *mon colonel*. You've done a great service for my country."

At that moment, Mario entered the room.

"Captain Mario Rossetti meet Captain Edouard Bolotatu." The men greeted each other and exchanged thanks for a job well done.

"Mario, get Stéphane, Frantz and Kwambe to check the motor pool for two trucks to return to the palace. You and I will ride with Kwambe."

"Captain, one more thing." François added, "I assume Colonel Kingambo is in town. Let him know we'll be driving through the center."

"I'll contact him immediately. I'll provide an escort for you."

"Thanks Captain, but there's no need. We'll make our way as we usually do."

"That doesn't surprise me. *Alors, bonne chance*."

François rounded up the remaining ten men of Gundhart's group. "Four of you with Stéphane and the other four with Frantz.

We'll go through the center of the city on our way to the palace. Let's get rolling."

They climbed aboard and headed out of the compound. They traveled only a few hundred yards when the first shots rang out. The mercenaries fired a few rounds to keep the attackers back while the vehicle drivers accelerated to create distance. As they proceeded further, the number of people by roadside increased, amidst both cheering and jeering. An independent audio vote counter would have declared 'cheering', led by '*Vive Kibali*', as the clear winner. The jeerers were definitely in the minority with their shouts of '*a bas les étrangers*', down with the foreigners, but they were the most demonstrative and agitated.

Shots were fired at the trucks but they didn't last long; bystanders took charge. In reverse action, the crowd attacked the fractious elements, subduing them and taking their weapons. An occasional wild shot was fired and rocks were hurled at the vehicles. The mercenaries were committed to avoid as much bloodshed as possible. Once again, mass killings could have repercussions. There was no serious threat with the majority of roadsiders jubilant, applauding and cheering.

While observing their reception, François spoke to Kwambe. "It's a good sign that the people are not associating us with the former colonials."

"*Mon colonel*, they know you're foreigners, but they see you as agents for change. They're fed up with Tombola. They know there wouldn't be change unless someone took action. We expect your group will leave once Kibali is here."

They noticed the change of scenery. They left behind a sea of fragile huts surrounded by fragments of cannibalized vehicles, emaciated chickens and sundry debris. Their new surroundings were paved streets, villas on plush grounds and multi-storied buildings. They had entered the capital city of Bandala. It was a transition from squalid conditions to a European look-alike setting.

François spoke to Kwambe. "Our mission is nearly over. We're getting out of here. This should please you, Kwambe".

"Please don't take offense, Colonel. There are aspects of our past we want to forget. No more outsider control."

"No offense taken, Kwambe. Pull over. I want to talk to these soldiers."

Kwambe had become more comfortable with his foreign companions. He took a liking to Mario, who seemed natural and without airs, treating people respectfully, unless they were hostile. All of the superiors he had known, in North Korea and Mandaka, were rigid and demanding. He observed that Mario's demeanor was different, and yet, he was a foreigner so one still had to be wary.

François and Mario alit from the vehicle and approached the soldiers, who moved into the middle of the street to block passage. The soldiers raised their weapons across their chests, challenging the two Europeans.

A corporal called out, "*Arrêtez!* Don't come any closer. Identify yourselves."

"I'm Colonel Morency and this is Captain Rossetti. We're assisting President Kibali and General Pastambu in their return to Mandaka. I'd like to meet with Colonel Kingambo. Could you direct me to him?"

"I'll radio ahead to check on you. The colonel may know who you are but I don't. Stand where you are until I get a response. My men will shoot if you make any move."

"*Très bien*, make your call. I assure you we're on the same team."

After receiving confirmation that the white foreigners were friends, the corporal beckoned François and Mario to come forward. He seemed to display displeasure with the outcome, likely preferring another disposition.

"I've been ordered to let you pass. My comrades have the same orders so you're free to move on. Colonel Kingambo awaits you in front of *la mairie*. City Hall is seven blocks down the road. Be careful how you behave. We'll be watching."

As they proceeded down the main street, *l'avenue de l'independence*, soldiers and armed civilians were at every intersection. Each of these groups interrupted their chatter as the vehicles approached. The European warriors received a good reception from these Mandakan patriots. Two men were standing on the front steps of City Hall. Two dozen soldiers stood on either side of the stairs. The older of the two men, who appeared to be in his mid-to-late 40's, displayed a measure of swagger and was bedecked in an officer's dress uniform. He had a golden cordon looped around his right shoulder and his chest was adorned with several ribbons and medals. Colonel Kingambo was a sight. Totally in conflict with the situation and in sharp contrast to his men in battle gear.

The second man on the stairs was in his early 30's and in civilian clothes. He waved to François and his men as they approached. He didn't seem intimidated by his companion's display.

"You must be Colonel Morency. I salute you for your success. My name is Claude Pelletier and I'm General Pastambo's adjutant. The armed men mingling with the soldiers are part of the general's group. This is Colonel Marcellin Kingambo."

"*Merci*, Monsieur Pelletier. I'm pleased to see the city under control."

"We ran into some disaffected, who tried to make trouble. With help from the *gendarmes*, we took care of them before the soldiers arrived."

Kingambo stepped forward to greet François and Mario, executing a limp and halfhearted salute. His formal education was limited to a few years of elementary school with the missionaries. He was maladroit when it came to social graces but he had a strong trait that was his salvation. His keen sense of loyalty to his superiors was constant regardless of who came to power. He advanced through the ranks under the colonial regime and was elevated to officer status soon after independence.

François spoke first to show respect to the colonel in front of his men.

*«Mes compléments, mon colonel», * as he returned the salute.

"I complement you, Colonel Morency. I'm impressed. From the start, I told Pastambu and Kibali your chances of success were minimal. I believe you have a term for the way you conducted the operation, 'a surgical strike'. While we don't want to become dependent on foreigners again, we have much to learn from you Europeans."

"In my judgment, it was the only way to go; light and quick."

"That's what is so impressive. Your planning, leading a small band of men and achieving your objectives in a limited time frame are noteworthy. We need to be mindful our military, from top to bottom, has a long way to go to achieve a degree of efficiency and effectiveness."

"It's been my pleasure to assist in Kibali's return. The arrival of your men at army headquarters was timely. It prevented further civilian bloodshed. I leave you to complete the duties of my mission."

CHAPTER FIFTEEN

As François climbed aboard his vehicle, he reminded Kingambo that Pastambu expected him at the airport.

"Yes, I'll be there shortly. I'll check my men to assure they are well dispersed."

"Do what you must, Colonel. I'm going to the palace and prepare to greet Kibali. My men and I appreciate your readiness and quick response."

Kingambo bade the European farewell while suggesting a speedy departure.

"*Au revoir et bon voyage*. May you have a safe journey home. If I may provide you with a word of advice, *ne tardez pas à quitter le pays."*

"Thanks Colonel, for your good wishes. I understand your meaning and we won't linger. My men are leaving as soon as

Kibali is in place. We don't want a backlash by overstaying our welcome."

François signaled to his men in the trucks that they were moving on.

"Kwambe, we return to the palace. You've provided valuable assistance to us and I appreciate it."

"Colonel, I'm honored to be involved in assisting Kibali's return. Mandakans will feel as I do. I'm of no consequence, but I thank you for what you've done for my people."

"It was a job Kibali hired us to do. It's satisfying it turned out well."

"Regardless of what you say, you have all staked your lives for us."

Mario was attentive as the two exchanged their appreciation. "Kwambe, your duties as our driver will end soon. I sense you'd rather not be a palace guard."

"Yes, but I don't have a choice."

"Kwambe, I have no official authority. But tell me, is there something you'd prefer doing if given a choice?"

"Now that I'm in the military, I believe it's my future. I'd like different responsibilities but it's very difficult to have changes approved."

"We may be able to arrange something for you. Will you trust us to look into it?"

Kwambe looked with some disbelief at Mario. He switched his glance to François. François nodded, exhibiting a smile that Kwambe hadn't seen before.

"Kwambe, you can believe Captain Rossetti. We'll discuss your situation with President Kibali and General Pastambu. We'd like to improve your situation. This is what we'll do, unless you object."

"I'm surprised that you would do this for me. Go ahead if you think you can help."

The three-vehicle convoy soon reached the limits of Bandala center and passed through *L'Arc des Martyrs.* The remainder of the trip to the palace was somewhat daunting but uneventful. Kingambo had dispatched some of his men to stand along the roadway, denying access to agitators who might attack the Europeans as they passed through. Countless people from the communes were there. They hooted and hollered. The crowd pushed closer to the passing vehicles. They clamored to reach out to the mercenaries, scuffling with the soldiers. People were pushed back and knocked down. Soldiers fired shots in the air to keep them back. The revelers were jubilant, but created a situation that could run amuck. François looked back to check on the two trucks carrying his men to assure their safe passage.

"Mario, this can be dangerous. Good to have the soldiers. These people, happy or angry, would have stormed our vehicles."

"We were nearly swallowed up by their gratitude."

"We can thank Kingambo for being on the ball."

At the entrance to the palatial grounds, several members of the military detachment stood by the sides of the three vehicles. Passage was allowed.

The scene as viewed by François and Mario did nothing to betray what had occurred on the grounds of the palace a short time earlier. Had they not known firsthand, there was no evidence multiple violent deaths had created a macabre landscape. The only indication life existed at this site was four white men sitting by a stilled fountain with weapons in their laps. All was quiet and there were no other signs of humanity, living or otherwise. François told Kwambe to drive up to the fountain.

"Seems you've just been lounging while we've been doing the heavy lifting."

"Use your imagination, François. Can't, you see this as a fine European-style spa."

"Very funny. I'm amused. What did you do with them?"

"We decided the area needed cleaning up, so we took care of things," replied another. "We figured dead bodies lying around tended to spoil the curbside appeal of this manor and we didn't want the next occupant to be repelled by its appearance. We found a cart and took them away to the rear of the palace."

"Good going. Where are Julio and the five others?"

"Julio is inside the palace lording over his authority and the others are there also."

The men from Gundhart's group alit from the trucks. Mario led Kwambe into the palace. François addressed his men. "Be here by the fountain in 20 minutes. We're nearly finished and must get ready for departure."

François hastened up the stairs and bounded into the palace. He exchanged greetings with the three men at the doorway. He spotted Julio astride the 'royal throne' shuffling through papers.

"You're right at home, my friend. You seem to enjoy this sense of power."

"It's great to see you also, *mi gran líder.* It's comforting to know you're still as cranky as ever."

"I'm pleased to see you have matters in hand, Julio. Counting you, I see only eight men where there should be ten. What happened to the other two?"

"One man is standing by the radio to handle communications. The other went to the hospital for further treatment. His wounds are non-life threatening but he needed minor surgery. Two others were treated here."

"There's hope for you yet, Julio. What are these papers you're leafing through?"

"A record of the Tombola regime's machinations. It provides details of wheeling and dealing and the names of those involved in pay-offs."

"Julio, good find. These papers will be valuable for Kibali and his people. They should help nail those who betrayed the country for personal gain. By the way, what have you done with Tombola and his entourage?"

"They're tucked away, François, under lock and key; Tombola in one room separate from the others. The guys check on them regularly."

"We're ready to receive Kibali. Preston and his men should arrive shortly. We need to gather to discuss our departure. Our mission is nearly over."

Mario was standing by listening to the exchange between his two friends. "Well done *amigo*. You look good in that seat of power. Say, François, what to do with Kwambe? We can't put him back with the others. Probably best he stays with us until we talk to Kibali and Pastambu."

"You're right, Mario. Keep Kwambe close by. He's ours for now."

François walked over to the room with the radio equipment and spoke to his man monitoring calls. "I'm gathering the men to discuss our departure, but I need you to remain here. Are there any messages?"

"Yes, François, a couple of dozen calls. Most from people who wanted to speak to Kibali. I have their names and contact information to pass on to him."

"Well done. Anything else?"

"There were three other calls. One was from Kibali, merely advising he was fine as he boarded the plane. He added that no one seemed to know who he is. Pastambu called to say he located a vehicle appropriate for the dignity of Mandaka's new president. Also, I just spoke with Preston. He's been relieved and is on his way here."

"We're in good shape. Let me know if there are any other calls. I'll pass on the messages to Kibali. I'll be by the fountain discussing our departure with the men."

CHAPTER SIXTEEN

Mandaka was similar in many ways to other newly emerging African countries. Their primary expectations upon attaining independence were control of their own destiny and respect of their sovereignty. They also fancied feeding at the global trough of economic and financial assistance.

Jean Paul Kibali was eager to begin the task of governing a country of considerable potential but with an unenviable record of mismanagement, corruption and failed economic policies. His arrival in Bandala on a BOAC, British Overseas Airline Corporation, de Havilland Comet was without fanfare, just as he wanted it.

Pastambu and Kingambo strode out of the terminal and proceeded across the tarmac to stand by the plane as it arrived. Kingambo commented on the paucity of activity at the airport, which was a clear indication of the lack of interest in Mandaka.

"General, there are only 2 or 3 passengers deplaning from Nairobi and none boarding for Lagos. It's as though Mandaka has fallen off the globe and the world community scarcely knows we exist."

"*Mon confrère*, it may well be they know about us, which could be reason for them to avoid us. We are being neglected but we've brought it on ourselves. I had a comfortable life in France but I was chagrined with the living conditions of our fellow citizens."

"No question a change is overdue. That's why I've thrown in with Kibali."

"Rest assured, Colonel, Kibali and I appreciate your loyalty. Kibali will need all the help he can get to put his plans in motion."

Only four of the thirteen passengers descended, Kibali being the last. The soldiers, who had accompanied Kingambo to the airport, took the other three passengers into the terminal building for inspection. There was some resistance among them, causing a soldier to strike a blow across a passenger's chest with his rifle butt. This elicited meek protests but full compliance.

Ignoring the fracas, Pastambu extended his hand to Kibali, greeting his friend with a warm embrace.

"*Bienvenu, mon président*. I trust all went well on your journey."

"Yes, the trip was uneventful. Traveling alone worked well. I went unnoticed, as far as I could tell."

"Jean Paul, it's a great feeling to be here and greet you back home."

"Gaston, you have to admit it, I was right about François Morency."

"I admit, I had doubts, but he's as good as advertized. We have a vehicle for your triumphal return. As our nation's president, you deserve transport equal to your position. This '*Déesse*' will serve you nicely."

"Thank you, General. It's certainly more than I expected."

As the three men piled in the rear seat, Pastambu introduced the armed man accompanying the driver in the front seat. "Guillaume has provided me valuable service. He might fit well in an appropriate position in your government."

"*Monsieur le président*, I feel I'm doing something worthwhile. I'm a school teacher, but if you decide I could serve our country better in another capacity, it would be an honor to do so."

"Guillaume, we'll see about that later as we get organized. However, it's rare praise this old curmudgeon has heaped on your behalf."

Kibali was anxious to get to the palace. He needed to form a government and establish a military hierarchy quickly to reassure the population and the world community.

"*Chauffeur*, take us through Bandala center. I want to see for myself how things are. Colonel Kingambo, I assume the city is secure."

"Yes, President. I have soldiers at road intersections along with General Pastambu's volunteers. The *gendarmerie* is also conducting motorized tours."

"Very well, let's get on with it."

As the *Déesse* proceeded on its journey, Pastambu and Kingambo briefed Kibali on their roles in the operation. A convoy of three trucks with armed soldiers escorted the Citroën through the city streets and onto the palace grounds. Mandakans, who were roadside, gazed at the convoy, hailing the sedan as it passed. François and Mario came forward to greet Kibali. François was gladdened by Kibali's arrival, as he was anxious to turn the palace over to him and move on.

"*Bienvenue*, *monsieur le président*, to Shangri-la. Good to see you here and I'm pleased to convey this fine establishment to you as your new home."

"Colonel Morency, your comment is amusing. I am pleased to accept on behalf of the citizens of Mandaka. You fully justified my faith in you. *Mission Accompli!* I believed in you from the first. The execution of your plan is impressive. For this, I'm eternally grateful."

"It's been my pleasure to assist you. I have a sense you'll succeed although you face many challenges. If I may, President Kibali, I'd like to prevail upon you to recognize my team members for their fine work. I know you have urgent business to tend to but this'll only take a moment."

"Of course, François, it's only fitting. I wouldn't be here were it not for them."

François walked over to the gathering with Kibali and introduced his men. Kibali shook hands with each one and thanked them for helping his country. Kibali turned to depart but François had another matter to take up.

"I must now get into the palace and confer with you, General Pastambu and Colonel Kingambo."

"Before we do, there's one more person I want to introduce. Mario, get Kwambe."

Kwambe was chatting with Kingambo's soldiers.

"Mister President, Mario has someone we'd like you to meet."

"Very well, François, but make it quick. Mario, go ahead."

"This is Kwambe, a former member of the palace guard. He's been loyal to us during our operations and assisted us out of dangerous situations. He's pleased with Tombola's departure and welcomes your return. François and I would like to speak to you further about Kwambe once you settle in."

"As you say, Mario, we can discuss this later. Now, François, will you join me in the palace?"

Kibali huddled together with François, Pastambu and Kingambo in the presidential chambers. François led the discussion, explaining the events as they unfolded. He gave Kibali a list of people who contacted the palace seeking to speak with him and the sheaf of papers discovered by Julio.

"Thank you François. Some of these people who called will be useful to the new government. Tell me, where are Tombola and Saferdatu being held?"

"Saferdatu is still at army headquarters in custody of Colonel Kingambo's men. Tombola is here in the palace, locked in a room. The two North Korean soldiers are locked in a room downstairs."

"I'll talk to Tombola and Saferdatu later. The papers you've provided will be useful in determining their fate. I will empower the judiciary. The courts will dispose of the criminals. My focus now is on the business of setting up a government so we can start functioning. You may not want to sit in on this, but you're welcome to do so."

"No thanks, Mister President. I appreciate the offer but I have other business to attend to. There are matters I'd like to discuss with you once you've taken care of the more pressing issues. Before I leave, I need to confirm the arrangements we discussed previously have been made for the departure of my men."

Kibali and Pastambu looked at Kingambo for a response.

"Yes, I followed up on this myself. After President Kibali contacted the Zandu President earlier this morning, I was in touch with a military colleague across the river. He's dispatching their VIP riverboat to ferry your men to Zandu for their flights. We agreed that we'll be relieved to see them depart the region. My men are standing by to provide transport to the dock."

"Thanks Colonel. I'll get my men organized for departure. Mario and I will remain to tie up any loose ends."

François returned to the courtyard and told his men the time had come to depart Mandaka. Trucks were standing by to take the mercenaries to the Lipongo River. Julio and Mario embraced, reminding each other of their planned get-togethers. Julio couldn't contain his emotions.

"Mario, it's difficult to appreciate that we've spent less than 12 hours in Mandaka when you consider what we've been through and accomplished. We've facilitated the empowerment of a government that could become the model for Africa."

"Julio, sometimes you get too idealistic. Don't get carried away with that notion. Maybe it'll work, and then maybe not. I'm convinced Kibali is sincere but he has a rough road ahead. The people aren't likely to accord him much time to prove himself. He must move quickly to gain their trust. For the immediate, he'll be riding on their hopes. The citizenry will continue to find it tough going because there'll be no overnight miracles."

Preston gathered his gear for departure as he listened to his two comrades.

"Julio, it's good to expect a positive outcome, particularly because of our role. I agree with Mario, who's more realistic. Anyhow, it'll be interesting to view developments in Mandaka from afar. My two friends, before we part company, there's something you should know."

Preston felt it his duty as an Englishman to put the Italian and the Spaniard in their proper places. His demeanor changed as he spoke again, a smug look on his face.

"I hear you are both engaged in a premature victory dance. This is about a *futbol* match? Madrid and Milan are fine teams. Winning the game is not victory—Manchester United looms ahead. You'll be awakened from your dreams."

Julio, ever the zealous patriot and *futbol* devotee, felt compelled to riposte.

"*Estos lleno de mierda,* You are full of shit. Madrid will whip Milan and take care of Manchester United. Even Milan would beat your English upstarts."

"Bugger off! Manchester United will show its mettle and send your Latinos back to romanticizing."

This set the stage for more wagers with an additional US $1,000. Mario and Julio each pledged half to cover the wager. "Preston, you have an excellent military mind. My *amigo* is correct that you don't have a clue about *futbol*. Where will we find you to collect our winnings?"

"All in good time, my dear chaps. You're delightful blokes. Your *naiveté* about the proper order of things causes me to feel sorry for you. Nonetheless, I'll relish the moment. The game will be played and we shall see who the savant is."

Mario couldn't resist getting his two-cents worth. "As my buddies might tell you in their own inimitable manner, *'che cazzo di stronzata!'*, this is fucking bullshit!"

PART II
ROMANTIC ODYSSEY

“Whatever you think,

be sure it is what it is what you think;

Whatever you want,

be sure that is what you want;

Whatever you feel,

be sure that is what you feel.”

T.S. Eliot

Anglo-American Critic,

Dramatist & Poet

CHAPTER SEVENTEEN

As Mario departed Mandaka, he had much on his mind. He was heading for Belgium to see Marianne. He was eager to talk to her but he was unable to control his uneasiness about the life-altering event. He intended to propose marriage but he had butterflies in his stomach thinking about it. He needed to muster the courage to articulate how he felt. Even then, there were no assurances Marianne's response would be favorable. He knew a key factor was his lifestyle. Certain elements were non-negotiable.

Mario settled in his first class seat, anticipating a long and tiring flight. To return to Europe, Mario flew to Kinshasa and continued on a Sabena flight to Brussels. He was restless, unable to relax as usual upon completing a mission. The nearly twelve-hour trip was full of anxiety and misgivings as he reflected on the person who emerged from youthful pranks and escapades. He retained his *joie de vivre* as a romantic but murkiness nudged its way into his persona. He was a killer, a person who extinguished lives when he was on a 'job'. His life was juxtaposed between violence and affability. He enjoyed life to the fullest, being gregarious and personable. But then, he lived on the edge, with his life on the line, engrossed in the darker side of humanity. Mario could walk away from the brutality, but he cherished the adventure. His work as a mercenary was intermittent and determined by the nature of missions. Casino security in Monte Carlo took up the balance of his time.

There were other matters related to the outcome of his Belgian visit. These involved both business and pleasure with Julio and Pietro. When he left François in Bandala, Mario told him he might not be available for future missions.

"I have important changes facing me. It's a life-altering discovery—Marianne is my *vero amore*, true love. I'll be with her tomorrow. *Questa bella signora*—this beautiful lady—won't accept me under my current state of affairs. I see it differently now. Our friendship is solid, but I have to tone down my behavior to have a chance of winning her."

"I hate losing you, Mario. Life goes on. Circumstances change. If a situation seems right, you have to seize it."

"François, you're a good buddy. We've been under the gun together, meeting challenges head on. I value your friendship. Let's keep in touch."

"The feeling is mutual. We have a common interest in Mandaka with our small equity in *Société Minéraux de Mandaka-Sud*. Kibali was generous in providing us minority shares in the government's diamond operation."

"Yeah, François, big deal! It's of little value at present, but has potential. Nothing to it. All it takes is a major infusion of capital and an experienced hand in management. Kibali is shrewd. It gives him a hook in case he needs us again."

"I agree. He was also quick in accepting our suggestion to appoint Kwambe as deputy chief of security for *Société Minéraux*. Now then, get a move on, your future awaits you."

The two warriors embraced and saluted each other as Mario's eyes began to moisten. They operated in a world where sentimentality was set aside to assure there was no conflict in performing the work at hand. The moment of parting caused the inured older veteran to choke up despite his best efforts to control his countenance. No one had ever accused François of being a romantic, but he felt a tinge of envy toward his *amico*.

"*Bonne chance*, *mon ami*, I'll miss you but I'm happy for you. You have a fine lady and you'll be lucky if she agrees to be your wife."

"*Au revoir*, François. I'll fill you in with details as they develop."

On the flight from Africa to Europe, Mario wrestled with his thoughts. If all went well, he needed a few days in Liège to begin wedding arrangements. If he got cold feet or if Marianne turned him down, he would be at liberty to hop on a plane for his next destination. After years of friendship, he didn't know the depth of Marianne's feelings for him. His heart was transmitting messages to his psyche that he needed to make concessions to win her over.

Another matter lay ahead: his involvement in the olive business. He had joint ownership of olive groves in Tuscany with Pietro. There was also Monaco. Mario knew he couldn't put off reporting back to his security job much longer.

Hopefully, Marianne would find his business endeavors reassuring. His life would be more sedentary, making the transition back to his innate disposition. He was uneasy as he fidgeted and stretched in his seat. He faced new challenges and it unsettled him. The prospect of becoming a family man and an entrepreneur brought on anxiety. He relished challenges, but this was different. He needed to regain his cool before meeting Marianne.

Another activity, diamond trade, might develop into a business venture. He had much to learn, with several possibilities to assist him. Benoît Duhammel, Marianne's oldest brother, worked in the diamond trade in Antwerp. Benoît was an apprentice designer and customer relations officer with a member of the Antwerp Diamond Bourse, Jaeckus Hoelebrand's Diamond World. Mario's intent was not to undermine Kibali and his government, but to be pro-active on their behalf. Kibali recognized foreign investors were needed to make the mining operations productive.

Mario felt guilty about Pietro. Sure, they had an agreement and Pietro wasn't one to complain. Their friendship was as solid as ever. Mario felt he was taking unfair advantage of Pietro's labor in their olive operation, while reaping rewards. A lifestyle change would allow Mario to become more hands-on.

Mario and Pietro kept in touch over the years, sharing information on their comings and goings. They served together in their youths with the partisan resistance movement, *"Giustizia e Liberta",* fighting against Benito Mussolini's fascist regime. Later, Mario did a brief stint with the Italian army in Italian Somaliland, administered by Italy as a United Nations Trust Territory. Pietro had no interest in serving in the military upon the defeat of fascism and returned to Verona. He went to work in tourism and married his Veronese sweetheart, Anna. They selected Mario to be godfather to the oldest of their three children, cementing further a lifelong friendship.

At a get together three years previous, Pietro raised the topic of olives.

"Mario, how long can you go on as an adventurer? You're not getting younger. You need to look ahead."

"I know you mean well, Pietro. Life is good. Health and fitness are fine. The pay is good and I can still handle myself."

"Be real, Mario. I know you have doubts. How confident are you on continuing without endangering your life and others around you? It's an issue you need to face up to. I want to share an idea with you."

"Okay, Pietro, let's have it."

"Mario, it's farming olives. I have an uncle in Tuscany who's getting on in years and wants to transfer his olive grove to a family member. He has generous outside offers but he's given me right of first refusal. He'll take less because I'm family. I told him about you and he'll sell it to us as partners. I really want to do this with you."

"Pietro, how can I? I can't be tied down. I need to be available for indefinite periods on missions. What about Anna? What does she think of this change?"

"Anna knows the area and the children vacation there with my uncle. They enjoy Tuscany. They'll help with the work. Anna likes the idea of you and I doing it together.

"Mario, this would be great for us. You can spare a few days to meet with Uncle Giovanni. He's in Lucca Province, right by *'la Strada del Vino'*—Road of the Wine—you fancy. In addition to fine wine, the best olives in Italy are grown here, perhaps in the Mediterranean area. We'll discuss the business operation and our possible involvement. At the very least, you'll have a few bottles of your favorite wine, 'the nice dark one' of Sangiovese grapes, *Brunello di Montalcino*. Its limited production and long aging process make it difficult to obtain. You'll leave Tuscany happy. How does that sound?"

Mario had scruples but he could be swayed with the right inducement. The lure of the *Brunello* was too much. He agreed to accompany Pietro immediately, knowing he'd likely find several reasons not to go if he hesitated. They packed quickly and were on route within the hour. With Pietro driving his Fiat *Millecento*, they chatted about their lives, Pietro as a homebound family man and Mario as an adventurous bachelor.

"Pietro, what about your tourism business in Verona?"

"I'll hang on to it. We're doing guided tours across the region, including Verona, Padua, Venice, Milan, etc. I hired a woman as a tour guide early on and she's proven to be very dependable. She's assisting me in managing the operation. We'll form a partnership if things work out in Tuscany."

They headed south on A22, connecting to A1 as they bypassed Bologna, and picked up A11 north of Firenze. As they drove west toward Pisa, the Lucchesi Hills loomed ahead. Pietro spotted the turn off and steered the *Millecento* toward the hills. Their destination was only a few kilometers south of Lucca. Arriving at Giovanni's *residenza,* on the fringe of the small village of Santa Maria del Giudice, Pietro reminded Mario that his uncle was from the old school.

"Mario, we both know the type. They're decent people who are accustomed to their ways. I know Uncle Giovanni loves me. He has difficulty with my manner and lifestyle, which isn't all that unconventional compared to yours. I'm certain Giovanni will accept you and you'll put your best foot forward. Just so you know what to expect."

"Not to worry, my friend. I'll have to remember I'm no longer in the jungle."

Upon their arrival, Pietro took Mario to meet Giovanni. Waiting to greet them was a trim, robust-looking man with sun-baked skin, appropriate for a life working the fields, and a full head of white hair. Giovanni walked with a slight gimp but appeared to be in fine physical condition, especially for a man on the verge of turning 80.

"Buono giorno, zio." Pietro embraced his uncle and introduced Mario.

Giovanni was known in the area as a fair-minded individual who had a love affair with his olives. He wanted to be sure his nephew and partner would take proper care of the grove. He expressed concern about Mario's occupation and periods of absence. Mario and Pietro had discussed this on route to Tuscany. Pietro and Mario had worked out some details of a tentative partnership and Pietro shared these with Giovanni. Giovanni, in turn, discussed his business proposition.

"I expect to be around for a long time. I'll be available to provide advice, but only if requested. Mario, I know you're a good boy. My youngest sister, Pietro's mother, has mentioned you often over the years. It's because of this that I've agreed to let Pietro take you on as his partner."

As the discussion continued, Mario learned that there were numerous varieties of olive trees, some thirty in Italy alone, just as there were with wine producing grapes. Mario confessed his ignorance. The three went on to discuss the business operation, the marketing, the employees, the cash flow, etc.

"It's obvious I know less about olives than I do about the liquid delights of grapes."

"Something else you might consider. I have a good friend about the same age as me who's thinking of selling his grove. It abuts mine. It might interest you. His only children, two sons, are in America and have no interest. If you did acquire his grove, you'd have to be prepared for the extra work. I don't think it's an urgent matter for him, so you'd have time to sort out your finances."

Giovanni told Mario, "You should be here for the *raccolto.* The annual harvest is in November and runs into December. It's labor intensive as you might expect but it's also festive. Additional workers are needed to gather the olives in their prime. People from the area show up to work the numerous groves; it's become a ritual. I'll provide you with the netting. The nets are laid out on the ground beneath the trees to gather the olives as they are freed from the branches."

Giovanni had to do little convincing. Mario had no problem in covering his half of the deal. There was no reason to delay. All of the appropriate legal documents were dealt with over the subsequent five days and ownership of Giovanni's olive tree orchard was conveyed to the new partners, Pietro and Mario.

CHAPTER EIGHTEEN

Marianne Duhammel thought she'd be a lifelong old maid if she wasn't married by her 33rd birthday. It was an artificial deadline, but she had a mindset. She wouldn't acquiesce on her criteria for a suitable man as her husband. She was comfortable with the person she had become and felt certain conditions and characteristics in a man were important to her. Marriage wasn't the be-all and end-all of her existence. The self-imposed milestone was nearly two years away but there were no prospects within her immediate entourage. There were suitors, but she regarded them more as escorts and friends than as potential husbands. She had renewed her numerous friendships upon her return to Belgium from the Congo, two and half years earlier.

Marianne, a product of a Walloon father and a Flemish mother, was a good-looking young woman, more attractive than pretty. Upon meeting her, her sweetness and geniality stood out. Other aspects of her character lay beneath; she was no 'shrinking violet'. Her congenial disposition could take a turn when provoked. Although known as a tolerant person, a fiery temperament surfaced occasionally when a cause or a principle dear to her was challenged.

Generally categorized as a 'girl next door', she carried a modest figure on her 5-1/2 foot frame. Her sparkling hazel eyes and a sprinkling of light wheat-colored freckles on her upper cheeks heightened her radiant and sometime mischievous countenance. Direct sunlight brought out a tinge of red in her shoulder length, auburn hair. Though she retained her youthful and vivacious demeanor, she became more aware of several older teachers who remained spinsters and were regarded as schoolmarms. She was devoted to her primary school students, who responded with great affection. Well educated, she achieved high honors at *Université Catholique de Louvain*.

Marianne had several close friends, male and female. They got together twice a week, '*toujours dans l'esprit de la bonhomie'*—always in the spirit of good-fellowship—as Marianne's closest friend, Claire Marie Blancke, would say. They both sang in the church choir and blended their dulcet soprano voices with a choral group that performed at schools and social events.

The Duhammels were staunch Roman Catholics. They carried on the tradition of several generations of Duhammels as parishioners of *l'Eglise Saint Jacques-le-Mineur* in Liège. The family of six was well balanced and close, getting together at the family home at least one Sunday every month. The oldest of four children, Marianne had assisted in looking after her three brothers. The two married brothers and their wives introduced her to their friends and acquaintances, hoping one might be 'Mister Right'.

There was one possibility whom she met in Africa. Upon completion of her university studies, Marianne began teaching primary school students in her hometown. Her well-ordered life deviated two years later when she responded to an appeal from the

Belgian Government in its effort to educate Congolese children. Hundreds of Belgian teachers were scattered across the African nation. Marianne was assigned to a primary school in Kamina, where she devoted three years. It was located in northern Katanga province, hundreds of miles from urban centers. Life was arduous. Her social contacts were limited mostly to other teachers and missionaries.

Shortly following her return from her summer vacation for the final year of her contract, Marianne met a person of interest. Marianne had gone to Elizabethville to retrieve a package. She was enjoying a glass of *Primus* beer and a *croque monsieur* at a *brasserie, le Coq d'Or*. A colleague who accompanied her had met some foreign members of Moïse Tshombe's militia previously. Her impression of the mercenaries she had met was that they were crude, crass and unrefined.

When three mercenaries entered the restaurant, Marianne's companion motioned them over. They drew chairs and introductions followed. Marianne gave Mario Rossetti the once-over at first sight. Conversation flowed easily. These mercenaries seemed different from others Marianne had met. While there was roughness in Mario's manner, Marianne figured it was a prerequisite for his line of work. She was intrigued with his display of tenderness and civility, traits not often in evidence in the Congo, especially among mercenaries. The breath of his knowledge and interests, as well as his sense of humor, fascinated Marianne. This positive first impression reinforced itself through other get togethers they had over the course of the year.

As she prepared to leave the Congo, Mario asked if he could visit her every now and again. Over the ensuing years, they exchanged phone calls and occasional brief visits. Marianne took comfort being in Mario's company but began wondering whether their relationship was destined to remain platonic. She found him caring and affectionate but he seemed unwilling to settle down and abandon his life as an adventurer.

Marianne did her best to converse with Mario in Italian, a language she was learning in evening classes at *l'université de Liège*. She was fluent in French, Dutch and German, and had a fair ability in English and Spanish. They discussed myriad topics. Neither was ever at a loss for conversation, often animated. Mario enjoyed the role of devil's advocate. There was one topic he considered off-limits, his mercenary activities.

She rationalized her relationship with Mario by labeling it a friendship, a category less stringent than her expectations of a suitor. He was handsome, charming, enjoyable and well mannered, at least in her company. He was a Catholic, schooled in the teachings of the Church as a youth. His ardor diminished gradually from serving as an altar boy to a more detached approach, attending mass sporadically. Marianne abhorred violence.

When Mario returned from missions in Angola and the Congo the previous year, he was aching to get together with Marianne. It was a grand reunion initially but Marianne kept testing him.

"Mario, you're a gentle person with compassion, so I'm baffled by how you can do what you do. Violence follows you wherever you go abroad. How do you reconcile with killing and destruction?"

"It's great seeing you too, Marianne. You sure know how to warm a fella's heart. It's good I know we're friends, otherwise I'd think you were condemning me."

"I know you, Mario, and yet I don't know you. I enjoy your company, more than I do anyone else. There's part of you, I won't call it sinister, let's just say a dark side that seems in conflict with all your fine attributes."

"We've been through this. I'm selective on assignments I accept. I believe I'm morally correct taking on missions that benefit people in need. I've refused missions to entrench despots or would-be tyrants."

"There you go again, Mario, rationalizing. Your actions run counter to the notion of Christianity, which champions the sanctity of human life."

"I consider myself a good and decent Christian," Mario spoke in his defense. "People of all religious beliefs have engaged in warfare and in taking lives of other human beings throughout history. You're conveniently forgetting the brutality of the Catholic Church."

Marianne retorted. "The Church had good reason to act as it did. You can't put yourself in the same category. The work of mercenaries is different. They're outsiders who choose to get involved for monetary gain."

"You're partly right, Marianne. The parties to conflicts in which I get involved don't threaten my life and safety prior to my engagement. It's my involvement that helps improve the lives of countless people. This is the work of a good Christian, looking after my fellow man."

"That's very noble of you, Mario, but you can't convince me with that argument."

"Noblesse Oblige! That's my motto."

It was early Friday morning when Mario arrived in Brussels. While Marianne expected him, she didn't know when it would be. Mario's departure from Bandala was uncertain until the last minute when a seat became available for his return. He didn't want to let on that there was anything special about this visit; he wanted to save his thunder for the right moment. The flight from Kinshasa arrived early enough in Brussels to phone Marianne.

«Bonjour, Marianne, c'est Mario.»

«Quelle belle surprise.»

"I just arrived in Brussels. I'm glad I reached you before you left for school."

"When will I see you?"

"I'm renting a car and will drive to Liège today. I have a couple of things to do here. I'll be at your home when you get back."

"Sono davvero eccitato—I'm really excited. How's that for Italian? I'm improving and I'll let you test me when we get together."

"Mia dolce signora, my sweet lady. You'll be a refreshing change for me. This afternoon can't come soon enough. I'll make a reservation at our favorite *liégeois* restaurant for this evening."

"That's great! I can't wait. I must go before I get scolded for tardiness by *la directrice*."

"Ci vediamo presto. Arriverderci"—see you soon.

Although fatigued by his recent activities and long flight, Mario felt an upward surge in his mood. Marianne had that effect on him. A major challenge remained; he needed to woo her. There was no doubt she liked him, but neither one had spoken the word 'love' to each other.

Mario figured it would take about 1½ hours to drive to Liège, fixing his departure at 2:00 pm. He had seven hours to accomplish what he wanted done. Mario left Brussels National Airport in his rented car and drove to his preferred hotel in Brussels, *l'hôtel Le Dôme,* on *boulevard du Jardin Botanique*. He was pleased with the service and its location, mere steps from the *Grand'Place*. He needed to rest for a couple of hours. Upon arrival, he sought out the concierge, Jacques. They greeted each other warmly with appropriate embraces. Mario asked Jacques to do a few things for him while he rested.

The phone rang as Mario was settling in. It was Jacques telling Mario he had Mme Christine Mertens on the line, and made the connection.

"Goedemorgen, mevrouw Mertens. That's pretty close to my limit in Flemish. I hope I'm not disturbing you. I'd like to speak to you about your brother."

"No, you're not disturbing me. What is this about?"

"My name is Mario Rossetti and I was with Roger in Mandaka."

"I see. His remains are due to arrive in three days."

"I'm truly sorry for your loss. I've just arrived from Mandaka and I'd like to meet with you later this morning if you're free."

"Yes, that's fine. What do you suggest?"

"I'm in Brussels, near the *Grand'Place*. Perhaps we can have lunch. I have a few of Roger's effects with me. Is there a *bistrot* nearby where we could meet?"

"Yes, there's one that's quite decent, called *le Papillon,* near the commune of Jette. It's not very far from you."

"I'll have the hotel *concierge* map the route for me. *A bientôt.*"

Mario awoke from his nap with a start as the phone rang, thinking he was still in Africa; it was a wake-up call from Jacques. He showered, shaved and dressed in a suit and tie. As he packed his bags, he phoned the restaurant, *Mame Vi Cou*, in Liège for dinner reservations. The *maitre d'* assured Mario he would have his usual table.

Leaving his travel bags with Jacques, Mario asked him to have his car brought to the front of the hotel at 11:30 am and walked to the KBC Bank to meet with his portfolio manager. While Mario had assets in banks in other countries, he maintained an account with KBC, which he opened in the Congo in the early 1960s. *Kredietbank-Congo* was a KBC affiliate at the time with a branch in Elizabethville. Mario began depositing some of his financial gains with the bank when he was operating with Moïse Tshombe's militia.

CHAPTER NINETEEN

Mario left in his rented Audi, following directions provided by Jacques. They were precise and Mario was soon parking in front of *le Papillon*. He entered the *bistrot* and asked a waiter if he knew Mme Mertens. The waiter led him to the table she reserved. Mario ordered *un verre de kir avec Chablis* while waiting. When the waiter returned with his cocktail, he was accompanied by an attractive woman in her mid-30s, with shoulder length flaxen hair. The waiter introduced Christine Mertens to Mario.

"*Enchanté*, *madame*. Thanks for meeting with me."

«De rien. C'est mon plaisir, monsieur»

"Mme Mertens, as you see, I've taken the liberty of ordering an *apéritif*. Would you like one?"

"It's probably a good idea given what we'll be discussing. *Garçon*, I'll have the same as Mr. Rossetti."

Mario, ever the discerning Latino, subtly observed the *décolletage* of his companion's dress, affording him a gratuitous view as she bent forward to be seated by the waiter. Considering himself somewhat of an expert on women's physiques, he graded her with a high mark—*seins* shapely and well conditioned.

"If it makes you more comfortable, please call me Mario."

"Very well, Mario, and I'm Christine."

"Christine, I was second in command of our unit on our mission in Mandaka. I have some of your brother's effects, which I'll pass on to you after *déjeuner*.

"Here comes your *apéritif*. *Santé*!"

"*Pareillement*! Do you live here in Belgium, Mario?"

"No, I don't. I had business to take care of in Brussels. I'm going to Liège this afternoon for a most important meeting. I pray the lovely lady with whom I'm dining will accept my marriage proposal."

"Do you think it's fair to the lady given your line of work?"

"That's a sensible question, Christine, and it's why I haven't asked her before. I'm abandoning my life as a mercenary, going in other directions."

"That's good to hear. I wish you success with your meeting."

"If it's okay with you, let's order and I'll share what I know about Roger. Would you like a glass of wine with your meal?"

"I'll go with the shrimp stuffed tomato and an endive salad. I'll pass on the wine."

"Garçon, les tomates aux crevettes pour madame, pour moi, les moules et des salades d'endive pour madame et moi."

They paused briefly as they sipped their cocktails. Mario resumed the conversation, telling Christine what he knew about Roger's death. She appreciated learning more about her brother.

Upon finishing lunch, Mario called for *l'addition* and paid the bill. Mario gave Christine the bag containing her brother's personal effects and she gave him her telephone number. They had discussed the small service her family would have for Roger. Mario said he'd call to check on the service. They embraced and gave each other the *grosses bisoux,* kisses on both cheeks.

It was shortly after 2:00 pm when he headed eastward. Mario was determined to keep his emotions at bay. He kept changing radio stations, seeking the right music for his mood. Finding nothing suitable, he began singing, enjoying himself more than anything on the radio. As he arrived within the city limits of Liège, he headed for the western sector of '*la cité ardente',* the fiery city, removed a bit from the left bank of the Meuse River. Marianne lived in the familial home on *rue des Augustins* with her parents, Maurice and Anika Duhammel.

Mario climbed the stairs to the Duhammel domicile and rang the doorbell. Anika Duhammel greeted him holding an open book. Mario could see it was a novel by Liège native son Georges Simenon.

"*Goede middag*, Madame Duhammel. I'm pleased to see you're looking well as usual."

"*Welkom*, Mario. You seem to be keeping yourself in good form."

"Thanks. It's becoming more of a struggle in my advancing years."

"Nonsense, I won't hear of it, you're still a young man. Now that you mention it, perhaps the aging process is catching up with you. You might want to evaluate some of your activities."

"Don't start lecturing me, *chère madame*. I'm here to enjoy a visit with Monsieur Duhammel and you, and spend some time with Marianne."

"I'm happy to see you, but you know what I'm talking about. So, I'll let it stand where it is. Marianne has a meeting with the parents of one of her students. She'll be along shortly. Don't just stand there, come on in and be sociable."

"I see I caught you absorbed in one of Liège's favorite son's writings. Another case for the good and efficient *Commissaire* Jules Maigret?"

"Yes, it is. Georges Simenon is clever the way he develops his plots and gets Maigret to solve the assortment of crimes Simenon sets up for him. A man smoking a pipe always had a special appeal to me."

They walked into the salon and she motioned to Mario to have a seat in the armchair across the coffee table from her. The furniture was clearly hand crafted. The artisan responsible for the unique styles and their creation was none other than Maurice Duhammel. He learned the woodworking/furniture trade as a youth in his father's *atelier*.

"Mme Duhammel, on my way here, I was reflecting on the Duhammel family and your origins in Brugge. I've been there a few times and find similarities to Venice. Did your youngest son, Lucien, settle in Brugge because of family ties?"

"He was uncertain where he wanted to head in life. I suggested he spend a few days there, to relax and consider his options. He agreed and I phoned my father, who introduced Lucien to an executive with Callebaut. Thus began his career as a *chocolatier."*

"*Mais oui*, Madame, Callebaut, the makers of the 'Finest Belgian Chocolate'. I wouldn't do well there. The good form you find me in would be no more. My sweet tooth would do me in."

The sound of a door closing drew their attention toward the front entrance.

CHAPTER TWENTY

Anika and Mario halted their conversation to check on the arrival. Marianne breezed in, looking as cheery as ever. Her cheeks had a bit of coloration from the coolness in the air. She displayed a carefree attitude as people often do when TGIF rolled around. It might not have been 'Thank God It's Friday' at all. The sight of Mario in her home, chatting with her mother could have done it.

Mario stood up to greet her and they embraced, giving each other the *grosses bisoux*. They held on to each other longer than a merely polite exchange would endure. They backed up slightly from each other, looking into each other's eyes, while holding hands. Mario thought it was a more intimate greeting than usual and wondered whether Marianne suspected his intentions.

Marianne broke the silence. "Mario, you made it tough to get through the day. When I thought I was done, I wasn't. I'd forgotten about an after-hour meeting. You got me distracted. I'm thrilled you're here."

"That's a good start because I'm delighted to be here."

"You look good. You seem intact. No scratches or bruises? Luck is with you."

"It's the good Lord looking after me because of my clean living."

"You've just opened yourself up to an argument but I'll let it go. This is a happy moment and I don't want a *battuta d'arresto,* setback. How's that for speaking the lingo, *mio paesano*?"

"Your Italian is coming along. I've been looking forward to relaxing with you."

Anika had remained seated, enjoying the moment. She was pleased with her daughter's self-contentment but sensed an added vivacity when she was with Mario. It was obvious they enjoyed each other. Anika stood up and approached the couple.

"Mario, have you plans for this evening? You're welcome to dine with us."

"Thanks, Mme Duhammel, but I've made a reservation at 'A Nice Old Lady', *Mame Vi Cou*."

"No matter. I think it's a respectful hour for an *apéritif*. M. Duhammel should be home shortly. You two care for one?"

"Yes, in a half hour. I'll run over to the hotel and check in."

Marianne chimed in. "I think that works all around. *Papa* should be here by then. *Maman* can fuss around in the kitchen as she's eager to do. I'll freshen up for the evening, while Mario looks after his accommodations."

«Je m'excuse. I'll be right back. *A tout à l'heure!*»

Mario gave Marianne a quick peck on the cheek and left. Anika stood by, gazing at Marianne.

"He seems to lift your spirits. Mario is such a good friend. It's a pity his visits are so infrequent."

"Mother, please! Yes, Mario is a dear friend and I do feel better when he's around. He has his life and I have mine; we carry on. Now, I must freshen up and see if I can transform this old schoolteacher into an attractive companion for Mario."

"Don't overdo it, Marianne; you're perfectly charming as you are."

As Marianne began her ascent on the stairs, the front door closed along with a greeting, "Anika, I'm home."

"*Bon soir*, *père*! I'm happy you got away early. I'll be down shortly. *Maman* just went into the kitchen."

"You seem to be in fine spirits, Marianne."

She took the steps two at a time and rushed into her bedroom to begin a lady's ritual for an evening with her favorite gentleman. Maurice joined Anika in the kitchen, where she was preparing some *amuse bouches*.

"*Bon soir, chérie!* I sense Mario has arrived."

"Yes, Maurice, Mario was just here and he'll return shortly. He left to arrange his lodgings."

"Why doesn't he stay with us? We certainly have room."

"That's his way. He doesn't want to impose. I suspect he likes to come and go, as he's accustomed."

"At least he's here. He seems to have quite an effect on Marianne. Do you think anything will come of it?"

"I sensed more electricity between them. Marianne hasn't said anything, but she seems ready to settle down. Mario is her only 'boyfriend'. The question is whether Mario is ready."

"We'll see how things go. He'll join us for an *apéritif* before going out?"

"Yes, he said he would."

Mario returned 45 minutes later. Maurice greeted him with a handshake and a light embrace, took a half step back, impressed. Mario wore a blue-gray tailored suit and a light blue shirt with a lavender floral silk tie. His tanned face was aglow, as he offered a broad smile to Maurice.

"Mario, look at you—hale and hardy, and none the worse for wear. Come in, I'm delighted to see you."

"Thank you, Monsieur Duhammel. Always a pleasure. I've brought *madame* and you small tokens for your gracious hospitality."

Mario always stayed at *Le Cygne d'Argent,* nearby on rue Beeckman, when he came to Liège. Invariably, he depended on the concierge to take care of things for him. In this case, he procured a liter bottle of the finest Belgian *Jenever* for Maurice and a dozen red roses for *madame*.

Anika was thrilled with the bouquet and promptly placed it in a water-filled vase. Marianne came down the stairs, looking radiant and fresh as a daisy in a lime green blouse and a black skirt.

Mario stood agape. "Marianne, you look like a princess. May I be so bold as to offer my fair lady this orchid corsage as we ready ourselves for our evening adventure?"

"I curtsy to you, my fair prince. I'm honored to accept the corsage."

Maurice had enough. "You have both passed the audition and have assured yourselves key roles. Now, let's get back to cocktails. I have the usual liqueurs plus a fine *Mandarine Napoléon,* a special blend of aged cognac and oils from tangerines."

All four opted for the *Mandarine Napoléon* and gushed over the sensuous bouquet. They chatted about events in their lives, as they swirled the libations in their snifters. Maurice had his own *atelier* with sufficient work and pending orders for his five artisans. Anika continued to enjoy her return to part-time work at the bank, BSGB Liège. Marianne was content with educating young students. Mario spoke on his African adventure, limiting it to its purpose and results.

They bid adieu to Anika and Maurice as they departed for dinner.

Mario told Marianne, "You look particularly lovely this evening."

"That's a fine complement. I take it you don't think I look so hot other times."

"Cher Marianne, 'où le Dieu vous a semé, il faut savoir fleuri'. Most appropriate French saying—'wherever God has planted you, you must know how to flower'. You have flowered."

"Mario, ever so charming. It's great being together again. Quite a change for you."

"You bring out the best in me."

They arrived at the restaurant on *rue de la Wache.* The *maitre d'* was pleased to see them again.

"This is the life. Here I am in a place we enjoy, no worries and you by my side."

"Mario, don't tell me you're getting romantic. It's great being here with you."

"Are you game for another *apéritif*? I'll have one before we order."

"Yes, I will. I'll go with an *Advocaat*."

Mario had something in mind. "I'll have an old favorite I haven't had in awhile, a German apple schnapps, *Berentzen Apfel Korn Liqueur*."

Mario gave their order to the waiter and looked around the familiar oak-beamed restaurant. When he looked back at Marianne, he saw her eyes fixed on him.

"This is nice. I'd forgotten how relaxing it is."

"It's amazes me, Mario, how you make the transition, from barbarism to civility. I'm glad you leave part of you behind when we get together."

"What you see is the real me. I've been doing some reflecting. I want to enjoy the moment. Here are our cocktails. *Salut*!"

They chatted, keeping it light with some of their usual banter, sipping their cocktails and ordering their meals. Each ordered the *salade Liégeoise*, while Marianne selected the *Carbonnades*

Flamandes and Mario picked the *lapin à la gueuze.* Marianne talked about events. They exchanged news on friends each of them knew. Mario delayed his primary topic for later. This carried them through the dinner. For dessert, Marianne went for the Chocolate Chestnut Truffle Mousse and Mario, the Pears Poached in Spiced Rodenbach Beer, each with an espresso.

As they sipped their coffee, Mario decided it was the moment to make his pitch.

"Marianne, I have something important to say. I'm making adjustments to my life. The symbolic olive leaves beckon me. I'm responding to a tugging that's been going on within me. I'm no longer a mercenary; I told François I'm through. I've had enough violence and brutality. Actually, olives are beckoning me back to Tuscany. I feel I'm being summoned to Lucca to work hand-in-hand with Pietro."

"Mario, that's wonderful. Do you expect it'll be that easy to change? I don't doubt you're prepared to give it a go, but can you be happy without being macho?"

"If I feel the need to be macho, there are other outlets. I've been content in all of my pursuits. I can be macho on my job in Monte Carlo. There's always a drunkard I can push around.

"I'm looking into a possible joint olive operation in Catalonia with Julio. The diamond trade is another possibility. I'll talk to your brother Benoît and others on this. François and I have a small minority ownership in Mandaka's diamond mines, thanks to President Kibali. They're virtually non-functioning but have potential. I'll have enough to keep me out of mischief."

"Well, Mario, I'll give you this. You seem resolved to turn over a new leaf."

"Sit back, there's more to come."

Mario reached his right hand into his coat pocket and took out a red velvet jeweler's box, which Jacques obtained for him in Brussels. He presented it to Marianne.

"The content of this box is special, which is how I think of you. Your friendship means so much to me. I ache to be with you when I'm away. Marianne, it's taken me too long to recognize that I'm in love with you. I've managed to repress it until now. It's erupted and consumed me. I want us together for the rest of our lives. Marianne, will you marry me and make me the happiest and luckiest person on this planet?"

"Wow! That'll knock any gal off her feet. Now that's it's out in the open, I've been in love with you for a long time. As another maiden assured your fellow Veronese romantic, 'I gave thee mine before thou didst request it, and yet I would it were to give again'. I've been waiting to recite this line from Romeo and Juliet, staged on your home turf. Such an opportunity seemed unlikely. Yes, yes, yes! I accept."

Mario rose from his chair and the two lovers exchanged lip-to-lip kisses for the first time. Marianne pushed Mario away so she could stand and give him a proper embrace. The first kiss was warm and affectionate but Marianne wanted more. She clung to Mario firmly, merging her lips to his for a timeless moment in complete abandon. The kisses were both sensual and lascivious, as they embraced each other with such voracity that they seemed to be satisfying appetites long left wanting. They ultimately unclenched, gasping for air. Mario wrapped his arms around her again, this time more tenderly, as they stood aside the table for a few more minutes. Repressed emotions were unleashed. Marianne hung on to Mario's arm and gently stroked his face as he returned to his seat.

Two couples, who were dining at a nearby table, stood and applauded while voicing "bravo, *félicitations*, *bien fait*". Other diners joined in with their cheers. It was a time of merriment as the restaurant came alive, in tribute to the gentleman from Verona and the *liégeoise* maiden lady.

"Marianne, you make me so happy. Now, please open the box."

"What is it? Are you teasing me again?"

"Marianne, it's your diamond. It's an uncut diamond of multiple carats. Your brother can advise us how to convert it into a gemstone. We can go see him in Antwerp."

"Sunday is our monthly family get together, so Benoît will be here. They're all pushing men on me to interview for the role of husband. So, you're a lifesaver."

"I'm pleased I've helped you out."

"Oh, come on, Mario. You know I didn't mean it that way."

«Pas de problème, ma chérie. I hope your family approves."

"Of course. They love you. They've been wondering how much longer it would take you to come to your senses and sweep me off my feet. It's taken awhile, but you've done it. Now, what about this rock? Did you find time to prospect your mine?"

"The diamond is a gift from President Kibali. He found it in the vault when he moved in the palace. It's his wedding present."

"I don't know, Mario. I have a feeling about this. It doesn't sit well with me. I'm concerned it was obtained through forced labor. I need to give this some thought."

"Whatever you say, but please take it."

"Okay, I accept it for now, and then we'll see. Take care of *l'addition* and let's get back. My parents have been waiting for this moment. Prepare yourself for hugs and kisses."

The waiter accepted payment but told Mario they had to stay. He presented a bottle of *Moët et Chandon* champagne brut that Mario rejected. When the waiter whispered that it was from the foursome at the nearby table, Mario invited them over to share the bottle. Mario and Marianne exchanged introductions with the two men and two women. They chatted for a few minutes, primarily about the nascent engagement.

Marianne displayed her rock. "As you see, it's a rock. My beau assures me that it's precious."

One of the women gushed over it. "It sure seems to have the makings of something significant. I vote in favor of your handsome brute, I think he's sincere."

The other woman interjected, "I think what's precious is the project in the making. It's so romantic and exciting to have such a big rock with exquisite promise in fashioning one's own ring."

Mario drained his glass and thanked their new friends. "We must get on. I can't afford to get on the wrong side of my future in-laws. Great meeting you. Thanks for the good wishes and the bubbly."

Mario and Marianne both felt giddy, light headed and entranced, as they headed to the Duhammel residence. They admitted to each other that it was fantastic, the sensation of *flotter sur un nuage*—floating on a cloud.

CHAPTER TWENTY ONE

«N'avez vous jamais eu cette sensation de flotter sur un nuage, de ressentir une émotion telle que vous oubliez ce qui vous entoure?»

The first thing Marianne said to her mother was to ask if she ever had the sensation of floating on a cloud, unaware of anything around her. Marianne pointed to Mario, who ran to catch up after she jumped out of the car.

"He's the guilty party; the one who put me in this condition."

"What's going on with you two? Are you *intoxiqués*?"

«Pas du tout! Nous sommes engagés»

"Maurice, take your nose out of that book and come here. Your daughter has something to share with us. Now, quickly, get over here."

"Yes, yes, I'm coming. What's so important that you have to hurry me along?"

"Father, mother, I present your one and only future son-in law."

Mister Grumpy transformed himself into Mister Cordiality.

"This is great news. Mario, you're taking away *notre petite fille précieuse.* I assume you're making other changes."

Anika was biting her tongue but couldn't hold back. "Maurice, settle down. Marianne may be 'our precious little girl', but she is a grown, mature woman, capable of looking after her interests. Let's sit and listen to what Mario and Marianne have to tell us."

"*Très bien*. This is special. I'll get a well chilled *Dom Pérignon* to celebrate."

Anika and Maurice couldn't contain their excitement when they returned from the kitchen and saw Marianne and Mario cuddling on the divan.

Maurice declared, "Mario and Marianne, you bring Anika and me great pleasure. Mario, I hear you're a decent baritone. We're a singing family. You can harmonize with my three sons on Sunday."

"Maurice, there you go again. Mario, pay him no mind. Mario and Marianne, we toast you. May the enjoyment and contentment you feel for each other at this moment continue through the years. Happiness is key and there'll be times for compromises. May you use good judgment in your relations with each other. *Mai Dieu vous guide et vous bénisse!"*

"Thanks, Madame Duhammel. Marianne and I will do our utmost to live up to your well-spoken sentiments and good wishes. We'll pray to God to guide and bless us as you have called upon Him to do."

"Please, Mario, let's cut the formality. We're family. We'd be more comfortable with Maurice and Anika."

"I don't mean to be disrespectful, but if that suits you."

"Mario, I agree with Anika. Since you'll be my first son-in-law, I have no experience with this, and I certainly don't want you calling me 'papa'. So, Maurice it is. *Salut*, *mes chéries*!"

Anika told her husband to hush up. "Maurice, let's listen to Marianne and Mario. It's their special evening. Now, the two of you, we're all ears."

"Well, mother and father, I don't know if it was hope or prayers or whatever. As we finished our meals, Mario spoke to me about changes he's making. He asked me to join him as he embarked on a new chapter in his life. He gave me a rock to get us started. That's our story so far."

Anika couldn't hold her tongue with a paucity of details. "Marianne, that was the Readers Digest condensed version. Mario, you're a good storyteller, take over."

"Maurice and Anika, your daughter has accepted my proposal of marriage. Marianne and I have a fine relationship, but I knew I had to make changes to have a chance of marrying her. When I allowed myself to admit it, I knew I loved your daughter. I was frightened at first because it required commitment. My heart and soul got together with my brain and they contrived to convince me that being in love with Marianne was a good thing. From that point on, all components of my persona went to work on the remaking of Mario Rossetti."

Anika, usually with composure under control, came back at Mario. "Look what you've done. You've got me down to a soap opera fancier, weeping away to please the band. Your revelation is already quite a change."

Mario went on to explain the changes he was making, as well as the story behind the rock. He promised to be true and steadfast.

Anika had instructions for Marianne. "Get in touch with your brothers first thing tomorrow. They need to know before they come."

"Yes, I'll phone them. I want my best friend, Claire Marie, as my maid of honor. As you know, she's already engaged and can give us some advice on what's needed."

The evening ended with hugs, kisses, handshakes, and more kisses and hugs. Marianne walked Mario to the door, where they embraced, their bodies firmly pressed against each other, accompanied by a prolonged kiss that neither wanted to end. Eventually, Mario bade Marianne a good night and headed back to his hotel to reflect. Pleased with the evening, he eased into a relaxing sleep.

Anika and Maurice were early risers, but Marianne was a step ahead; the aroma of coffee was a giveaway. She was at work on batter that would become the local version of Belgian waffles, crunchy, caramelized, oval shaped *gaufres de Liège*.

"Marianne, you have much to do. I'll finish up. Go phone your brothers. Have you spoken to Mario this morning?"

"Yes, I did a while ago. He's joining us for breakfast, then we'll go to the *Parc d'Avroy*, and enjoy the fresh air. We'll get started on what we need to do. I'm asking Claire Marie to join us."

Parc d'Avroy was an attractive green space between two boulevards, located a short distance from the city center and on the west bank of *la Meuse,* the river bisecting the city. The park was close by; the Duhammels used it as their playground and meeting place.

Anika had more advice to offer. "You should speak with Father LeBlanc about the ceremony. Even though *l'église Saint Jacques-le-Mineur* is our traditional church, you might consider the *Cathédrale de Saint Paul*. The renovation work at Saint Jacques will continue for some time. Something to think about."

"I have Father LeBlanc on my list and I'll phone him after I speak with my brothers. Mario and I will try to see him today and decide on the venue."

When Mario arrived, Maurice and Anika were at the dinner table, chatting over coffee. Marianne had returned to the kitchen after her phone calls. She was pouring coffee and filled a second cup when she saw Mario. A series of embraces and kisses ensued. Marianne was animated, as she related her chats with her brothers and their eagerness to see her. She managed an occasional nibble of the *gaufres* as her audience cleaned off their plates.

It was a fine Saturday morning and the early autumn air was invigorating. The sky was azure with bright cotton-white puffy cirrus clouds scattered about, contrasting with the greenery of multiple shades in Avroy Park.

Mario knew what was coming. The discussion would be genial at first as they agreed on the easy issues. Mario knew Marianne had a vision of the reconstructed Mario Rossetti.

They sat on a bench in silence for several minutes, enjoying a mother duck gliding along the pond's surface with her six ducklings in tow. An avian symphony filled the air, accompanied by the gleeful sounds of children at play. The vehicular traffic on the boulevard was light and sounds emanating from there were muted to being inconsequential.

"It's such a beautiful day, Mario. I woke up this morning to the best feeling I've had in ages. You seem relaxed, but I wonder. With your head tilted toward the sky, you seem to be gazing wistfully at the contrails from aircraft heading south."

"*Pas du tout*! I'm just enjoying the day and the moment as you are."

"No problem then. We have time before Claire Marie joins us. Let's start with the wedding ceremony. We'll discuss this further with Father LeBlanc this afternoon."

After some back and forth, they decided to marry in Liège following a year to get to adjust and get to know each other better.

"There we are, two issues resolved, time and place. I'll put the interlude to good use to tie up loose ends. I suggest Tuscany for our home, as I labor in the olive groves."

"That seems reasonable. I've thought about Tuscany and what it might be like to live there. I don't know the area well but I sense I could be content. I'll need to speed up my Italian lessons to feel more at ease. Your annual *raccolto* is in November, right?"

"Yes it is. This would be a good time for a look-see."

"It'd be a good opportunity to get involved. We can check out the housing. I'll request some time off."

"I'll be content to live in or near Lucca, Pisa or Florence, wherever you prefer. There's also my apartment in Monte Carlo. This will depend on my job there. My boss has been understanding. I think I'll be able to put in enough time to satisfy him."

Mario and Marianne continued their discussion of what lay ahead. Before long, Marianne brought up the dicey topics of Mario's lifestyle and his less-than-avid religious dedication.

"Marianne, we've been over this before. My conscience is clear. I lead a reasonably good Christian life."

"I'd like you to accompany me to Sunday mass and get involved in our parish."

"Listen to me, Marianne. It's not in the cards that I'll return to the degree of devotion I had as a youth. I'll give it my best shot and that should be sufficient."

"Obviously, Mario, this is an issue we need to consider further."

"It is important. I agree. In fact, it might be critical. When you say 'we need to consider further', you mean 'you'. I've considered it further and I stand fast. I'll tell you this, I'd be heartbroken if you choose to undermine our engagement over this."

"Mario, I want this to work. I need to reflect some more. Perhaps Father LeBlanc can give us guidance."

Claire Marie's timely arrival salvaged the neonate romance for the moment. They both put on a happy face as they greeted Marianne's best friend.

Claire Marie was engaged to a childhood friend, who attended school with Marianne and her. She told them a civil ceremony was required, despite a church wedding. She spoke about publishing the banns and gave them a sheet listing the required documents, including certificates of birth and of residence.

As time approached for their rendezvous with Father LeBlanc, they thanked Claire Marie while exchanging embraces. Mario and Marianne strolled the few blocks along the boulevard to St. Jacques in tempered conversation. After their spat, Mario wasn't keen about the meeting with the padre. He hoped to avoid further controversy.

Father LeBlanc and Marianne greeted each other warmly as they embraced. He shook hands with Mario, covering their handshake with his left hand, as he tried to convey warmth and friendship. Mario broke out his patented smile.

"Mario, I'm delighted to meet you. I'm very fond of Italians, having spent some time in your country pursuing my religious studies."

Mario's immediate thought was 'oh, please don't go on and patronize me'. However, he merely nodded and smiled.

"Marianne and Mario, you've requested my assistance for your nuptials. I'm here for you. We'll discuss the details in a moment. There's something I feel obliged to share with Mario. You've chosen to enter into a lifetime union with Marianne, who in my view is a child of God. I ask you to consider that this is a hallowed union you seek with a genteel person. I've heard of your lifestyle, with your insouciant demeanor, which may well be the antithesis of Marianne's. I'm told you're not very dedicated to your religion. You must admit the two of you have disparate lifestyles."

"Father, before you go any further, let me set this straight. I mean no disrespect and I don't intend to offend. First of all, I don't allow myself to be harangued by anyone. Secondly, it's abundantly clear we need to get beyond this damn religious issue. To be perfectly blunt Father, I don't care what you think of me as a person or as a husband to Marianne. How I choose to practice my religion is my business. Father, I know God hasn't instructed anyone to squeeze Mario Rossetti to pay more homage to Him. I also know you mean well in looking after Marianne's interests, but she's very capable of doing this on her own. We're working on our issues and we will resolve them. If, at the end of the day, either of us finds contentment isn't achievable, we'll walk away from each other. Marianne, if you feel our differences are irreconcilable, we'll terminate our engagement now."

Mario's rebuke met with stunned silence. Mario was usually affable, but Marianne knew he could be resolute. Father LeBlanc was dealt a blow that rocked his foundation. It was totally unexpected from a person who proclaimed himself to be God-fearing. After a moment, Father LeBlanc stepped into the breach.

"Mario, let me say this about . . ." Marianne cut him short.

"No, Father, it's for me to speak. Mario, I apologize for putting you through this. I didn't intend for Père LeBlanc to lecture you. It is an issue that must be resolved. I think I'm a compassionate person and I'm seeking common ground with you. I don't want to lose you. *Scusi*, Mario!"

"I'm afraid you will if this keeps up."

CHAPTER TWENTY TWO

Mario and Marianne sat quietly in the rectory exchanging glances with each other. Father LeBlanc sat silently, struggling to regain his composure. He wasn't knocked out, but he was clearly dazed. He braced himself as he readied to stand. The fervor in his earlier voice had abandoned him.

"Perhaps it would be best if I recused myself. It wouldn't be prudent for me to continue as your advisor. Father Doucet has recently arrived to the parish. I believe he will serve you well. *Je m'excuse, pardonnez moi.*"

After Father LeBlanc left the room, Mario whispered to Marianne. "Like I said, I didn't mean to offend anyone. It's unfortunate it came to this but I felt I was being browbeaten."

«Ne t'inquiet pas. Father LeBlanc has been close to our family for many years. He seems to feel a need to look after me. I want this marriage to work."

The door to the room opened and a priest entered. He stood a few inches taller than Mario, had long blond hair and a reddish face that seemed to have been recently in the sun. Father Doucet introduced himself and apologized for appearing disheveled. He explained that he had just returned from sailing on the river.

"Marianne, I believe I met you briefly once after mass. I'm still learning my way around the parish and about the city itself. Mario, I'll assist Marianne and you in any way I can. Father LeBlanc asked me to take over for him but offered no explanation and none is needed. The two of you want to get married in the Church. That's the extent of my knowledge. So, let's take it from there."

Mario piped in, "It seems to me you're settling in quite well, already sailing on the Meuse."

"Unfortunately, I don't have a boat here yet, but a parishioner was kind enough to invite me. It's such a lovely day I had to put other things aside and take advantage of the offer. Perhaps, Marianne, you can get us started."

Marianne filled Father Doucet in with their plans. Father Doucet turned out to be a simpatico individual who impressed the betrothed with his candor and insights. He offered suggestions when asked and provided alternatives when appropriate. They spent slightly over two hours with the priest and left feeling it was time well spent.

As they departed the rectory, their intent was to return to Marianne's home. Marianne stopped on the sidewalk and pulled Mario back toward her. She was still unnerved by the scene with Father LeBlanc and the threat she received from Mario. She wrapped her arms around him and hugged him tightly as though she feared he might get away. He kissed her forehead and she lifted her head to receive his kiss on her lips. She melted in his arms as they stood coupled together in the middle of the sidewalk. They were oblivious to the passers-by and the gawkers in vehicles. The romance had a temporary reprieve, rekindled from the fading embers.

"Mario, let's go to a *brasserie* where we can relax and mull over what we've been through."

"That's the best suggestion you've made all day. I could use some refortification before we meet with your family."

"We don't owe my family any explanations. We'll stick to simple details."

"That's fine with me, Marianne, but your mother won't rest until she learns what happened with Father LeBlanc. She'll seek the answer, if not from us, then from him. Let's not get ahead of ourselves. First things first. Some good *bière belge* will get us on track for what comes next."

"Let's go to the *quais*. There are several *brasseries* near the river. We'll find a fairly quiet one where we can chat."

"Marianne, that's fine, but I'm all talked out for today. We'll get lots more advice from your brothers and their wives, whether we want it or not. So, let's get lubricated."

They walked a few blocks to the quay area and found a pub to their liking. They returned to their comfort zone, discussing sports, books, friends, ethnic cuisines, etc. After a period of relaxing and imbibing Liège's finest brew, *Jupiler* pilsner, Mario's stomach reminded him they hadn't eaten since the *gaufres* that morning. He said he was in the mood for *boulets à la liégeoise.*

"I can't come to Liège without stopping by *Café Lequet* for of its renowned fried meatballs and *frites*. It's right around the corner, on the *Quai sur Meuse*."

"D'accord, Mario, j'ai faim aussi. I'll let *Maman* know we won't be back until after *souper*. Two of my brothers might be here this evening."

Marianne managed to dodge her mother's questions on the phone. It was crowded as usual at *Café Lequet*. People were waiting for tables to clear. Mario noticed a woman of Marianne's age waving.

"Marianne, someone you know?"

"Yes, that's a school chum, Camille. You've met her. Let's go over and say '*bonjour*'."

Camille rose from her seat and embraced Marianne and Mario. She introduced her four companions at the table, two men and two other women. She indicated an empty chair and invited the couple to join them, which Marianne accepted.

"Mario, see if you can find a spare chair. It could be a bit of a wait."

Mario grabbed a chair and joined the group. The libation of choice for the quintet was the red house wine. Marianne and Mario opted to make it unanimous. The wine was robust and would go well with their fried nourishment.

Camille remarked on Marianne's countenance. "There's something afoot. What's with this glow? Your face betrays you."

"It's no secret, Camille." Marianne stretched her arm out, reaching across Mario's shoulders, pulling him closer. "My special friend, Mario, is also my *fiancé.*"

Their five companions rose in unison, wine glasses in hand, and shouted out, *'à la votre!'* Diners at other tables, who knew one or more members of the group, came by to see what was happening. Soon, there were a dozen or so well-wishers surrounding the table, hoisting their glasses in good cheer. The waitress struggled to gain access to the table, but pressed onward to deliver the *boulets et frites* to Marianne and Mario. It was a gay time, just the medicine the betrothed needed after the stress of the day.

The evening hour advanced without notice, as the merriment within the café carried on unabated. Eventually, reality set in and Mario acknowledged Marianne's signal that it was time. They bid their adieus, making their way through the still-crowded café, and hailed a taxi. Marianne told Mario her oldest brother Benoît, a year younger than Marianne, his wife Chantal, and their two young children, Dirk and Giselle, would have arrived from Antwerp. The youngest, Lucien, and his Flemish wife Hennie would arrive a little later from Brugge. The middle and unmarried brother Emile was a bit of a *roué,* who considered himself a Don Juan. He showed up Sunday mornings, sometimes with a woman with whom he spent the night, joining the family at church for mass.

Mario was eager to get back to his hotel room but he knew he couldn't leave Marianne alone to be interrogated. Despite his varied experiences, these were unchartered waters and he would have to navigate as best he could, hoping not to run onto unexpected shoals. He had to put on the happy face. He met the brothers before and they got along well. Fatigue was making him apprehensive. He resolved to be low-key and congenial.

As they alit from the taxi, Marianne observed Benoît's car parked just ahead. Lights shone throughout most of the house but they heard no sounds when they entered. Maurice, Anika and Benoît sat in the salon, engaged in conversation, but speaking softly. Chantal was upstairs putting the toddler Dirk and the infant Giselle to bed. Upon seeing the new arrivals, Benoît rose and exchanged the *grosses bisoux* with his sister, settling on a handshake and a hug with Mario.

"I'm very anxious to see that rock of yours. I'm intrigued."

"I'll get it for you. I have concerns about it."

Anika felt compelled to step in. "Marianne, *bon soir*! Don't you have a greeting for your mother and father? We've been waiting your return."

"*Je m'excuse*, *maman.* It's just that I was excited to see Benoît."

"Mario, please sit down and join us for awhile so we can chat."

"Thanks, Anika. I'll stay but I must leave shortly. It's been a long day."

"Maurice will get us beverages and the two of you can to tell us about your day."

Benoît spoke up. "If any of you want some excellent, authentic Trappist beer, Lucien, Emile and I have some from our area monasteries. Emile is bringing Rochefort 8 from here and Lucien, Westyleteren 12, from the western-most monastery. I brought a supply of *Westmalle Tripel* at 9.5%. Feel free to dip in."

Mario wasn't keen on drinking any more but he accepted a *Westmalle.* Marianne went to the kitchen with Maurice; she prepared tea for her mother and herself. Benoît seized the moment to chat with Mario while he had a chance before Anika got going.

«Dites-moi, mon vieux, comment ça va?»

"Frankly, it goes quite well, Benoît. I'll let Marianne fill in the details, but it feels good having gotten this far. I'm certain this is where I want to be but it's been agonizing. We're making adjustments and it's a process that we'll be going through."

"I know what you mean. Fortunately, Chantal made it easy for me. I wouldn't change a thing. My family is so precious to me, a lovely and compassionate wife and *mes deux petits gosses*. Being married is one thing, but fatherhood is truly special."

"I've observed how you and your wife relate to each other. It's obvious the two of you are content. I sense a couple needs to find the right balance in their lives before they can determine their comfort zones."

"Mario, it seems to me you've just made a crash landing. You don't seem damaged. It'll be awhile before you know how you've fared. Coming from Africa, you've just weathered turbulence. Frankly, I don't know how you do it. It can't be as easy as you make it seem. My advice is take your time. Don't allow yourself to be rushed. I want my sister's happiness but I also know her quite well. My apologies for going on, but I think you understand what I mean."

"D'accord, Benoît, je comprend. Marianne and I have agreed not to rush. We've had good discussions today and that will continue. When Marianne returns, we'll explain where things are."

Mario saw Anika straining to hold her tongue; she was anxious to put it in motion but awaited Marianne's return to unleash it. Maurice came back with beers for the gents and Marianne followed with tea for the ladies, including one for Chantal who was coming down the stairs. Marianne beckoned Chantal to join the group.

"Chantal, *vien.* You're just in time. We've made a bit of progress but it's tentative. The only thing that's not tentative is our love for each other."

Chantal's excitement was apparent as she embraced Marianne. "I'm so thrilled for the two of you. I can't wait to get the details." She reached over and gave Mario a hug.

Marianne took a sip of her *thé* and cleared her throat.

"Let me start with time and venue. Mario and I have discussed this at length and I've taken both of our interests into consideration. I want to comfort Mario as much as possible and I've arrived at a decision. Mario and I will *s'enfuir* au Congo. We'll elope next week, returning to the Congo where we first met. It'd be too much of an ordeal to do it the traditional way, with the rituals, the families and all the hoop-la."

Five pairs of eyes were frozen on Marianne, with all mouths agape. Marianne leaned back in her seat, nonchalantly sipping her tea. The bombshell had stunned everyone, including Mario. He looked quizzically at Marianne while the other eyes transposed themselves onto to him, searching to understand.

After a moment, best described as a 'pregnant pause', Marianne spoke again before bedlam had time to erupt.

"Gotcha! The truth is Mario and I have agreed on a tentative date of a year from now. The wedding will be at St. Jacques in a conventional manner. How's that sound?"

Anika scolded her daughter, "What possessed you to say that? You nearly precipitated *une crise cardiaque*, if not with your father, certainly with me. You wouldn't be so pleased with yourself if either one of us had a heart attack."

No one dared to speak until Maurice came to his daughter's defense. "There's no harm. My heart did skip a beat. I take no offense. I understand what the two are going through and it's good to throw in a little levity. Tell me Mario, it appeared to me that you weren't privy to this little charade."

"I was as surprised as you. No one should be offended. We should be pleased instead, as I am, with Marianne's sense of humor. I believe it's an important element in a healthy relationship."

Benoît jumped in to obviate his mother from speaking. "I was aghast as Marianne spoke. I agree with Mario. We all know Marianne has a little devil in her and it's refreshing to have her display it. There's no doubt today has been stressful for both of them. Humor is a good release. It provides a healthy outlet for tension."

Anika lamented, "Well, it seems I'm a minority of one, so I'll hold my tongue. Marianne and Mario, are there other details you might share?"

Marianne filled her family with some of the things discussed with Claire Marie and Father Doucet. Anika felt sufficiently rebuked that she didn't inquire about Father LeBlanc. This would carry to another day. Chantal offered to assist Marianne in any way she could. Mario rose from his seat and bid everyone '*adieu et bonne nuit*'. He kissed Marianne and wished her sweet dreams. Benoît reminded Marianne about the diamond, which she fetched for him. He took it to study over night.

As Mario descended the stairway, he noticed a couple walking toward him.

"*Bon soir* Lucien! *Bon soir* Hennie! The others are still up. Marianne was just explaining what we've accomplished so far."

«Vien ici Mario et donne moi un baisser.»

"Hennie, I'm so pleased for you and Lucien. Marianne told me that you're *enceinte*, pregnant. Your face radiates joy even in this darkened street."

Hennie explained her delight. “Every system in my body is alive with happiness. I’m in the second trimester and all signs are solid.”

“Mario, you old rascal,” Lucien remarked. “I figured it wouldn’t happen for my sister and you. I’m delighted. You’re doing our family a great service by taking her off our hands. My brothers and I did our best to get her hooked up. She turned all of our candidates away, obviously waiting for you. She’s chosen well; welcome to the family.”

“It’s a fine family to be part of but it won’t be official for another year. We decided this’ll give us time to get to know each other better.”

“Sorry we missed your presentation. We got delayed departing Bruges.”

“Never mind, you’re here. What do you have for me from the finest *chocolatier* in Belgium?”

“You’re in luck, Mario. I have a couple of morsels set aside for you. I knew I had to indulge you with that sweet tooth of yours. Here is my special concoction of Callebaut’s best African cacao mingled with pralines and truffles. Enjoy!”

«Merci, mon ami. Tu es plein d’égards!»

“ *De rien* ! It’s the least I can do for my new brother.”

“I’ve got phone calls to make. I’ll see you at mass in the morning.”

Mario walked back to the *Cigne d’Argent,* checked reception for messages and went to his room. It was too late to phone his mother but he decided it was early enough to return Pietro's call and to phone Julio.

"Pietro, it's been a long day . . ."

CHAPTER TWENTY THREE

Mario was a sound sleeper, requiring five to six hours to be in top form. He awoke at 5:50 on Sunday morning, dressed in a warm-up outfit and walked west on *rue du Jardin-Botanique* as he limbered up. He was determined to get a fresh start on this new day and decided to avoid the *parc d'Avroy*. He opted instead to jog around the Botanical Garden of Liège, a few steps away. He ran for about a ½ hour in tranquility amidst a variety of plant life from around the globe.

Mario's thoughts returned to the previous day and his confrontations with Marianne, Father LeBlanc and Anika. Not a bad start, stepping into controversy with little effort on his part. He came to Belgium disposed to be accommodating and avoid wrangling. He learned this was not possible. He had to draw the line. 'I have to live with myself'. He felt romance could carry them through initially, but more was needed for the long haul. He resolved to be amenable on Duhammel family day. He would pray to keep the contentious issues dormant for the day.

He recalled his conversations with Pietro and Julio. They were both ebullient and pressed Mario for details. He told them Marianne and he were working to strengthen their relationship. He confirmed to Pietro he would be his best man, and to Julio he would be in the wedding party. He still needed to call his mother.

As he ambled back to the hotel, he was relaxed and ready to face the new day. He ordered a light breakfast, *le petit déjeuner Européen*, to be sent to his room. He collected the newspapers he requested, including 'Le Soir' of Brussels. He had nearly three hours before joining Marianne and her family on the 15-minute walk to St. Jacques. He was used to cold-water showers. There was no choice in most places he'd been. He preferred the brisk feel of the water, which he found invigorating. As he showered, it was reassuring to know the water was sanitary.

Mario emerged from the bathroom, wearing a plush hotel bathrobe, and answered the knock on the door. The waiter laid out the coffee and croissants on the table by the window. Mario brought the newspapers and the telephone to the table and settled in. He knew his mother was an early riser. He wanted to reach her before she left for 8:00 am mass since he'd be occupied the rest of the day. He took a moment to reflect on what to tell her. He had to be upbeat as he was with his two friends. There could be no hint of his concerns. He tried to distract himself by reading the newspapers. It wasn't working. Time to put on the 'happy face' and phone his *madre.*

"Hello, may I speak to Mrs. Rossetti?"

"*Allo*, Mario, I know it's you. I've been expecting your call. Are you in Liège with Marianne? Are you okay?"

"*Salve, mamma! Lo sto bene! Si,* I'm in Liège, getting ready to attend mass with the Duhammels. Marianne and I are *una coppia di fidanzati.* Yes, I proposed and she accepted, so we're an engaged couple. We met with the priest at the Duhammel family church and discussed the wedding. It'll be a year from now, giving us time to know each other better."

"You catch me by surprise but I'm pleased, *mio figlio*. She's a nice girl. Can you change enough to settle down and be with a wife? It's not only your *madre* who'll worry, you'll have a *moglie* and, God willing, some *bambinos*. You need to pray to God for guidance. Pray to Mary, she's a mother who also worried about her son. Maybe you'll learn how to be a good husband and father."

"*Mamma*, are you trying to talk me out of getting married? I've considered everything. Marianne and I will be happy together. Don't fret about it. Now, let me feel that nice smile of yours."

"Mario, there you have it, my best smile. *Io sono felice!* I am happy. Marianne will make you a fine wife. I have these concerns about you."

"Okay, fair enough. I'll spend another day or so in Liège and come to Verona on my way to see Pietro in Lucca. *Ti amo*, *mamma*! *A presto*! "

"*Buon coraggio*, Mario."

Mario understood his mother's concerns. She hadn't seen Marianne's domineering trait, which was his main concern. He expected this would mellow over the coming year as they adjusted to each other. His self-assured nature prevailed, encouraging him to trust his instincts. He finished his breakfast and glanced through the newspapers, making sure to check on the *futbol* world. He reviewed 'Le Soir' for information on the Belgian League, Division 1. Marianne's middle brother was a midfielder, an adept dribbler, with Royal Standard de Liège, a soccer club in the country's top category. Mario would team up with Emile later in a brief soccer session against the two other brothers.

The ringing telephone brought Mario out of his reverie. Marianne wanted him to come over sooner. Benoît was anxious to speak to them about the African rock. He completed his ablutions, got dressed in a dark blue suit with fine light blue pin stripes, a white shirt and a vermillion tie. Time to get a report card on his so-called treasure.

He walked over, arriving at the same time as one of the neighbors. The teenager would look after the two children while the parents attended mass. Marianne greeted them cheerfully and called to Chantal. Marianne was decked out in green, sporting a jade skirt and a chartreuse blouse, covered over by a lime green bolero. Benoît sat in the salon while the rest of the gang was putting finishing touches on their Sunday finery.

"Marianne, Mario, sit down and I'll explain the best I can."

Mario was unsure how to take this opening. "Benoît, you look a bit glum. Does this reflect what you see in the rock or is it a contrived poker face?'

"Mario, sometimes things aren't as they seem. Take this rock of yours and my visage. One is what it seems and the other is not. Which is which?"

"I know my brother well enough and it is his sour puss that's the phony. We await your judgment."

"Marianne, you do know me too well. The rock is true to its promise; it's a gem, in the best usage of a jeweler's term. I figure it to be at least eight carats. It needs to be examined under a *loupe* by our graders, but from what I see, it might qualify for the exquisite Hearts and Arrows cut."

"Benoît, Marianne and I are novices in your world. Translate."

"Hearts and Arrows is perfect symmetry. You have a top quality stone. If I'm correct, its value is probably in the range of high five/ low six figures in US$s. My colleagues in Antwerp will determine the actual quality and how you might choose to have it cut as a gemstone."

Marianne was blown away. She wrestled with ownership of the diamond through a restless night. "Now I know it's more than a trinket, I can't accept it. I told you both earlier I have concerns. It has to be tainted, obtained through drudgery."

"Are you crazy, sister? You're making assumptions you know nothing about."

"Benoît, I know enough of that part of the world. Forced labor is used to enrich the masters. I'll have no part of it."

Benoît looked at Mario. "I can't think of a single woman who would turn up her nose on this bauble. Rest assured, Mario, my people at Jaeckus Hoelebrand will be interested.

"Now, Marianne, don't be foolish and get off your high horse. *C'est idiot!* This is bullshit! Wake up to what this is about. You have the person you love who loves you. You need to show trust in each other. Mario came to this stone honestly and gave you a special gift. Speculating on its origins leads nowhere. You don't know, Mario doesn't know, President Kibali doesn't know. It doesn't bode well for your relationship with doubts that reflect on your fiancé. I can't speak for Mario, but I'd be insulted by your reaction."

Well, well, just what I needed, more controversy, Mario was thinking. Nobody told me it was going to be easy. Good ol' Benoît. Nice to have him on my side.

"Marianne, I honestly don't know where the diamond came from. All I do know is it was in the safe in the palace. I accepted it as a gesture of appreciation for what our group accomplished. It's pure speculation to assert this diamond is tainted. You would never have seen it if I sensed it might be.

"I don't get it, Marianne. You profess your love for me. You seem pleased with our engagement and happy about our forthcoming marriage. Yet, you keep coming up with problems. First, it's my mercenary activities, then it's my religious devotion, now it's the diamond. What's next, the way I chew my food?"

Saved by the bell. Chantal entered the salon, saying it was time to go. The others had already started. Mario decided it best to let Marianne mull things over. He felt discouraged, as though he was in a tailspin. Benoît was right on the mark when he told Mario he had 'crash landed'. He'd have to abort the engagement and the relationship if everything became so contentious. As Benoît also said, 'it does not bode well'. Mario knew one of his strengths was resiliency. He needed to reach deep down within himself.

The rest of the morning was uneventful. Father LeBlanc, who had celebrated the mass, greeted the parishioners as they left the church. Mario overheard Anika ask him why he wasn't serving as advisor to Marianne and Mario. He replied that she should ask her daughter. On the walk back to the house, Mario looked up and thought he saw a banner floating in the air with the message 'TROUBLED WATERS: The Soap Opera'.

CHAPTER TWENTY-FOUR

Upon returning to the house, Mario and the three brothers changed clothes and went to the park to show off their prowess in soccer. Maurice accompanied the women in the salon. Marianne expressed her concerns, telling the group she didn't want to lose Mario. She admitted she needed to employ greater restraint. Sometimes she couldn't help herself when she blurted out her thoughts rather than engaging in a low-key discussion. She knew she had to be less contentious and convince Mario she could be more agreeable. Chantal and Hennie told Marianne she had a fine person in Mario and needed to avoid scaring him away.

Marianne's middle brother Emile, accompanied by his friend Yvette, had joined the family at mass. Yvette considered whether to speak up, deciding to have her say.

"This may not be my place to speak, but I'd like to share some of my experience. As you know, I'm an *avocat*, specializing in family law. I've had many cases where couples are clearly incompatible. I admit I don't have the full story of what's involved between Mario and you, but I've a sense the two of you are deeply in love. A sound marriage can't exist without compromises by both parties. I can tell that Mario isn't a *louche*; he's a solid individual. Emile has told me about your fiancé and I admit I've seen him only briefly. I sense he'll make a fortunate woman a fine husband and companion."

Maurice was usually comfortable letting others speak, unless it was a pile of *merde*. He figured it was time to weigh in. "Marianne, you're my daughter and very dear to me. I want you happy and content. You have to decide how badly you want Mario as your husband. I don't know all the details either but, based on what I'm aware of, I'd already be running away from here if I were Mario."

Anika took her turn. "Don't be so hard on Marianne. She has every right to stand up for her principles."

Maurice came back. "My dear, you know very well there's a time to stand up and a time to stand down. If she does as you say, she'll go through life as a *vielle fille*, holding tightly to her principles, a champion of causes, but with no companion."

Marianne seemed bewildered. "This is what's called family loyalty? None of you seems to appreciate my concerns. I feel you're all ganging up on me. How about some understanding? Mario and I have issues to work out and we'll do just that."

It remained quiet for a moment. Anika went over and gave her daughter a hug. Chantal arose saying it was time to prepare *souper*. Hennie and Marianne followed her in the kitchen to gather the ingredients for the meal. The two wives chatted on the phone earlier in the week, deciding on a menu for Sunday and who would bring what. The trio discussed the tasks and agreed on assignments. Everything was on hand to prepare the courses from appetizer to dessert. The menu for the day was:

- *Moules Hoegaarden*

- *Asperges a la flamande*
- *Braisé belge endive*
- *Waterzooi de poisons* (an eel, bass and vegetable stew)
- *Tarte au sucre*
- *Café de choix—espresso ou café belge avec Elixir d'Anvers*

Yvette looked in on them and offered to help. The response was thanks for asking but we're all set. She wasn't put off because Emile had alerted her not to take rejection as a personal rebuff. He told her it was their way and it worked well. Instead, she walked down to the park and watched the guys at play. Meanwhile, Anika was looking after her grandkids and Maurice had settled in with a book.

The three brothers and Mario came back to the house after an hour of *jeu sportif*, grabbed some beers and went to the back yard for some *pétanque*. The ladies heard them having a grand old time while they worked in the kitchen. Chantal and Hennie chatted with Marianne as they prepared the meal. They tried to reassure her and get her to soften up with Mario. The lads came back in the house from time to time to replenish their beers, tapping the gals' fannies to show their appreciation. Playtime was soon over. Time to head for the showers and dress up.

When Mario returned from the hotel, it was nearing dinnertime. Contrary to European custom of late dining, the Duhammels had their family reunion meal late afternoon to afford a reasonable hour for the travelers. This was Maurice's moment; he was in charge of entertainment. He had selected a few songs for his sons and Mario to pick from and sing to the ladies. Marianne usually accompanied on the piano or guitar. When Maurice called the gents together, Mario spoke up, telling him he'd like to lead off with a solo and accompany himself at the piano. Maurice was surprised but pleased with Mario's initiative.

«Pourquoi pas? Allez-y!»

The audience was attentive as Mario worked his fingers across the ivories. He started right in with his vocalization without introduction.

«Ne me quitte pas

Il faut oublier

Tout peut s'oublier . . . .»

He continued with his pleading 'Don't Leave Me', giving his best Jacques Brel imitation. His voice was smooth and mellow, his accent close to authentic. As he sang, he moved on to the Flemish singer/songwriter's Flemish version. He sang a few lines of '*Laat Me Niet Alleen*' and finished with a silky Italian version, '*Non Andare Via*'. He conveyed sensitivity and sensuality.

Maurice was on his feet, overwhelmed. He rushed over to Mario and gave him the full treatment—tight hugs and kisses. This was a first. The ladies were standing, ardently applauding and brimming with tears. The three brothers stood to the side stupefied but sufficiently aware they heard something special.

«Chapeau!» «C'est incroyable!» «Bravo!» «Magnifique!» «Formidable!»

As the din settled, the three brothers remained bemused. They realized Mario's performance cast their program awry. They conferred and came up with an alternative; stick to the theme set out by Mario. They discussed this with Maurice and decided to devote the entertainment session to fellow Belgian, Jacques Brel.

Each would render a different Brel *chanson*, with Marianne on the piano. Benoît led off with '*Quand On N'a Que l'Amour*', followed by Emile with '*Les Bourgeois*' and Lucien doing the finale with '*Les Bonbons*'. Each selection fitted the performer, seemingly a kindred spirit with Brel.

There was sustained applause and shouting. All were rapturous, the audience as well as the performers. It was time for jubilation. Faces were gleaming. Wives hugged husbands. Anika relaxed her guard, embracing Maurice tenderly and moving on to give Mario an emotional hug. Marianne was feeling contrite but swollen with pride for her man. She approached Mario demurely, chagrined with her behavior. Mario stepped forward, grabbed her in his arms and kissed her. Emile figured their efforts earned them more refreshments. Lucien helped fetch the beer as they awaited the call to *souper*.

The *bonhomie* carried over to the dinner table. Spirits were uplifted. The guys had their sporting engagements, *boulevardier* performances and the monks' brew, whereas the gals had the splendid entertainment and the compliments for their cuisine. Maurice was more animated, while Anika was less so, satisfied to smile and take in her family's joy.

The meal was a total success. With stomachs full, the men expressed their thanks and admiration to the women for their epicurean labors. Upon getting their fill, they all assisted in clearing the table, laughing as they bumped into each other. Yvette chased them all out of the kitchen.

"I need to finish this. This is my input to a splendid meal. Now then, get out of my way."

Upon getting kicked out of the kitchen, they returned to the salon to relax a spell. Chantal headed up the stairs to gather her sleeping infants for the trip back to Antwerp. Maurice spoke up about one element of the wedding he hadn't heard mentioned.

"I realize the wedding isn't for another year but it's not too soon to make arrangements. I'm thinking of the reception. If the two of you are agreeable, I can ask a long time friend about using his place."

"Who are you talking about, papa?"

"You know him Marianne. Grégoire Parmentier and I grew up together and we've maintained our friendship over the years. He's been a faithful customer of mine as well. *Il a un château près de la Citadelle.*"

"I think I know where it is. If it's the one I'm thinking about, it would be great."

"All I want is your okay to inquire. I won't presume myself on your arrangements. The University's Castle would have been a good spot but it's unavailable because of the fire. M. Parmentier's castle may be your best option if he'll allow you to use it."

Mario liked the offer. "Maurice, it's a bit early to commit, but it'd be good to know if he's agreeable."

"Consider it done. He has functions there from time to time. We've been to a few over the years. I'll inquire about catering as well."

Chantal was soon ready to travel with the children. Benoît took the uncut diamond to have it analyzed. Lucien and Hennie had the longest drive and were eager to hit the road. Yvette thanked everyone for including her. Time for hugs and kisses.

Benoît and Chantal secured Dirk and Giselle in their Volvo Amazon wagon and followed Lucien and Hennie in their fresh-from-the-factory Peugeot 504 Saloon. Emile and Yvette departed soon after in his Mercedes 250 SE white and black convertible. Mario thanked Maurice and Anika, excusing himself to take care of a few things. He gave Marianne a light embrace and kiss, telling her he'd see her in the morning.

Mario sat pensively in his room, reflecting on what he'd been through. As he headed to Liège two days earlier, he thought he'd be euphoric. Instead, doubts were raised. Could he be happy with Marianne? Issues remained unresolved. Marianne was taking the next day off, giving them another day to work out their differences.

He had phone calls to make: Mme. Mertens, his mother, Pietro, Julio, François, Alitalia and his concierge in Monte Carlo. Upon calling Mrs. Mertens, he learned the service honoring Roger was set for Tuesday at 11 am. He wrote down the particulars, telling her he would be in Brussels to catch a flight and would do his best to be there. When he phoned his mother, she told him she wanted him to contact his estranged brother. Mario reflected that it was seven or eight years since his last contact with Marcello, who was five years younger. Marcello was in Milan and Mario would be passing through. When he heard Mario was getting married, he told his mother he'd like to speak with Mario. She had no idea what Marcello's concern was after years of avoiding Mario.

Mario and Marcello were the progeny of Manuccio and Teresina Allegretti Rossetti. Manuccio was a handyman, a jack-of-all-trades, repairing anything that needed fixing. Teresina and he were lifelong residents of Verona. She was a seamstress and between the two, they were able to scrimp enough *lire* to purchase their own home.

Marcello wandered off at a young age. After their father was killed while fighting in a partisan group against Mussolini and his black shirts, the brothers went in different directions. Mario joined the fight against fascism in his early teens, while Marcello got an early start with petty crime, eventually graduating to mafia-type gang activities.

Teresina attended mass daily to pray for her departed husband and her two sons. She was a parishioner of *Sant'Anastasia*, a venerable, centuries-old, august Gothic structure. She enlisted priests and nuns to send special messages to the saints to look after her wayfaring son, but especially her wayward *secondo figlio*. Teresina was proud of Mario with his steadfastness in broadening his education, attending university courses wherever and whenever he could.

In the midst of his phone calls, Mario heard a sharp rap on his door, accompanied by a frantic voice calling his name. When he opened the door, he saw an agitated Marianne. She was still panting from her run to the hotel.

"Mario, I tried phoning but your line was busy. It's Hennie. There was an accident. Benoît called. She's at the university hospital in Brussels, CHU Brugmann."

"Easy now, Marianne. Here, sit down. Take a minute to catch your breath. What else did Benoît say? What about Lucien?"

"Lucien was driving on the Brussels bypass when a BMW came roaring onto the roadway. Apparently, the young German driver thought he could make it to the gap ahead of Lucien's car.

The BMW slammed into the right side of the Peugeot, where Hennie was seated."

"It sounds like Lucien didn't see the BMW coming."

"Benoît and Chantal were directly behind preparing to veer off for Antwerp. Benoît said the accident happened in a blink of an eye and there was no time to react."

"So, how bad is it?"

"Lucien and Hennie are undergoing tests but Lucien seems okay. Hennie has lacerations and contusions. They're taking x-rays to check for broken ribs. She's quite shaken and was given a sedative. Benoît said he would phone again a little later."

"Marianne, I'll take you to Brussels in the morning if you like."

"I'd like that Mario. I'm taking the day off, expecting to spend with you."

"You'll probably be busy looking after Hennie for awhile. Our wedding plans can wait. I'm going back to Italy and Monaco to sort things out. How about your parents? Are they going see Lucien and Hennie?"

"My father has work he can't put off. Emile will drive my mother to Brussels."

PART III

QUANDARY REIGNS

"Any Idiot
Can Face a Crisis
—It's This Day-to-Day Living
That Wears You Out"

Anton Chekhov
Russian Writer and
Physician

CHAPTER TWENTY FIVE

Le fond du verre devenant un trou noir qui vous attire, vous transporte!

Mario felt his life had turned topsy-turvy. A principal participant in a soap opera, he was the leading actor in a plot of romantic turbulence, trepidations and contentions, along with family and religious entanglements. It was as though he stepped into a quagmire, the bottom of a glass became a black hole, drawing him down. *Spiaggia di una vita!* Bah! Contrary to the popular expression, life was not a beach; it was strewn with rocks.

François was still in Paris when Mario phoned Sunday evening. Mario told him of Roger's service in Brussels on Tuesday, and asked him to come; he needed a friend. François agreed and Mario arranged to meet him at the train station.

When Mario drove up to the Duhammel residence the following morning, Marianne was sitting on the stoop. He saw her grave expression and soon learned it fronted a saturnine demeanor.

"Mario, this is the saddest moment of my life. I feel so bad for Hennie."

"How is she?"

"She has two broken ribs and she lost the baby."

Mario tried to comfort her. "I'll have you there in no time. You can cheer her up."

"Hennie is inconsolable. I'm not fit to be any help. As you can see, I'm not in a good frame of mind."

"She has Lucien, Chantal and Benoît by her side."

"Chantal is there. Benoît drove back to Antwerp to take care of the kids."

"Marianne, could have been worse. They'll bounce back. Be positive."

"I can't talk about it anymore."

Silence prevailed on the drive to Brussels. Mario tried to lighten the mood but Marianne would have none of it. She kept lamenting the poor baby who never had a chance. After being rebuffed, Mario remained close-mouthed for the remainder of the trip. He also knew efforts to resolve their issues would be for another day.

Marianne rushed into the hospital while Mario parked the car. He had to negotiate with the hospital staff to learn where Hennie was and then to be allowed into the area. When he finally joined the group, he saw Lucien, Chantal and Marianne sitting in a waiting room, chatting with a man and a woman in white frocks. Lucien introduced Mario to Dr. DeVos, an orthopedic surgeon, and Dr. Van den Broeck, a gynecologist.

Mario expressed his concern. "Lucien, how are you holding up?"

"Thanks for coming, Mario. You never know what to expect when you join our family. I lucked out with only a few bruises. The impact propelled me onto the steering wheel. I have contusions on my chest and left arm, plus these cuts on my face."

Dr. DeVos explained his findings. "The breaks in Hennie's ribs are clean and there's no threat to internal organs. She's in no danger. She'll make a full recovery and can have follow-up treatment in Brugge. You'll have a full report for her physician."

Dr. Van den Broeck followed with her comments. "Lucien, I understand your concerns. I'm optimistic about Hennie. There are different aspects."

Lucien was chomping at the bit. "Come on doctor, out with it."

"It could be much worse, Lucien. You can be thankful. Hennie is in good health. I agree with Dr. DeVos; Hennie will make a full recovery. The loss of the baby is tragic but there's no evidence of permanent damage to Hennie childbearing ability. This requires further evaluation. Be optimistic and help her get through this."

"You're saying we can still have children."

"Yes, Lucien, most likely. I'll provide a full report for her gynecologist. Her doctor will advise her after Hennie recovers from her injuries."

"What haven't you told me?"

"Lucien, this is the tough part, Hennie's mental health. It's important for her to face up and accept the loss of her child. This will take time with lots of love and understanding from family and friends. Hennie is traumatized. Counseling might be advisable."

Mario found both doctors candid and compassionate, helping to ease some of the anxiety in the air. Dr. Van den Broeck told the group Hennie was sleeping and not in pain. She should awaken within the hour, when they can visit.

Mario suggested going to the cafeteria for coffee but got no takers. He went alone. Marianne was withdrawn, understandable given the circumstances. He recalled his earlier resolve never to settle down with a woman with temperamental proclivities.

When he returned to the waiting area, he found Benoît, Chantal and Emile sitting and chatting. Benoît stood and greeted Mario.

"Fortunately, our nanny was available despite her day off. Hennie is awake and my mother, Marianne and Lucien are with her."

"Can you spare a few minutes to chat?"

They moved to another area of the room to converse.

"Benoît, you've stood up for me and I appreciate it. There's nothing phony about me. I am what you see. I'm not perfect and I know it. I'm making meaningful changes in my life for the sake of Marianne. I love her and I believe she loves me. My concern is this—can we find happiness together? Given what we've been through these past couple of days, I have serious doubts. You're her brother and I expect you to stand up for her. I'd appreciate your candor on how you see this going."

"Yes, I think dearly of my sister and I want her to be content. Frankly, I don't know if it's in the cards for her to find comfort in a husband. Marianne needs to take a few steps back. She's a delightful and intelligent person but she can be sanctimonious. I like you Mario, and I sense that you would adapt well to marriage. Unfortunately, I can't forecast how a union with Marianne would be. Her love for you is genuine but she needs to come to grips with herself. And now, we have this. Marianne is preoccupied with the new life taken away. It will take time for her to sort through all the issues."

"Thanks for being forthright. I've been reflecting on the past couple of days and I've come to the same conclusion. Marianne and I are still engaged; that hasn't changed. I'll marry her if issues can be worked out. Wedding plans are up in the air. I'll head back to Italy. Marianne needs time to consider what she wants. I'll keep my options open. Time will tell."

"You've done as much as you can, Mario. Keep in touch. I mean it when I say I'd like this to work for both of you."

"Thanks, Benoît, I appreciate that. These are numbers where you can reach me. I'll give you a call to check on things."

"That's fine, Mario. I'll try to move Marianne along."

"That's all I can ask. Right now I feel I'm in limbo."

"You're in a tough position. What about the famous, or is it now the 'infamous' rock?"

"I'll take it and place it in the bank vault. It needs to rest in peace for a while. The poor thing has gone through a lot of turmoil."

"I have it with me. I didn't dare leave it anywhere."

"I'll see Hennie and bid *adieu* to Marianne, then I'm off."

"Don't forget about coming to Antwerp."

"Agreed, Benoît. We'll talk and set a time. *Au revoir*!"

"A la prochaine!"

Mario visited Hennie and expressed his regrets. He wished her a speedy recovery and kissed her on the forehead. He saw Marianne as he left the room. She still looked glum. He told her he was leaving and gave her a kiss. She appealed to him to be patient.

Mario left the hospital and checked in at *l'hôtel Le Dôme*. The concierge Jacques was happy to see him again. He changed his flight to Milan to late Wednesday afternoon. Roger's service and François' arrival were on Tuesday. He contacted people he knew in Brussels. Through his exploits, Mario knew many accomplished individuals who straddled the fence between legal and illicit activities.

Mario awoke Tuesday morning refreshed. He had a light breakfast after a brisk run around the *Grand'Place*. When he met François at the train station, Mario embraced him as though it had been ages.

"François, it's great to see you. I know it's only been five days but much has happened."

"You seem unnerved, Mario. It's unlike you. You going to tell me about it?"

"I'll talk to you after Roger's service. Some of our colleagues might show up."

Mario found the small church in the commune of Jette without difficulty. It was across the street from *le Papillon*, where he had lunch with Christine Mertens. More than fifty people were at the service. Roger was active in the community, including coaching youth soccer.

Mario introduced François to Christine, who thanked them for coming. The service was solemn but brief. Everyone was invited to *le Papillon* for refreshments. The restaurant owner, Hervé du Champ, was a friend of Roger.

The feature of the reception was the beer. Hervé's offerings were catholic. The choices of brews paid justice to the nation's reputation and culture, affording diversity to suit all tastes. Mario whispered to François that Roger must have been a real good friend because Hervé wasn't sparing the expenses.

«Hervé a fait un festin à tout casser.» It was a smorgasbord.

Some of the selections included: *gaufres belge*s with fruit, *chicon gratin* (endives & melted cheese), *jambon d'Ardenne*, Belgian meatballs braised in beer, *choucroute*, *andouille*, Brussels sprouts in sour cream, *boudin*, asparagus, *langouste*, mashed potatoes with leeks, etc.

Christine Mertens and her early teenage twin daughters arrived from the private burial as the feast was underway. Christine's mariner husband was away at sea. She petitioned for a divorce and obtained a legal separation nearly a year earlier. He was a heavy drinker and abusive and she was determined to protect her daughters.

Mario took such apparent notice of her arrival that François felt compelled to nudge him. Mario found Christine's pulchritude distracting, despite her mourning attire.

Walking back to the car, François admonished Mario for his lasciviousness.

"*Entre nous*, your behavior surprises me now that you're engaged to a woman whom you profess to be 'the love of your life'."

"Relax, François, it's not what you think. Christine is a nice lady. I was merely paying my respects. Besides, there is nothing wrong with admiring objects of beauty. I need to speak to you about my situation but I'll wait until we get to *l'hôtel Le Dôme*. I reserved a room for you in case you decide to stay the night."

"Why would I want to do that?"

"It concerns what I'll be discussing with you. Once you hear what I have to say, you might want to stay a little longer."

"Mario, you sure know how to make your plot suspenseful. I'll be patient and wait until you're ready to reveal your deep, inner secrets."

CHAPTER TWENTY SIX

François and Mario settled themselves in the hotel lounge, each ordering a *café au lait*. Their physiques were diminished by the floral damask velvet chairs that threatened to swallow them.

"Mario, it's time of reckoning. Come clean and tell me what this is about."

"François, we're friends, so here goes. I'm in a different position than I expected to be. If Marianne accepts my proposal, I'm ecstatic, right? If she refuses, I'm at liberty to continue my life unaltered, right?"

"So, what's the problem? She accepted your proposal. This is what you wanted."

"Yes, it is, and then, it isn't. I'm neither in heaven nor in hell. I've been sentenced to spend an undetermined amount of time in purgatory. My lifestyle has caught up with me; not enough religion and too much violence and debauchery."

"You'll need to spell it out for me. I must be missing something."

"Marianne declared a definitive 'yes', as I told you. Concerns emerged. She is conflicted by an image of her ideal. She wants to marry me. There's the problem of me being a killer. There's the problem of me not being religious enough. To advance this further into limbo, she refused the uncut diamond because of suspected origin."

"Mon pauvre ami, tu es vraiment en purgatoire. I feel for you, my friend. It's an unsettling situation. What are you going to do?"

"Take it one step at a time. Marianne could awaken tomorrow, convinced we truly belong together, or it may never happen. Being in limbo, I can still do as I please."

"I see your point, Mario. I'm not trying to inveigle you back into action. Just to let you know, there are two possibilities, a back burner and a front burner. Both involve training military groups in Africa. An English-speaking country in west Africa needs more time for the right conditions to evolve. The second activity might interest you. It concerns Mandaka. Do you want to hear it?"

"I'm not sure. Don't tell me Kibali has already been overthrown."

"Okay, I won't. That's because he hasn't. Pastambu phoned two days ago. He said Kibali held a weekend meeting that included him, Kingambo and six carefully selected middle and junior grade officers. We met two at army headquarters, Commandant Florien Tanandu, the officer who stood up to the mutineers, and Captain Edouard Bolatatu, who led the army unit that relieved us. Both have been promoted. They're restructuring the military. Most changes can be handled internally. They want to set up an elite corps. It'll be staffed by the most promising soldiers, who'll be put through a rigorous, performance driven training program."

"Anything said on the state of affairs across the country?"

"It's been little more than a week, but the populace is giving Kibali some slack. He is moving quickly to get his new army in place. So far, pockets of disturbances are isolated."

"Now, François, who's keeping whom in suspense? You haven't told me what this is about."

"It's the elite corps. They want us back. We impressed them. Pastambu asked me to put together a small unit to train several dozen soldiers to be based at three locations: the presidential palace, army headquarters and the mines. I told him I'd look into it."

"I'm inclined to join you. I would be protecting my investment."

"Kibali's group mentioned both you and Gundhart specifically. I think eight of us would be right for this job. I'll be getting more details. Tanandu will have overall command of the unit along with other duties and Bolatatu will have direct command. Both officers will go through the training."

"There's something else François. I've been thinking about the diamond. I've developed a friendship of sorts with Marianne's brother who's with a diamond enterprise. I intend to drive to Antwerp to meet with him and his colleagues."

"That makes sense, Mario, you old devil. You've been working up to this. You play your cards close to the vest. I should've guessed when you wanted me to stay the night. I'll go with you but it has to be early morning. I have to get back to Paris."

“Same for me. I need to leave for Milan.”

Mario placed a call to Antwerp. “Benoît, Mario here. How’s Hennie?”

“In somewhat better spirits, Mario. She’s anxious to get back to Bruges. She’ll remain in the hospital under observation for at least another couple of days.”

“Any chance of seeing you tomorrow morning? I’m still in Brussels and I could drive to Antwerp first thing. My colleague is with me.”

“I’ll set it up. Be sure to bring the rock.”

François checked in and went to his room to rest, while Mario went to retrieve his treasure. They went out two hours later to a nearby *bistrot* for a light dinner of mussels and Belgian fries. Mario looked forward to going back to Mandaka.

On Wednesday morning, François joined Mario in the Audi and headed north for *Antwerpend*. The jeweler, Jaeckus Hoelebrand, was located in the Diamond District on *Hoveniersstraat*. Mario told Benoît of his possible return to Mandaka. He explained that it was a training mission, intended, in part, to improve security at the mines. Benoît cautioned Mario on the delicacy of this new development when informing Marianne.

François and Mario met with Benoît and three diamond specialists for two hours. The experts were diligent in examining Mario’s rough diamond. They confirmed its exceptional quality.

“Little is known of Mandakan diamonds,” the marketing specialist added. “The area is remote in the tropical rainforest and the mine was discovered by the French toward the end of colonial rule.”

Mario responded. "That's what we learned. The French made a lighthearted effort. They weren't willing to expend the resources needed with the colony headed for independence."

The geologist gave the two novices a quick course in Diamond Mining 101. "Your diamond, Mr. Rossetti, is likely alluvial, taken from a riverbed. It would be good to know if there was excavation in the area to determine the existence of kimberlites. The natural pipe mining exploration process could be either open pit or underground."

The marketing specialist provided a scenario on how the situation could develop.

"This is unofficial. If this diamond's origin can be confirmed to be Mandaka, Jaeckus Hoelebrand Diamond World might be interested in entering into a joint venture. Many details would be needed before this would be considered. Collaborating with DeBeers would be a possibility along with the Government of Mandaka."

Benoît escorted François and Mario to the car, wishing them bon voyage. He embraced Mario, wishing him *bonne chance* with his sister. "Marianne is still devastated with the loss of the baby. You need to tread easy"

Mario drove back to Brussels and dropped François off at the train station.

"Mario, Marianne isn't the only one you need to mollify. You need to square yourself with your casino boss. There's also your olive partner, Pietro, and you have Julio to deal with. You've made arrangements with him you might not be able to keep."

"Yes, there are things to take care of. Are you in Paris for the next few days?"

"Yes, I'll be at there at least through the weekend."

"My little brother wants to speak to me. He's in Milan and we haven't been in touch for several years. I'll see what's on his mind and move on to Verona."

"Happy to have you on the mission if you feel right about it."

"*A bientôt*, François! I've got to get going. I'll get the diamond stashed and head out to the airport."

CHAPTER TWENTY SEVEN

Mario had a way of bouncing around from one place to another, and he had a preferred hotel at each location. He checked in at Hotel Cavour on *via Fatebenefratelli* in Milan late afternoon and began making phone calls. He preferred this hotel because of its location; it was near the Public Gardens and a few blocks from the *Teatro alla Scala*. He tried his brother at the number his mother gave him. It was an answering service. Mario said he was Marcello's brother and left his number.

"Pronto!"

"Mario, is that you?"

"Yes it is, Marcello. Just arrived in Milan. Good to hear from you. Momma said you wanted to talk to me. What's up?"

"I'm glad you're here. Can we get together? I know I've gone out of my way to avoid you, but I need to speak with you."

"Marcello, I have no idea what you're up. If you're in trouble, count me out."

"It's not that. I'm not in trouble. If I were, I wouldn't dump it on you. Can we get together?"

"I haven't had dinner yet. You can join me."

"Sure, I haven't eaten since this morning."

"The restaurant here is decent. Meet me in an hour."

"*Gracie*, Mario. Momma reminds me you're a good guy."

Mario phoned his *madre* next.

"Momma, I'm staying overnight in Milano, so I'll see you tomorrow. I just talked to Marcello on the phone. We're meeting for *cena* shortly."

"Mario, you be careful with your brother. You must be *delicate.*"

"I promise I'll be nice to him."

His other call was to Pietro. He held back telling him about Mandaka and Marianne. He told him he'd be in Lucca in a couple of days after visiting his mother in Verona.

Mario sat in the reception area. His own appearance hadn't changed much but figured his brother's probably had. There was considerable activity, to and fro, with visitors enjoying Milan's amenities, especially when La Scala opera was in season.

As he sat people watching, a tall slender man with a Prince Valiant hairstyle and dark hair approached. He had olive skin with

Roman centurion features, and wore a gray custom tailored suit with a violet silk tie. His carriage was erect and his stride assured. His visage, with its pale blue eyes, displayed a hint of a smile. The stranger gazed at Mario and gave him a slight nod.

"Mr. Mario Rossetti, I presume."

"I know the voice, but I don't know the body. Quite an outfit, Marcello. I'm pleased to see you looking well. Momma worries."

"It's been a long time, *fratello*. Before we start, I owe you an apology. I've been *schifezza* toward you and Momma."

"Let's eat, Marcello, and we can carry on from there."

The maitre d', Fillipo, stepped forward to greet Mario and his guest.

"*Benevenuto, signore* Rossetti! It's a pleasure to have you here with us again. Let me show you to your table. I set it aside as usual."

"You're a good man Fillipo, and you always treat me better than I deserve. But, I do appreciate it."

Marcello was reminded of earlier times. "I don't get it, Mario. I knew there was some kind of magic with your manner, but this is my home turf. I've been here before and Fillipo knows me, but with you, I'm a stranger."

"Well, Marcello, maybe we're getting somewhere. Go on, explain what's bothering you."

"Mario, this is what I think. You're five years older than me. When I was a youth, you were my hero. You excelled in everything, sports, school, making friends and had uncommonly good looks. As for me, I was scrawny and considered myself ugly, and average at best in everything. Hero-worshiping developed into jealousy as I grew older and, eventually, hatred. I had to erase you from my mind; otherwise, I would have driven myself mad. That's what I was trying to get away from."

"I appreciate you're telling me. I thought it might be something like that. Why now?"

"I hear you're making changes. I need to do so also. I want to break away from the underworld and become respectable. I'm making an effort, taking courses at the university, one or two each term. I've accumulated a bankroll over the years. I want to do something worthwhile that'll give me a sense of fulfillment."

"You look terrific. You speak well and you seem in good health. Seems to me, it's tough to cut loose from the 'family' once you're in."

"I can leave. My *padrino* took me in over a decade ago and treated me as a son, replacing his own son who was killed by a rival gang. I've done good work for him and he looked after me, encouraging me to further my education. Several months ago, he told me he'd do what he could to assist me if I decided to leave the *famiglia*. I've made a good living, but I'm spent."

"It's hard to understand your godfather would let you walk away just like that."

"My *padrino* told me he sees a softer side of me. My sense of anger at everything has subsided. He's afraid I'm losing my edge."

"Are you free to leave right now?"

"You mean now, as in today? The answer is yes, but tomorrow would be better."

"Nice, a touch of humor. Tomorrow will be fine. You can accompany me to Verona and visit our *madre*. After that, I'm going to Tuscany to see Pietro in Lucca. You remember Pietro DiSanto, my friend from Verona?"

"Yes, he was nice. Momma told me he and you are partners in an olive business."

"If you like we can go to Tuscany together. I'll be spending more time there, helping with the business. It might be good for you to get away from Milan for a while. It'll give us time to know each other better. I'll be frank, Marcello. Your Mafioso connection leaves me uneasy."

"I'll go with you to Verona. Tuscany, maybe. I don't want to force myself on you. I understand how you feel. The past is the past. Whatever I do, I'll sever my old ties."

"Okay, Marcello, fair enough. Let's make Momma happy. She's invested a lot of prayers on us. She'll be pleased to see us together. We'll just take it as it comes."

"All I need is a time of departure. Let's make it in the afternoon."

"Done. Let's meet here at 2 pm. Do you have a car or should I rent one?"

"I'll pick you up in my Ferrari."

"Life has been good, at least in material things. Let's finish the Chianti and get some rest for tomorrow."

Marcello was on time the next day. Even with sunglasses, Mario was compelled to look askance by the luster of the yellow Ferrari 275 GTS parked by the hotel entrance. The day was clear with bright sunshine. Mario climbed aboard and the two brothers embraced lightly. A degree of reticence was evident, but the previous evening's meeting began the journey of reconciliation. On the ride to Verona, Mario explained his situation with Marianne. They reminisced about the better memories of their early days.

Teresina Rossetti sat by the window, anticipating their arrival. Mario told Marcello she'd been there since she got out of bed. Her face was radiant; a prouder mother couldn't be found in all of Italy. They watched her as she blessed herself, moving her lips in a prayer of thanks. As they approached the entrance, they saw another person. Mario walked in followed by Marcello. The atmosphere was somber. Most of the drapes were drawn to keep the sunlight out. Mario couldn't understand his mother's reasoning, closing out natural light of day and using artificial light of dull lamps. She explained sunlight was too harsh for the eyes and it faded the texture of her furniture.

In earlier years, her husband-to-be worked for Alessandro Venier, who founded a furniture manufacturing company in Treviso, outside of Venice. Alessandro appreciated Manuccio's dedicated work and gave him two brown and red damask upholstered chairs and a sofa to celebrate his wedding to Teresina. Mario told her many times he would buy her new furniture. Despite wear and tear, she insisted the furniture would live as long as she did.

Mario was first to speak. "*Salve*, *madre*! *Salve*, *nonna*! It's a blessing to see you lovely ladies looking so well. Grandmother Allegretti, you look fit as a fiddle."

Teresina's mother waved her hands at Mario. "Posh, you foolish boy. It pleases me that you haven't changed, my *nipote*."

"Speaking of change, check out your other *nipote*. I didn't recognize him last night."

Baci e abbracci, kisses and hugs ensued. There was a lot of that going around in Europe; gender immaterial. Teresina extended her arms and invited her two sons so they could wrap themselves around each other. Nonna kept her calm while her daughter burst with excitement. Teresina had been praying, including novenas and anything the Church had available in its arsenal. She was determined to employ any means to achieve her last major goal in life—to see her two sons together in her house, hoping it happened sooner than her funeral.

No time was wasted upon gathering in the *salotto* as the two women pelted Mario with questions about the engagement, marriage plans and future activities. Mario tried to be circumspect. Just give them the soft sell, he thought.

"This is where we are. Marianne and I are engaged to be married. We're making adjustments to prepare for our lives together. Marianne feels she needs time to get her thoughts together. I've left the mercenaries but I might return to Africa in a different role. This would be as a consultant and trainer, looking after my diamond interests. It's short term and I wouldn't be engaged in battle."

Marcello was not immune from the inquisitive ladies. They bombarded him with questions on his life in Milan and his intentions. Nonna asked him a pointed question about his work.

"Tell me, Marcello, did you ever kill anyone in your work for your *padrino?*"

"My *padrino* shielded me from this and never put me in such a position. I'll admit to using strong-arm tactics, but that's in the past. I did shoot some men who attacked me, but I never killed anyone.

"I'm feeling my way around. My life over the past two decades is history. I'm moving on. Mamma *e* Nonna, the tug from all of your prayers is working on me. Don't overdo it with the spooky spiritual stuff. I want to decide for myself and not have a thunderbolt strike me down."

"Marcello, that's no way to talk. All I ask is for God to guide you."

Mario added his comments. "Prayers and religion are good, Momma. They seem to have worked in getting Marcello and me together, something I wasn't expecting. The problem is people go too far using religion as justification for anything they do."

Nonna felt that she needed to step in as the reigning elder statesperson present.

"Mario and Marcello, your mother and I are old-fashioned. We're still committed to what we learned as children and this has changed very little for people of our generations. These are different times, and we know that. Each of us needs religion and it's up to individuals to decide for themselves the nature of the relationship that's right for them."

"Bravo, Nonna!" the two brothers applauded.

Teresina spoke and called an end to the discussion and a return to a more felicitous conversation. She asked Mario to tell her more about his involvement with diamonds, which he did. He mentioned that people in the business told him Mandakan diamonds might be valuable, so he needed to gather more samples to be analyzed.

"Before I leave tomorrow, I want to stop by Sant'Anastasia and discuss my wedding. Which priest do you suggest, Momma?"

"That's good, Mario. Come to mass with me in the morning. Padre Augusto is the one to talk to. You've met him. He should be available after mass."

"*D'accordo*! I'll do it. I'll phone to set it up."

Teresina gave Mario the phone number for the church. He went to the kitchen to make the call while Teresina spoke to Nonna about preparing *cena*.

"I need to cook something for my two big boys and I could use your help."

Marcello spoke up on hearing this, "No way! You two fine looking ladies are Mario's and my dates. We're taking you out to show you off. No sense in resisting. We insist."

"I'm an old woman", Nonna protested. "I don't stay up late evenings. I certainly don't kick up my heels like you youngsters. Life is more sedentary."

Mario heard some of the conversation as he returned. "Tomorrow morning is set. I'll meet Padre Augusto after mass. Now, what's this about being too ancient to enjoy life? *Sociocchezze*! Nonsense! We don't have to go to a fancy restaurant but ours is an offer you can't refuse. We'll walk three blocks to the *trattoria*, where we've enjoyed Fabiano's food preparations. Marcello and I are sensitive about our reputations. We wouldn't be able to show our faces if we were turned down by two of the prettiest ladies in all of Verona."

Nonna admitted that Mario wore her down and she relented. "Okay, *Senore Incantatore*, you have won me over with your charm. We need time to get ready."

"You're both gorgeous as you are. But, if it makes you feel better, do what you must."

The ladies were ready to go in a half hour. Despite their claim to being stogy old fogies, they set a sprightly pace afoot and their banter was in tune with the times. The foursome agreed to share a large platter of antipasto with an assortment of *carne* and *verdura,* followed by individual preferences of pasta dishes. Nonna toasted the return of the two prodigals with the slightly acidic and pleasant bouquet of the house red wine. Teresina probed her sons to try to understand how they had changed.

"Marcello, you said you were determined to change your way of life. How do you know you won't go back to your old ways?"

"Momma, I stayed away from visiting you because I was ashamed. I was on drugs and alcohol. It was convenient and I only dealt with the immediate. I don't know what he saw but my *padrino* said there was goodness in me. He took me on as a pet project. He challenged me to believe in myself. He assigned a *consigliatore* to provide guidance. Education was the key to an improved self-image. As I gradually emerged from my long-term stupor, my *padrino* took notice of my diminished ardor toward work. That's when he spoke to me about letting me move on to something more self-fulfilling. So, I'm committed to the change and there's no turning back."

"That's a nice story, *mio caro figlio*. I've always believed in you. Life has been rocky for you but you'll put that behind you. As for you Mario, you seem to have developed an attitude toward religion that concerns me."

"Momma, I have spiritual beliefs. I believe and trust in God. You may not see it, but I'm the same person who served at *Sant'Anastasia* as an altar boy, although less naïve. I've learned priests and nuns aren't divine, aren't infallible and don't have a monopoly on interpreting the word of God. I believe in prayer. I also believe a church setting isn't necessary to engage in fervent prayer. I believe I'm a compassionate human being and I'm sensitive to the feelings and needs of others. I believe one should be true to his conscience, which I am."

Mario was feeling uncomfortable in baring his soul, but he needed to finish his thoughts. His three dinner partners were looking at him with stunned expressions. He paused a moment, catching his breath and taking a sip of wine.

"There's no ambiguity in our relationship, between God and me. I'm a member of His flock, but I'm not a blind follower. I do pray to thank and to ask His intervention. I believe that it's useful to pray for the good of others. I believe prayer can have a healing and cleansing effect."

Marcello piped in, "Well done, brother!"

Silence prevailed at their table. Teresina had never heard such a blunt elucidation of religious devotion, all the more disconcerting because it came from her son. The gelato was being served, which was most propitious. Nonna, Marcello and Mario dug in while Teresina drifted off in her thoughts, playing in her dessert with her spoon. Nonna asked Mario about his friend Julio, whom she had met and thought he was a nice boy. This reminded him to check with him about arrangements to meet in Tuscany as they had discussed the previous evening.

The chatter was subdued as they made their way back to the Rossetti homestead. Upon entering the house, the two women made their excuses, saying they were exhausted and it was time for bed. Marcello gave each warm hugs and kisses, expressing his love to each. Mario followed Marcello's lead, but added that he hoped his remarks didn't upset her. Teresina told Mario she would reflect on what he had to say but would continue to pray for him.

Marcello broke out the *Peroni birra* he had stashed in his car. The brothers' conversation bounced around sundry topics but the hot agenda item at dinner resurfaced.

"Mario, I sensed that you were drawing a line in the sand. Not so much with Momma, but with your fiancée. I don't know her, so I can't judge. I get the impression she's a person who clings to her convictions at all costs with no regard for compromise. Your inner feelings poured out with such passion, I felt you'd been put through the ringer."

"You're perceptive, *mio fratello*. Yes, my remarks were motivated by what transpired between Marianne and me over the last few days, but there's lots more to it."

Mario felt he was getting to know his brother better. Feeling more comfortable with Marcello, he explained the full story that led to his dinner remarks. He had a sense of relief in unburdening himself to Marcello. The beer gave him a temporary boost, but eventually, the glow subsided and he felt spent. Time for a quick phone call to Julio and crawl into his old bed.

CHAPTER TWENTY EIGHT

When Mario awoke in the morning, it took a few minutes to get his bearings. Sometimes it was quicker, but it always seemed to take a moment for his head to figure out where he was. There were mornings when his life depended on recognizing his situation before taking his first step. He sat for a while to reflect. At first, he thought he was back in Africa. Shaking off his mental cobwebs, he realized it was Friday morning and he was in Verona. One week had passed since Mario's return to Europe from Africa. He recalled the past evening and his agreement to accompany his mother to mass.

Teresina and Mario strolled the several blocks to *Sant'Anastasia*. They exchanged glances indicating they cared for each other and chatted about people in the neighborhood. They both exercised diligence in avoiding the previous evening's hot topic. After mass, Mario met Padre Augusto in the sacristy and they adjourned to the rectory for their chat. Teresina remained fixed in her pew, fully enthralled in prayer. Mario emerged from his *tête-à-tête* with the padre in a little under an hour.

Padre Augusto was the right religious person at the right time. He never wagged his finger at Mario, never smirked at him, never lost his even-tempered, soothing voice, and never was condescending. Mario left the session feeling validated. Padre Augusto reassured Mario he was on the correct path and to deal with God in his own manner.

"*Dio ti aiuta*."—May God help you.

Mario carried one of his infectious smiles when he rejoined his mother in the sanctuary. She was happy again because Mario had made his peace.

Marcello and Mario had a light *pranzo* with Nonna and Momma before jumping in the Ferrari and heading south. Marcello awakened in the morning thinking of Mario. He liked him but sensed his brother wasn't keen on having him around very long. Perhaps it might be worthwhile to test the chemistry. Marcello decided to do just that.

It was a day fit for a drive through picturesque Italian villages of Veneto, Emilia Romagnia and Toscana regions on a late summer day, in an elegant open-air, high powered V-12 sports car, with your brother by your side. The sky was clear with a few small scattered clouds, the air resplendent with fragrances of changing seasons, a mixture of the sweet aromas from fading blossoms and fecund scents of the land. They bypassed the larger cities of Bologna and Firenze, as they drove south and west toward the Mediterranean.

Julio was joining them in Pisa, where they would overnight. Mario came frequently to Tuscany but his visits were usually short. His domicile on these visits was the Royal Victoria Hotel on *Lungarno Pacinotti*, on the north side of the Arno River. Since the Ferrari was a two-seater, Mario retrieved his own two-seater, an Alfa Romeo Giulia TZ1 sports car, which he kept in the hotel garage.

When Marcello and Mario checked in the hotel, Julio was waiting in the lounge. Mario introduced his brother, and after exchanging howdy-dos, Marcello excused himself and went to his room. This gave Mario and Julio time to chat. Julio wanted to hear the full story on Marianne.

"Wow! That's a ball buster. I never figured her to be so rigid. I'd have a tough time with that. How are you handling it?"

"Julio, it leaves me at sixes and sevens. I don't know if we'll wed. I'm engaged to Marianne for now but we have issues. There's a proposition I want to discuss with you."

"I knew it. You're reneging on your promise to Marianne."

"Not quite, Julio. It's not that clear cut. François and I have a continued interest in Mandaka. Also, there's another appeal to François for further assistance there."

"We did our bit for that *maudit pays*, pardon my French. We're done."

Mario explained what occurred in Bandala after Julio and the rest of the group departed. He spoke of Kibali's gifts of the diamond, of the small equity in the mines François and he received and of Kwambe's assignment. He described the quality and value of the diamond. He discussed Pastambu's contact with François.

"I'll phone François shortly to tell him I want in. It's easy to justify and be true to myself. It's a training mission. The elite force will provide security for the mines. All members of this mission will benefit. If the quality of the diamonds is confirmed, and with enhanced security, it could become attractive for investors."

"Mario, that's all well and good, but it sounds Pollyannaish. You saw what they're up against in *il paese dimenticato da Dio*, pardon my Italian. We did run into a few bright individuals. It takes lots more to turn a country around and establish an attractive setting for outside investors. You and I are in role reversal. Preston and you told me my optimistic outlook for this godforsaken country, pardon my English, was pie-in-the-sky. Now, you're the blind optimist."

"Is this your way of saying no thank you, 'I am perfectly content'?"

"I'm here because you badgered me about olives. I've looked into possibilities in Catalonia. You said Pietro and you would show me the ropes. You're now suggesting I head out with you to *el pais de Dios maldita*, pardon my Spanish."

"Despite what you think, I'm going. Pietro and I will do what we said. Regarding the new mission, details need to be worked out, including timing. It'll be within the next few weeks. François would like you on the mission. So what is it? We'll be a team of eight including François and me."

"Okay, count me in. You haven't sold me but you managed to arouse my curiosity. Despite my reluctance, you need me to watch your sorry ass, *mi amigo*."

Julio went to his room while Mario stayed in the lounge to make a quick call to Pietro. He told him he was in Pisa with Marcello and Julio. Pietro told Mario he'll drive over and make it a foursome for dinner. Mario gave him his room number and told him to come right up. He took the elevator to his room and called François, leaving a message. He said Julio and he wanted to be included on the team and suggested François call Kibali to get his blessing on the project. A half hour later, Pietro was in Mario's room, listening to Mario recite his Marianne story, the tale of the diamond and his rationale for returning to Mandaka.

"Sorry you won't be here for the *raccolto* in a few weeks. I'll miss you."

"I regret the conflict in timing. I'll have more funds to pour into our business. Plus, there's potential for greater riches if we can help pave the road to a profitable operation of the mines."

"I get what you're saying, but this mission is loaded with risks. The rhetorical road you're talking about may be paved over minefields. I hate to see you go, but it's alluring in terms of the potential. I'll hold the fort, as always."

"Think of the positives. We'll be able to close out our payments for the adjoining grove. We could expand our holdings, reach out to broaden our marketing efforts and become an important player in the refining area. These are ideas to evaluate as we go. We might consider folding Julio into our business with an operation in Catalonia. Keep a good thought, Pietro."

"You overwhelm me, Mario, I never knew you to be such a dreamer. It does make sense. You know I'm an advocate of positive thinking. Remember, I'm the guy who sold you on the olive business. You weren't enthusiastic, but it's obvious you've converted. You've been beckoned by the olives and you're heeding the call."

"There's something else—It's Marcello. He's looking to change his ways. He says he has a mutually agreed severance with his *padrone*. Let's show him our operation if he wants. He knows I'm uneasy with his Mafia connection. He has funds, but we haven't discussed investing with us.

"Enough of this. Let's get together with Julio and Marcello and celebrate our reunion. I think you will find Marcello an upright person."

The foursome walked over to an upscale seafood restaurant that Pietro and Mario frequented. They made liberal use of a Tuscany favorite, Chianti Classico. The oenophile among them, Mario, preferred a higher quality product but the selection was satisfying. They were spirited and each relished the occasion for his own reasons. They were together to enjoy the moment; tomorrow would take care of itself.

They feasted on *friuts mare*, gorging themselves, and then some. Ultimately, they bowed to temperance and swapped the *vino* for some *caffè*. Despite their intentions, they were subverted when the lads laced the sobering brew with *grappa*. After a few hours of revelry and feasting, they made their way to the hotel, feeling blissful.

The following morning—it was now Saturday—the four merry-makers gradually assembled in the hotel restaurant for breakfast with a heavy demand for *caffè*. Sobriety had returned along with a moderate degree of eagerness to get on with the day. Mario told the others to go on ahead. He phoned François and caught him before he stepped out for the day. He brought Mario up-to-date.

"I might have *i cinque amici* for the mission. Gundhart's wound is still healing but he'll probably join us. This gives us seven men, including Preston, Julio, Stéphane and Michel."

"Are you contacting Kibali? He's top dog and we should get his approval."

"I'll phone him Sunday, and follow-up with Pastambu to work out the details."

When Mario caught up with the trio, Pietro was already into his orientation. He was giving Julio and Marcello the same spiel Giovanni gave to Pietro and him three years earlier. They were walking through the grove as Pietro added his own comments to provide a fuller explanation of the process.

Giovanni still lived on the premises but he had moved to a small cottage that Pietro and his workers had built for him. Pietro occupied Giovanni's house with Anna and the three children. Giovanni helped Pietro with small tasks but limited his participation in the *raccolto* to the festive portion. He noticed the group tour in the grove and joined in, listening to Pietro. Giovanni couldn't resist bragging about the olives.

Mario was impressed with Pietro's delivery. His partner was an entrepreneur who knew his business and was articulate explaining it. Marcello and Julio thanked Pietro and Giovanni for their presentations.

Anna came out of the house to greet Mario, whom she always regarded as someone special. She welcomed Julio and Marcello, telling them it was nice seeing them again. Anna invited the trio to join them the next day for Sunday dinner, an offer readily accepted. Mario asked Anna if he could use the phone to call Marianne. Anna replied, "*ma certo*!" Julio and Marcello said they were going to dinner at a restaurant in Lucca. Mario told them he'd catch up with them.

He hadn't spoken to Marianne since Monday. He found it odd defending her with his comrades the previous evening after explaining his situation. He phoned her in Brugge where she was spending time with Hennie.

"*Bon soir*, Lucien. Is Marianne available?"

"Yes she is, Mario. Hold on a second and I'll get her."

"*Buona sera*, Mario. I'm glad you called."

"I've been thinking about you. How you doing?"

"I'm even more confused. Hennie's situation and the baby weigh on my mind. I do love you and I want to be with you. I'm sorry for putting you through this."

"I understand, Marianne. I love you too. We'll take it a step at a time and see how it goes. Our wedding next September is highlighted on my calendar."

"That's sweet, Mario. Please be patient with me."

"I am but there's something else I need to tell you. I'm back with Pietro. I have an opportunity to get more funds to expand our olive business. It's complicated but it entails going back to Mandaka. This time it's a peaceful mission. I'll be training soldiers to become an elite force. It'll provide security for the mines."

"Well, that's a surprise. It makes me wonder whether you really want to change."

"It's not like that, Marianne. A better trained security force will allow the diamond operations to develop, enhancing the value of my share. Greater revenue from this will provide funds needed to expand the olive operations. At that point, I'll be a full-fledged Tuscan, looking after you and our *bambini,* if we're so blessed."

"I understand your rationale. It still seems more of the same."

"That's not so, Marianne. By training soldiers, I'll also be protecting my diamond interests. I'll not be fighting, I'll be teaching. These soldiers will learn skills to defend their country. It's a good thing to do. Believe me, Marianne, this is different."

"Obviously, I'm not in a position to stop you. I wish you wouldn't go but I expect you will. I want you to keep in touch. I do want to marry you, Mario."

"I'll talk to you again soon, Marianne. Be well, *mon amour*."

«*Toi aussi, Mario. Bonne chance!*»

CHAPTER TWENTY NINE

Mario was back in Monte Carlo, trying to relax on the beach, *les Plagues du Larvotto*. Julio kept hassling him since their trip to Milano, where Mario lost his bet. Julio accompanied Mario to Monaco on Thursday morning after the *futbol* match. They stopped for lunch on route in San Remo, the picturesque *la Cittá dei Fiori*—the City of Flowers—on the Italian Riviera.

Mario kept telling Julio to stifle it but Julio was keyed up; Mario needed to tone down. He spent an hour at the beach and left Julio to his own devices. Mario returned to his apartment for a few hours sleep before reporting to work. He resumed his security management responsibilities at the casino that evening.

Mario had earned his way up the ladder at the Monte Carlo Casino to become one of the Chief of Security's three assistants. There were considerable perquisites that came with the job, but it demanded spending time working. This entailed availability and responsibility in supervising and coordinating a large security force to take care of problems as they developed and ensuring the smooth operation of the casino.

Mario had ingratiated himself with his boss through his social skills coupled with *une main ferme et une tête solide sur ses épaules*—a firm hand and a solid head on his shoulders. His boss provided Mario considerable latitude but he had certain demands that Mario knew to respect. Christophe Pouliot was a *Monégasque*, born and reared in Monaco. He was a staunch participant in Monaco rugby, both as a player when he was younger and continuing as an advocate.

Christophe became a favorite of the Rainier family, endearing himself as a member of the royal family's private guard. A bear of a man, his strength was as great as anyone Mario had encountered. His body was the large size model, not truly extra-large, but with a very muscular V-shaped torso. Christophe's physique reminded Mario of François, except Christophe was three inches taller and brawnier. He was solid from his tawny crew cut cropped head to his size 13 shoes. His deep but somewhat raspy voice added to an image that commanded respect.

Christophe had a daughter in Boston, Massachusetts, who had completed medical school at Harvard University and was an intern at Massachusetts General Hospital. He was waiting for Mario's return to Monaco so he could take a few days to visit her. When Mario phoned from Brussels about the mission to Africa, he assured Christophe he would be back as agreed.

While Mario was still in Tuscany, François gave him the latest on the mission.

"Kibali confirmed what Pastambu told me. The French want to resume military assistance and training. Kibali said he'd likely accept it. He wants our group ahead of this, to get started without politics."

"François, don't you think this is ironic? The French are anxious to resume a military program in Mandaka. Kibali wants them back, but not quite yet. Kibali wants us to have first crack at his best soldiers and he'll pay us to do so. Where does he get the money? While the French aren't funding military assistance at present, they're providing economic and budgetary assistance to Mandaka. The French want in, Kibali says not so fast, he reaches out to us and gives us funds he received from the French."

"It does make sense, Mario, and it is ironic. You can bet the French will be monitoring us closely once we launch the program."

Mario felt he was on an emotional rollercoaster. He was on edge on the flight to Europe as he thought of what lay ahead. His time spent in Belgium didn't go very smoothly. His efforts to woo Marianne lay fallow. The need to keep expressing his attitudes on religion was unsettling. The recently emerged anxiety about Marcello and his mother added to his concerns. Thrown into the mix was the guilt he felt in abandoning Pietro yet again.

Up to a few days earlier, Mario hardly gave a thought of Marcello. He now felt that he bore some responsibility for his brother's welfare. He was pleased that Julio and Marcello stayed in Lucca for a few days to help Pietro in the olive grove. Marcello spent time with Pietro in getting a better grasp of the operation. No offers and no decisions were made. Marcello didn't indicate he wanted in. Mario thought it best for Marcello to come on board as a worker if he was interested. This would give the two partners time to resolve their concern about Marcello and his former associates.

Marcello told Pietro, "The olive business seems interesting. Before I left Milan, my *padrone* suggested viniculture could be a worthwhile activity."

Pietro responded, "Mario and I might expand into grapes/wine eventually."

Toward the end of the visit, Marcello inquired, "Any thoughts about me joining up with you guys? Perhaps we could expand into a wine-making operation together."

This caught Pietro by surprise. "Marcello, are you saying you want to invest with us?"

"Not necessarily, it's a feeler. My brother and you are partners, but you run the operation. That's why I raise the question with you. I'm just exploring possibilities."

"Marcello, I'll be frank. Mario and I believe you're sincere in starting a new life. It might be a good opportunity to take you on. Then there's the submissive relationship between the godfather and his foot soldiers. He has his tentacles wrapped around each of them. You still refer to your *padrone*. If you have an interest, we'd like you to work with us in the grove. We could look at the question of partnership later. We need to feel more comfortable that your prior connections are indeed in the past."

"I don't know what'll take to shed this black mark lingering over me. I'm going back to Milan to think this through."

Before parting, Mario told Marcello, "There's one condition that's inviolate; no money from your *padrone* in our business. From what you say, he treated you well. That's good. Your boss and his thugs are brutes. You're my brother and I'm eager to embrace you fully. We'll chat more on this."

Marcello drove back to Milan to discuss his prospects with his *padrone* and his *consigliatore*. Whereas, Mario and Julio went to Milan to witness combat in an arena. The *Stadio Giuseppe Meazza* in San Siro district was overflowing beyond its 85,000 capacity. It was *España* versus *Italia*; Spanish *La Liga* Champion Real Madrid Club *de Futbol* versus Series A Italian Football Champion *Associazione Calcio* Milan; Julio versus Mario. Expectations were riding high on both sides of the field and throughout the stands. This was European *futbol* at its best, with the winner slated to confront the plucky Manchester United Football Club Red Devils.

It was a tight match with the AC Milan *Rossoneri* (Red-Blacks, color of jerseys) displaying greater ball control early. They scored a goal and led 1-0 at halftime.

"Julio, get ready to pay up. Your guys are pretty shabby."

"Mario, as an opera buff, you're aware it ain't over till the fat lady sings. All I'm hearing is your wish that this match lasted only 45 minutes."

"Wake up to reality, Julio. I feel bad for you. The first half set the tempo for the second half."

"Mario, it'll be such a thrill to see you fall off your high horse."

"Let the match resume. Onward to victory."

Well! A soccer match does take 90 minutes to complete. The second half began as the first half had been played, with Milan the more aggressive team. However, the turn-around began at the 61st minute of the match with Madrid's first goal. It's second goal a few minutes later concluded the scoring. The final whistle blew with the Spaniards victorious and Mario's pocketbook lighter by $1,000. Slam-dunk for Julio!

Mario pulled his shift at the casino, taking care of a few minor problems, mostly unruly customers. He retired to his apartment for a few hours sleep before joining Julio for a couple of sets of tennis at the Monte Carlo Country Club, followed by nine holes of golf at the Monte Carlo Golf Club. Access to these exquisite, world-renown facilities with their spectacular views of the Med, was part of Mario's package of perks that came with the job. Mario got his revenge for the lost bet by soundly beating Julio in tennis and by eking out a 2 and 1 victory in match play on the golf course.

Mario put in eight 10 to 12-hour days before flying to Paris to meet up with François. He was happy to be back at work at the casino, finding it therapeutic, but he was also looking forward to the mission.

François assembled his men to draw up a training program and identify the materiel needed. He sought input from the group. He had his full complement of seven men in his Parisian apartment in Auteuil for the planning sessions.

Mario got first licks joshing Preston. "It's amazing this old English chap was able to roll out of the hammock and abandon his *Costa del Sol* retirement getaway to join us."

"No way of keeping me away, Mario. When I learned you were on this mission, I had to sign up to protect the poor Mandakans you'll attempt to teach. I had a nightmare that you pierced a trainee with a bayonet while showing him techniques. So, I can't retire as long as you're active."

"Good show, mate! I'm delighted to have a good warrior on my flank. Great seeing you again, Preston."

Gundhart's availability for the mission was uncertain, but the few weeks of recovery allowed his wound to heal. The muscular tone of his legs accelerated his return, but he still relied on a cane for support. Also present were Stéphane and Michel. Mario hadn't expected to see the Austrian. François explained Frantz's presence.

"Frantz is here at Gundhart's suggestion. We need his martial arts expertise. It's an essential component of the program. We're all good, but he's the master. Frantz will have the lead role on this, helping to refine our techniques."

François began his orientation by reminding his colleagues of their commitment.

"I'm pleased you're all able to do this. We engaged Mandakan soldiers on our prior mission and you know what shape they're in. This is quite a task. Clear your calendars for at least 1 ½ months; the program is for thirty days excluding weekends.

"French military interests have rekindled. Military assistance and training may be in the offing. The French Military Attaché will be looking in on the training, but only as an observer. President Kibali assured me he'll not tolerate any interference. We control content and execution. Our former driver and now deputy head of security at the diamond mine, Kwambe Musambu, will be a trainee."

The first day's session was devoted to reviewing François' outline of his concept of the program, with give and take throughout the day on inclusions and deletions. The agreed plan was to break down into four groups with two instructors each. The training would be less cumbersome and allow greater individual attention.

On the second day, the men went out to the nearby *Bois de Boulogne* to practice some of the tactics they'd be teaching to the Mandakans. Frantz worked with the seven others to build up their abilities.

The final session was a review and finalization of the program. There could be no confusion on any aspect of the program with the trainers and the trainees. The written program underwent scrutiny and some word changes. Upon reaching agreement, a discussion followed on equipment, each man weighing on the needs to run the program. François said he would obtain the materiel through his sources in Paris and Marseille and send it ahead through the Mandakan Embassy in Paris.

François briefed the men on conditions in the country.

"The country is relatively peaceful but some problems could be looming. There are at least three potential threats to Kibali's honeymoon. Public awareness of an imminent return of French military on Mandakan soil could resurrect negative images of colonialism. The impending public trials of Tombola and his cronies could arouse tribal partisan agitation. The sightings of black Cuban soldiers in the south of the country could disrupt further safety in the area where the principal mineral mines are located."

Preston broke in. "I'd include us as a fourth element. Our return could play into the hands of anyone looking for an excuse to make trouble."

"You're right, Preston. This mission differs from our previous one in a number of ways. Let me explain.

You're not going in as aggressors but with the sanction of the ruling government;

You'll not be facing soldiers in an adversarial role but rather soldiers motivated to improve their skills;

Your presence in the country will not be measured by hours but rather by weeks;

You'll not be considered military in any guise but rather as private civilian consultants;

You will not be the law but rather subject to the laws of the country;

You will not be limited to Bandala but will be able to travel to other areas of the country on days off and dependent on conditions on the ground;

Your entry into the country won't be clandestine but rather will be announced publicly by the President."

François urged his cohorts to begin the mental transition to conditions in Mandaka. Respecting the customs of the people would enhance their acceptance. Anyone going astray of the country's laws would be at the mercy of the appropriate local authorities. Any untoward public behavior, such as drunkardness or scurrilous comments or actions, would be grounds for immediate dismissal and repatriation without compensation.

Prior to dismissing his men, François gave them further instructions.

"Gather your gear upon returning home to have it ready to go. Our departure is in two weeks. No weapons. I told Pastambu the deal was off if we weren't given arms for self-protection. We will get our 9-mm MAC-50 semi-automatic pistols when we arrive. We're returning to Mandaka because the country's leaders trust us. I want to be sure each of you understands the situation and agrees to the constraints we'll be under."

All seven men voiced their acknowledgement and approval.

CHAPTER THIRTY

Mario returned to the *Côte d'Azur* to join hordes of tourists, sportsmen, businessmen and gamblers. However, his was not to play and frolic, but to resume work and prepare for his departure for Africa. Christophe gave his two other assistants time off to take advantage of Mario's availability. Mario worked longer days but thought it was fair since Christophe would make do again without him. He had worked out an arrangement early on with Christophe and agreed to by upper Casino management. It proved to be workable with some minor inconveniences.

The recent vicissitudes of his life brought on a behavior modification. While still personable, Mario became more reticent. His emotions vacillated whenever he thought of Marianne.

In his last phone conversation before leaving for Africa, Mario told her, "I'll see you in Liège as soon as I conclude my mission. It'll be about six weeks. We need to get back to planning for the wedding, if it's going to happen."

"What do you mean by that, Mario, 'if it's going to happen'? Are you looking to break our engagement?"

"No, Marianne, that's not what I'm saying and it's not what I mean. We'll see what needs to be done to move on beyond our present stalemate. We're in neutral. I don't want to go in reverse and lose you. I want to get into low gear at least and gain momentum so we can cruise ahead."

"I want that too, Mario. Take care of yourself. Don't let any harm come to you. I love you, Mario."

"Not to worry, Marianne. I'll be okay. I love you. See you soon."

There would be resolution, one way or the other. He would regain his joie de vive, either as a married man to someone he loved or continuing as a very eligible bachelor.

Marianne confided in friends and family. Claire Marie Blancke did her best to get her friend to clear her head and go with her heart. Even Father Doucet counseled her to ease up on Mario. If Mario was to be her mate, the 'ball was in her court'. The attitudes she held, which she considered a blessing, had become a liability.

The two weeks went by quickly. The eight team members made their way to Bandala, Mandaka. Mario Rossetti flew to Paris to join François Morency, Michel Langlois and Stéphane Chappuis at Orly Airport for an Air France flight to Zandu. Gundhart von Stoessel and Frantz Brunner boarded a Lufthansa flight in Frankfort for Nairobi, while Preston Langford went to Heathrow for his British Overseas Airways Corporation (BOAC) flight to Nairobi. Julio Valesquez took an Iberia Airline flight to Cairo, connecting to a BOAC flight to Nairobi.

Surreptitious, indeed! Quite the opposite. One month had elapsed since their departure from Mandaka as mercenaries. Each man was greeted upon arrival as a VIP, in Nairobi and Zandu. Although absent diplomatic status, two officials, one each from the Mandakan Presidential Staff and the Defense Ministry, were on hand for their arrivals and escorted them on their final leg to Bandala. Kibali held nothing back in acknowledging his gratitude for past deeds and his expectations for services to be rendered. They were taken to the Bandala Hilton, which would be their home for the following several weeks as guests of President Kibali. Chauffeured vehicles were at their beck and call.

The French contingent, plus Mario, was first to arrive. The Hilton *gérant*, Philippe Ziegler, told Mario and François he was *enchanté* to see them return. François reviewed the arrangements with Ziegler. He asked Ziegler to alert him if his men caused any problems.

Their former driver, Kwambe Musambu, traveled from the south the previous day and awaited François and Mario in the lounge. As they greeted each other, Kwambe's emotions were unrestrained. He expressed gratitude for the intervention by his two European friends. He was proud of his newly acquired *sous-lieutenant* uniform and insignias. When he settled in, he painted a picture of conditions at the mines.

"It's going from bad to worse. Diamonds are out in the open but you can't enter the mines. Operations are at a standstill. The equipment has degenerated, the work force has dissipated, funds are unavailable and security is virtually non-existent."

As Kwambe was describing his woeful tale, two men approached François and Mario. They remembered meeting Claude on their previous mission. The second person was Guillaume, who was with Kibali and Pastambu when they arrived at the palace from the airport.

Claude introduced himself anew and presented his colleague. "We met when you drove through downtown Bandala on your way to the palace. I'm *Capitaine* Claude Pelletier, *aide-de-camp* to General Gaston Pastambu. This is Guillaume Wabitale, President Kibali's *chef de cabinet.*"

"Captain Pelletier, I assume your officers have selected the trainees carefully. If they have, these soldiers should be self-starters with no need for a *coup au cul*—kick in the ass. Discipline is your responsibility. Anyone causing problems will be terminated."

Guillaume spoke up. "Mr. Morency and Mr. Rossetti, President Kibali extends his *complements* and welcomes your return. We met briefly at the palace. I served with the military but left a few years ago to become a teacher. President Kibali will greet your unit personally tomorrow. Captain Pelletier and I will give you and your men a briefing and discuss how we can cooperate and provide support. Two officers you know, Lieutenant-Colonel Florien Tanandu and Commandant Edouard Bolotatu, will go through the training with the men. These soldiers will be under their command."

"When are you coming back for the briefing?"

"It'll be about an hour after the four others arrive. Time for them to freshen up after their journey. *Alors, à bientôt.*"

Guillaume and Claude arose and stepped aside to chat with Kwambe briefly before leaving. Whereupon, Kwambe resumed his discussion on conditions at the mines. Mario was eager to learn more on diamond sightings.

"Kwambe, continue where you left off. Tell us about the diamonds."

"Yes, there are diamonds, Mario. I picked up some stones myself. They're in a vault the *Société Minéraux de Mandaka-Sud* has in the compound. The vault is set in concrete and one of the few pieces of equipment that still works."

Mario inquired further. "Do you know if the diamonds have been examined by an expert? Also, have you seen signs of excavations in the area where you found the diamonds? Are people in the area searching for diamonds?"

"No one has examined the diamonds since I've been there. There haven't been any official visitors. I've walked through the entire area, following the Rimbaud River upstream. There has been some digging. Rusted excavators are nearby, abandoned and inoperable. I remember a French company was involved around the time of independence and hired some local people. They found a small amount of diamonds and this is how my government became interested in the area.

"People still search the riverbed and occasionally find diamonds of varying sizes. More poachers are now crossing our southern border. Members of my tribe say they've been staying away because it's become riskier. Armed black men, who are not African, come across from their base in the country to our south, Runhantia, seeking diamonds. They beat up anyone they find. Our security isn't dependable. My boss, the head of mine security, is a lackey. His rank is commandant, but he has no understanding of the job and shows little interest in it. I have only three men I can count on. They'll join me in the training program."

François reflected on the country's export data, indicating minimal activity within the mining sector. He intended to pursue this further.

"Kwambe, Mario and I will travel south for a tour of the mines after we complete the training. We want you with us along with your three associates."

The second foursome arrived at the Hilton two hours later. François and Mario had retired to their rooms, as had Stéphane and Michel earlier. Preston phoned François from the reception desk to announce their arrival. Their escort alerted them to a briefing in an hour at the hotel. François told him to settle in and relax.

Guillaume and Claude returned to meet with the group, armed with information packets for each man. They contained summary sheets on the economy, imports and exports, known mineral resources and the best information on reserves, population indicators and listings of key government and military officials. The kit also had a listing of diplomatic representation accredited to Mandaka with key personnel and another list of foreign economic/commercial interests registered in the country.

Mario was impressed. "You guys did your homework. This is better than we get in more developed countries."

Guillaume took a graceful bow, arms spreading in swanlike fashion. "We debated how much to include but decided all eight of you have a stake in our country and the success of our government. It's in our interest that you know us better."

"We're delighted to have you back," as Claude joined in. "You're friends of Mandaka. General Pastambu will greet you tomorrow after you've met with President Kibali. The General is pleased with your program. He insisted the group includes members of several of our tribes. In his view, a multi-tribal elite military force could set an example for the rest of the military as well as the country."

François responded. "We look forward to the meetings tomorrow morning, after which we'll visit the training venue at army headquarters. Assuming all is in order, the men should be ready to start early afternoon."

Guillaume and Claude took turns briefing the men, providing highlights of material contained in their information kits. Guillaume said manpower was the key to success.

"Both the President and the General are persuasive in approaching people to join their team. Exiles are coaxed to return, urged to set aside personal agendas temporarily. Well-qualified and educated men and women are responding to create an on-going dialogue on our future. Many were schooled in Europe and America. New ideas are being offered. There's a tangible resolve. Despite our woes, an uncommon feel good buzz is in the air, energized by the influx of creative thinking."

The meetings the following morning with Kibali at the palace and Pastambu at army headquarters went well. Kibali, normally reserved, was ebullient in expressing his appreciation for the return of 'his mercenaries'. Pastambu reviewed the program details and pledged his full support. The two Mandakan leaders spoke of the renewed interest of the West. An important element of French foreign policy was to keep economic and military links open with its former colonies. Other countries were also showing interest.

Pastambu forewarned the trainers to expect observers. "Military attachés and counselors of embassy will be by to witness developments. This will include the Soviet Union, East Germans and North Koreans. The French, Americans and West Germans, in particular, have tendered interesting possibilities for military training and assistance."

Kibali regarded this interest as a stamp of approval for his government by the international community.

After the meeting with Pastambu, Claude led the eight men on a tour of the training venue. The two superior officers of the new unit joined them. François and Mario saw a different compound from the one they occupied thirty days earlier. The area was spruced up, buildings were being refurbished, a perimeter fence was being erected, flowering shrubs were planted around command control and a new flagpole stood tall bearing a crisp Mandakan flag. On François' initiative, an assortment of equipment was delivered and installed in the building housing a rudimentary gym. An outdoor firing range was prepared in a safe area with a supply of targets. The field for training exercises was cleared. A tower was nearly ready for basic airborne jumps. Straw dummies were set up for close combat exercises.

"I'm always amazed," Mario said, "with what can be done in a short time when there's the will to do it."

Lt. Colonel Tanandu responded, "It's a surprise to us. There's a new attitude within the military. We owe you our thanks. The soldiers feel they have a purpose. Everyone is hoping it'll last. At least for now, the military is backing our president."

François declared, "Everything I requested is in place and the materiel I expedited is here. We're good to go. *Allons-y, mes amis!*"

The trainees were assembled and François stepped forward to inaugurate a program replete with great expectations.

"*Bon jour, patriots!* I'm delighted to see so many eager faces. President Kibali and General Pastambu have asked the eight of us to work with you and help develop your skills as soldiers. You have the ability to be special. We've been asked to help prove your leaders right. This is our task. Yours is to learn as much as you can from us. If you're to become the elite force your leaders expect, you'll need additional training, but this program will get you started.

"I'm pleased your superior officers, Lieutenant-Colonel Tanandu and Commandant Bolotatu, have agreed to go through the training program with you. I'm also pleased the Deputy Chief of Security at the *Société Minéraux*, *Sous-Lieutenant* Musambu, will be participating, along with three of his comrades. This program demands total commitment. A word of caution and a guarantee—**your lives will depend on how attentive you are to each element of the program**. You'll be in situations when you'll apply some part of this training. In most situations, you'll be a member of a team. You'll find it isn't enough to know the proper action to take; you'll expect your comrades to know as well. It's up to each of you to make sure others are fully involved in the training because you don't know who'll be at your side in a life-and-death situation.

"You will not walk away from here as experts after thirty days of training. Maintaining and improving your skills is an ongoing process. Never allow your ego, regardless of how good you think you are, to take an adversary for granted. We'll limit ourselves to PT this afternoon. Physical training is part of your program. We'll get started on the rest tomorrow. Your effectiveness will increase with different types of exercises we'll be doing to develop body strength and stamina. We'll split into groups and my men and I will lead you through sets of exercises that'll enhance your fitness as soldiers."

Some of the soldiers went to the revamped gym, while the remainder broke into groups on the adjacent field. All were led in stretching exercises and calisthenics, running sprints and pumping iron, and the use of other bodybuilding equipment. All the soldiers were quartered on location. They were encouraged to do the exercises on their own.

The following morning began with a 'gung-ho' inspirational session. Guillaume and Claude presented the President's and the Army Commander's welcome and best wishes in the program. The French Military Attaché was introduced, with the comment that he'd be present only as an observer, but with a view of how he might expand the training later. Guillaume explained that representatives of other embassies would be by as well. Finally, Tanandu and Bolotatu spoke of the high regard they had for the participants and committed themselves to giving their best effort.

François took over and explained the program briefly to the trainees.

"The focus will be close quarter combat and hand-to-hand combat. We'll do numerous exercises that will be set up under different conditions. We'll work to get you to think and act quickly with the action you believe most appropriate for each situation. You must be prepared to use deadly force. You can't hesitate and allow your adversary to take the initiative. Your effectiveness and survival will depend on your ability to incapacitate your enemy. Your weapon of choice might be a firearm, depending on distance. This could be a carbine, submachine gun, shotgun or pistol. If you're too close for a firearm, options might include bayonet, spear, knife, machete, garrote, tree branch, rock, knee, elbow, palm-heel, forearm, head-butt and fingers. This list is not exclusive, but you get the idea. We'll demonstrate and practice various techniques including sniper firing, elementary airborne jumping, stealth advancement, engaging armed enemy close range, martial arts and the Israeli *Krav Maga* hand-to-hand combat system."

The program proceeded as planned. There were no interruptions and the trainees attacked their challenges with vigor. The gym and the training field resonated with audible grunts and groans, along with shouts of coaxing and prodding. The scene was a beehive of activity. The arena had its gladiators, compelled to prove they were worthy, and its soldier spectators, either relieved they were non-participants or wrapped in envy for not being included. The trainees were hurting; the trainers were pleased. At the start, some soldiers begrudged the trainers, mumbling their resentments and accusing the 'colonials' as sadistic for the 'punishment' they had to endure. They were soon dissuaded from their griping by their comrades. On the first day of training, there were 91 soldiers, plus, Tanandu, Bolotatu and Kwambe. After 23 days, the contingent had lost six through physical incapability or poor attitudes. All involved were pleased with the low level of attrition. Friday had rolled around again and it was time to stand down; weekends were for diversions, not training.

PART IV
CONFRONTATIONS

“A true knight
is fuller of bravery in the midst,
than in the
beginning of danger”

Sir Philip Sidney
English Poet, Courtier
And Soldier

CHAPTER THIRTY ONE

"You are listening to BBC World News—(pause)—In the hapless country of Mandaka, deep in the heart of Africa, the sound of gunfire was in the air. A destitute child of the colonial era, poverty and misery have been the norm in a country whose leaders have become the exemplars of ineptitude. Despite the travails the populace has been enduring, relative tranquility has been the rule, with only occasional isolated incidents occurring. When violence broke out in the capital city of Bandala last evening, it became a guessing game whether a staged uprising had been unleashed or if it was merely a disgruntled group acting on its grievances. At daybreak, an eerie calmness pervades the city and has enveloped the downtrodden citizenry in the communes, where nearly 30% of the country's population is crammed in flimsy shacks. A curfew is in place with soldiers and gendarmes patrolling the streets. Preliminary casualty reports indicate numerous fatalities and at least several dozen wounded. There has been mention of foreigners among the casualties, but no details have been provided.

"President Jean Paul Kibali came to power two months ago through the intercession of European mercenaries. Mandakans

have been giving him a grace period to begin the process of redressing the years of neglect. Some of these same mercenaries are presently in the country at Kibali's invitation. They are involved in a program to train an elite Mandakan military unit. Last night's action demonstrates the need for such a unit. Hopefully, for the sake of the Mandakans, these private consultants, ex-mercenaries, are limiting their actions to training. If this is indeed the case, perhaps their efforts will have salutary results."

It was Saturday morning and Marianne was lazing at home, getting ready to take on chores. Suddenly, she felt apprehensive as she listened to the news report on the radio. She had taken up the habit of listening to BBC to keep up with world events, but also, to help improve her English. Her body tensed in panic. She knew only too well how volatile Africa could be; spontaneous combustion, no external source needed. As her thoughts deepened, her concern for Mario darkened her mood. Her imagination carried her into a funk she never felt previously. All she could visualize was Mario lying unattended in the street, bleeding profusely from his wounds. She wept as she tried to reach out to him. She saw his beloved visage and thought she may never see him alive again. She felt empty, overcome with profound sadness.

When the training concluded for the week on the fifth Friday of the program, the trainers and the trainees disbanded and returned to their housing, the Hilton for one and the barracks for the others. While the Hilton contingent was relaxing in the lounge with cocktails, the others were elbowing each other for lavatory space. This was TGIF time, 'Thank God It's Friday', an unfamiliar term in Bandala but, nonetheless, it was a notion few people would have difficulty relating to. No training until Monday morning. No care, no worries until then, unless something unexpected cropped up. The only concern was to decide on the mode of relaxation and possible entertainment. The same decision that Asians, Europeans, Americans faced, but in Africa, and especially in Mandaka, decision-making was less complicated because the options were limited.

Despite the exodus of Europeans in recent years due to the deteriorating economy and an uneasy security situation, they remained in sufficient numbers to operate viable businesses, including restaurants and nightclubs. As in many African countries, there was an array of expatriates in Mandaka, willing to endure risks for opportunity. Among these were French and a fair number of Greek, Portuguese, Indian, and others. In addition to the Hilton and its amenities, Bandala had one medium size hotel with a nightclub, a favorite of foreigners of questionable origins and designs, who managed to slip in and out of the country without leaving an imprint. There were four smaller hotels, three nightclubs and numerous restaurants/bars of varying size, cuisine, quality of food and sanitary conditions. Realistically, the nightclubs were lounges until around midnight, when they transformed into truly 'night' clubs. Customers poured in around the bewitching hour, ready to cavort until sunrise. The only requirement for admission to these 'up-scale' establishments was the ability to pay. This precluded 95% of the Mandakans from the fruits enjoyed by foreigners and their affluent countrymen.

The eight Europeans usually remained at the Hilton to dine. However, this Friday evening they went into town to the French-Lebanese restaurant, *L'Espalier*. They were replete after consuming entrees ranging from *bouillabaisse* to *coq au vin* to *steak aux poivres*. François, Mario, Preston and Gundhart were content to relax with espresso and *Armagnac*. They had no interest in prolonging the evening and headed back to the hotel. Julio, Frantz, Stéphane and Michel were not through. It was time for revelry. They had been to the nightclubs twice without incident and there was no indication of any fomenting disturbances.

They entered *Le Chat Noir* at 10:30 pm, joining 18 other patrons scattered at six tables; the club was ¼ full with subdued recorded music playing.

The shooting began at 12:43 am as the foursome exited the nightclub. Pedestrians were either arriving or leaving the *boites de nuits*. The atmosphere was convivial. Guffaws reverberated from the buildings, contributing to a devil-may-care ambiance. Suddenly, popping sounds were heard. Some of the streetlights were *en panne*, resulting in blackout spots along the street. The shooters were hidden behind parked cars near an intersection of *l'avenue de l'independence.* People collapsed on the streets as pandemonium broke out. They ran to find shelter, breaking storefront windows to gain entry. Some fired back with pistols they carried for protection.

Julio and Frantz were walking to their vehicle ahead of Stéphane and Michel. They unholstered their weapons as soon as they heard the shooting. They returned fire in the direction of the sounds, about 100 meters away to their right. People were falling all around them. Julio, Frantz and the chauffeur joined the casualty list. All three were struck by blasts from automatic weapons as bullets filled the air indiscriminately. Had they been targeted or was it a coincidence the shooting began as the four foreigners emerged from the nightclub? The question was of no consequence at that moment.

Stéphane and Michel, who were still near the nightclub doorway, ducked back in to assess the situation. They realized the entrance was in an unlit sector of the street. This was to their advantage as they scrambled back out to reach their stricken comrades. Keeping low behind vehicles, they counted on remaining undetected for as long as possible. They didn't return fire for this reason, hoping the attackers would think that all four had been hit. Stéphane and Michel reached the chauffeur first and checked for a pulse. There was none. They needed to get Julio and Frantz to safety. People ran and crawled toward buildings and cars, trying to get out of harm's way. Some made it unscathed, while others were struck as they fled. The shooting was unrestrained with bullets whizzing by every which way.

Stéphane told Michel, "We have to get out of here. Best bet is that alley; about 15 meters to there. It's closer than trying to get back to the restaurant."

Michel agreed. "Stay low. Minimize our exposure."

"Michel, I'll take Frantz. You go first with Julio. He's lighter and you'll be able to move more quickly. Here, let's get him across your shoulders."

Michel, who had Julio in a fireman's carry, hunched down, leaned forward and made a diagonal beeline for the alley. There was no let-up in the firing as bullets ricocheted off cars, walls and sidewalks. Fortunately, the shooters were not marksmen. Michel reached the alley with a minor grazing of his buttocks.

Stéphane's task could be more difficult, although he had no way of knowing if the shooters were anticipating him to follow. Frantz was conscious and told Stéphane to leave him and he would get himself to safety. Stéphane told Frantz to move his legs but he couldn't. Stéphane's broad shoulders and bodybuilding physique enabled him to pull Frantz onto his back. He figured he would improve his odds by taking a different path to the alley; a ninety degree dash to the alley rather than diagonal. He crawled on his hands and knees half-way, hugging the edge of the sidewalk by the parked cars. He got to his feet, crouched and checked Frantz's hold around his neck. Stéphane's strong legs propelled him across the sidewalk to the alley. It was a game of chance because a lucky bullet could strike them despite the aim. It was survival in the absolute; the real deal of life and death. It worked. Stéphane heard more buzzing than he cared to hear, but he made it unscathed and with no further damage to his passenger.

With attention drawn to their right where the shooting commenced, bullets began cascading from the opposite direction. A second wave of shooters was advancing on their left. This was clearly an ambush. Stéphane and Michel knew they couldn't shoot it out from the alley with attackers on both sides of them.

The shooting was sustained as the distance to the alley narrowed. Stéphane and Michel had been in life-threatening situations where they had to extricate themselves. It went with the job. They would soon be pinned down with no apparent relief on the horizon. Their position was precarious. The *gendarmes* who were on duty in this sector had either been taken out of action or cut and ran. Suddenly, howling and yelping filled the air. The aggressors were moving in for final disposition.

Stéphane and Michel were ready to give as good accounting of themselves as they could. They would take several bad guys down before their time ran out.

Stéphane told Michel, "We're sitting ducks. The alley is blocked at the other end. There's no way out. We need to take action."

Michel asked, "What choice do we have? We can't leave Julio and Frantz."

"We can't stay here. You and I will dash out behind those cars. One thing going for us is we're in a darkened area. There's a group coming from each direction. You take the one on the right, I'll cover the left."

"Let's do it. It's good we have extra ammo; looks like we have some shooting ahead."

Frantz spoke up. "Julio and I will hang on to our weapons. Take our spare bullets. You can put them to better use."

"Thanks, guys. We'll get us out of here. Move out, Michel."

With no light on them, the two men scooted out in low crouches, and made it to the parked cars. As the two groups came closer to the alley, they were unaware two of their targets had left the alley. Both groups had the misfortune of walking with streetlights lit behind them. It hadn't occurred to them to shoot those lights out. Stéphane and Michel commenced firing as though they were on a firing range. Both groups of attackers were out in the open in the middle of the street. They suffered several casualties, exposed to the precise shooting of Stéphane and Michel. The remaining attackers sought cover while spraying bullets with their AK-47s. The onward assault was thwarted for the moment. Both men reloaded their weapons.

"Keep covered, Michel. We've stalled them for now. They're confused and uncertain where we are. Maybe they'll end up shooting each other as they try to move from opposite directions."

"They'll be more cautious as they try to close in. Let's get them before they're on top of us."

The attackers regrouped but were less brazen as they resumed their dual approach on their targets. They fired more shots, but Stéphane and Michel had moved one car closer to each advancing group. As members of the two groups came closer, Stéphane and Michel opened fire, causing more casualties and another halt on the assault. Both men reloaded their weapons.

The attackers were considering their next move when Stéphane and Michel heard gunshots coming from beyond the group on the right. The cavalry to the rescue? Not likely. A third wave of attackers? Hopefully not. The situation became more confused. Attackers from the group on the right began groaning and falling in the street. Someone was shooting them from the rear. The tables were turned. The attackers on the right became the prey, caught between the new arrivals and Michel.

Stéphane, Michel, Julio and Frantz were fortunate François received Philippe Ziegler's phone call at the hotel about trouble in town. He alerted Mario, Preston and Gundhart and they hastened to town with their weapons. They arrived in the nick of time to take out an armed group just ahead of them at one end of the avenue.

The attackers on the left were attempting to move in on Stéphane. As he braced himself for a charge, he heard unexpected sounds coming from the direction of the enemy. There was gurgling, wheezing, gasping and groaning. It sounded like the aggressors on the left side were also being attacked. The shooting continued, but there was less of it. Stéphane peeked out but saw no one standing. He scanned the area ahead, expecting to draw fire. Nothing at first, then he saw movement. He was ready to fire when he realized that another group had come to their assistance.

Some of the trainees had come to town to unwind. They were in another nightspot, further down the street, to the left of Stéphane and the others. When the shooting began, the trainees had no idea who was involved. They came out of the building to see what was happening; it was a macabre scene. Bodies were splayed across the street, some immobile, others squirming and pleading. The wild firing of the attackers was indiscriminate. There was no safety from assault; it was left to chance. Kalashnikovs were fired, local and foreign people were falling. The men behind the guns were on a rampage.

There were seven trainees and they knew they had to act. They acknowledged the perpetrators were reprobates, who had to be eliminated before causing further harm. What could they do? They were unarmed because of their status as students. They went back into the nightclub to discuss the situation and review their options. There was unanimity that they couldn't ignore what was happening. Walking away was not an option. As they talked, they psyched themselves into believing they could take control of the miscreants. One of Kwambe's men was among the group; Kasadi took charge. He urged his six comrades to keep their cool. He reminded them the Europeans trained them to deal with such a situation. He sent them to scout the building for available weapons. They returned with ropes, knives, cleavers, electrical wiring and broom handles.

Kasadi told the men, "Spread out and move forward as though your target is a lion. You don't want the lion to know you're coming. Think about what the Europeans taught us."

Another man expressed his concern. "We're outnumbered. They'll turn around and shoot us."

"Trust what you learned. Stealth, that's the deal. One man at a time. Our targets are focused on what's ahead, not on their rear. Let's go, pick a target and get it done."

Using techniques they learned in training, they approached the aggressors from behind as the latter engaged their targets. The commotion created by the gunfire, the yelling and wailing prevented the aggressors in the front line from knowing what was happening to their mates in the rear. The trainees acted methodically and simultaneously. The results of the first round: seven trainees standing, seven bad guys incapacitated. It was a laboratory experiment in real life. Some of the trainees looked awkward and reticent in practice, but having their lives on the line brought focus and resolve. Close quarter techniques recently learned were employed.

The show was a spectacle. A teacher would fluff his feathers in pride. One trainee used a wire to take his target down by garrote, another chopped off a head with a cleaver, yet another stabbed his target through the heart as he lunged toward him. Four other attackers went down in similar fashion. One of the insurgents managed to fire his weapon. This caused the attackers who had their backs exposed to the trainees to turn and direct their fire at the trainees. However, the trainees were concealed behind cars and were now armed with AK-47s taken from their victims.

As the attackers on the left exchanged gunfire with the trainees, Stéphane and Michel returned to the alley for cover and to protect Julio and Frantz. The attackers on the right exchanged gunfire with the new arrivals behind them. Both groups of renegades were distracted from their intended targets and became targets themselves. They had expected easy pickings; an in-and-out shoot 'em up. The intent was to show there were opposing forces to be reckoned with, and walk away until the next foray.

The trainees' objectives were to save lives, stay alive themselves, quickly incapacitate the aggressors and return to the nightclub for a couple more beers. They never hesitated to take action because they were members of Mandaka's elite force.

The guns became quiet, the street was a disaster area, and survivors were moaning and crying for assistance. The assault had ceased. All insurgents were incapacitated; dead, wounded, disarmed. The attack was repelled.

François remained anxious. "We've taken care of this group, but what's happening up ahead?"

Gundhart responded. "Two separate groups are advancing. There are men shooting at the group in front of them."

As the four Europeans moved cautiously, they halted abruptly to get a grasp of what lay ahead. One group was taking down the insurgents. In the dim lighting, they could make out some silhouettes.

Mario spoke up. "Some men are standing over a number of bodies on the ground."

François identified himself and called out. "One of you, come forward unarmed. No harm will come to you. Identify yourself and approach."

Mario and Preston moved closer to the seven men. It was enough to identify them. Mario called out to François, "Stand down, François. These men are our trainees."

As instructed, the leader came forward. "I am Kasadi, friend of Kwambe."

"Yes, of course, Kasadi. You men have done well. I'm pleased with your action."

The scoreboard results were tabulated. François and his three colleagues incapacitated the attackers at one end of the avenue, while the newly trained Mandakan soldiers dispatched those at the other end. Mario counted fifteen armed attackers felled by seven trainees, six others wounded and taken prisoners. Credit Stéphane also. At the other end, François' foursome eliminated eleven renegades and wounded five. Credit Michel also.

The sight of the students standing in victory over an opponent three times their size was exhilarating. However, François couldn't afford to gloat over his teaching success; he was responsible for the lives of the seven men he brought with him. He knew his four men had taken a lot of gunfire, but he didn't know what shape they were in. Mario and he rushed over to check on them, while Preston and Gundhart went to the trainees to congratulate them.

Stéphane jumped up to greet François and Mario. "I wasn't hit, but Michel has a *mal au cul* and might not sit for a while. Julio's and Frantz's injuries are more serious."

At that moment, Guillaume appeared on the scene accompanied by a dozen *gendarmes*, with more on the way. He took charge, barking out orders. The normally well-groomed *avenue de l'independence* was littered with bodies. People poured out of buildings to assist the *gendarmes* in checking those gunned down in the enfilade. The surviving attackers were rounded up and taken into custody. All of these required medical attention. Vehicles were commandeered to take the injured civilians to medical facilities. Guillaume contacted General Pastambu, telling him he needed to come to the scene of the assault and to bring troops with him to set up a patrol. He instructed the *gendarmes* to maintain crowd control until the soldiers were in place. He called his boss, President Kibali, and briefed him on what occurred and actions he took. He urged Kibali to impose a curfew to let things cool down.

Julio and Frantz needed immediate medical care and faced surgery that couldn't be delayed. Kibali had a missionary physician who looked after his medical needs before he went into exile. Upon his return, Kibali persuaded the American, Frank Doyle, to be his attending physician. Guillaume contacted Reverend Dr. Doyle, explained the situation, and asked him to contact the two surgeons he had in mind to be available immediately for surgery.

François and Mario didn't know the extent of the injuries visited upon Julio and Frantz, but the considerable bleeding, the nature of the wounds and agony seemed ominous. Michel aggravated his wound while scrambling in thwarting their enemy. They stabilized the three wounded men as best they could and took them to a hospital run jointly by the government and missionaries. Dr. Doyle was at emergency admission, waiting for the patients. He told François one surgeon was already scrubbing and the other was on route. Dr. Doyle did a quick examination of the three men and determined Frantz should be taken to surgery immediately. There were three entry wounds and two exit wounds, with the possibility a bullet could be lodged near the spine. Frantz took hits to his abdomen, left shoulder and right calf. Julio's situation was less grave. He had a single entry wound in his right hip and no sign of an exit wound. The second surgeon, who just arrived, examined Julio and sent him to surgery. He directed that Michel be taken to surgery as well to clean his wound for suturing.

Guillaume came by the hospital to assure everything possible was being done. Because of missionary involvement, *Maison du Bon Berger*, was better staffed and supplied than *l'Hôpital Général,* where the wounded insurgents were taken. He sat down with the five anxious Europeans in the surgical waiting room.

"How serious is it? One of your men looked in tough shape."

"Yes, Frantz is in critical condition. The doctor said his injuries could be life threatening, but he won't know until he examines the internal damage in the abdominal area. Julio's condition is dicey with a bullet in his hip, which could affect his spine. Michel needs to be patched up. Nothing for us to do but hope and pray."

"I'm with you on that, François. I'm embarrassed. It's an omen for our country. We must have law and order to give other improvements a chance."

Mario interjected his thoughts. "Guillaume, you're 'Johnny-on-the-spot'. It's obvious why the president has such confidence in you. A person such as you is rare in countries like Mandaka. You'd normally be seen in Europe or America, leading a comfortable life. What keeps you here?"

"As you probably figured, I have European blood within me; a Tutsi father and a Belgian mother. Mandaka is my country. This is where I was born and raised. Both parents are well educated and instilled in me a love for learning. I was home taught early on and sent to Belgium for my secondary education. I went on to the

Sorbonne in Paris and King's College in London. Unusual for me to be here with all this education? Yes, but I was touched by what I saw every time I returned home on holiday. I felt compelled to use my abilities to help my compatriots."

"I'm not easily impressed," François pronounced as he measured the man, "but you've managed to do just that. Now, tell us what you can about this incident."

"This is what we know. There were at least 37 attackers, consisting of a dozen or so disgruntled soldiers, ten members of Jacques Tombola's tribe, some opportunists and several outsiders, including five black Cubans. The Cubans use their black soldiers to blend in with Africans. A quick casualty tally indicates 26 attackers dead (3 Cubans) and 11 wounded (2 Cubans). We believe there was a larger number of renegades and some slipped away in the darkness. The defenseless and innocent victims are 8 Mandakans civilians killed, 6 foreigners killed (2 French, 1 Chinese, 1 Indian, 1 Portuguese, 1 Greek) and a total so far of 27 others wounded. The captured Cubans provide solid evidence of encroachment by an unfriendly country. I'm meeting with the president later to explore our options. We'll consult with the French, make a *demarche* to the Cuban Government and appeal to the UN Security Council. The Soviets will likely block any action at the UN, but it shouldn't deter us.

"We learned your men were the principal targets despite the wild shooting. The assault was intended to discredit the 'colonialists' by displaying your vincibility, spread fear among the populace and instill distrust in our new government. I grieve for your injured men and wish them a complete recovery."

François responded. "Thanks Guillaume. There is some good that's come from this."

"I agree. You must be heartened by the way your students acted. The saplings flourished beyond expectations because of the rich nourishment they received. Such a transformation in 23 days is impressive. We'll declare the men heroes. It'll give a positive spin to a brutal event. It might take some of the edge off that the people no doubt feel."

"Guillaume, I'm thinking about our remaining time. Fortunately, we have the weekend to look at the situation realistically and sensibly. I'd like to finish the rest of the program. The wounded need to be evacuated to Europe. Mario and I want to visit the mines in the south. Kwambe should be with us as well as his three comrades."

Stéphane asserted his intent to stay on and finish the program. "If we continue, I suggest we resume with an opening act. Let's have our seven heroes re-enact the techniques they used against a superior enemy. We could comment on the techniques and offer suggestions."

"Great idea!" Mario declared. "Even if we re-convened for only one day, this would be most productive and, if we continue, it would be a great lead-in to get the rest of the trainees to think beyond the training. There's no down-side, François."

"Sounds good. I'll put it in the hopper to consider when we evaluate the situation tomorrow evening."

As the clock ticked away, the group grew in size. Pastambu stopped by briefly to pay his respects.

François greeted him. "We appreciate your visit, General. Three of my men are wounded, but they're being cared for. How is it out there? Any more problems?"

"The situation is under control for now, François. We've cleared the streets, closed all establishments and asked everyone to return to their homes. A curfew in the cities is in effect and soldiers are patrolling the communes in armored vehicles. We're seeking to root out any Cubans who might still be in the area."

"What about other parts of the country? This doesn't seem like it was either impromptu or isolated."

"This event was staged, François. The attack in Bandala was planned in advance. When they learned you were in town, they decided it was an opportune time to strike. There were minor skirmishes in two other towns, one in the south and the other in the east. Our *gendarmes* reacted quickly, repelling the insurgents and army units chased them into the forests. We're working on an action plan to launch a sizeable military operation in the south and reclaim our border."

A somber mood shrouded the group of contemplative and taciturn men. The group grew larger. The trainees' superior officer, Edouard Bolotatu, and Kwambe accompanied Pastambu and stayed on, joining Guillaume and the five Europeans. Edouard had additional information. "Mario, you recall the incident at headquarters when seven soldiers tried to attack and you shot one? Well Colonel Tanandu told me to tell you those six others were involved in this attack. Two were killed, one wounded and three escaped."

"Thanks Edouard. It certainly confirms they were rogue elements."

When Michel emerged into the domain of the healthy, he was greeted with exuberance. He was carrying a donut cushion for his *derrière*. It would be some time before they'd know the condition of the two other patients.

Eventually, Dr. Doyle, who was assisting the surgeons, came out of surgery. He told the group the two surgeons would be out shortly to explain the situation. He reassured everyone both men were alive and the surgeons did a fine job.

The eyes and attention of nine apprehensive individuals focused on the two surgeons, a Swiss and a Swede, as they pushed through the doorway. They explained their diagnoses and extent of damage both patients had endured. Their prognoses and recommendations for treatment followed. They chose to discuss Julio first.

"The bullet was located and removed. Fortunately, the spine was unaffected. The internal damage was repaired and the wound closed. The bullet entered just above the right hip on a trajectory that caused it to lodge in his left pelvis. It probably ricocheted before entry, reducing its impact. There is bone damage but it appears slight and should heal with no adverse effect. He needs rest but he should begin physical therapy as quickly as possible.

"We've done everything we can for Frantz. His shoulder and leg injuries have been repaired. The grim news is he's paralyzed from the waist down. The bullet is lodged near the spine and we don't have the means to do the very delicate procedure required to extract it. We're unable to evaluate the duration of paralysis, which will be addressed by surgeons who are better equipped to probe further. Both men need to be evacuated to an appropriate European location. We recommend you charter a Med Evac aircraft, if one is available in the region. Time and minimum disruption are key. Before Frantz was sedated, he insisted on his home country for further treatment. Julio agrees to go to Vienna as well if it makes arrangements easier. Frantz's condition doesn't allow for delay."

François thanked the three doctors for their consideration and attentive care. He told them he would move straight away on securing an aircraft for an expeditious evacuation. He asked his five men to stay at the hospital to visit with Frantz and Julio when the time was right to do so. He left with Guillaume for the presidential palace to arrange transport and alert the hospital in Vienna.

CHAPTER THIRTY TWO

The international airport in Nairobi, Kenya, served as a regional hub with numerous intercontinental connections. An unmet need became painfully obvious with the dearth of quality medical resources and facilities in most African countries. A medical evacuation service was established at the airport to operate as an airborne 'ambulance'. It transported the gravely ill and seriously injured to destinations where they could receive proper treatment. This Med Evac enterprise had undertaken a number of flights from African airports to destinations across the Mediterranean. Fortunately, a converted DC-3 with Pratt & Whitney PT6 engine turbines was available to service François' needs.

The aircraft arrived in Bandala shortly after noon on Saturday, with the patients ready to embark. Medical attendants alit with litters and transferred Frantz and Julio from the hospital's gurneys. It was a risky maneuver but, through great care and assistance from their colleagues, the two patients laid strapped on the litters with no additional damage or pain. They were made as comfortable as possible with free movement of their arms.

Two other passengers boarded the aircraft. While Michel's injury was not severe, the doctors feared infection and felt it prudent for him to leave as well. He needed follow-up attention for his wound. The fourth passenger was a reluctant Gundhart. He strained his previously injured leg during the shootout and François was concerned it would be aggravated if Gundhart stayed. However, François had no success in his urgings until he convinced Gundhart to board the plane; Frantz needed him by his side. No time was wasted. The DC-3 was on the ground less than an hour before heading north.

François, Mario, Preston and Stéphane remained to chat with their contacts, Guillaume and Claude. A collective sigh of relief was exuded as they congratulated each other for getting through the ordeal. They went into the terminal building and each savored a Stella Artois. Guillaume inquired on the status of the training program.

"I'll decide on Sunday, when I review the situation."

"François, I'm not pressing you for a decision. We prefer you to defer until Monday. President Kibali wants to meet with the four of you to evaluate the program. In view of last evening, he wants to review what's been accomplished and what remains."

"So, we won't resume until Tuesday. Okay with me. We'll be ready. Tell us when."

"10:00 am Monday at the palace. General Pastambu, Lt. Colonel Tanandu, Commandant Bolotatu, Claude and I will be present. *Nous allons bavarder avec des donner et prendre*. It'll be useful to have your input in a relaxed give-and-take session. President Kibali invites the four of you to have lunch with him following the meeting. May I tell him you accept?'

François looked at his three colleagues, who all nodded. "We're pleased to accept and thank the President for us. That takes care of Monday. Looks like we have Sunday free."

"No you don't, unless you want it that way. I have another invitation to convey. A French plantation owner of long-standing has made his property available to you to relax for the day. He phoned his close friend, President Kibali, this morning when he learned of last night's violence. They chatted about the situation and he inquired about your men. He's in France looking after his other businesses but his staff is present at the plantation and, they are ready to pamper you. The property has a swimming pool, horses and billiards among other amenities. You'd be the only guests. What do you say?"

Mario was the first to respond. "Count me in. It'll be a well-needed change. Tell us more about the owner and the property."

"René Archambault is a *colon* and a patriot who resides in Nice, France, when he's not on his plantation. He's a former French army officer who came to Mandaka with a military unit thirty years ago and stayed. Son of a French father and a mulatto mother from Martinique. Claude Pelletier's mother is René's younger sister. Monsieur Archambault, who is now in his early 60s, enjoys a good reputation here and abroad. Some Mandakans, spurred on by outsiders such as Cubans and Chinese, threaten the plantation from time to time. All attempts have been repulsed rather handily by a combination of militia, employees and sharecroppers. As a *patron,* M. Archambault has treated his staff and workers fairly over the years and they've been faithful to him. He's the most influential expatriate in the country but maintains a low profile.

"The plantation is southwest of Bandala, about an hour's drive. It's been consistently productive, even through the transition period from colony to independence. M. Archambault's secret to success has been in maintaining a balance between production for export and for local consumption. The primary crops are groundnuts (peanuts), coffee, cacao and bananas. As you can imagine, the plantation requires a sizeable workforce."

François was familiar with abuses local workers suffered on European plantations in Africa during the colonial period. René Archambault's attitude and experience were the exception rather than the rule.

"I'm intrigued by this *patron*, who seems to tread lightly on the high wire of political upheavals. Obviously, he's well connected to President Kibali. How did this come about?"

Guillaume provided more background. "They met at an official function here in Bandala 10 or 11 years ago and have been friends ever since. They visited each other in Paris and Nice when Kibali was in exile. M. Archambault urged Kibali to return to Mandaka and contributed to the payment for your earlier services."

François remained curious. "Many expatriates abandoned their African properties when colonies became independent. Of course, circumstances differed from country to country, but many colons left hastily, fearful for their lives. How was M. Archambault able to persevere?"

"What you say was true in Mandaka, François. We have been learning the lesson of cause and effect. With the flight of Europeans from Mandaka, as elsewhere, economic production diminished, leading to a downward spiral for our nation's economy. Fewer exports and no way to pay for imports. M. Archambault was threatened during those uncertain times. He refused to be intimidated. His workers remained loyal. They realized they were better off than most Mandakans. When you arrive on the plantation tomorrow, you'll meet a person who played an important role at that time, and continues to do so. Boniface Lissouba began working on the plantation as a teenager about 22 years ago. He was born in a French military camp in Mandaka to parents of Sudanese origins, who worked as a laborer and a servant at the camp. His parents were killed in an insurrection at the camp when Boniface was nine. Camp officers took him in. He began as an errand boy, while being tutored. This is where M. Archambault met Boniface several years later, eventually hiring him to work on the plantation. Boniface has been plantation overseer and the *patron's* alter ego for the past nine years.

"Another thing about Boniface, you'll note his appearance when you meet him. He's a Dinka and was known as Majak Arop in his early years. After his parents' death, the French changed his name to a more traditional Mandakan name. Are you accepting the invitation?"

All four chimed in their acceptance. Claude, who had been silent throughout the discussion, spoke up.

"I won't be going with you to my uncle's plantation, but I'll see you off. A trusted driver with a Land Rover will call for you at 8:00. While we don't anticipate trouble on route, I'll return four of your Uzis to you. It's merely a precaution that'll make us all feel better. You'll be well protected while on the plantation. We'll take the Uzis back at the end of the day. We want to avoid giving a wrong message. Our detractors would seize on this for their propaganda. I hope you understand our concerns."

«*Je n'ai aucun problème, Claude*.» François understood the need for prudence. He agreed it would not be wise to be seen carrying the Uzis in public.

The four mercenaries/consultants took leave from Guillaume and Claude and returned to the Hilton to rest before a quiet dinner. They retired early to compensate for their adrenalin-filled and sleep-deprived night.

The next morning, Sunday, Claude entered the hotel and approached the four men in the café. They proceeded to their vehicle, where they met the driver and took possession of their weapons. They were soon traveling on two-lane (just barely), rutted, dirt roads. The driver's competence was evident as he displayed familiarity with the roadway when approaching obstructions.

When they were a little over an hour on the journey, the scenery changed suddenly. A gate stood as a point of demarcation. The dense forest, with no display of habitation, gave way to a village of brick houses on the left side of a well-maintained road that led to the plantation's main buildings. The sturdy housing and tidy grounds within the village, constructed and established for the workers, belied the appalling conditions that Mandakans living in the communes had to deal with. A timberland, consisting of zebrawood, bubinga and padauk, covered the right side of the 1.5 mile road. These exotic trees were for occasional use only as lumber for the plantation.

The main building was as imposing as any structure they had seen in Africa. At 17,500 sq. ft., it appeared massive as they approached. There were several outbuildings, including guest quarters, servant quarters, stables, barn, water tower, etc.

Mario was first to comment. "René Archambault seems to be doing okay for himself. He had to have his act together to hang on to this."

François pointed ahead to a figure standing in front of the main building. An elegant looking woman and four children were by his side. The man was garbed in a two-piece blue dashiki with gold embroidery and the woman was attired in a purple brocade caftan with yellow embroidery. They both wore sandals while the woman was adorned with a necklace of ivory carvings, a bracelet of carved wooden beads on her right wrist and bangles of assorted colors on her left wrist.

"We're about to meet a person who's largely responsible for Archambault's ability to retain his property."

Boniface Lissouba was a large man with erect posture. Standing a touch over two meters, a physically fit body at 100 kilos enveloped in ebony skin with a phosphorescent blue/purple hue, he had a majestic presence. He exhibited self-assurance and genuineness as he welcomed his visitors. His trim body was muscular and his demeanor, while not daunting, was reassuring and commanded respect. Boniface was a person who was comfortable in his own body. The woman, who was about twelve centimeters shorter than her companion and a shade lighter in skin coloring, was the picture of classical beauty and refinement. Ayar Mathiang was a member of an esteemed Dinka family in southern Sudan.

«Messieurs, vous êtes bienvenu. Je vous présente ma femme et mes gosses.» Boniface had a good command of French, reflecting the special effort made to educate him after he lost his parents. "This lovely lady is my wife, Ayar, and these four *gamins* are the issue of our union. Ayar is my talisman sent to me by God to look after me, which she has been doing to perfection. Ekene, Ngozi, Kunto and Anan are our pride and joy. The good Lord spared us and allowed us to have a girl. Kunto holds her own with her three brothers.

"We are honored and delighted to have you with us for a day, which will be as restful or as active as you want it to be. I'll give you a tour of our facilities and I'll be available to you throughout the day, as you may need. Ayar will introduce you to our *cuisinière* and her staff. Monsieur Archambault insists you feel at home. He's a generous man and a consummate host. I assure you he'd be disappointed if you felt ill at ease. So, shall we get on with the tour?"

François spoke for the group. "We're indebted to M. Archambault for his generosity and thoughtfulness. We appreciate your and your family's gracious acceptance of our intrusion into your domain. We'll try not to be a distraction to your quietude."

"Mister Morency, spoken as an accomplished diplomat. Please disabuse yourselves of any notion that you need to be wary of your wellbeing while you're here. We have a sizeable sentinel force scattered around the plantation perimeter so you should have no concern for your safety. You'll observe on your tour that we have equipped our men with appropriate weaponry and communication gear. The household staff is accustomed to entertaining guests. We're all grateful for the assistance you've provided to President Kibali and we're the ones in your debt. So, please, make yourselves comfortable.

"We have a specially equipped van we'll use. We'll go to the periphery and show you the operation that keeps this place going. On our way back, I'll show you the facilities at your disposal."

Boniface showed his guests some sentinel stations, and drove through the coffee, banana, groundnut, cacao sectors and a well-stocked vegetable garden. The tour continued with a look at eight horses awaiting exercise in the pasture adjacent to the stables, a few dozen cows ruminating in the meadow near the barn, chickens pecking on feed by the coop and pigs wallowing in the sty. It concluded in the kitchen after passing through the game room and the library. Ayar took over and guided the visitors through the main building. Fruit, pastries and coffee awaited them upon completion of the tour.

"Any of you fancy equestrian? I'll have the stable boy saddle the horses."

"Yes, we'd all enjoy it. Do you have a map of the trails?"

"I could give you a map but my two oldest sons, Ekene and Ngozi, are eager to take you out and test your horsemanship. They'll show you the trails, but don't be surprised if they challenge you for a run."

"That's just fine with us. We thrive on challenges and competition."

"Once you're done, feel free to use the swimming pool, play bocce, shoot billiards or pool, and browse through the library. Beverages and snacks are available in the game room. We'd like you to join us for dinner late afternoon before you head back to Bandala."

"Thanks, Boniface. You pamper us and we appreciate your hospitality."

The afternoon was filled with a blend of sporting activities and competitions mixed with relaxation. The two young Mandakans held their own against the determined Europeans, who begged off eventually, settling their horses into a gentler trot. Despite their bravado, they found a slower tempo more to their liking after the events in the city. It was shortly after noon when the quartet splashed into the swimming pool with assorted entries. After a light lunch and beverages, they played *pétanque*, shot billiards, took reading material from the library and settled down for respite on lounge chairs by the swimming pool.

Preston gazed at Mario, who was stretched out, reinforcing his body's nut-brown hue under the equatorial sun. "Mario, I'm impressed with your fortitude. You strike me as the picture of repose despite your setbacks. Your bravado in our contests today didn't quite hold up. Then there's your financial hit betting against Manchester United. But, this is the thing. We know you're engaged to be married, but then again you're not. First she says yes and then she says, hold on, not so fast."

This was their cue. François and Stéphane joined Preston in good-natured ribbing. They gathered by Mario's chair and harmonized, vintage Ames Brothers (Sid Robin/Charlie Shavers).

"First you say you do, and then you don't

And then you say you will, and then you won't

You're undecided now

So what are you gonna do? . . . ."

The trio spared no lyrics as they serenaded their Italian friend. Mario lay unfazed, allowing a hint of a smirk to show his appreciation for the fraternal affection.

"I'm touched by your caring. I'm also pleased the three of you could provide some competition. It gets lonely standing on top of the hill. Your ballad selection was clever; 'Undecided Now' seems to have been written for me. A word of advice. Don't bank on theatrical careers with your creaky voices. The only thing I regretted while listening to your warbling was the lack of an oil can to lubricate your vocal instruments."

"Mario, you never disappoint. You always come up with a clever retort." François tousled Mario's freshly combed hairdo. "You're a good chap and we're concerned about you. Where are you with Marianne?"

"My intentions haven't changed. What I know for certain is that I love her and she loves me. Perhaps, there's something to the saying, 'absence makes the heart grow fonder'."

Preston couldn't resist. "So, what's your game plan? You need to consider us as well. Our social calendars are rather tight. We need to be present to see you properly cast off. We fear you'd foul things up if left on your own."

"Okay, *mes amis*, this is the deal. I forgot what social animals you are. Block out the third week of September next year to be in Liège. All that remains is to determine whether there'll be a wedding. My sense is there will be, but then, I'm an eternal optimist. I'll travel to Liège when our business is done and meet with Marianne. If she still harbors qualms about matrimony, there'll be no wedding, at least not with me."

Preston tried to assuage Mario's feelings. "Don't pay any mind to my teasing. You're a good bloke and you'll do what's right for your lady and yourself. Happiness is elusive and you need to grab it when it presents itself."

"Thanks for the vote of confidence. I appreciate your friendship, Preston. That goes for you too, François, Stéphane and the rest of our gang. It'll work out, one way or the other."

Boniface approached and told them dinner would be served in 15 minutes, giving them time to freshen up.

The dinner was savory, to the delight of the four guests. They feasted on *ratatouille*, *roti de porc au lait* and *pommes de terre au gratin dauphinoise.* The atmosphere was congenial as all ten dinners, adults and children, participated in the relaxed conversation accompanying the meal, sharing their views on various topics, discussing aspects of their lives and projecting Mandaka's future.

The visit concluded with embraces and an outpouring of gratitude from one party to the other, one, for assistance to Kibali and Mandaka, and the other, for well-appreciated hospitality. The drive back to Bandala was uneventful and the Uzis were returned to army headquarters. The four men called it a day and retired to get sufficient rest for their meeting with Kibali in the morning.

CHAPTER THIRTY THREE

The four comrades gathered in the Hilton coffee shop on Monday morning, feeling refreshed and revitalized. They ate a light breakfast and discussed how they might handle the conclusion of the training program. They agreed to begin the meeting by listening to ideas and concerns from the presidential party and see how these could be melded into the final training sessions.

Their chauffeur arrived at 9:30. They rode through downtown Bandala on route to the palace. Some progress was made in the clean up, but debris remained on *l'avenue de l'indépendance*, including burnt vehicles. Blood, gasoline and other splattered stains marked the scene of the conflict. Some limited commerce resumed, but there was little activity other than the conspicuous military patrols. Blown out windows were boarded up adding to the degradation of the city as a war zone. Prudence was the watchword for the day. Mandakans were accustomed to strife and were somewhat resilient. A return to normal on the next day was likely if no further incidents occurred.

Palatial guards were in evidence along the hillside road leading to the palace. The Neptune fountain was no longer feeling neglected; an effort was underway to restore its splendor and regain the water flow. Landscaping improvements were evident. The beautification projects were funded by donor nations under the accommodating label of economic development.

The four intrepid warriors ascended the stairs to the palace and were greeted by Guillaume and Claude, who escorted them into the grand parlor. Kibali was expansive in welcoming them, while the remainder of the cabal was less effusive. In addition to François, Mario, Preston, Stéphane, Kibali, Guillaume and Claude, the other conferees were *Général d' Armée* Gaston Pastambu, *Général de Brigade* Marcellin Kingambo, Lieutenant-Colonel Florien Tanandu and Commandant Edouard Bolotatu.

«S'il vous plaît, messieurs, soyez à l'aise.» Kibali embraced the four men. "We've been discussing Friday's event and our need to prevent future occurrences. It's obvious your efforts have already proven effective. We'd be delighted to have you here longer to train more of our troops, but we realize your time is limited."

As the men settled into their seats, François initiated the discussion. "Your Excellency, before we get to our main topic, I'd like to share some observations on Friday evening's incident, if I may."

"Please feel free. It's evident we're not well prepared. All suggestions are welcome."

"Your first priority is to develop an elite military unit and expand its capabilities. That's why we're here. You have a solid cadre to build on. Friday evening revealed a functional vulnerability that invites further insurrections with greater threats to Mandaka's stability. You were correct in saying the *gendarmerie* was apolitical. What you omitted was they are ineffectual and undependable. Those at the scene on Friday who weren't shot, ran and hid. The *gendarmerie* should be your first line of defense in the face of domestic uprisings before the military is brought in. Attention should be given to proper training, including a dedicated recruiting and dismissal initiative. The Americans run an effective police action program that might be available to Mandaka.

"Another key weakness is intelligence. It's obvious your people don't know what the Cubans are doing. I hear references to Cuban incursions as ghost-like movements. They're probably operating a training camp in an isolated area of your country. In my view, a special military unit should be established and trained to reconnoiter. It's important to gain the trust of the local population to facilitate information gathering. Perhaps the French could help you in this regard."

"François, your men were the principal target on Friday but we learned the assault would have occurred regardless. All Mandakans are in your debt and we would benefit from more of your assistance."

"Mister President, we are gratified you find our service to your satisfaction. We need to move on to other commitments. You've assembled a worthy team around you."

"François, you've endeared yourself and I look to you as a brother. Enough of this. Let's get on with our business."

As agreed, François let Pastambu and his fellow officers take the lead. They reviewed what was accomplished in 23 days. They focused on the new mindset of the trainees and the take-charge attitude of the seven soldiers on Friday evening. Skills learned and skills to be developed were identified. Sources of funding for military training were discussed. Caution was expressed to avoid politics as much as possible and to address needs in military and security terms. Kingambo was impressed with the *Krav Maga* hand-to-hand combat system. Another suggestion was to have each trainee do one more jump from the tower. It would help evaluate personnel for intensified airborne training. With François' group cut in half, Tanandu and Bolotatu volunteered to assist with the training.

François responded on the agenda. "We believe four days will be sufficient. We prefer Friday as the last day rather than going into another week. When training resumes tomorrow, we'll start with a demonstration by the seven heroes of the insurrection."

Edouard spoke up on the show-and-tell. "It'll be a morale booster for our heroes, their fellow trainees and other soldiers who'll be watching. Best to keep it quiet until they're called upon tomorrow. It'll be more spontaneous."

Preston agreed. "That's a good point. If they knew in advance, we'd be watching a well-rehearsed drama."

François continued. "We accept Colonel Tanandu's and Commandant Bolotatu's offers to assist as trainers. We'll meet both of you later to review what remains to be done. At the final session on Friday afternoon, I suggest a graduation ceremony to honor the trainees. New assignments could be handed out. It's worth making a big splash; it's a good publicity opportunity for future trainees and the population."

At lunch, Kibali was expansive on the outlook for his country despite the distress of the people and a foundering economy. He regaled about the opportunities to make the country more productive in several sectors, focusing initially on agriculture and mining. After listening to the Mandakan leader's exuberant prognostications, Mario felt compelled to interject some realism, while wondering whether Kibali had consumed some *khat* prior to lunch.

"I don't mean to dampen your enthusiasm, but the enterprises you mention take considerable time, effort and financing to get started. Do you expect the people will give you the time and make the effort needed to get these sectors going? You'll need external sources of assistance and financing, which doesn't happen overnight."

François frowned at Mario, expecting Kibali to be offended by Mario's bluntness, undermining the host's geniality. Kibali smiled at Mario.

"What you say, Mario, is at the heart of my problem. Unfortunately, I don't have an answer for you. I may be a dreamer but it's with dreams that goals are established and their pursuit unleashed. Think of your own goals and accomplishments. Didn't they emerge from earlier dreams? I don't delude myself about the challenges that lay ahead, but I have to be the motivator to get the engine running."

Mario's comment and Kibali's response opened a frank discourse for the remainder of the meal.

The training went as expected for the balance of the program. When the trainees reconvened on Tuesday morning, they were greeted by Kingambo, who spoke briefly on behalf of Kibali and Pastambu.

"You're justified to be proud of your accomplishments in a rigorous and specialized training program. You can't allow yourselves to be pompous. Your fellow soldiers will be looking to you to set the example of good military conduct. You've earned the right to consider yourselves the best, but it's your behavior that'll determine whether others will consider you the best."

François spoke to the men on the remaining schedule. "The program will conclude on Friday. You've already learned the techniques and we'll be running through them again to get you feeling more comfortable with them. Since we're down to four trainers, we're fortunate to have two volunteers. Lieutenant-Colonel Tanandu and Commandant Bolotatu will assist my men and me as trainers. Your immediate superior officer, Commandant Bolotatu, will explain the remainder of the program."

The trainees had no advance word on the remaining agenda. Edouard spoke of the Friday event.

"What occurred Friday evening is something you must be prepared for. Other incidents could arise with no forewarning. You're the foundation of the new Mandakan army. Insurrections need to be nipped in the bud. These can be averted through greater knowledge. You'll be looked upon to thwart any threats to our country and our people. The casualties suffered on Friday are regrettable, but it would have been much worse without the intervention of our European friends."

The audience broke out with murmurs and shouting. Edouard had scripted it well and got the trainees enlivened for the opening act of the program's final week.

"Now, now, give me a chance to finish. I know there were others involved and I was just about to mention them. Several citizens came to the assistance of the wounded and the distraught. The *gendarmerie* acted responsibly once they were told what to do. Our medical providers reacted promptly and performed well with emergency service."

More interruptions. Someone with a booming voice bellowed, "What about our own men?"

"I'm so glad you reminded me. I do recall some of our lads had a hand in this affair. In fact, we have a surprise for you. I'm calling these men to come forward."

As the seven men stood and walked to the front of the assembly, their fellow trainees gave them a raucous reception.

"The seven of you are brave men. You're national heroes for your timely action. We have a special treat for your comrades. They've received the same training as you, but only the seven of you have put it into action. Kasadi, since you seem to have emerged as ringleader, select a dozen or so of your *confrères* from the audience to assist you."

Edouard explained the scene as it existed on Friday and placed the actors in their positions. He told the seven men the stage was theirs and to proceed with their actions beginning with hearing gunfire while in the nightclub. He also asked them to tell the audience what they were thinking and discussing. There was no evidence of reticence. Testosterone was on display; adrenalin was unleashed. On a few occasions during the drama, the observer-trainers interjected with queries to keep over enthusiasm and embellishment in check, and to comment on the application of techniques in play. A blanket of absolute silence enveloped the audience. All were fascinated their *sept camarades avaient les coquilles*—having the balls—to act as they did and wondered how they would have acted.

François allowed the stage show to run until the lunch break. It was time well spent. Probably the most valuable training session of the entire program. The hands-on application of the training instilled greater confidence in the men. To describe them as upbeat would be putting it mildly; they were inspired, eager to take on all comers.

The remainder of the week was devoted to repeating the lessons and techniques taught. Each of the 85 trainees was put through the paces and evaluated on performance. François was delighted when dark clouds covered the sky on Wednesday morning. The rain began as a sprinkle but the heavens opened up, releasing the floodgates. Except for three days, the weather was sunny with clear skies and moderate temperature. He wanted to see the trainees perform under more adverse conditions. Sloshing over the sodden soil and sliding through the muck, the trainees were unsteady but purposeful.

When Friday afternoon arrived, the stage was set for a grand ceremony. The venue was army headquarters in the area in front of command control, where the mercenaries and Mandakan soldiers had confronted each other a couple of months earlier. The top brass turned out along with every military attaché accredited to Mandaka. Members of the press were also on the scene. Advance publicity played the event up as the most significant since Independence Day. President Kibali opened the ceremony.

"I'm enthused by what's been accomplished and the special occasion we're celebrating. This program is testimony to a genesis occurring in Mandaka. The people are clamoring for change, for a new beginning.

"Admittedly, the training of 85 soldiers and three officers isn't newsworthy. If you allow yourselves to view this as embryonic as I do, you'll see it as tangible evidence of commitment. Security within our borders and the safety of our citizens are sacrosanct. The new *chasseurs parachutistes* unit we celebrate today is the foundation of a revamped military. We want to assure *nos amis à l'extérieur* that they're welcome to come to Mandaka where they shouldn't be concerned for their safety."

General Pastambu followed with his personal pledge. "Accountability is important. I hold myself accountable to President Kibali and my fellow citizens, while every member of the military answers to me. A needs assessment is underway to identify shortcomings in capabilities and skills. A thorough evaluation has been initiated to determine which soldiers should be retained, advanced or terminated. My staff is exploring training opportunities with friendly nations."

All speakers extolled the honorees. It was a time for macho posturing. The atmosphere became more electric with gung ho commentaries by François, Edouard Bolotatu and Florien Tanandu. Each member of the new special unit was greeted by the dignitaries on the stage. Tanandu gave each new airborne soldier a certificate of accomplishment, an insignia of his new unit and assignment orders.

A typical African banquet was set up. It was a smorgasbord of delicacies. The ubiquitous staples of cassava, groundnuts, plantains, yams and bananas appeared in various guises. *Viande de brosse*—bushmeat (wild boar and monkey)—goat, chicken and insects (crickets, grasshoppers, termites and caterpillars) were added to other ingredients such as palm oil, peanut paste, hot pepper sauce, palm nuts, millet, sorghum, cassava leaves and *fufu*—ground cassava tubers. A few different *pièces de résistance* were put together by varying combinations of ingredients. The non-Africans were attracted to the *brochettes*—skewers of beef and pork. The selection of beverages included palm wine, coconut juice, *pombe*—millet and sorghum beer—and *jus de tamarin*—seedpods of tamarind tree.

CHAPTER THIRTY FOUR

Four men stood on the riverbank engaged in conversation, their camaraderie fully evident. One pair was leaving the country, the other remaining to journey deep into its bowels. The six-week training mission concluded to unqualified acclaim. The eight-man team, diminished to four, was down to two. Preston and Stéphane were embarking the ferry to cross the Lipongo River to Zandu for a flight to Paris. Preston was returning to his *Costa del Sol* refuge, while Stéphane was heading to his domicile on the outskirts of Paris. François and Mario were remaining to visit the mines in the south.

François finalized arrangements for the trip to the mines during the training program reception. The French Military Attaché, Colonel André Chouinard, was more than willing to fly down in his aircraft. It provided a good excuse to snoop around the area with presidential blessing. The flight to Pliganta Province was early Saturday afternoon as was a special Air Mandaka flight, hauling two dozen soldiers and 15 members of the new airborne unit on their assignments.

In addition to François, the passengers on Chouinard's plane were Mario, Guillaume, Edouard and Kwambe. Edouard took six Uzis along in case of need. Upon arrival in Mandaka's southernmost region, they went to the compound of the *Société Minéraux de Mandaka-Sud.* Kwambe told the others the buildings hadn't gone asunder and remained habitable. It was obvious at first sight they needed extensive rehabilitation to remedy deterioration and replace pilfered items. The group checked out the compound and inspected the living quarters. Kwambe introduced his travel mates to the company's meager staff and security guards. They walked over to check the adjacent military encampment, replenished with new manpower.

François and Mario were anxious to take a look at the upper Rimbaud River, where diamonds were found. They left the others and Kwambe drove them in a company Land Rover. It was late Saturday afternoon when they arrived. The light was dusky as the sun sank below the tropical forest tree line. Several people were visible, squatting along the riverbed. The trio was cautious about approaching. They were concerned about Cubans in the area.

Mario asked Kwambe, "Can you tell who these people are?"

«Nous sommes bien pour l'instant.» Kwambe responded that there was no problem. "Yes, I recognize two. They wouldn't be here if they felt threatened."

Years of experience taught François and Mario to be instinctively suspicious; no one could be taken as they seemed. Kwambe had earned his way as a trusted ally. He led François and Mario, armed with their Uzis, to the people he knew. He spoke to them in their tribal dialect. He inquired whether they felt safe at the riverbed and if they sensed a threat from outsiders. Kwambe translated.

"It's the end of the day. This is the only time they come, except sometimes early mornings. They stay away during the day because *les démoniaques* come and butcher them. They watch and when the intruders leave, they feel safe."

"Who are the *démoniaques*? Do they know where they come from?"

"These evil ones have a camp about 20 to 22 kilometers southwest from here. It's near our border with Runhantia. They've seen the camp and there are Mandakans with weapons and *des étrangers*. There are *blancs* also at the camp."

"*Merci*, Kwambe. François, this confirms what we anticipated. Cubans do have a training camp for revolutionaries down here."

"No doubt about it, Mario. Cubans act as stooges for the Soviets. No question we need to check this further."

Mario remained focused on diamonds. "Kwambe, ask them about diamonds?'

"Yes, they have seen some. The interlopers pick some up, but they overlook others the locals find. The natives are more diligent and know what they're looking for."

Daylight was fading; time to get back to the compound and return in the morning. The next day, the six men set out to observe the riverbed from the brush overlooking the river, dispersing in pairs. Mandakans appeared at the first light of day from nearby villages to wash their clothes and cooking utensils, collect water supplies and quickly disappeared into the forest. There was no activity for over an hour. Suddenly, eleven men emerged and approached the river. Mario and the five others remained concealed. Mario and Kwambe were positioned behind trees near the riverbed. The eleven men walked closer to their location, but on the other side of the narrow river. Mario and Kwambe stepped out in the clear and called out to the new arrivals. Guillaume, François, Edouard and André provided cover. Mario greeted them in French and Kwambe tried to communicate in tribal dialects.

Kwambe told Mario some of the men were foreigners and others were not from his tribe. None of the new arrivals responded. They had a surly demeanor that discouraged good fellowship. Some of the men began to raise their weapons. Mario and Kwambe scampered back to the trees. A barrage of gunfire opened up. The *démoniaques* hurried to nearby boulders for protection, leaving four bodies. Gunfire continued from both sides. Additional shots were fired from the woods on the other side of the river.

François told Guillaume, "Sniper rifles would be handy right now."

"We can strafe them from our different vantage points, shoot a few more and wear them down."

André whispered to Edouard, "We'll be more effective with these Uzis if we move forward a bit, especially to get at those in the woods."

"Go ahead. Get behind those rocks. I'll provide cover and join you."

Mario said to Kwambe, "These foreigners must be Cubans. We need to take one dead or alive for evidence."

"They can't advance on us. Maybe they'll retreat to their camp."

"I don't think they want to fight us, Kwambe. They're the *démoniaques* who beat up on your people. We're not so easy to pick on."

The Cubans and comrades put up a good fight. They realized they were out-gunned and out-positioned. A few men shouted from the woods, saying they'd been hit. They saw they weren't inflicting damage on their opponent, while they suffered seven casualties. Their guns fell silent as they disappeared deeper into the woods.

Mario went over to check the victims; five dead or mortally wounded, two wounded less severely. Four black Cubans and three Africans. The four shooters descended from their perches and joined Mario and Kwambe.

François expressed his concern. "We need to get these bodies and wounded out of here quickly. Edouard, this is your action. The men who got away will sound the alarm when they get back to camp. You should think about beefing up security."

"I agree, François. Kwambe, is there a medic with our unit? Get a vehicle here."

Guillaume interrupted. "Before you move the bodies, get lots of photos we can use as evidence. We have a case to make. I have to return to the compound and alert the President. Mario, you come with me. The four of you remain here until the truck and troops arrive. This is another situation with the Cubans and our neighbors in Runhantia, with possible Soviet collusion."

Mario and Guillaume returned to the compound in the Land Rover, chatting on the way. Guillaume spoke on the need to augment military presence.

"Mario, this tells us General Pastambu needs to activate his plan. The President may want us to return to Bandala. Be prepared for that. I'll support François and you, but you need to make your case if you want to stay longer."

"I understand it'll be difficult to allow us to remain another day. You have sufficient military to repulse any threats for now. The danger is they might target villagers for retribution. We must verify the quality of the diamonds if we're to help get the mine going again."

"Mario, the big unknown is the rebel camp; we have no information. You may be right about our military presence but we need to reconnoiter the site."

"Guillaume, I don't think the Cubans want to fight you. It's not their way. They're here to incite rebellions and train dissidents. This group we just encountered came here as bullies, not fighters."

"I hope you're right, Mario, but we have to be ready. Let's make our phone call and chat some more."

They were waved through the gate and proceeded to the main building. Guillaume got two bottles of water and joined Mario in the lounge adjacent to the office. They exchanged views on the situation at the camp.

"As you know, Mario, the commanding officer of this detachment was *soûl* when we arrived. He knew we were coming but he couldn't stay sober. He's restricted to quarters and he'll learn his fate in Bandala. For the moment, Bolotatu is in charge but he expects to be on the plane with us. In my call to the President, I'll propose that Edouard remain here as interim commander until it can be sorted out. I want Kwambe as his deputy, but with specific responsibility for the special unit component stationed here. I'd place Kwambe's top man, Kasadi, as the top non-commissioned officer to coordinate the training of the regular soldiers by the *chasseurs parachutistes*, when they can be spared."

Guillaume placed the call, explaining the incident at the Rimbaud River and sought Kibali's and Pastambu's approval on the detachment leadership. Mario made his pitch to remain another day to obtain diamond samples. Kibali told Guillaume and Mario he would have answers for them in an hour.

The truck returned with the bodies of the five slain men and the two wounded, who were treated by a medic. François and André returned on the truck, leaving Edouard and Kwambe to position the security detail. Mario called them in as Guillaume answered the call from Kibali.

Kibali told Guillaume, "I agonized over pulling your group out, but decided to trust your instincts and our military. You have one more day to take care of what needs to be done. General Pastambu and I approve all three of your personnel recommendations."

"Thank you, Mister President. We're pleased to have the extra time. We'll do our best not stir up trouble."

"Hang on, Guillaume, I'm not finished. Ask Colonel Chouinard to fly to our border near the Cuban camp. We need photos to examine the setup and as proof of their presence. Take great care not to violate Runhantian air space. It's important to identify the exact location of the camp."

Guillaume responded. "I'm sure Colonel Chouinard will be please to comply. I'll go along and take Kwambe. He knows the area. If the camp is where the locals said, we should get a good view without straying over the border."

"Use utmost caution, Guillaume. I don't want you making this incident worse."

The three men were on their aerial mission by mid-afternoon. François and Mario returned to the river and followed it into the hillside. They spent the remaining daylight hours uninterrupted as they wended their way slowly up stream. They found some promising specimens but were unable to complete the course before nightfall. The three others were back when François and Mario returned. Guillaume felt the fly-over was a success. At least half of the camp appeared to be on Mandakan territory. They saw white soldiers as well as black. Magnification of the photos would provide better details. There were vehicles at the camp but no access road to the river. Incursions were on foot.

On Monday morning, the men dispersed to handle different tasks. Guillaume sent runners to invite elders in nearby villages to meet with him later that morning. Edouard took his interim assignment in stride and worked with his men on assignments. Kwambe assisted Edouard initially and joined Guillaume for the meeting with the elders. André spent time with his aircraft preparing for the return to Bandala in the afternoon. François and Mario went to the Rimbaud to conclude their exploration.

The attack came as Guillaume was meeting with the elders and as François and Mario were probing the hillside in the excavated area of the mine. The security detail responded to the dual assaults with gunfire, alerting everyone in the compound, military camp and at the riverside. It was a brazen response to the deaths of their malevolent comrades. Guillaume herded the elders out of harm's way into an interior room of the office building. The security force, augmented by other soldiers, didn't anticipate an attack on the compound. The assailants entered the compound before security had time to react. No one thought the aggressors would be so brassy to take on the newly reinforced detachment. They took positions behind equipment and buildings and began firing at the soldiers as they scrambled to set up a defense. Some soldiers were shot as they mobilized. Fortunately, some elements of the detachment had been dispersed to other sections of the compound. They led a counter attack on the intruders, inflicting sufficient casualties to cause withdrawal of the enemy. The soldiers prevailed as their foe aborted its attack on the compound and withdrew into the forest.

Meanwhile, the riverside was the site of a companion siege. François and Mario had climbed into the excavation pit and were finding more diamonds. This second batch of intruders swarmed along the river and up the hillside, firing their weapons as they advanced. They seemed unfazed by the returning fire of members of the elite corps on the periphery. As the assault continued with greater penetration on the hillside, François and Mario began firing their Uzis at the rebels who were endeavoring to surround them. Unlike the previous day, the enemy came to fight. The group was a rabble, undisciplined and poorly trained, but seemed determined to inflict damage. They were at least two dozen in this assault. Their bravado held up for awhile despite the success of the elite unit; they were getting results, cutting down the enemy one by one. François and Mario managed to keep the enemy from entering the pit. The obdurate opponents relented after a 20-minute engagement, as they sought defensive positions and a way to extract themselves. They endured more casualties as they fled, fading away into the woodland from whence they came.

There were no Cubans, only men from tribes of the border region. Edouard took stock of his men, praising them for their performance. There were a few injuries among the soldiers, none life threatening. An enemy bullet found its way to François, causing a laceration of his upper left arm. Mario tended to it and stopped the blood flow.

When things quieted, the tribal elders returned to their villages. Guillaume gathered his five colleagues in the company lounge. All soldiers queried asserted they saw no Cubans among the Africans. It seemed a desperate act of vengeance. More than likely, it was a test of the military detachment's resolve. The Cubans might have used the assaults as a training exercise for their conscripts. In any event, they came firing weapons, created a stir, inflicted some damage, and withdrew after dual engagements. All six men agreed the action didn't compute under conventional rationale.

Guillaume contacted President Kibali and briefed him on the recent occurrence. He also assured his boss François, Mario and he would be on André's aircraft within the hour, heading to Bandala. The six men agreed the trip was a success. They had significant photographic evidence of a hostile training camp involving foreign troops and of the attacks on Mandakan soil. François and Mario gathered numerous rough diamond crystals, including some previously gathered by Kwambe. Testing the *chasseurs parachutistes* under fire provided another benefit.

Edouard and Kwambe were saddened as they stood by the aircraft, embracing François and Mario. They realized there was little likelihood of seeing their European friends again. They promised to keep in touch, but then, good intentions often have a way of dissipating.

Upon arrival at the airport, Guillaume contacted Dr. Doyle to be available to suture the gash in François' arm. General Pastambu and *General de Brigade* Kingambo were with Kibali at the palace. André accompanied Guillaume, François and Mario and sat in on the initial part of the debriefing. Kingambo was intent on getting details.

"I'm eager to hear what you can tell us and see your photos."

Chouinard responded, "I'll develop and enlarge the photos as soon as I'm finished here. We'll have a better idea of the camp's activity."

Kingambo assured the gathering, "I have a battalion on stand-by, a full regiment if need be. Once we have your reports, we can proceed with our plans to deploy troops to Pliganta and other southern provinces."

Kibali urged caution. "Let's be sure of what we're doing before we launch. I'm anxious to do a definitive clean-up of the region.

We need this to get mining operations underway and ensure safety. We're dealing with delicate issues. We have every right to defend our borders. This will be a good test of our diplomacy. Cuba and Runhantia are involved, perhaps others."

When discussion of military matters concluded, Pastambu, Kingambo and Chouinard left the palace. Kibali kept François, Mario and Guillaume to chat further.

"I continue to be impressed with the two of you and your men. The training program bodes well for future programs. Your trainees have met the challenges."

François responded. "You have a fine cadre. They were eager to learn and submitted readily to the training."

Kibali had a request. "François and Mario, we've been candid with each other since our first meeting. Tell me what you think as we wrap up."

François reminded him of his previous comments. "You should be mindful of the old adage, 'Action speaks louder than words'. International donors, lenders and investors hear lots of talk, but they look to commitment and performance."

Mario spoke of Mandaka's citizens. "If you're to succeed with your programs, there's a limit to promises. People want changes that touch their lives for the better. I believe you're a good man with good ideas, but it won't take you far unless you're seen to be delivering on promises."

Kibali listened intently as his two European friends spoke as outsiders with insider perceptions. Guillaume kept a sober visage, hoping the two combat veterans weren't going too far with their commentary. He could speak in such fashion to Kibali, but these were foreigners. Kibali wasted no time in providing his reaction;

he smiled and agreed they gave good counsel. He mentioned diamonds only in passing. François told Kibali he'd convey all pertinent information in that regard when he obtained it.

Guillaume walked François and Mario to the vehicle waiting for them.

"The fewer people who know about the diamonds, the better. We don't want to advertize their mode of transport to Europe. I'll take them now, as we agreed, and see that they're in the next diplomatic pouch to our embassy in Paris. They'll likely be on the same flight with you tomorrow. This is the name of our diplomat in Paris, whom you should contact to collect the diamonds."

François placed the paper in his pocket. "You're a good man Guillaume, and I sense you're destined for even bigger and better things."

"Thanks, François. I've no thoughts of being elsewhere. I'll be by Kibali's side for some time to come."

Mario expressed his feelings to the President's right hand man. "I've also been impressed with you, Guillaume. We went through some good productive days and stressful moments together. It was reassuring to know you were there to take care of things. I might even consider sending you an invitation to my wedding, if it ever happens."

"Thanks, Mario, for your conditional invitation. I hope the lady is worthy of you and it goes the way you want."

"Bien dit, mon ami. I won't bore you with details but I'll soon learn where I'm heading."

"I know you're quitting this stuff. Whatever you do, you'll do well."

François had enough. “Let’s get on with it. We could be here for the rest of the day with your sweet talk. Let’s get the hugs and embraces out of the way and move on.”

“See what I have to put up with, Guillaume. It’s a wonder I lasted this long with this guy.”

PART V
RECONCILIATION

"To be happy you must have
taken the measure of your powers,
tasted the fruit of your passion,
and learned your place in the world"

George Santayana
Spanish Novelist
and Philosopher

CHAPTER THIRTY FIVE

Marianne was devastated upon hearing the BBC news broadcast on the fighting in Mandaka. Despite exerting her willpower to believe Mario was unharmed, she couldn't get herself to accept it. Her innate sense told her Mario was critically wounded and possibly dead. She couldn't shake off the vision of him lying helpless amidst the turmoil. She was desperate to be with Mario and decided the best way to be closer to him was to be with his friends. Her daze notwithstanding, she remembered Mario mentioned Pietro was his emergency contact. Impulsively, she contacted her superior that Saturday morning and told her she needed time off to tend to urgent family matters. She made an airline reservation for the next morning to fly to Firenze and phoned Pietro.

"I've decided to come to Tuscany. It's time for the *raccolto* and I want to help. It'll be good to get hands-on experience."

"This is a surprise, Marianne. I know you wanted to be here with Mario. Are you sure you're up to doing this?"

"I need a break. Working the harvest will be good medicine. Besides, it's an opportunity to become more familiar with the area."

"Sounds good. You'll stay with Anna and me in our guest room. When are you coming?"

"Tomorrow. I'll be on Sabena arriving in Firenze at 1:30 pm."

"I'll meet you at the gate. Have a safe flight."

When Pietro met Marianne at the airport, she told him of the BBC news report, enhanced by information gleaned from newspapers. She learned Europeans were among the dead and injured and European mercenaries were involved in repelling the attack. Reports suggested that the mercenaries were the primary targets. Pietro had no knowledge of this. He tried to comfort her as she related the dread she felt about Mario. When they got to the house, Pietro spoke to Anna and asked her to take Marianne under her wing, but to give her space to breathe. He told her what he just learned about Mandaka and the foreboding that had Marianne traumatized.

Marianne was emotionally deflated but the physical labor in the grove had a therapeutic effect. Otherwise, she remained withdrawn, restricting conversation to pleasant, brief responses when spoken to. She was particularly diffident with Mario's brother, Marcello, who returned to help with the harvest. Pietro surmised Marianne was embarrassed by her melancholy disposition.

Anna was a godsend for Marianne. During Marianne's first ten days in Tuscany, Anna persuaded her to spend a few afternoons with her and have lunch in town. They explored some of the area, in Lucca and Pisa, looking at churches, schools, museums, theaters and various types of housing. Anna observed to Pietro that Marianne seemed more relaxed on these outings. One week after the BBC broadcast, Marianne still had no information on Mario. There was brief mention of Mandaka's special unit ceremony in news coverage, but there was nothing to ease her fear. Her premonition of doom continued to dominate her thoughts. Anna contacted Mario's mother on Marianne's behalf, but she hadn't heard anything.

Pietro discussed Marianne's state of mind with Anna. "I fear that Marianne's melancholy will become more entrenched the longer uncertainty continues with Mario's condition."

"She does have moments when she appears a bit more upbeat, but I agree with you. Even when I take her out, she has periods when tears start flowing. She apologizes and says she can't rid herself of her premonition about Mario."

"I hope we hear soon from Mario or François. I sense they came through their scuffle unscathed. I always dread that I will lose my friend when he goes off on one of his adventures; this time, I feel differently."

"Too bad you can't reassure Marianne about your vibes, Pietro. She's like the doubting Thomas; seeing is believing."

Anika Duhammel phoned her daughter several times during the first ten days, speaking to either Marianne or Anna. She was assured Marianne was in good company and doing her best to deal with the situation. Halfway through Marianne's second week in Tuscany, Anna answered the phone; it was Anika again. She insisted on speaking to Marianne, who was working in the olive grove. It would take her awhile to fetch her, but Anika preferred to hold and wait. When Marianne greeted her mother, Anika told her there was someone who wanted to speak with her. Marianne dreaded the news she was about to hear. After a brief pause, a male voice came over the line. She was so emotionally distraught, she had difficulty identifying who was speaking. He repeated his name three times before recognition set in. *«Marianne, c' est Mario.»*

Marianne was beside herself and couldn't speak. She handed the phone to Anna.

"Who is this? I'm Anna. Marianne needs to catch her breath."

"Anna, this is Mario. I understand there was concern and I'm sorry information François sent didn't get through to any of you. I'm well and at the Duhammel home in Liège. Thanks for looking after Marianne. If she's able to get back on the phone, please put her on."

"Mario, is it really you? I've been so worried. I need to see you. I'm so sorry. I've been a jerk. Why are you in Liège? Will you wait for me to return? I love you, Mario."

"I promised I'd visit you in Liège as soon as I returned from Africa. I'm coming to Lucca. I'm making arrangements and will let you know."

"I thought something happened to you. I can't wait to see you."

"I love you, Marianne. Wait for me at Pietro's. Try to relax. I'll be in Lucca before you know it. *A bientôt*!"

Mario arrived in Paris the previous afternoon and accompanied François to his apartment in Neuilly, where he spent the night. Mario told François he'll arrange a meeting in Antwerp to view the diamonds. Mario left the next morning for Liège in a rented car. After speaking with Marianne, Mario accepted Anika's invitation to chat awhile over a glass of wine.

"Marianne has been in a deep funk since she heard an account of your shootout on BBC. She made an impulsive departure for

Tuscany. She moped around before leaving, hardly uttering a word except to mumble that you were probably dead and she'd never see you again. It was heartrending to see my daughter in such a state, but it might be the wakeup call she needs. So, what's with you? You look none the worse for wear."

"I managed to dodge my fair share of bullets. We suffered some injuries, but they're all mending. It was a worthwhile trip overall."

"It's such a relief seeing you, Mario, all in one piece. Marianne had to be excited with your call."

"She's in good hands with my friends. My intentions toward your daughter haven't changed. Actually, I'm more optimistic now than I was in Mandaka. As you said, this incident might help her get a grip."

"There's something else. Marianne confided in me on how Père LeBlanc treated you. I don't blame you for reacting as you did. Whenever we see him, he glares at Marianne as though he's on a special assignment to save her soul. It's become spooky. He says nothing, just an intense stare. It's bothered Marianne and she's questioning the function of priests. I sense she's become more aligned with your way of thinking."

"Thanks for sharing, Anika. It does sound unnerving."

"It's been a roller coaster ride for all of us, Mario. As you've learned, Marianne is strong willed, but she's also fragile. She needs love and tenderness."

"That's what she'll get from me. Beyond that, we'll see how it goes. Hopefully, there'll be a wedding. I must get going. My fiancée awaits."

As Mario was leaving the Duhammel residence, he was convinced Anika was praying for a successful reunion. He knew she was on his side, routing for him to seduce her daughter. Anika displayed more emotion than he'd seen from her. Her relief in seeing him and the tears streaming down her face were good signs. It was reassuring to know his potential mother-in-law was in his corner.

He kept the rental car and drove through France, arriving in time to bed down in his Monte Carlo apartment. He phoned his boss, Christophe Pouliot, to announce his return. Mario also called François and Pietro that evening.

"Christophe, I've just pulled in. I'll be here briefly, but I'll be back. I need a couple of days in Tuscany. Can we talk early morning?"

"I'm delighted you survived another adventure. Let's meet for breakfast at 8:00."

Mario's phone call to François was brief, since he had just seen him. "Marianne is in Tuscany with Pietro. We spoke on the phone and she seems better disposed. I'm in Monte Carlo and I'll be with her tomorrow."

"Mario, you need to keep me up-to-date. I'm intrigued and hanging at the edge of my seat for the next episode of your soap opera."

"Very funny! I am keeping you *au courant, mon ami.*"

"Don't let your romantic imbroglio interfere with other important matters."

"Not to worry, François. I'll attend to the diamonds and set up another meeting in Antwerp. I'll be back to you on both topics."

Mario's call to Pietro was to let him know he was in Monte Carlo. "I'm driving to Tuscany tomorrow. I think we should chat after I meet with Marianne. She sounded excited when I spoke with her. I'll be glad to get back to Lucca."

"When do you expect to get here?"

"Mid-afternoon. I have a breakfast meeting with Christophe about my situation at the casino."

"Marcello returned and he's helping with the harvest."

"I didn't know. How's he doing? Any further discussion of partnership?"

"We'll discuss all of this when you get here, Mario. He's rolled up his sleeves and is pitching in. He hasn't broached the partnership issue. So, don't get excited over it."

The next morning, Christophe was sympathetic but realistic. "I don't want to lose you, but I need you to put in more time. You're well regarded and respected by our clients and management."

"I need a few days to sort things out. I want to continue working at the casino. The thing is, I have to ascertain whether I'm heading for marriage or not. My fiancée has been playing me like a yo-yo."

"Hope it works out. I'll give you five more days. We'll work out a schedule when you get back. If you can't commit, we'll have to part company."

"Understood, Christophe. You're more than fair!"

Mario was accustomed to being fully engaged, but he felt like a circus juggler. Along with the casino and olives, he was more involved with the fortunes of Mandaka and his diamond interest. His standing with Marianne had to be resolved before any other issues could be dealt with.

When Pietro spoke to Mario on the phone, the most fitting term he thought of to describe Marianne was *taciturno* (taciturn). When Mario drove into the DiSantos' yard the next day, *euforico* (euphoric) seemed most apropos, as Pietro watched Marianne leap off the front porch and sprint toward Mario. The ensuing hugs, embraces, caresses, and pecks concluded with an enduring open-mouthed kiss that would have thrilled any romantic film director. They walked arm-in-arm into the house. Marianne was so effusive that Mario scarcely had a chance to utter a word. Eventually, emotions settled down and they discussed their relationship and their commitment to each other.

"Mario, I repent. I've done a lot of soul-searching since we last saw each other in Brussels three months ago. I'm annoyed with my behavior and embarrassed with the way I've treated you. I've been a pain-in-the-ass ever since you proposed."

"My consolation, Marianne, is that you've been my sweet 'pain-in-the-ass'."

"Don't make fun. I realize now I can't live without you. My idiosyncrasies created a barrier that the dread of your death broke down."

"Marianne, I'm sorry for what you went through, but I'm delighted with the results. It's music to my ears. I've been waiting for this moment. I love you."

Mario remained dubious the slate was wiped clean. He didn't want to probe too deeply about her changed attitudes—time would tell. He decided to savor the moment and see where it led. He had a five-day reprieve from Christophe.

As he readjusted to Marianne's declaration, she suggested they go to Pisa for a quiet dinner. Mario agreed and settled on an atmospheric riverfront restaurant. Mario ordered his favorite *Brunello di Montalcino* to ease some of the weariness he was feeling from his adventures and travel. Dinner went smoothly and the wine worked its magic. As they left the restaurant, Mario headed for the car to return to Lucca.

"Mario, let the car be. I don't want to share you with anyone. I'm selfish and want you all to myself. Let's check into a hotel for the night."

"Are you sure, Marianne? It seems sudden."

"I've given this a lot of thought while you were away. I didn't know whether you were dead or alive."

"I don't want you to act on a whim you'll regret later."

"As you told Father LeBlanc, I'm grown up, a big girl, and I can make my own decisions. Relax, Mario, I know what I'm doing. I've even picked our sign-in names: Mr. and Mrs. Rocco Maggiore."

"What's with the name?"

"RM is the reverse of your initials. Rocco is a name I fancy. The surname is because you're great."

Mario did as instructed. Who was he to resist. This could be the ultimate test. Once again, he decided to see where it led. It didn't take long. They restrained themselves on the way to the elevator. As soon as they were in flight to their floor, Marianne snuggled up to Mario and began groping. Mario responded instantly with an erection larger than in Marianne's dreams. By the time the elevator doors opened on their floor, Marianne was panting. They clung to each other as they staggered to their room. Once inside, Mario was attacked by a famished animal. He was quickly stripped to his bare naturalness. He began to remove Marianne's clothing but she slapped his hands away. She French-kissed Mario as she stroked him.

With his pride of manhood firmly in her grasp, Mario managed to inch them forward onto the bed. He got her to disengage her hold long enough to shed her clothes. She had suppressed her sexual appetite for so long that she lost her habitual propriety. She fondled and kissed him. Mario was having trouble controlling himself. He pulled her up and began kissing her breasts. Marianne moaned and dug her fingernails in Mario's back. She reached down to his groin. As he gained entry, her ravenous appetite took over. She thrust herself upon him with such pulsating vigor, it was over in an instant. Despite her aggression, Mario managed his orgasm to coincide with Marianne's. She had worked herself up for their moment of intimacy. There was no fuse to light. A mere spark ignited the dynamo. Marianne collapsed on Mario, spent, sated and exhausted. She was soon asleep with a smile on her face. It was an abrupt transformation. Mario reflected on this, musing on what had just transpired—was it an aberration or did it signify real change in Marianne's mindset? It could be that a new Marianne emerged from the agonizing she endured. It made sense to him that her fear of his death, her experience with Père LeBlanc and the Hennie ordeal might have led Marianne to fundamental changes. Once again—time would tell.

The intense lovemaking night brought gratification to the two newly christened lovers. It also had a profound effect on the nature of their relationship. There were no regrets the following morning. Rather, Marianne awoke before Mario and embraced him with a smile of contentment on her face. After some smooching, they went at it again. Mario eased her eagerness with tenderness.

"Marianne, lovemaking is more than what we did last night. It should be less ravenous and more tender. Last night was great, but it can be even better. It was like a full-fledged assault resulting in cataclysmic eruptions. There's another way, more like a skirmish. Let me guide you through it. You'll get more pleasure and greater satisfaction. You seem comfortable with this now, so lend me your body. Relax as best you can and let me show you the way."

"I never thought I'd be doing this with anybody, but especially you, Mario. Yes, I've wanted you but I always blocked it out in my reverie when it came to doing the deed. I can't believe I'm so comfortable here and now. In reflection, I detested the animal-like sexual fixation of humans. Yet, that's what I did last night, and I enjoyed it."

"Believe me Marianne, if you enjoyed last night, I guarantee you'll be enthralled with this morning. Lay back and let your body go limp. Let me bring pleasure you haven't felt before. There'll be time to act together, but let me get things started."

"I don't know what you intend, but I'm in your hands."

Mario caressed her breasts, kissing them and working his way down her torso. When he reached her pubic area, he used his fingers to massage her erogenous zone. Marianne started squirming and heaving as Mario manipulated her most sensual part. She climaxed amid convulsions, uttering incomprehensible sounds. Mario lay by her side as they held each other closely. Marianne reached down for Mario, but he pushed her hand aside. He mounted her in the traditional style, and eased his organ into the well-lubricated and welcoming opening. She pleaded for his entry, but he told her to take it slowly and gradual. Restraint early and let it build up. He began his thrusts deliberately with deep penetration, allowing her to feel him within her. It was slow and easy with the pace building up gradually. That it did. The well-orchestrated crescendo brought on a simultaneous climax.

Things moved quickly following the night of seduction and the morning of intimacy. Issues were discussed calmly and resolved over breakfast in their hotel room. The wedding was definitely on. Both parties reaffirmed their agreement. The date was moved up a few months. There would be no more harangues about 'good' Catholic/'bad' Catholic.

"Marianne, I make you a promise. I'll enroll as a parishioner at the church in Tuscany where we decide to live. You have to give me room to do what I'm comfortable with."

"I know, Mario. I've been hearing this from everybody, even the less rigid priests and nuns. They tell me, 'to each his own'. As long as one is true to God, each person should choose how the relationship with God works. I make no demands but I'd like to have you accompany me to mass."

"We'll see how that goes. I'll take some baby steps to test the water and perhaps, if I'm not repulsed by what I encounter, I might immerse myself to a greater degree."

"Another thing, Mario, I won't get on your back again about your mercenary activities. I'm pledging to look forward."

"I'm not doing that anymore. However—you expected a 'however' didn't you? There's a disclaimer. The exception involves my diamond interest. A need could arise. Some action might be called for to protect my stake in the mines."

"I'd rather your abandonment was unconditional but I know you're intent on keeping that option. I'm grateful for letting all else go."

CHAPTER THIRTY SIX

Mario and Marianne met up with Pietro and Anna later that afternoon.

"Thanks for inviting us to dinner. Marianne and I will fill you in on our situation."

Anna read their expressions. "Mario, you needn't say a word. The glow in Marianne's and your faces give you away. It's obvious you've reached an understanding. Is there more to say?"

Marianne responded. "Yes, there is. We've rededicated ourselves to each other, issues resolved. There's going to be a wedding. Date to be sooner rather than later—sometime next spring."

Mario broke in. "We're leaving in the morning, Pietro. We have business to discuss. We're best friends and lets be sure we're in agreement."

“That’s fine with me, Mario,” Pietro assured. “Let us know what we can do for Marianne and you. We’re happy to help.”

“Thanks, Pietro. We’ll keep your offer in mind. We’re spending the night in Pisa and driving to Monaco in the morning for a chat with Christophe. After an overnight in Monte Carlo, we’ll drive to Liège. I’ll continue on to Brussels to meet François. He has the diamonds we gathered at the mines. Then, it’s on to Antwerp to meet with Marianne’s brother, Benoît, and his colleagues at Diamond World.”

“All I can say is WOW! I don’t know how you do it, Mario. You always seem to have a full plate, yet you display equanimity.”

“I manage, Pietro, but then, I don’t see you getting much leisure time. Speaking of work, let’s adjourn to your den for a chat.”

The two friends and business partners brought each other up to date. Pietro told Mario the *raccolto* was going well. Mario gave a brief accounting of his recent mission.

“Pietro, now that my life is changing, I can spend more time with you, taking some of the burden from you.”

“Yes, of course. We agreed on this when we set up our partnership. It’ll be great seeing more of you, but there’s the question of revenue. You need to look at the figures more closely.”

“I know what they are, Pietro. You’re making a decent living for Anna and your kids. I won’t intrude on that. This is what I’m thinking. I’m earning a generous income in Monte Carlo. If Christophe and you agree, I intend to split my time between the casino and the olives. I won’t draw any additional income until our new projects are in place. With no more missions to pull me away, I think I can work out an acceptable schedule at the casino.”

"That would be a good solution for all of us."

"One more question before I go. How's my brother doing? I probably won't see him before I leave in the morning."

"Marcello is fitting in. He's made friends with some of the workers. He's with them now. He doesn't seem to have an agenda other his day-to-day involvement in the *raccolto*. His attitude is good. I think his work here is having a cleansing effect."

"I'm pleased he's fitting in, Pietro. Tell him I asked about him and sorry to have missed him."

Mario and Marianne left and returned to the hotel in Pisa, where they spent another amorous night. They left the next morning for Monte Carlo, staying overnight in his apartment. He spoke with Christophe.

"Mario, I need to depend on you. You haven't failed me. This is why I'm agreeing to this arrangement. There's no room to maneuver."

"I'll be true to our agreement. I value working at the casino. I'll spend time in Tuscany but I'll be here at least two-thirds of the time."

"I'm glad we were able to work this out. You have a positive presence and do your job well. We'll review the situation after your wedding to see where we stand."

Mario drove Marianne to Liège the next day. He visited with Maurice and Anika briefly. Marianne's parents didn't know what to expect. Anika greeted them at the door.

"I'm relieved to see you two together. Come sit and tell us what's going on."

"*Maman et papa,* the wedding is on and will be earlier. It'll be springtime."

Anika couldn't contain herself. She jumped up and hugged her daughter and her dauntless future son-in-law. "I'm so pleased. Marianne, you're a different person than the one who left two weeks ago."

"Yes, it's been two weeks, but it's been a tough three months."

Maurice chided his wife. "Let it be, dear. Don't spoil things. Marianne and Mario are together and they're happy. I think that's great."

Mario was quick to interject. "Anika and Maurice, we're okay with each other—no looking back. Our focus is on getting our wedding plans squared away."

Maurice had information to share. "Good news, *mes enfants.* I spoke with my friend, Grégoire Parmentier. He says OK. Actually, he told me he's delighted to make his home available for your reception. I'll introduce you to him, Mario. You can coordinate your new wedding date with him."

"Thanks Maurice," Mario responded. "I'll stop back here for a couple of days to get things started. I'm meeting your son Benoît and his colleagues in Antwerp. My friend François will join me. That's it for me. I'm out of here first thing in the morning. *Je fait mes adieux.*" Mario spent a restful night at his favorite *liégeois* hotel.

Mario's journey across Europe resumed with the dawning of a new day. He met François at the train station in Brussels. "I expect good news for us today, François. You do have all our diamonds?"

"Yes, they're all here. I got them from Guillaume's contact at the embassy yesterday afternoon. Ease up on your expectations, Mario. The stones look good to us but the experts have the final say."

"You have it all wrong, François. It's not emotional for me. This is scientific."

"No doubt, we'll ride our way to wealth in your chariot fueled by your expertise. Back to the real world. Did you pick up your uncut diamond from the bank vault?"

"The bank is just opening. I'll get it as we head to Antwerp."

François removed his injured left arm from the sling, resting it on his lap as they proceeded to the diamond capital. When they reached their destination, Mario asked to see the diamonds.

"This is the one I picked up in the excavated crater. I think it has possibilities."

"Are you sure, Mario? How about this one from Kwambe. Take it."

"No way, François. I'm not visiting that scene again. I know about this one, exactly where it came from and who found it. I can swear on a stack of bibles to Marianne I got this diamond from the mine with my own hands. I'm hanging on to it."

Benoît greeted Mario and François. "I'm relieved you made it back safely. The news on the shoot-out painted a grim picture. Mario, Marianne phoned this morning. I'm happy for the two of you."

“Thanks to you and others, Marianne has done a one-eighty. Your advice was right on the mark. She’s done a remarkable turnaround.”

“There’s more to it than that, Mario. I grant you, we didn’t let up on her. I think Hennie’s accident and loss of child, plus her belief you were dead or critically wounded were more decisive. She has a new attitude toward life. The soul-wrenching agony she endured during your three month absence gave her a new perspective on your importance in her life.”

“Thanks again, Benoît. Sounds promising. Hope it lasts.”

François was thrilled for Mario and the change of fortune in his love life. “Let’s see if these people can help finance your wedding. It’s show-and-tell time. Let’s get it on.”

The sight of Mario’s rough diamond at the earlier meeting elicited interest throughout the company. Joining Benoît in the meeting were the company CEO and four experts. Before showing their stone collection, François and Mario described the location where the diamonds were found. They provided details on the site. The CEO led the discussion as he probed to gain a better understanding.

“We’ll look at your stones shortly. This is what I get. The mine is in an isolated tropical rain forest at the opposite end of the country from the capital. Rough diamonds were found along a riverbed. The French did half-hearted exploration and excavation some years ago. There’s been little activity since then. Cubans have been showing up at the site. The two of you visited the site and brought samples you found on the riverbed and in the mountainside excavation crater. Is this correct?”

François acknowledged the CEO’s summary. “Yes sir, that’s it in a nutshell. We brought back seventeen stones, twelve found at the site by either Mario or me. Four others were collected at the site by the mine's head of security. The remaining stone is the one that caused some excitement at our previous meeting."

"Obviously, we have an interest. Show us what you have."

François had the rough diamonds in a satchel with a strap he carried on his right shoulder. Mario removed the stones and placed them on the table to be examined by the experts. The CEO picked one up and then another, scrutinizing them.

"I must tend to other matters. I appreciate your coming to us. My experts will give you an honest appraisal. If they're as good as they seem, we might be able to do business. Pleasure meeting you, François and Mario."

The experts carried the stones to an adjacent lab. They got down to business, each picking up a stone, jotting observations. Benoît joined François and Mario carrying three cups of coffee. They chatted as the experts did their work, examining the stones with their equipment. The experts huddled to compare notes after they inspected each of the seventeen stones. After awhile, they came up for air.

"Gentlemen, you'll be pleased with our findings." The senior expert declared. "The four of us concur. The CEO authorized us to share our conclusions but with the understanding the ultimate appraisal and rating will be determined after further review."

Mario was eager. "I think you know our questions, so give us the answers."

"Very well, here they are. We'll need to clear some of the crust from the diamonds to evaluate them properly. The diamonds are gem quality with good possibilities. With your permission, we'll work the diamonds over to provide an appraisal of value."

François inquired about Mario's original diamond. "Does the diamond we showed earlier compare with the new ones?"

"Yes, it does, which is why we're enthused. All seventeen diamonds come from the same source. In our judgment, our company should make further inquiries with the Mandakan government about a site visit. Our CEO and his senior team will decide how we should proceed. What's your intended disposition for these diamonds?"

Mario arose and picked up one of the stones. "Fifteen will be available for purchase at a fair price to be determined. This one will be fashioned for my fiancée's engagement ring. After you've examined it further, I'd like your opinion on its grading and best use. François is keeping one as is."

François picked up the diamond he wanted. "When the value is determined and a fair price is offered and agreed on, we'll be disposed to sell the fifteen diamonds."

"If you'll entrust us, we'll clean the stones to display their qualities. Benoît will be your go-between. We'll do your diamond first, Mario, and give Benoît a full evaluation along with our recommendation to pass on to you. Is this okay?"

François and Mario voiced their approval. They all shook hands. François recouped his diamond and exited the building with Mario and Benoît. As they parted, Benoît assured the two men the diamonds were in good hands.

"You needn't worry. We do this all the time. Here's a receipt for each of the sixteen diamonds we're holding and copies of the photos the experts took when they were examining the stones."

Mario felt somewhat reassured. "Thanks Benoît, it's a bit worrisome leaving the stones behind, especially the one intended for your sister."

"Don't sweat it, Mario, do you think I'd fuck over a guy who could easily beat the shit out of me. Then, there's your more intimidating pal. Are we OK?"

François answered for the two. "Yes, we're golden. Get in touch with Mario when you have information and he'll pass it along."

It was early evening by the time François and Mario returned to *l'Hôtel le Dôme* in Brussels. They placed a call to Mandaka, hoping to catch Guillaume Wabitale in his office at the palace. He was catching up with paperwork. François briefed Guillaume on their meeting in Antwerp, alerting him they'll call again after hearing from Hoelebrand.

Parting company with François the next morning, Mario drove back to Liège to focus on wedding arrangements. He was feeling upbeat. The diamond situation was in the hands of Hoelebrand. He had an understanding with Christophe to remain at Monte Carlo Casino. When Pietro told Mario he was pleased with Marcello's hands-on effort with their olive business, it allowed Mario to be away from Lucca and spend time on his job in Monaco. Once married, Marianne would accompany Mario, whether in Lucca or in Monte Carlo. Mario assured Christophe he could depend on him to be available whenever Christophe needed to be away from the casino. He gave the same assurances to Pietro to cover their olive business whenever Pietro needed time for his tourism business in Verona or his new tourism venture in Tuscany (mainly Pisa/Lucca area).

Mario received the phone call from Benoît. The diamonds all passed muster. The conclusion of the company experts and executives was the diamonds justified a look into possible exploration of the mine to ascertain the viability of exploitation. François' phone call to Guillaume put the wheels of a partnership agreement with the Mandakan Government in motion. Numerous meetings followed between Hoelebrand executives, the Mandakan Ambassador in Paris, members of Kibali's inner circle, and eventually involving DeBeers. A deal was struck. Mario and François retained a small piece of the action. The fifteen uncut diamonds were sold to Hoelebrand and the proceeds disbursed equally to the eight members of the training team. Diamonds would take as little or as much of Mario's time as he was willing to put in.

Regarding Mario's mercenary career, he was determined to be true to his promise to Marianne. The training mission in Mandaka was his last. He turned down an opportunity to join François and other buddies on a mission to a West African country. The olive leaves beckoned him to make love, not war.

CHAPTER THIRTY SEVEN

The selected day in May could not have turned out better. The weather in Liège was splendid, sunny with few scattered clouds. The ebullient ambience was contagious. There was harmony among all key participants. Not a single untoward word was uttered, or at least heard. Anyone unaware of the antecedent tempest would avow it was the perfect marriage made in heaven. The bride and groom, attendants and family members were aglow.

L'Eglise Saint Jacques-le-Mineur had the largest crowd in attendance in recent years. Mario's friends came from all over Europe and elsewhere, including North and South America, Australia and Africa, with Middle East sheiks and Hong Kong Chinese magnates among them. Mario had many lasting contacts from his various exploits, especially his work in Monte Carlo.

Father Doucet performed the ceremony, assisted by Padre Augusto. Claire Marie Blancke served as maid of honor and Pietro DiSanto was best man. Julio Valesquez, who had fully recovered from his injury, was present and in the wedding party. Pietro proffered the wedding band to accompany the excellent quality, multi-carat Mandakan diamond, already a fixture on Marianne's finger.

When Mario gave Marianne her engagement ring, he didn't want to resurrect the issue of her earlier refusal.

"Marianne, I'm determined to get this right. Benoît's people crafted this diamond from a stone I personally picked up in the mine excavation area. The only labor involved was mine as I scrabbled around, searching with my hands and dodging a couple of bullets."

"I hope you understand my apprehension."

"I do understand. Will you accept this engagement ring? I even have a Certificate of Authenticity. Let me read it.

> '*This document certifies the authenticity of the accompanying diamond. It was obtained from an excavation pit in Pliganta province in the country of Mandaka in November 1968. The encrusted rough diamond was removed from nature by Mario Rossetti. He is solely responsible for the labor involved in acquiring the stone.*
>
> *Signed and sealed by Mario Rossetti.*'

"There you have it. You can't go wrong with this product, *mademoiselle*. It comes with two certificates, one from the experts on details of the diamond and the other on its provenance. I highly recommend you accept it."

L'Eglise Saint Jacques-le-Mineur is an imposing church, generally considered the most beautiful medieval church in Liège. It's a mixture of architectural styles: Gothic, Romanesque and Renaissance. The church was founded in 1015. Construction of the present church began in 1155 and concluded in 1538. It was the perfect setting for a grand old-time wedding. This was Mario's show and he went all out with flowers, buntings, organ and choir. The two proud mothers, Anika Duhammel and Teresina Rossetti, met for the first time and it seemed one was trying to outdo the other with tears of joy.

Grégoire Parmentier, friend of Marianne's father, came through on his earlier commitment. Grégoire spared no expense in festooning his chateau with a carnival atmosphere. He got to know Marianne and Mario quite well during the time leading to the wedding and found both endearing. Being a man of means with a successful business, he decided to finance the reception and do it up in glamorous and majestic fashion. He felt Maurice's delightful and whimsical little girl and her handsome squire deserved the full treatment. He became more convinced of this when he saw Mario's guest list; he was impressed with the power and wealth represented.

Mario and Marianne were sky-high with emotions. It was a day both parties questioned would ever happen. The large gathering of people pulled the couple apart to mingle with friends and meet other guests. Mario was a major domo. He was in his element being personable, determined to greet and chat with each invitee. Some guests he hadn't seen for some time, yet they remained on his contact list. Claire Marie accompanied Marianne as she moved from one group to another. The waiters seemed to have specific responsibility of looking after Marianne's thirst. She was never left wanting. As soon as she drained one glass, another glass of champagne was in her hand. She became mellow and giddy.

Ignoring the quartet that was playing dancing music, she inveigled Claire Marie to sing with her. What came to mind was '*Sur le Pont d'Avignon'*. They sang gaily, making the bows and motions according to the words and then some. Many of the dancers stopped for the sideshow. The quartet picked up the impromptu entertainment and provided accompaniment. Mario was in another room chatting with some of his casino contacts about diamonds. When he realized the music had changed suddenly and heard singing, he returned to the main room and discovered his new bride on center stage. Fortunately, she was in her 'let's-have-fun' mood. He also saw she and her friend were tipsy. The gathered crowd encouraged the duo to go on. Emboldened by the attention, they moved on to the 'Can-Can', stumbling with their leg thrusts. Mario to the rescue. Amid hoots and shouts of 'Encore!', Mario managed to corral his wife and settle her in a chair. Comments from the crowd could be heard: 'She's loose as a goose', '*Bon Dieu*, what a change in that gal', 'Poor chap, he's got no idea what he's in for', 'She was such a sweet girl', etc.

So, welcome to married life. It began with a bang as the newlyweds went off on their honeymoon. The well-wishers sent them off into the sunset.

The *lune de miel* in Tahiti was everything a honeymoon was designed to be. They rediscovered the great camaraderie that had drawn them together initially as friends. They romanced incessantly, professing unremitting love and commitment to each other. They found time to SCUBA dive, play tennis, walk the beaches, and other activities. There was no reminder of contretemps of the past as they both rose to the occasion, exhibiting the best romantic and alluring aspects of their make-up. It was evident to any on-looker these were two people were not only in love with each, but also liked each other very much.

EPILOG

Mario was pensive as he reflected on how his life had become the antithesis of what it was a year earlier when he left Mandaka the second time. He had a good life then but faced uncertainties. The question was marriage, whether or not it was going to happen. In his willingness to change his lifestyle, he expected the path to his renaissance would be along a smooth and straight boulevard. It was not to be. He persisted, struggling to advance along a route replete with crags and curves.

It was November once again. The contentious issues were resolved. He glanced at the chair across from him in the parlor of his own home. His face gleamed as his eyes met hers. An evocative contentment was felt across the room. Mr. and Mrs. Mario Rossetti were smug with their lives as they relaxed in the pastoral surroundings of Tuscany. Marianne put in a full day by her husband's side, harvesting olives. It was the *raccolto,* the second for Marianne. Mario spent more time in Tuscany with the harvest in progress.

Mario was faithful to the schedule he worked out with Christophe at the casino. Marianne usually accompanied him to Monaco when he worked there, staying at his apartment. She was getting involved with activities in Lucca, which called for her to stay there occasionally while Mario went to his job in Monte Carlo. The separation every now and then worked well for them. Pietro and Anna were happy to have Marianne close by and seeing Mario more than in the past. Mario grew more comfortable with his brother. Papers were being drawn to bring Marcello into the partnership; he passed the test of cutting ties to the Mafia. Momma Rossetti and Nonna were delighted with the developments. Another partnership was created between Mario and Julio, to operate the olive grove they purchased in Catalonia. Hoelebrand and DeBeers formed a joint venture with the Government of Mandaka granting them exploration and exploitation rights. For their part, François and Mario had no financing obligations but could reap rewards if the operation was successful.

Marianne and Mario moved into their rented villa upon returning from Tahiti, six months earlier. They both enjoyed the surroundings near Piazza San Giovanni, in the heart of the medieval walled city of Lucca. It was convenient for them, given Marianne's somewhat ungainly situation. Her body size had expanded to make room for two new Italians who would come forth after the turn of the year. She was into her sixth month of gestation, carrying twins. Mario and Marianne were at peace with each other and within themselves. They had achieved contentment.

AUTHOR'S NOTE

Although this is a book of fiction, some of the characters are a compilation of people I have known. There are no countries of Mandaka, Zandu and Runhantia. The situation described in Chapter One did occur, with some embellishment of literary license. I was there at the time and knew some of the mercenaries. I have not known any of them to be ruthless killers. Rather, they enjoy life and I have found them to be good company socially and good drinking buddies. With the exception of Bob Denard and Jean Schramme, all mercenary names came out of thin air.

A further word about this type of warrior, known under various names, i.e., mercenary, soldier of fortune, hired gun, etc. Such men have been engaged for millennia at the behest, and in the interest, of others. They fought alongside the Romans during the Crusades and many subsequent instances of aggression, including the American Revolution. Thousands of German and Swiss nationals fought side-by-side with French and British troops during the 18th century. More recently, foreigners have participated in numerous militant encounters across the African continent, as well as in Asia and Latin America. Today's mercenaries, for the most part, are hired under contract by private companies that have been engaged by national governments to assist their militaries.

Who are these individuals who put their lives on the line for someone else's cause? Generally, the term "mercenary" evokes an immediate negative impression. The thought sometimes is of psychopaths who enjoy killing and inflicting misery on others. However, if one met a professional soldier of fortune in a casual setting, it is not likely he would be revealed as such. These men are usually battle-hardened veterans who served in a nation's regular military force. Upon returning to civilian society, they learn their unique skills are in demand. The rewards are compelling.

ACKNOWLEDGMENTS

I owe a debt a gratitude to the Department of State, for looking after my needs as I developed as a diplomat. When I returned to Africa in the mid-1960s, I was embraced by the finest diplomats representing our country abroad. George McMurtrie "Mac" Godley, Ambassador; Robert O. Blake, Deputy Chief of Mission, and James P. Farber, Political Officer, made me feel welcome at my arrival in Leopoldville, Congo, and never deviated from the support I received from them.

I grew as a writer through my experiences and having a job requirement of reporting on my observations and insights on various assignments with the Department of State, with other end-users, including the White House, the National Security Council, the Defense Department and the CIA. Among other things, writing a one-page report for the President, while in the Office of the Secretary of State, on significant occurrences abroad overnight for his early morning reading was a challenge on the use of language.

In a previous published endeavor, I have attributed a significant stimulus to Marvin Kalb, political commentator and communications virtuoso. Mr. Kalb's early encouragement continues to be an impetus as I embark on new attempts to put together nouns, verbs, adjectives and adverbs in a meaningful way.

I am indebted to my best friend, my wife, Dailyn. She endured the various versions of my manuscript I turned over to her for scrutiny. The final product is mine, but Dailyn's handiwork is manifested throughout.

It was my good fortune to meet Patrick LoBrutto. Pat is a seasoned and accomplished editor. He read my draft manuscript and led me through the process to convert drabness into vitality. He was critical in an agreeable way and all of his suggestions were right-on the mark.

ABOUT THE AUTHOR

William Boudreau is a retired career diplomat and international consultant. A considerable amount of his experience involved African issues, on assignments in Africa and in Washington. While in the Congo, Mr. Boudreau met and befriended several mercenaries, who at that time were working for the Congolese Government. When they rebelled against the government, chaos ensued. He has written a memoir on these times in the Congo and Madagascar. "A Teetering Balance: An American Diplomat's Career and Family" (AuthorHouse) depicts American activities to thwart Soviet in-roads in Africa during the Cold War.

Mr. Boudreau is a writer and lecturer, who also assisted the United Nations on missions. He and his wife Dailyn reside on Seabrook Island, SC. Their three grown sons remain in their native New England.